The Web
of
Iniquity

# The Web of Iniquity

## EARLY DETECTIVE FICTION

## BY AMERICAN WOMEN

CATHERINE ROSS NICKERSON

Duke University Press   Durham & London

1998

© 1998 Duke University Press

All rights reserved

Printed in the United States of America

on acid-free paper ∞

Designed by C. H. Westmoreland

Typeset in Adobe Minion with Mistral display

by Tseng Information Systems, Inc.

Library of Congress Cataloging-in-Publication

Data appear on the last printed

page of this book.

*To My Teachers*

# Contents

# Preface

This book traces the rise and development of a tradition of detective fiction by women in the period between the end of the Civil War and the beginning of World War II. Its subject may come as a surprise to those who have long associated American detective fiction with the expression and dissemination of a hard-boiled style of masculinity. In fact, several women were highly successful authors of detective novels in the late nineteenth and early twentieth centuries; their books sold briskly and the authors achieved a certain level of literary celebrity in their day. Their novels were published in hard covers, for a middle-class audience of women and men, and the plots generally revolve around murders committed in middle- and upper-class homes.

When people hear me talk about the women's detective novels this book examines, they almost always ask, "What are they like?" They are like this:

In Anna Katharine Green's *The Mayor's Wife* (1907), our narrator, a young woman named Saunders, goes to a domestic service agency seeking work and is granted an interview with none other than the mayor of the city. He is concerned about his wife, who is in a state of nervous exhaustion and claims to be haunted by a ghost. He feels there is more going on in the household than his wife is telling him, and he wishes to hire Saunders as an ostensible companion for his wife and also as an extra pair of eyes for himself. Saunders is desperate enough for work to accept this morally dubious position, and she moves into the mayor's house. While showing Saunders to her bedroom, the maid makes slyly disquieting remarks ("I guess you never heard about this house") and hints that she has plenty to say about Mrs. Packard, the mayor's wife. Saunders is startled to discover an "uncanny" old woman staring fixedly into the room from a window of the house next door, and puzzled by the contrast between the supposed chaos of Mrs. Packard's mind and the thoughtful and tasteful arrangement of the room, which indicates a "wholesome nature."

Saunders is about to discover a set of intertwined plots of bigamy, theft, and false identities, all connected literally and figuratively by a secret code, but we might linger at that moment in her bedroom as more or less paradigmatic of early detective fiction by women. Surrounded by evidence of domestic virtue as expressed by the decor, of household intrigue in the hints of the maid, and with the knowledge that she is being paid to do "a spy's duty," Saunders suffers from a sense of confusion that has cultural, moral, and epistemological components. In this novel, as in many others of this tradition, mystery is the beginning of wisdom, an ultimately positive sign that, as Saunders puts it, there is "something worth my knowing." And while these novels are not always narrated in the first person, that narrative form is paradigmatic in the sense that it foregrounds the processes of learning, feeling, and discovering that these novels explore.

At this moment in Saunders's bedroom, we see a kind of layering of surveillance that is also characteristic of these novels. While Saunders hears hints that the servants are keeping their own tabs on their mistress, and as she attempts to read the lay of the interior landscape, she is herself being watched by someone else. In early detective fiction by women, investigative work always includes an element of spying (listening at doors, snooping through the mail, trailing, and eavesdropping) that at first pricks the conscience of the neophyte detective and later raises the hair on the back of her neck when she discovers that she is the object of someone else's inspection. The detectives in these novels are not always women, especially in the earlier works, but they are all concerned, in some way, with how suspicion and investigation intersect with ideologies of genteel womanhood. Female detective figures like Saunders are frequently sidekicks or rivals of professional or police detectives; we can call them detectives (as we do Agatha Christie's Jane Marple) when they compete with, supplant, supplement, or correct a more official, male-headed investigation. In that sense, this scene, which is structured by what women know and don't know about each other, expresses another basic concern of this tradition.

The fact that this moment from *The Mayor's Wife* is set in the domestic sphere is also exemplary, and so central to this type of fiction that I call this subgenre of detective writing by women the "domestic detective novel." Almost all of the action of Saunders's narrative takes place in private quarters, in a series of homes that range from the grand urban mansion of the mayor to a wooden shack in rural Minnesota. The main locus of domestic detective fiction is the domestic spaces of the wealthy professional and mercantile classes, and the belief that such places needed the services of the new literary and historical figure of the detective was, I argue in the course of this book, the basic, socially critical premise of the genre. Finally, this scene includes a gothic element — in the strange, unblinking figure of the woman in the window — that is another definitive part of the tradition. In *The Mayor's Wife,* as in many other novels, the problems in the household manifest themselves in ways that people interpret as supernatural (footsteps, moving lights, and missing objects are attributed to ghosts), and although the haunting of a house is always debunked at some level, certain structures and tropes associated with the gothic mode demand to be taken more seriously. These novels abound with metaphorical and literal doubles, live burials, secret letters, and madwomen in attics, conventions that constitute a language for expressing female anger and rebellion in this literary tradition and in several others.

By demonstrating the existence of a sequence of extremely popular women writers of the genre in America in the period between Poe and Dashiell Hammett, a period most standard histories of detective fiction refer to as "a gap" or as "fallow," this book offers a corrective history of detective fiction. I am most centrally concerned, however, with this tradition in relation to the history of women's writing and social criticism, and as a part of the development of mass culture in the United States. Taken collectively, these novels offer a series of tales about American crimes and punishments, popular tales that were engaged with the various discourses on public and private morality of their day. They offer a new source for understanding the lived experience of the policing and the transgressing of gender norms that vexed and energized middle- and upper-class culture in the decades around the turn of the century. Both the fact of their popularity and the content of their plots suggest a historical need for a new discourse on crime, its investigation, and its punishment or eradication that also worked as literary entertainment for the upper classes.

Both my argument and my method work to take this form of popular literature seriously, by which I mean several things at once. Popular writing is significant on its own terms, partly because of the sheer depth and breadth of its appeal (what we might in our own age call "market penetration"), and partly because exactly those elements that are its sources of entertainment (the jokes, the tragedies, the terrors) reveal much about the configurations of common anxieties at any given cultural moment. At the same time, any in-depth study of popular writing requires examination of the relation of "high" and "low" cultural products, because, as the work of several scholars over the last decade has shown, members of the elite and powerful classes consumed many low or popular forms of entertainment with gusto, and high and low genres influenced and shaped each other to a remarkable extent. So, in this study, when I use such terms as *popular* (or *low*) or *elite* (or *high*), I use them without pejorative connotation or an inflated sense of their precision as descriptors. I have found *middlebrow* a useful term to characterize the ways these novels appealed to an educated, middle- and upper-class audience who were not interested in, or who sought a respite from, the particular kind of linguistic and thematic difficulties presented in elite literary forms of modernism. Methodologically, I take these works seriously by focusing the kind of attention on them that some literary scholars reserve only for elite forms. As I outline in the first part's discussion of generic conventions, detective fiction has a complex narrative structure that, I believe, demands close narratological reading, especially because detective fiction is a literature in which plot is very much the point of the text.

I might add here, while discussing terminology, a word about labels for class, which tend to be overly inclusive and inexact. The novels I examine here focus mainly on family circles in which the head of household is a white, native-born lawyer, doctor, minister, banker, stockbroker, or an executive of a manufacturing or importing company. I use the term *professional class* to refer to the families of the lawyers, doctors, and clergy, and *mercantile* or *capitalist* to refer to the others; in the period under study, they together began to form an elite of cultural authority, and thus I call them upper middle class or, when their wealth is their most distinctive feature, moneyed. However, the professional class consciously espoused what it saw as the more stable values and ideologies of the middle class and consumed such middle-class entertainments as the domestic novel (especially in the immediate postbellum period). The more leisured reaches of the upper class often shared those values by default; when referring to all these groups at once, I use the encompassing terms *middle class* and *upper class*.

The first part of this book examines several of the most important threads of mid-nineteenth-century popular fiction that domestic detective fiction knots together: Poe's tales of ratiocination, the sensational story-paper, popular nonfiction crime and trial narratives, the domestic novel, and the social-critical use of the gothic mode as exemplified in the works of Harriet Beecher Stowe, Louisa May Alcott, and Charlotte Brontë. I begin with a discussion of these multiple origins, then move on to a close examination of what is generally accepted as the first full-blown American detective novel, Metta Victor's *The Dead Letter* (1866), and a lesser-known novella, *The Figure Eight* (1869), the latter in conjunction with Pauline Hopkins's *Hagar's Daughter* (1901). Victor's novels, which imperfectly integrate dime-novel formulas with more genteel romance and domestic novel structures, celebrate lawyers and doctors as the ascending arbiters of public and private morals. Although these first novels are narrated by male detective figures, they establish the emphasis on erotic entanglements among the suspects and victims and on the emotional involvement of the narrators in ways that show their ancestry in mid-century sentimental culture and set the pattern for the works that follow. Hopkins's experiments in detective fiction (which also include a short story, "Talma Gordon" [1900], that I discuss near the end of the Rinehart section) use the trope of mistaken identity to comment on the construction of race in a prejudiced society.

Anna Katharine Green, the subject of the second part of this book, more fully blended the detective novel and the domestic novel. *The Leavenworth Case,* her first novel and the best-seller of 1878, drew on and stabilized the recipe of detection, domesticity, and gothicism concocted by Victor and made it into an appealing entertainment for a middle- and upper-class audience. In the 1890s, she created a spinster detective, a figure that became important to many women writers of detective fiction, and she used her female detectives to critique the greed and hard-heartedness of masculine mercantile culture. Chapter 5 explores the relation between the upper-class female detective and the reform culture of the Gilded Age and Progressive eras, and argues that the revival and revision of the older female gothic plot served as a way to express deep ambivalence about the changes in women's roles and opportunities.

Mary Roberts Rinehart, the subject of the last part of the book, took up the motifs of Green's work and inflected them with more terror, more humor, and more feminism. Her work is, even more than Green's, engaged with the remaking of womanhood in the first four decades of this century. Chapter 6 examines *The Circular Staircase* (1908) and argues that both Rinehart's use of the trope of the haunted house and her retrospective, first-person narration foreground epistemology and storytelling in ways that challenge the normative female roles of mother, housewife, and helpmate. Chapter 7 places Rinehart's use of spinster detectives in the cultural context of the 1920s and 1930s and argues that *The Album* (1933) is a powerful example of the ways Rinehart's tales of murder, terror, and investigation serve as a commentary on women's experience of and in the beginning of the twentieth century. In that novel, Rinehart articulates what was understood even at the time as a generational conflict over female sexuality and economic freedom by constructing a story of matricide out of a famous murder within an upper-class family. The readings of Rinehart's novels are the culmination of the fundamental line of inquiry in this study: the relation between these novels about the investigation of crime in the domestic sphere and the changing (and sometimes retrenching) ideologies of gender and domesticity in the long transition from the Victorian age to the modern era. The Afterword discusses the decline of the domestic detective novel in the 1930s, attributing it to many of the same historical and cultural shifts that made the advent of hard-boiled detective fiction both possible and phenomenally successful as a discourse on the newly interesting question of masculinity.

The other question that academics and detective fiction fans alike frequently ask me is that perennial and vexing query posed to scholars of women's popular novels: "Are they any good?" I can only answer that I personally find these novels satisfyingly complex in their engagements with cultural history, sometimes hilarious in their feminist wit, and unexpectedly self-reflexive about their status as a literary discourse of secrecy and disclosure. If these texts rarely question the predominant ideologies of race and class of their day, they do challenge normative notions of gender. They have a kind of literary and cultural density that makes them worth restoring to our present cultural memory, if only for the way they complicate our sense of what has actually gone on in the pages of popular fiction. I hope this book will prompt some readers to seek out the few editions of these works that are still in print (at this writing, one of Green's novels and several of Rinehart's) or to find them in libraries. For readers who are already fans of the detective genre, these novels will offer both a history lesson and the more immediate satisfaction of well-crafted mysteries. For those who combine a taste for mystery with an affection for the domestic novel of the nineteenth century, these works offer a potent blend of satisfactions and surprises.

# Acknowledgments

Mary Roberts Rinehart used to write her fiction so quickly that she had to dip her already filled fountain pen into a bottle of ink because no pumping mechanism worked fast enough to keep up with the flow of her words. In the course of researching and writing this book I had many occasions to envy both her speed and her confidence. I needed, and received, a great deal of help along the way. This project began as a dissertation in the American Studies Program at Yale University, and I am deeply indebted to Alan Trachtenberg, who served as a wise, challenging, and generous director, and to my advisers Michael Denning and Laura Wexler, whose enthusiasm for the study of culture was both bracing and inspiring. Jean-Christophe Agnew, R. W. B. Lewis, Katherine Snyder, Susan S. Williams, and Bryan Wolf all offered important advice and encouragement at key junctures, and Ruth Bernard Yeazell gave the completed dissertation a clear-eyed reading.

At Emory, I have found an equally stimulating intellectual community in the Graduate Institute of the Liberal Arts and the English Department. Amy Schrager Lang and Cristine Levenduski both read the manuscript at several stages, offered sustaining advice, and helped chase away my demons. Many other colleagues shared wisdom and insight of several kinds, and I heartily thank Julie Abraham, Angelika Bammer, Cynthia Blakely, Rudolph Byrd, Frances Smith Foster, David Hesla, Walter Kalaidjian, Ivan Karp, Cindy Patton, Jonathan Prude, Mark Sanders, Steven Springer, Allen Tullos, and Lynna Williams.

I am extremely grateful to the readers for Duke University Press, who understood what I was trying to do and offered me invaluable advice on how to do it better. Jan Cohn very generously read and commented on an early version of the Rinehart chapter. Dale Bauer, Harriet Chessman, Gordon Hunter, and Suzanne Juhasz showed an interest in this project that helped me through the rough patches. Throughout, Candace Waid was an irresistible voice of encouragement and a model of scholarly seriousness and creativity. Stephanie Thomas gave me the generous gift of her sensitive reading, and Frank and Deirdre Menchaca have taught me much about the discipline and joy of the creative process.

Ken Wissoker, whose insightful and patient editing made this book far better than it would have been otherwise, acted like Peter Falk toward this project, by turns Columbo ("There's just one more thing") and guardian angel. I also thank Katie Courtland for her warm and cheering attention to this book, Pam Morrison and Anna Haas for making publication such a pleasant process (at least for me), and Mindy Conner for copyediting the manuscript with intelligence, skill, and care. Sara Clough of the Feminist Press graciously furnished me with the galleys of *Unpunished* before the book appeared in stores. The burden of revising and preparing this manuscript was lightened by the work of several research assistants over the years, and I thank Kerry Soper, Christopher Green, Lisa Spadafora, and, for a level of engagement far above and beyond the call of RA duty, Amy Wood. A series of Junior Faculty Development Awards allowed me to devote several summers to research and writing, and I thank Emory University for this crucial financial support.

This book is dedicated to the teachers named above and to several other extraordinary ones, especially to Ruth Williams of the Park School; to Lucy Withington, Dale DeLetis, Alan Proctor, and John Charles Smith of Milton Academy; and to Henry Louis Gates Jr., my undergraduate thesis adviser. My family have been my most influential teachers. My mother, Mary Nickerson, has always had an unreasonable and infectious faith in my abilities, and my father and stepmother, Donald and Margaret Ann Nickerson, early taught me the saving power of work and words. Spencer Merz taught me to think big and to pay attention. My brothers—Jeff, John, Nate, and Mike Nickerson—my sisters-in-law—Debie Morris, Edie Nickerson, Karen Covey, and Sue Wooldridge—and my brother-in-law Bill Wooldridge have kept me laughing and kept me grounded. My mother- and father-in-law, Irene and Rupert Covey, have shown tremendous generosity toward this work and its demands on me. This book would not have been possible without the help of my husband, Bruce Covey, who read every draft of every chapter with care and greeted my writerly moods and obsessions with patience and humor. The fact that I found such warmth and strength in my own family while reading about so many catastrophically unhappy ones is my fondest memory of this work.

# Part One

## THE ADVENT

## OF DETECTIVE

## FICTION

## AND THE

## POSTBELLUM

## PERIOD

*C* apitola Black, heroine of E. D. E. N. Southworth's *The Hidden Hand* (1859), is a realist, but she is comfortable in a number of popular literary genres: the rags-to-riches story, the gothic mode, the sentimental-domestic novel, the adventure story, the urban exposé, and the criminal narrative.[1] Just as she pragmatically trades in the clothing of a girl for the more protective clothing of a boy while living on the streets of New York City, she is able to negotiate the challenges of each generic situation with startling success. When she finds herself held captive by the evil Craven Le Noir in the lair known as "the hidden house," she knows to "do the sentimental up brown," which includes "piling up the agonies," refusing meals, and weeping loudly, as part of a plan to free herself and another young woman from his clutches.[2] And in this situation, Capitola not only *uses* "the sentimental," she uses it to thwart a classic gothic plot of female captivity that has been laid against them. She and Clara have been shut up in the mansion, which is populated by an ambulatory ghost and a grim housekeeper, to await Clara's forced marriage to Le Noir. In her decision to "do the sentimental," Capitola simultaneously steps into the role of the helpless heroine of the gothic novel and uses that role to sabotage Le Noir's plot. By swapping clothing with Clara, Cap plays the part of the victim-bride with gusto until she can humiliate Le Noir at the wedding chapel.

Capitola acts out a relationship between the gothic mode, sentimental discourse, and domestic narrative that I find very suggestive for the study of American women's popular writing in this period. In the immediate postbellum period, certain alignments of culture and congruences of these genres produced a style of detective novel written by women that maintained a substantial presence in the popular literary marketplace well into the 1930s.[3] The first chapter sketches out the generic origins and characteristics of what I call the domestic detective novel, including the first appearance of a detective in American women's letters, in a story by Louisa May Alcott. The second and third chapters discuss specific works by Metta Fuller Victor, who wrote the first full-fledged detective novels in the United

States, examining narrative structures and themes having to do with secrecy, disguise, surveillance, and emotional regulation and their historical contexts. The third chapter concludes with an examination of Pauline Hopkins's socially critical experiment in detective fiction, *Hagar's Daughter.*

# 1

## "To Trace a Lie, to Discover a Disguise"

### GENRES OF CRIME AND SECRECY

The Detective Story and the Gothic Mode;
or, Dupin and the Ourang-Outang

Despite its penchant for violent mayhem and general sneakiness, detective fiction is the teacher's pet of popular genres. It has surely received as many pages of scholarly attention as its closest rival, the western; it has been meticulously catalogued by connoisseurs, subjected to minute taxonomies of subgenre, arrayed in long lineages of influence, and has received the additional flattery of scrutiny by such academic luminaries as Jacques Lacan, Umberto Eco, Tzvetan Todorov, Roland Barthes, Fredric Jameson, and Geoffrey Hartman. It might be tempting to extrapolate some sort of collective psychological profile of the humanities professor from this phenomenon, but it is probably more fruitful to consider what the fact of this large and various body of criticism reveals about detective fiction. This genre remains as fascinating to the academic as to the general reader because it lends itself to so many kinds of reading and cooperates with so many demands from historians and literary critics. Because it is a narrative about the detective reconstructing the story of a crime, a detective novel is a rich textual object for readers interested in metafiction, self-reflexive language, and narrative structures that highlight storytelling. More historically oriented readers can find a wealth of information about the definition and imagination of crime, the policing of cultural norms, the experience of shame, and the ideologies that have surrounded those phenomena at different points in our history. Detective fiction's sheer popularity makes it useful to historians of mass culture as well as to those who wish to analyze the specific structural and thematic appeal of formula fiction and the relation between popular genres.

This study of early detective fiction by women will, at different moments, look at the genre from almost all those angles, but is most interested in two of them: the narratological study of the way the stories of crime and investigation are presented, and the ways these novels are both a product of and a commentary on ideologies of domesticity and gender. These two approaches, I have found, are mutually reinforcing: certain patterns of storytelling in the novels can be fully understood only when (re-)connected to specific features of the cultural moment of their production and original reception.

As I suggested above, there are many possible approaches to a discussion of detective fiction, but in practice, there are two main critical avenues. They differ mainly over the question of whether detective fiction is at heart a kind of puzzle that readers find mentally stimulating in the manner of a crossword or whether it is most properly interpreted as a mirror of the work's historical moment (in both the broad and minute senses).[1] Of course, these two angles are not mutually exclusive, and can be brought to terms with each other by considering the ways in which the *kind* of puzzle popular in a particular time and place reflects history and culture.[2] But I highlight this rift because I believe it is part of a pattern in the standard histories and in generic (and subgeneric) definitions of detective fiction wherein something labeled as "intellectual" is set up in opposition to violence, emotion, and realism.

Among the authoritative histories of detective fiction, there is solid agreement on the "main line of development" (and these accounts are strongly evolutionary). Almost everyone concurs that Edgar Allan Poe's "tales of ratiocination" (beginning in 1841 with "The Murders in the Rue Morgue," "The Mystery of Marie Rogêt," and "The Purloined Letter") initiated the detective story.[3] After that, the focus shifted quickly to England and France and the emergence of what is called the "classical" or "golden age" style of Arthur Conan Doyle, Agatha Christie, G. K. Chesterton, Dorothy Sayers, and their lesser American imitators. The British supremacy was broken only by the abrupt advent of the "hard-boiled" style of Dashiell Hammett and Raymond Chandler, which is understood to be essentially American in the way that the classical style is understood to be essentially British.[4] The classical style is also understood to be primarily devoted to the production of intricate mental puzzles and astound-

5

ingly clever detectives — Sherlock Holmes and Hercule Poirot, for example — to solve them. The hard-boiled style, on the other hand, is generally described and apprehended as more realistic, more interested in basic instincts and motivations (e.g., rage, greed, and lust) in its criminals and in its detectives, and shot through with violence and disorder, even in the investigative stages of the narrative. These oppositions of brains and brawn, order and chaos, and intellect and emotion were articulated forcefully by Chandler himself in the 1930s. He skewered the "utterly unreal" classical style as "the same old futzing around with timetables and bits of charred paper and who trampled the jolly old arbutus under the library window" and praised Hammett as the writer who "gave murder back to the kind of people who commit it for reasons, not just to provide a corpse; and with the means at hand, not hand-wrought dueling pistols, curare, and tropical fish." [5]

The fact that this history of golden age and hard-boiled revolt ignores an entire, and quite distinct, tradition of American women's writing from the 1860s through at least the 1930s is only one reason why I rehearse that tradition here. [6] The standard histories set up detective fiction as a genre with two divergent national streams: one fork British and soothingly intellectualized, the other American and satisfyingly violent. This historical narrative both reinforces and is reinforced by a similar opposition of intellect and violence in the fundamental definition and conceptualization of detective fiction. Again, we turn to Poe and the classic readings of what is at issue in the Dupin stories and how they relate to Poe's equally important and influential stories of horror and the supernatural. In Joseph Wood Krutch's famous formulation, "Poe invented the detective story in order that he might not go mad." [7] The detective story, according to this way of thinking, neutralizes terror and horror by demonstrating how the intellect can identify and control evil. "The Murders in the Rue Morgue" demonstrates this point nicely because it puts the highly analytical thinker, Auguste Dupin, on the trail of a vicious animal. We can see how such a reading of the founding text of the genre, which begins with some coy remarks about draughts, chess, and whist, lines up nicely with the idea that the first golden age of the genre was the production of the British puzzle style.

But what if Krutch has it wrong? What if the relation between

Dupin and the Ourang-Outang is more like that of Jekyll and Hyde? Richard Wilbur gets closer to the heart of the matter when he writes that Dupin "uses his genius to detect and restrain the brute in himself, thus exorcising the fiend," and when he deduces that Dupin and the corrupt Minister D—— of "The Purloined Letter" are brothers.[8] Perhaps we need to read the tales of ratiocination not as the repudiation of Poe's narratives of terror, but as an even fuller expression of the gothic imagination. William Patrick Day, in his acute and richly original study of gothic fantasy, argues that "the detective story develops because the inner logic of the Gothic demands such a development." He explains that in the gothic novel the "Gothic world overwhelms the human world, for no character can understand, or stand against, its evils. The detective challenges the encroachment of its terrors, the disorder brought on by crime and the monster in the shape of the criminal, returning the world to order and stability."[9] Day urges us to think of the detective as a figure constituted by the gothic mode, by the crimes that demand investigation and the mysteries that need to be dispelled. In addition, he argues that "Poe invents the detective to provide within the world of the story a character who can explain and organize the events into a meaningful pattern," suggesting that the detective is a kind of gothic narrator as well as a gothic character.

Day's argument allows us to reconnect the foundational text of detective fiction to a long tradition of gothic narrative. The gothic mode, or style, is recognizable through a long list of conventions, including its setting in a large, architecturally complex house, repeated problems with doors, windows, and cabinets (and the corollary locks and keys); the importance of veiled women, curtains, and secret rooms and passages; the visitation of the living by the dead and intentional or accidental live burial; the confusion of dream states and waking states, and of both sanity and insanity with inebriation; the fear of foreignness and racial difference, often manifested as Orientalism; an insistence on associating sex with danger, including obsessive interest in the rape of virgins and incest; a deep ambivalence about figures of authority, especially demanding, remote, or inept mothers, tyrannical fathers, and dissipated uncles; and many anxieties surrounding questions of identity, which are expressed in plots of mistaken identity, false or hazy paternity, switched babies, and, perhaps most pervasively, in the figure of the double. Gothic plots are driven by several principles, including the identity plots just mentioned, repetitions (which are like doubling at the level of narrative), and secrets, which are surrounded by the energy of repression and its logical, almost mechanical counterpart: the inevitability of every secret being told in the end.

Eve Sedgwick, the most elegant theorist of the gothic novel, sees several tropes that give these gothic conventions what she calls "coherence." One of the most important is the theme of the "unspeakable," which is manifest in the frequent repetitions of that word, but also in "a character who drops dead trying to utter a particular name," in letters mutilated or written in code, and in "a kind of despair about any direct use of language."[10] Sedgwick is especially interested in the way these thematic patterns affect the narrative structure of gothic fiction, and offers the following analysis of Maturin's *Melmoth the Wanderer* (1820):

Take, for instance, the famous Chinese-box structure of Melmoth, which at two points comprises a story within a story within a story within a story. Although all the stories do get more or less told in the novel's course, their very distinctness is a token of the divisive power of unspeakableness. The novel could, but does not, take the form of one continuous narrative, in which a character facing one situation would be from the start heir to gradually accumulated knowledge. . . . The plots, . . . closely parallel, are nonetheless kept rigidly separate by those devices of crumbling manuscripts, conventual secrecy, taboos on the communication of a family curse, and narrators who fall into convulsions at the word "Melmoth." . . . If in a story-within-a-story-within-a-story-within-a-story, all the stories are similar and parallel . . . then clearly the focus of formal energy must be these strange barriers: how spontaneously they spring up and multiply, and what extremes of magic or violence are necessary to breach them.[11]

Sedgwick's insight into the crucial and contradictory impulses of the gothic mode—to throw up barriers to knowing and telling *and* to provide the means of overcoming the barriers—allows us to see how the world of the gothic novel can not only accommodate but actively demand a figure like a detective. It is a detective's business to learn things and to make them known; he or she is, in structural terms, an incarnation or agent of the "magic or violence" that leads to understanding and coherence for characters in the novel and for the reader. The magic is usually the dazzling speed and thoroughness with which the detective reads and connects the physical evidence and the facts, lies, and lacunae in witness testimony. The violence is sometimes physical, whether it involves breaking into locked closets or chasing and shooting suspects, but it is also sometimes more metaphorically an act of violence against social convention, as when a male detective insists on searching the bedroom of an upper-class lady.

Structurally, detective fiction offers a streamlined and specialized version of the Chinese-box, story-within-a-story arrangements so common to eighteenth- and nineteenth-century gothic novels. As Tzvetan Todorov has illuminated through structuralist analysis, a detective novel is a narrative with two stories.[12] One story is the narrative of the investigation of a murder: the discovery of the body, the search for and interpretation of clues, the surveillance and questioning of suspects, the apprehension of the murderer. The second story is that of the actual murder: why and how it was done, how the murderer concealed his or her identity. The investigative story moves forward in time from the discovery of the murdered body to the moment of solution; the tale of the murder is being reconstructed backward from any efforts to disguise identity or confuse the police, through the moment of murder, and back to the earliest formation of motive. This second story is a concealed one — one that has been deliberately fragmented and made inaccessible to the detective by the murderer. We might think of both murderer and detective as authors or plotters, in which case the two figures become rivals struggling over the question of what will be made known about the secret crime.

We can see, then, that both the form and the content of detective fiction center on the tension between secrecy and revelation in a more structured and codified version of the oscillation between those impulses in the gothic mode. Mary Roberts Rinehart, in a formulation that predates Todorov's, offers a series of gothicized images of the "magic or violence" that accompany the breaching of the barriers between the two narrative streams. She writes that the detective story "consists of two stories running concurrently, the one which the reader follows, and the other a story submerged in the author's mind. . . . Every time this subcurrent story sticks its head above water, it makes a clew." Those "baffling clews and inexplicable mysteries" are what keep the reader reading, and "just when you are convinced that the pockmarked man committed the crime, a hand minus a thumb appears through a shattered window and sets you off on a new wild guess." [13]

In practice, though, clues, as points when the concealed story of murder becomes partially visible in the process of investigation, are only *like* fists through windows or creatures surfacing from under water. Detective fiction retains the gothic preoccupation with texts within texts, and in a detective story, written texts of all varieties (letters, wills, monogrammed handkerchiefs) almost invariably function as clues. With its attention to the ordering of disparate pieces of information, fragments of writing, and physical evidence, the detective novel has to be understood as not only about murder and solution, but also about the process by which narrative becomes coherent and authoritative. Peter Brooks takes this idea a step further in his brilliant study of "design and intention in narrative": "The detective story may . . . lay bare the structure of any narrative, particularly its claim to be a retracing of events that have already occurred. The detective retracing the trace of his predecessor . . . represents the very process of narrative representation." [14]

The doubled structure helps to foreground the steps by which a solution is reached (rather than the solution itself), something that is highlighted even further by the first-person retrospective narration of novels in the domestic detective tradition. Rinehart goes so far as to state that the ending of a detective story is always an "anticlimax," claiming that the necessary final chapter of tidy explanation of the crime is never as interesting as the ones that precede it, and that this problem is "a weakness no amount of technique can overcome." [15] This effect may be a large-scale manifestation of the gothic preoccupation with barriers to knowledge and to articulation of that knowledge. Between saying that mysery and bafflement keep us reading and that firm solutions are anticlimatic, Rinehart indicates that the middle of a detective novel is the most engaging and energized part.

Some of these energies include fear and confusion; as brilliant as some detectives are in this kind of fiction, all must engage in an epistemological battle with the materials of their case, if not a physical or emotional one. The gothic tradition demands that we take states of fear and confusion seriously, as emotional and epistemological experiences to be thoroughly explored before they are, in most cases, settled by the endings. Ann Radcliffe, whose *Mysteries of Udolpho* helped establish the popularity of the gothic novel, wrote that terror "expands the soul, and awakens the faculties to higher degree of life," and that phenomenon describes the reader's relation to the story as well as a character's reaction to the events of the plot.[16] Ellen Moers puts it as well as anyone can when she writes, "What I mean — or what anyone else means — by 'the Gothic' is not so easily stated except that it has to do with fear" (both of these comments are especially pertinent to the female gothic, which we will consider at greater length below).[17] Certain types of detective fiction retain this celebration of terror, including the early detective novels by women examined here, and, I would argue, Poe's foundational texts. In the gothic scheme of things, fear, suspicion, and the excruciating awareness that there is something one doesn't know are not false ideas that hinder true knowledge, but are crucial to the process of learning, knowing, and negotiating the real barriers between oneself and the truth. Of course, the heroine (or hero) of a gothic detective novel has to keep her wits about her, but it is fear that awakens her faculties, just as it is the mystery that makes her into a detective.

These questions — about whether detective fiction is a tidy puzzle or a reflection of the violence of its age, about whether Dupin exorcises the ape or is his double, and about whether to read detective fiction as a genre centered on solution or on bafflement — are all versions of each other. All of them point to a central issue of this study, the potential for detective fiction to act as social criticism. The recent work of Kathleen Gregory Klein has raised important and difficult questions about the cultural politics of the genre. Klein, in her trenchant study of female detectives in literature, finds the genre incapable of meaningful social critique and antithetical to feminism, though it is important to add that she does not treat the domestic detective novel with any depth. She writes, "The conservatism of the genre can be seen from the beginnings: structurally, the successful stories depended on a regular and familiar sequence of events; thematically, they reinforced a capitalistic, traditional, moralistic, and nostalgic world view."[18] She argues that the genre upholds the deeply ingrained cultural hierarchies of male/female and mind/body, so that the detective is "definitionally male" and the victim is always female. Indeed, Klein sees a kind of constitutional misogyny in this genre in which "the detective — and before him the criminal — writes his story on the ever available body of the victim."[19] Her survey of detective fiction tells her that even when detectives are played, as it were, by female characters, they are undercut by the events of the story, and the novels in which they appear are always a species of parody.[20]

Klein's arguments are penetrating and theoretically informed, but she gives too much weight to the law-and-order endings of detective novels. Although all forms of narrative have, as Brooks puts it, pleasurable structures of delay, detective fiction seems especially insistent on this point, offering one solution after another as the detective investigates and works out scenarios for a series of suspects. I hope in the course of this book to make a case for reading for the middle as an approach to at least the tradition of domestic detective fiction. The work of these authors is both chronologically and thematically close to the gothic traditions of the nineteenth century; Victor, Green, and Rinehart take their subject to be fear and confusion as well as knowledge and resolution (as do the experimenters Alcott and Hopkins). They also use the gothic elements of encroaching evil and disorder as a way to name iniquities in the sunny ideology of middle-class domestic life. These critiques are moderate and very much incorporated, to use the term in the way Raymond Williams has defined it, into the value systems of the middle and upper classes. When these authors criticize capitalism, they blame it for producing greedy, hard-hearted men who disown their daughters at the drop of a hat, not for producing a permanent underclass. Yet, though written by and for members of the middle and upper classes, these novels still have a certain bite, especially on questions of gender expectations. In this sense the authors' use of gothic tropes is quite different from the use of the gothic in the "dark-reform" literature of mid-century, which deploys the most graphic and violent configurations of the gothic mode to paint a picture of the upper class as corrupt and monstrous.[21] The novels I examine in this book are, however, squarely in the tradition of domestic fiction, both in the specific ways they treat and deploy the gothic mode, and in the more general tone and goal of their social criticism.

## The Domestic Novel and the Gothic Mode;
## or, The Authentic Ghost Story

In some ways, the gothic and domestic modes would seem to be antithetical: the domestic novel is solidly realist (though in a style somewhat different from the social realism of Howells or the psychological realism of James) and genteel, while the gothic is given over to many kinds of excess.[22] However, there are many examples of British and American women writers who explore the congruences between the domestic and gothic modes. When they do so, writers like Alcott, Stowe, Southworth, and Charlotte and Emily Brontë take up the style of gothic established by Ann Radcliffe in the eighteenth century, a style called the "female gothic."[23] In the female gothic, the emphasis is on fear rather than on horror, outrage, or disgust. The gothic heroine is alternately immobilized within a domestic space and chased through its hallways; escape remains a fantasy, but any movement is terrifying because it seems to promise pursuit rather than liberation. Almost always, the heroine must be rescued by a man of virtue from the conspirators who surround and threaten to corrupt her. Imprisonment, flight, and rescue are darkly eroticized in this tradition, but knowledge is also a focal point of tension and energy in the female gothic mode. Even as she is being pursued, the heroine pursues an epistemological quest of her own through the house, castle, or convent in which she has been confined. Her investigations usually teach her that another woman has been wronged or murdered in the past, and lead her to a secret room or hiding place associated with the crime.[24] This woman is always in some aspect a mother figure and is often a repellent or disturbing trope for the female condition and a cautionary example to the heroine. As that plot point suggests, the female gothic sets up a narrative of personal development through confrontation, although the gothic heroine's tendency to repeat her mistakes largely occludes it. The heroine's explorations of the ghostlike mother or the stories told about her are undertaken in a state of fear so carefully detailed that it operates as a heightened state of consciousness, With every physical sense aroused, she must evade and outsmart her captors, she must exert tremendous self-control, and she must take a careful measure of her own abilities and resources in order to undertake the dangerous work of investigation. Of course, most gothic heroines don't succeed in learning their captors' secrets while evading further punishment (since they tend to faint at crucial moments), but the desire to unravel mysteries, the ability to resist moral corruption, and the impulse to challenge tyranny are characteristic of the gothic heroine.

That emphasis on surviving tests of moral strength and intellectual acuity is an element that the female gothic mode shares with the American domestic novel of the mid-nineteenth century. Like the gothic heroine, the domestic heroine is literally or figuratively motherless near the beginning of the story, and the ensuing narrative charts her temptations and troubles as she attempts to find a place in the emotional and economic order of the middle class. The domestic novel, substituting more realistic terms for the deeply symbolic vocabulary of the female gothic mode, posits that the heroine must come to terms with her dead, lost, or invalid mother by becoming her own governess and counselor. The domestic heroine must learn to discern the difference between real love and emotional playacting, between wholesome delight and hollow dissipation, between true Christian devotion and cynical religiosity. She develops a keen moral sense and eventually comes to understand self-sacrifice as pleasure instead of duty. In short, she becomes a woman who is happily ruled by her conscience.[25] The gothic heroine of the eighteenth and nineteenth centuries, being by definition beset from all sides, never achieves this level of serenity. Yet, there is a certain overlap in the narrative trajectories of these two modes. Both valorize intelligence in women, and both suggest that all serious learning involves self-knowledge. Both center on domestic life as a fabric of activities and relationships that matter, and both explore the psychology of motherhood and daughterhood with great intensity, even ferocity.

Many writers of high and low fiction mix gothic and domestic elements in their fiction. Southworth's *The Hidden Hand* bristles with plot devices from the gothic: symbolic birthmarks, trapdoors and bottomless pits, captive maidens, a bedside ghost, and highway robbers. It also has what Sedgwick calls the "Chinese-box structure" of some gothic novels, in which several subplots that have seemed separate eventually turn out to be parts of a single story.[26] Yet it is also a quite complete bildungsroman, in which the young Capitola learns self-control, cheers the lives of the people around her, and gets to marry the man she has always admired. Southworth's novel is an exemplar of the way the domestic and gothic modes can be used to reinforce each other; in this case, the terrors of the hidden house make vividly clear the importance of developing an independent spirit and nerves of steel.[27]

Likewise, domestic detective novels evoke the images, themes, and plots of the American domestic novel of the mid-nineteenth century. The setting of the action is almost exclusively within private homes, and the drama of the plot is based almost entirely on the dynamics of the relationships among the members of the household. We see certain plot elements from the domestic novel, such as the proof of the heroine's virtue by her personal attention to the deserving poor. Most of these novels have urban settings, and even in those set in suburban or rural areas, the capitalist city is always on the horizon. The city is not so much the setting for the investigation (the interior of the home is where most of the clues are) as it is the setting for the temptations that lead to the crime. As in the domestic novel, the main problem in the world of these books is male greed; men warped by capitalist longings for money are often murderers or parties to murder. And as in the domestic novel, the good woman is an anchor of stability in the family and the administrator of class identity, teaching her husband, her children, and anyone else who comes under her care how to be morally middle class and responsibly genteel.

But, having raised the framework of the domestic novel, the writers we will examine then go about questioning its assumptions in more and less subtle ways; that evocation and subversion are the core of the social critique these novels make. Ultimately, they argue the same case that the domestic novel does: that the woman's sphere can provide the values, practices, and attitudes to ameliorate or repair the social ills of the day.[28] But by making gothic tropes like the haunted house central to their work, these authors emphasize even more strongly that strain of discontent within the domestic realm that we can discern in many works of the genre.[29] The symbolic language of live burial, for example, makes a critique of the waste of women's talents both inescapably clear and viscerally disturbing. Other gothic tropes of mistaken identity, masking, coded messages, and forgery work as allegories about hypocrisy and mendacity in the upper echelons of society.[30] The gothic, in other words, has potential for social criticism, even—or especially—when embedded in a middle-class novel of domestic life. We might even understand the gothic mode as a discourse through which certain writers have attempted to articulate the mutual influence of the public and private realms of experience, especially in matters of morality and money.

In *Gothic America,* Teresa Goddu offers multiple insights into the convergences and divergences of domestic and gothic modes of discourse on the home. Particularly helpful for our understanding of the uses of the gothic mode by the authors I discuss here is Goddu's argument that we can "locate the gothic in relation to the public sphere of the nineteenth-century American marketplace." In Louisa May Alcott's fiction, in particular, the marketplace is gothicized as a world of shadowy seductions and mysterious power.[31] Goddu bases this part of her argument on the depiction of Jo March's visit to the offices of the *Weekly Volcano* in *Little Women.* We might also think of the anecdote of Meg March Brook and her impulsive and self-indulgent purchase of a length of expensive silk she can't afford to make an evening dress she doesn't need. Immediately regretting her purchase after she returns home, she puts the fabric away, but "it haunted her, not delightfully as a new dress should, but dreadfully, like the ghost of a folly that was not easily laid."[32] We can also see in Meg's struggle with gothicized luxury goods an undercurrent of bitterness that she must learn to be content with what her husband's salary can provide. As Goddu puts it, there is "poison at the heart of the sentimental sugarplum: . . . the domestic realm is already the site of the market," a "workplace where women are expected to give their labor for free." The gothic mode, Goddu argues, is called on to depict "the market demons that penetrate" the middle- and upper-class home, especially in the tropes of the veiled lady and other dramatic figures of mistaken identity (which, like commodities, operate by gaining power not from intrinsic worth but from assigned value). One of the scary effects of the gothic mode in this context is the insinuation that the home is like a stock exchange where emotions, loyalties, and women's minds and bodies are traded. "The gothic," Goddu asserts, "enacts the maneuvers of a commodity culture that the sentimental strategically veils." Goddu's analysis calls for us to rethink the way we tend to "imprison" the gothic mode in the private realms of psychology and domestic ideology, since by "dissolving the boundaries between the public and private spheres, the female gothic in mid-nineteenth century America does more than expose female entrapment within and rebellion against a patriarchal culture; it also reflects how the anxieties and dislocations of a new commodity culture were mediated through the female body." [33]

The gothicization of "market demons" and the critique implied by the process of making them irrationally powerful is even more pronounced in domestic detective fiction. Money is a corrupting influence, of course, especially when a capitalist yearning for increase causes a man to engage in criminal versions of market speculation, such as high-risk, high-yield embezzlement strategies, long-term investment in blackmail schemes, and the consolidation of holdings through the murder of partners in crime. More important, domestic detective fiction expresses both the certainty that the domestic realm can never isolate itself from the competitive, cutthroat world of capitalism and the anxiety that this fact should be true. Early detective fiction by women almost always includes extended scenes of searching the middle-class home and interrogating the middle-class family and its servants as demonstrations not only of the difficulty of breaching the obstacles to the truth put up by social barriers of class privilege and material wealth, but also the importance of rooting out and removing the contagion of self-interest implied by the heiress's gunpowder-spotted handkerchief stuffed behind the sofa cushions, a blackmailer's logbook hidden under the floorboards of a study, or a gold coin offered as a bribe to a servant girl and tucked away in her spare pair of stockings. The kinds of secrets domestic detective novels centralize and expose often result from quandaries from the domestic realm compounded by problems of the marketplace, like an elopement made in secret because the woman will be disinherited if she marries the penniless man she loves against the wishes of her father.

As Goddu so acutely observes, the gothic mode was used by nineteenth-century women writers to record and to critique what they saw as capitalism's insidious effects on women, including the literal and figurative marketing of their bodies in marriage, rape, prostitution, and slavery. That tradition of deploying the gothic mode as social criticism was continued by the domestic detective novel tradition from the mid-nineteenth century into the early twentieth century, with the added emphasis on the need to investigate the murders that can result from the commodification of women (usually these murders involve women killed by men who think they own them, sometimes women who kill men attempting to enforce their masculine prerogatives). This strain of gothic social criticism adopted by Victor, Green, and Rinehart was developed in part by Harriet Beecher Stowe, whose story of Cassy and the haunted plantation evokes gothic terror in service of the larger moral argument of *Uncle Tom's Cabin*.[34]

Simon Legree's plantation is a place of brutality and terror ruled by a corrupt and troubled tyrant. Cassy, one of his slaves, plays on his guilty (though hardened) conscience in order to mount a successful escape from the plantation. Building on a rumor that the garret of the house is haunted by the ghost of a murdered slave woman, Cassy sets a glass bottleneck into a knothole to shape a draft into eerie moans and uses her own assertions of fear to terrify Legree. Having ensured that he will never set foot in the attic again, Cassy uses it as a place to secrete herself and another female slave after staging their escape into the swamp. Her trick works — she and Emmeline are shielded from discovery until they have a chance to slip away from the plantation for good. Although she is restored to a gentle motherliness by her experience in rescuing Emmeline, Cassy is for most of these chapters a resident madwoman, cursing Legree and her fellow slaves and ranting about the tortures awaiting them at Legree's hands.

The whole episode is a narrative of female rage within the home; originally, Cassy plans to kill Legree with an axe. When Tom warns Cassy that "[t]he Lord hasn't called us to wrath. We must suffer, and wait his time," Cassy replies in a voice both murderous and desperate: "Haven't I waited? — waited till my head is dizzy and my heart sick. . . . His time's come, and I'll have his heart's blood!"[35] Stowe is not, it seems to me, suggesting that gothic rage is a desirable mode of self-expression for women. Cassy is a woman cornered by physical brutality, sexual abuse, legal bondage, and spiritual starvation who becomes desperate enough to plot a murder (but plots a haunting instead). Thus Cassy's roles as gothic madwoman and as manipulator of the gothic each serve Stowe's larger argument that slavery perverts the Christian-maternal complex that is the source of true morality in public and private life.[36] It is because the gothic mode, with its structures of barriers and its tropes of mistaken identities, proves so apt for describing the horror of enslavement and racism that Stowe can call this part of her moral fiction "an authentic ghost story." It was authentically scary and authentic to the reform agenda of the northern middle class at mid-century.

Cassy is crucial to our understanding of the uses of the gothic in the domestic detective novel because of the way she deploys her gothic "stratagem." Invoking the gothic plot can be a tricky thing for a female writer or a female character, for the position of the female heroine is that of the pursued and imprisoned, even if she is finally rescued from her terrors. The powerful positions for women in the gothic, Cassy's story tells us, are the ones occupied by the angry ghost and the author or plotter. As it was for Capitola Black, the role of gothic heroine can be desirable only when it is clearly a kind of playacting entirely under the control of the woman in question. In those cases, the gothic mode can set up very effective plots of escape and revenge for its female characters and compelling parables of social criticism for its authors. Cassy's stratagem sketches a paradigmatic gesture for domestic detective fiction, for the plots of those novels tell us the same thing over and over: it is better to be the author of a gothic story than to be its heroine, and it is better to be a wraith than to be haunted by one.

Stowe and our detective novelists also suggest that to tell gothic stories about the realm supposedly ruled by contented, orderly domesticity is to say something more truthful than genteel forms would allow. It is this particular moral purpose in using the gothic tradition that marks the main difference between the American domestic detective novel and the British Victorian sensation novel. Sensation novels, wildly popular in the 1850s and 1860s and mirroring the sensational press, often feature legal and social crime among the upper classes—bigamy and divorce, assumption of false identity, withholding of inheritances, theft—as their subject.[37] Generically, the sensation novel is quite similar to and contemporaneous with early examples of the domestic detective novel, and Wilkie Collins was an influence on both Victor and Green. Collins's *The Moonstone* (1868) is widely accepted in histories of detective fiction as an important link between the short stories of Poe and the full-fledged detective novel. However, the police detective, Sergeant Cuff, never solves the mystery of the stolen diamond; instead, his efforts only delineate the impenetrability of the wealthy private home to public scrutiny. The domestic detective novel is far more interested in and optimistic about the efficacy of surveillance by the police or other moral arbiters, which means that detectives are not only more important figures in these novels, but also more effective ones. As part of their interest in states of fear and confusion, the novels of Victor, Green, and Rinehart share with the sensation novel the ability to produce somatic effects in the reader with their narratives of continual suspense and frequent bursts of terror.[38] But the American novels, at least those of Victor and Rinehart, are more interested in how women can foil the gothic plots laid against them than, as is the case in the bulk of sensation novels, in spinning out variations on that theme.

In the way they combine the moral worldview of the domestic novel and the structures of encroaching crime and energetic investigation from the foundational works of detective fiction, domestic detective novels seem to be in some ways successors to the domestic novels of mid-century. I offer this idea tentatively. I am not trying to argue that *The Leavenworth Case* was read by the same people who read Elizabeth Stuart Phelps's *The Gates Ajar*. Instead, I am suggesting that the domestic detective has to be understood as coming after the domestic novel and as reflecting many of the transformations and redactions of sentimental culture in the postbellum period. The domestic novel, which was the most important forum for commentary on the domestic arrangements of the middle class at mid-century, began to lose its cultural ascendancy sometime after the Civil War.[39] The domestic novel did not disappear entirely, however; novels such as Maria Susanna Cummins's *The Lamplighter* (1854) and Susan Warner's *The Wide, Wide World* (1850) were reprinted—the former notoriously so — in many editions through the turn of the century, and *Little Women* (1869) is still standard reading for young girls of the middle and upper classes. What we can say about the domestic novel of the mid-nineteenth century is that it lost a great deal of its cultural currency after the Civil War and that publication of new work took place in comparative obscurity.

But, as I have noted in this discussion of gothic, detective, and domestic traditions, popular genres hybridize and linger within a culture long after their zenith of influence or popularity.[40] In her study of the western, Jane Tompkins gives a model for sketching the relationship between the domestic novel, which so dominated the middle-class fiction market, and the multiple popular genres that seem to have followed in its wake. She summarizes the "main features" of the sentimental domestic novel in this way:

[A] woman is always the main character, usually a young orphan girl. . . . Most of the action takes place in private spaces, at home, indoors, in kitchens, parlors, and upstairs chambers. And most of it concerns the interior struggles of the heroine to live up to an ideal of Christian virtue — usually involving uncomplaining submission to difficult and painful circumstances. . . . In these struggles, women give one another a great deal of emotional and material support, and they have close relationships verging on what today we would identify as homosocial and homoerotic. . . . Emotions other than anger are expressed very freely and openly. Often there are long, drawn-out death scenes in which a saintly woman dies a natural death at home. Culturally and politically, the effect of these novels is to establish women at the center of the world's most important work (saving souls) and to assert that in the end spiritual power is always superior to worldly might.[41]

Tompkins concludes that "the elements of the typical Western plot arrange themselves in stark opposition to this pattern, not just vaguely and generally but point for point."[42] The domestic detective novel, which was ascending to a point of some cultural potency just as the domestic novel was waning, does not place itself in opposition to the domestic novel in the same way the western does. Instead, it continues some aspects of domestic fiction, downplays or heightens others, and makes strategic substitutions elsewhere, often of female gothic tropes for strictly domestic ones. Where the domestic novel focuses on the deathbed farewell as the apogee of the all-important activity of feeling, the domestic detective novel centers on the discovery of a corpse as the initiation into fear, confusion, and the desire for knowledge. Emotional expression is still an important discursive mode in the domestic detective novel, with the added twist that emotions need to be analyzed carefully for fakery, for undertones (of guilt, most specifically), and for appropriateness. The novels we will examine take a great interest in relationships between women, especially between mothers and daughters, but the anger and suspicion surrounding the crimes tend to make those relationships stormy as often as supportive. They tend to portray the homosocial world of the domestic novel as anachronistic and to show moments when women must challenge the sexism of the public sphere and of traditional domestic arrangements.

The heroines of these detective novels fall into two distinct types: in the early period, in the work of Victor and in the first novels of Green, the detectives are male and the heroine is a woman falsely accused of a crime or orphaned by the murder of a relative. She must, like a heroine in a domestic novel in painful circumstances, submit nobly to the public humiliation of gossip, newspaper headlines, and legal proceedings; her goal is to regain her place of respectability within the ideologies of race, sex, and class. The crimes often jeopardize her inheritance or income, and financial hardship threatens her entire way of life. The later work of Green and that of Rinehart features female detective-heroines who likewise face their trials. They are shaken out of their upper-class complacency by the murder and have to learn physical and mental courage as they work to correct an inept police investigation or protect a member of their family who is wrongly suspected of the crime. Those later novels, to echo Tompkins, establish women at the center of the urgent work of saving the professional and upper classes from their own corruption and venality.

In domestic detective fiction, the middle- or upper-class domestic interior is still the stage for the most significant activities, but it is now understood as a realm of high anxiety and deep flaws. Often the domestic space presents itself as a haunted house, but it is always a place where fierce emotions and libidinal impulses run just beneath the veneer of gentility. The domestic sphere is no longer a simple model of a higher moral and spiritual order to be used for social reform. Instead, the idealized home is clearly in the realm of the imaginary: it is something people believe in and hope to bring about by solving crimes, but the ideal is continually shown as ruptured by the forces of the marketplace. The detective fictions of this tradition insist on the need for intervention in the dangerous configurations of greed, rivalry, lust, and the suppression of women that are the direct or indirect result of the pervasive desire to trade up socially and to dominate every emotional or material transaction. When women writers took up the work of writing detective fiction, they placed the detective in the home, asserting a need for a new kind and level of investigation into the domestic arrangements of the middle and upper classes. The significance of that strategy will be made clearer as we turn from this examination of literary-historical origins to a discussion of the earliest appearance of detectives in fiction by American women and its cultural context.

## The Advent of the Detective

The fiction of Louisa May Alcott might seem to be an unexpected point of arrival for the fictional figure of the detective, but it does seem to be the case that her 1865 story "V. V., or Plots and Counterplots" features the first appearance of a detective in American women's letters, though it cannot be called a fully developed detective story in the sense that I have outlined above.[43] This development might seem less surprising when we consider that Alcott's works exhibit a confluence of literary modes that almost perfectly represents and recapitulates the broader literary-historical moment of the 1860s. The discovery that Alcott, known to generations as the unrelentingly virtuous "children's friend," wrote scores of thrillers for the story-papers has forced critics and historians to reassess where she belongs in the literary landscape.[44] Richard Brodhead has shown that study of her career demands that we revise our maps of that landscape; he puts her at the center of what he calls "a major rearticulation of the literary field" in the 1850s and 1860s.[45]

Before that period, Brodhead argues, the literary marketplace had been shaped by a "domestic culture of letters," which is to say "the newly formed middle class's creation of a newly central place *for* literature among its organizing habits and concerns." Beginning in the 1850s, the literary world was reorganized through a proliferation of specialized periodicals and the development of new literary commodities such as the dime novel. Cosmopolitan magazines like the *Atlantic* helped to demarcate "the nonpopular 'high' culture that came to exist 'above' the domestic or middlebrow world of letters in the later nineteenth century just as the new story-papers of the 1850s helped organize the 'low' one that came to exist 'below' it." This period, in other words, saw the development of high literary culture (what we call the American Renaissance), of sensational mass culture (story-papers and dime novels), and of middlebrow reading (which Brodhead sees as at least partly occupied by holdovers of the middle-class domestic novel). Alcott's career, which included publication in all of these "zones" of literary culture, "can teach us that late nineteenth-century cultures typically studied in isolation came into existence together, through a unified process of cultural development." [46] I would add here that while we should heed Brodhead's warning not to collapse the differences between Alcott's "proto-high and proto-low" performances (and we might add, thinking of *Little Women,* the ones that are "ur-middle"), we can certainly take into account that while she was writing for different sectors of the market, she always wrote from one class position. This may help explain why the women's detective novel, which began on the pages of the story-papers, quickly "rose" (as we shall see in our discussions of Victor and Green) to the level of the genteel hardbound novel and from the beginning seemed to speak to particular nodes of middle- and upper-class anxieties.

The detective figure likewise needs to be understood as a product of certain "rearticulations of the literary field," especially those accompanying the waning of "sentimental hegemony" after the Civil War.[47] Alcott brings in her detective to help when a young aristocrat, Dougal, must determine if the pretty young widow who has infiltrated his social circle murdered his fiancée (she did). Dougal further suspects that this woman is in disguise and is in reality an actress and *danseuse* named Virginie Varens, who was married to and probably murdered his cousin (she is). The detective, Antoine Duprès, is clearly modeled on Poe's Auguste Dupin (even taking the alias of M. Dupont) and arrives in the Scottish setting of the story from Paris. He is not an official policeman, but seems to have made a name for himself as an investigator of delicate and violent family matters such as this one.

Although this thriller is not a detective story according to our structural definition, Alcott understands several things about the detective's potential as a literary and a cultural figure. Duprès, having quickly determined who the widow is and what she has been up to, does not wish to expose her immediately. If literary critics have struggled to articulate the ways in which a detective is a metaphorical author, Duprès does so directly and enthusiastically. He says to Dougal, "[P]romise me that you will not call in the help of your blundering constabulary, police, or whatever you name them, until I give the word. They will destroy the éclat of the *dénouement,* and annoy me by their stupidity" (VV, 382). Like Dupin, who is the embodiment of Poe's description of an "analyst" who "glories" in "that moral activity which *disentangles,*" Duprès "adore[s] mystery; to fathom a secret, trace a lie, discover a disguise" (VV, 382).[48] But there is a double meaning in Duprès's words; for him, "to trace a lie" can mean to inscribe as well as to pursue, and "to discover a disguise" can mean to acquire as well as to unmask. Even more than Dupin, who places an ad in the paper to lure the owner of the escaped Ourang-Outang, Duprès delights in weaving a web to catch a criminal.[49] He tells his client, "[T]his brain of mine is fertile in inventions, and by morning will have been inspired with a design which will enchant you by its daring, its acuteness, its romance" (VV, 383).

Just as Duprès can be read as a kind of paradigmatic fictional and fictionalizing detective, so can his work be seen as establishing certain patterns of investigation and intervention. Virginie combines two of the most dangerous mid-century female types — the actress and the adventuress — with the almost unthinkable evil of bad mothering (she has abandoned a child from the marriage to Dougal's cousin). She must be unmasked as only playing the part of the virtuous and genteel widow, and she is subjected to a quite literal reading by Duprès and Dougal when they drug her, put her to bed, and read her letters, her monogrammed jewelry, and the secret tattoo on her arm (a scene repeated in many early detective novels).[50] But while he wants to know everything about her, Dougal wants to have her stopped and punished quietly, to avoid bringing dishonor to his family. The detective, then, must possess discretion as well as discernment. He must know all the codes of conduct of the upper class so that he can detect imposters like Virginie, so that he can understand the moral measure of their violations, and so that he can restore the proper order of things through his activities (as when he sets up a duel to restore Dougal to a more manly state of mind and to kill off the insincere, homicidal, and incestuous cousin of Virginie).

We might begin to think of detective fiction as arriving not just in the aftermath of the domestic novel as a general phenomenon, but in answer to the needs of the continuing anxiety over sincerity, self-control, and moral governance in the middle and upper classes.[51] If, as Brodhead argues, the domestic novel operated as a medium and a model of "disciplinary intimacy" for the middle class, the domestic detective novel has to be seen as introducing new agents to detect and correct improper behavior in the domestic sphere. The overwhelming and sometimes supernatural power of the mother to know what the members of her family are doing and should be doing, which is the basis of disciplinary intimacy, is replaced, in the domestic detective novel, by a detective who likewise examines and regulates the behavior of a family in turmoil. This particular point will be clearer when we get to the development of female detectives in the later work of Green and Rinehart. But even in this prototype by Alcott, the experiments of Hopkins, and the novels of Metta Victor, we can see that the work of the detective is hygienic and disciplinary. The men who are the first of our detectives come onto the scene not just to learn the truth, but to untangle and measure the transgressions against domestic ideology and to reroute the problematic erotics of lust, jealousy, and selfishness. Even when the detectives are paid professionals or policemen they are motivated as much or more by genteel ideas of rightness as by the interests of the state or the letter of the law. The fact that they are welcomed in these texts and in popular culture more generally is an indication of the permeability of the private and public spheres around questions of morality, for the private sphere of these novels clearly needs regulation, and the emissaries from the criminal justice system are aware of the needs and desires of the middle and upper classes.

That assessment of the advent of the detective in women's fiction is reinforced by evidence from other contributing literary and historical phenomena. In his richly worked account of the way various literatures of crime came to constitute popular culture in New England between the 1670s and the 1850s, Daniel Cohen argues that colonial execution sermons, the first of these genres, emphasized a straightforward relationship of crime and punishment, but later forms, especially the annotated texts of trial testimony that became popular in the early nineteenth century, stressed the "intervening process of adjudication."[52] Cohen examines the many newspaper reports, broadsides, and books that narrated one particularly sensational murder trial in 1802 and traces the use of sentimental discourse, especially in relation to questions of sexuality and sexual transgression, in both trial reportage and the attorneys' arguments. He concludes that these texts document how "the dry husk of the last-speech broadside was exploded by an infusion of motifs from the sentimental novel . . . and early trial reports stressed the legalistic components of the new cultural regime." He observes that "far from being the antithesis of sentimental expression, nineteenth-century legal advocacy could be its very essence," and speculates elsewhere, in a formulation that resonates strongly with Brodhead's analysis of disciplinary intimacy, that this type of sentimentalized legal narrative "exposed frustrations inherent in an emerging regime of Victorian gender relations that celebrated romantic engagement while demanding sexual restraint" and "exposed some of the darker contradictions of a moralistic consumer culture that alternately mandated self-discipline and self-indulgence."[53] In her work on early American murder narratives, Karen Halttunen argues, with her characteristic distilled clarity, that "any narrative of murder involves a fictive process which reveals much about the mental and emotional strategies employed within a given historical culture for responding to serious transgressions in their midst" and contends that the execution sermon was succeeded by a "variety of secular genres," including "trial reports, criminal biographies and autobiographies, journalistic accounts of the crime, and detection narratives."[54]

Detective fiction might be understood as an elaborate new structure for the consideration, interpretation, and even control of narratives of crime. The emergence of the middle-class domestic detective

novel shows how important to genteel culture narratives that enacted dramas of self-indulgence and self-control had become in the
postbellum era. As I have already noted, detective fiction of this type
foregrounds problems of knowing, especially in regard to social
identity, that were of an increasingly complex and vexed nature in
middle- and upper-class culture in the late nineteenth century. In
the studies of detective fiction by Victor, Hopkins, Green, and Rinehart that follow, I will show how those concerns were inflected and
expressed through their stories of crime and its investigation within
the domestic sphere.

# 2

## *"The Eye of Suspicion"*

### THE EROTICS OF DETECTION IN

### *THE DEAD LETTER*

Metta Fuller Victor was a prolific and successful writer and editor of popular fiction in the decades around the Civil War, but very little is known about her life. Her name is probably best known today to collectors of detective fiction, for as far as anyone can be certain about "firsts" in American publishing, *The Dead Letter*, published in book form in 1866, is the first American detective novel.[1] Victor was born in 1831 and grew up in Pennsylvania and Ohio. The fact that she attended a private female seminary suggests that her family was at least middle class. Victor began publishing regularly at thirteen, and most of her early publications were poems, some of which she wrote with her sister.[2] Her adult career as a writer of dime novels is a startling mixture of commercialism and reform politics; she was clearly a writer who knew how to work the literary marketplace, but she seems also to have been genuinely impassioned by the questions of intemperance, slavery, and Mormon plural marriage that she took up in some of her most successful dime novels, such as *Maum Guinea and Her Plantation Children* (Beadle, 1861), and her temperance novel, *The Senator's Son* (1853).[3]

She wrote a remarkable number of dime novels in a wide range of genres, shrewdly marketing herself as several authors by using a different pseudonym for each genre: for boys' books she was Walter T. Gray, for domestic novels, Corinne Cushman, and so forth. In 1856, she married Orville Victor and worked with him to build up the Beadle publishing house; she later became the editor of the Beadle magazine *Home* and of *Beadle's Monthly*. She was thus well versed in the discourse of domestic ideology, and she wrote articles on deportment and housework and compiled cookbooks. She had, in addition to this busy and prolific writing career, nine children. She wrote a book, *Passing the Portal* (1876), that presents itself as autobiography but conforms utterly to the conventions of the domestic novel. In it, a young girl from the country comes to stay with her rich relatives in New York City; she softens up her curmudgeonly uncle and resists the temptation to frivolity and fashion, and we never see the heroine write anything but letters. What this autobiography tells us is that Victor preferred to remain behind the shield of pseudonyms and pseudobiography—whether for the sake of modesty or career is a matter of speculation.

Victor wrote two detective novels under the pseudonym Seeley Regester: *The Dead Letter* and *The Figure Eight; or, The Mystery of Meredith Place* (Beadle, 1869), and one novel that includes the pursuit of a criminal, *Too True: A Story of Today,* under her own name.[4] Both of the detective stories were marketed as fifty-cent hardbound novels, which is to say to a middle- and upper-class audience.[5] Both *The Dead Letter* and *The Figure Eight* integrate the distinctive narrative structure of detective fiction with older popular styles; we can pick out many of the tropes of story-paper gothic, pirate tales, and, as an appeal to its middle-class audience, the calmer strains of the domestic novel's values and worldview. They are full-fledged detective novels in the sense that the entire narrative centers on the investigation of the murder and they include figures who are professional detectives or driven amateurs. Both of Victor's detective novels are explorations of what spying and surveillance might expose and accomplish within the homes of the well-to-do. Both are narrated by rising young professional men whose experiences in investigating domestic crime both solidify their sense of upper-class identity and justify their sense of being part of an elite within that class. Both books are thus documents of a moment in cultural history when the young professional seemed to hold the promise of mediating between the cloudy-minded nostalgia of the landed class and the unprincipled greed of the merchant and capitalist classes.

Like *The Figure Eight, The Dead Letter* makes the family of the professional class into an arena of suspicion and secrecy. It features two detective figures: a police detective named Burton and a young lawyer named Redfield. Burton is not a regular member of the police force; he is a private citizen of independent means who has become an expert on the "dangerous secrets of a community" and the "whole web of human iniquity" that connects even the wealthy and powerful to crime and corruption.[6] Victor is at pains to explain to us that Burton is a gentleman, and that he accepts no fees for his services. She outlines the story of how he was converted from a businessman of integrity to a detective by his discovery of the depth and range of corruption among his fellow import-export merchants, "high and mighty potentates, against whom to breathe a breath of slander, was to overwhelm the audacious individual in the ruins of his own presumption" (*DL,* 68). Having discovered their operation involving arson and insurance fraud,

> he went to work, quietly, and singly, to gather up the threads in his cable of proof. . . . [H]e threatened them with exposure, unless they made good to him the loss [of uninsured merchandise] which he had sustained through their villainy. They laughed at him from the stronghold of their respectability. He brought the case into court. . . . Banded together, with inexhaustible means of corruption at their command, the guilty were triumphant. . . . Burning with a sense of his individual wrongs, he could not look calmly on and see others similarly exposed; he grew fascinated with his labor of dragging the dangerous secrets of a community to light. (*DL,* 68–69)

Victor clearly means to distinguish her detective from the morally ambiguous detective figures that her readers might have known from the newspapers and the newly popular genre of the detective memoir (genteel readers would likely have had little personal contact with police detectives in this period).

The police, especially the police in cities, had changed their mission in the middle decades of the nineteenth century, shifting from a force that functioned as a constabulary to an agency tasked to prevent crime by aggressive investigation of criminal activities.[7] By the last decades of the century, most departments were promoting detectives out of the ranks of uniformed officers, but from the 1840s into the 1870s, detectives were more often private citizens who contracted their services to the police. Many detectives not only asked a fee of their client — private citizen or police department — but also expected a share of any stolen goods they successfully recovered or a bribe from a criminal willing to pay for the detective's silence. The propensity for corruption among detectives arose, in part, from the strategy urban police used to apprehend criminals. They attempted to know the names and whereabouts of all criminals in their city; when a crime was committed, they brought in the "usual suspects" for questioning. A useful detective was therefore one who knew a lot of criminals and could induce them—by trickery, bribery, or friendship—to talk about their colleagues. The work of the police, then, was based on surveillance of the most direct kind—the observation and recording of the faces of criminals. The chief of detectives of New York, declaring that "there is nothing that professional criminals fear as much as identification and exposure. . . . With their likenesses within reach of all, their vocation would soon become risky and unprofitable," published a rogues' gallery in book form that included photographs and biographies of two hundred criminals from across the country.[8] The detective memoir, written by both police and private detectives, was highly popular in the 1870s and 1880s, and the genre often included lighthearted and affectionate portraits of criminals and exposés of police corruption and chicanery.[9] As Marcus Klein puts it in *Easterns, Westerns, and Private Eyes,* in the mid- and late nineteenth century, "in the regard of all decent people acquainted with the ways of the law, detectives and most especially private detectives had been no better than the scoundrels whom they supposedly detected, if indeed they were not worse."[10]

Victor is not interested in modeling her detective on the scoundrel type, and she makes Burton a man of unquestionable morals in part by making him a palpably fictional hero. Burton is endowed with several extraordinary gifts: eyes that look into, rather than at, people; expertise in analyzing character from a person's handwriting; the ability to follow people almost invisibly; and a clairvoyant daughter. He employs all these in solving the case, and he also draws in a neophyte to aid him, a young man named Redfield, a lawyer and the narrator of our story. Redfield is sensitive, highly ethical, and fiercely smitten with one of the principals in the case. This pairing of a wise, good, but slightly remote police (or police-employed) detective with an amateur, emotionally involved member of the upper class establishes the predominant pattern in the domestic detective tradition. Here, the two work in concert, though in many other works, especially when older female detectives are introduced, the amateur and the detective become rivals.

The fact that Redfield, the book's center of consciousness and protagonist, is a lawyer is especially interesting. He seems to come from several places at once and to align several cultural phenomena: the popularity of the criminal trial report, a tradition of fictional representations of lawyers, and the constitution of a professional class in the postbellum period. According to Maxwell Bloomfield, the type of the "lawyer-gentleman" became quite clearly delineated in a certain kind of antebellum novel.[11] Redfield fits the mold quite closely: he is white, old-stock Anglo-Saxon, and Protestant; he is self-made, having been left fatherless at a young age; he is the protégé of an older lawyer who hired him and taught him the ways of the law and of the lawyer's life; and he is both diligent and idealistic. In the gentleman lawyer's development, what Bloomfield calls "the big case" is key, and it usually involves winning an apparently hopeless acquittal for an innocent man. Southworth's blockbuster *Ishmael* is the most famous of these novels, in which the big case involves challenging the legal disadvantages to women who seek property rights in divorce proceedings as well as the necessity of proving murder, conspiracy, and kidnapping.[12] This kind of case forces the lawyer-gentleman to ally himself with the victims of injustice and the noblest ideals of the justice system and the law. The counterexamples of the dissipated young hotshot, the litigious pettifogger, and, in the late nineteenth century, the soulless corporate lawyer show what can happen to him if he does not govern himself carefully.

In *The Dead Letter,* the corruption of the court and its role in making Burton a detective lingers in the background, as does the example of the pampered and unprincipled lawyer in the character of James Argyll (whom we shall meet shortly), so Redfield's choices are a matter of some import. Here, the investigation of the murder of Henry Moreland stands in for the big case and the big trial. However, there is no lawyering whatsoever in this novel—no trial scenes, no discussion of the law per se—an absence that suggests that Redfield is not a lawyer's lawyer, but a more general figure for someone who is an agent of the adjudication. His job in the novel is to root out a murderer, but, in this domestic-fictional world, to do so is synonymous and conterminous with restoring the harmony of the domestic sphere. In the process and in the ultimate goal of his investigation, the lawyer becomes the kind of presence that Brod head calls "a monitory intimate": someone who watches, judges, and punishes from within the erotic circle of an extended household.[13] Redfield's investigation is also geared toward the purging of the debauched and insincere from the rising professional class — but I get ahead of myself.

The murder that requires investigation is the killing of a young banker named Henry Moreland. One evening, on his way to visit his fiancée, Eleanor Argyll, he is overtaken on the road and killed with a single stab to the back. The Argylls, who reside in "Blankville," a short train ride from New York City, are a wealthy professional family. Mr. Argyll is a lawyer, and his dependent nephew, James, is a law student. Mrs. Argyll has been dead for some time; besides Eleanor, there is another daughter, Mary, who is also of marriageable age. Richard Redfield, our narrator, is a close friend of the family — actually, he is the son of Mr. Argyll's best friend — and a young lawyer who has hopes of being made a partner in the Argyll firm when Mr. Argyll retires. This is a family situation full of ambition, jealousy, and erotic longing, for James and Redfield are not only hostile rivals for the partnership in the law firm, but also are both secretly in love with Eleanor, even as she prepares to marry Henry Moreland. When the case baffles the local constables, Redfield goes, at the request of Henry Moreland's father, to the New York City police to ask for help from the legendary Burton.

Although the novel combines many modes, it doesn't do so seamlessly, and the more gothic moments stand out as disruptions in the harmony of middle-class life, as signs that something is terribly wrong. The most obvious gothicism of this sort is the haunting of Henry Moreland's house after his death. The Irish caretakers of his estate report seeing "dead-lights" emanating from the empty house; they find a ghostly imprint on Henry's freshly made bed; they find footprints in the snow on the porch of the house. The Irish — always servants — are depicted throughout the novel as figures of superstition and ignorance. When Mrs. Scott, the caretaker, first begins to talk about the haunted house with Redfield, their conversation seems to privilege Redfield's rational, analytical, middle-class mind over Mrs. Scott's foolish, stubborn, lower-class emotionality. We expect

Richard's investigation of the haunted house to produce a rational explanation of the supernatural visitations. And indeed it does, for the ghost turns out to be a missing witness whom Burton and Redfield want to question, a seamstress named Leesy Sullivan. But the episodes in which Redfield, then Redfield and Burton together, explore the house are nevertheless excursions into the gothic mode; in some experiential sense, this *is* a haunted house. When we enter this villa, built in—what else—"the Gothic style," we are in the realm of a "moldy smell," creaking floors, involuntary shudders, and the swift passing of silent figures in the dark. The first time Redfield enters with Mrs. Scott, they find Moreland's bedroom disturbed; someone has been lying in his bed, wearing his slippers, and reading his books. Mrs. Scott is convinced that Moreland has come back from the dead. There are also foods missing from the storeroom and scrabbling noises in the attic, which Mrs. Scott and Redfield attribute to rats and cats. By this point, even the most obtuse reader knows that the "ghost" is Leesy, and the whole episode works to show what a poor detective Redfield is at the beginning of his career.

Another important gothic note is the grief of Eleanor Argyll. Technically not a widow, she plays the part of one with gusto, dressing entirely in black, refusing meals, and remaining secluded in her room, except when she wanders dramatically through the barren December garden. On the day on which she and Henry were to have been married, she dresses herself in her wedding gown and veil and sends for a bouquet of flowers. Her sister Mary reports: "[S]he says that to-day they will be married, the same as if Henry were on earth instead of in heaven; that their vows shall be consummated at the hour appointed and that thereafter she shall hold herself his wife just as surely as if he had come in the body to fulfill his part of the contract" (*DL,* 136). Little could be more gothic than Eleanor's fantasy of consummation, yet her madness is in some ways simply a logical extension of the domestic ideal of monogamy. Eleanor is so fully shaped by domestic ideology that she wishes to fulfill her marriage contract in its fullest sense, disdaining the loophole in her prayerbook that states "until death do you part." Eleanor is simultaneously the most gothic and the most domestic figure in the novel; her obsession with monogamy is the point where Victor conjoins domestic and gothic modes of discourse.

Even with its gothicism, *The Dead Letter* is, at bottom, a courtship novel. It is, however, a marriage novel of a new kind, one that not only offers a tale of the need for caution in evaluating erotic possibilities, but also provides a narrative of the eros of suspicion itself. There are a number of love triangles sketched around Henry Moreland, and the investigation of the murder proceeds by tracing the lines of desire connecting the characters to each other and to the murder victim. There is the Eleanor-Moreland-James triangle: James Argyll has an excellent motive for murdering Henry Moreland: if he could marry Eleanor, he would fulfill his secret passion for her and consolidate his position with his uncle, the law firm, and the formidable Argyll bank accounts. James is our prime suspect, for he is unpleasant to our narrator and turns strange colors, quivers, and runs away whenever anyone discusses the murder. Furthermore, we learn that he has serious gambling debts; Eleanor's money seems his only hope to avoid ruin. And worst of all, he begins spreading suspicion in the Argylls' minds about Redfield, our narrator, claiming that Redfield killed Henry Moreland in a jealous rage and that his efforts to investigate the crime are simply a ruse. And that is our second jealous triangle — James-Eleanor-Redfield — with James and Redfield competing first with Moreland, and then only with each other, for Eleanor's affections and a powerful place in the family. Another triangle with strong motives for murder involves Moreland and the Argylls' seamstress, Leesy Sullivan. Leesy, along with Moreland's reputation, comes under suspicion when it is recalled that Moreland used to double, out of his own pocket, the wages Leesy was paid by the Argylls. Things look even worse when Burton and Redfield discover that Leesy has the care of a baby whom she claims is the daughter of her deceased cousin. Leesy was seen on the Argyll grounds on the night of the murder but disappears when police try to question her; later she is discovered hiding in Moreland's abandoned house, worshipping his portrait and his belongings. Moreland looks like a philanderer, and Leesy looks like an abandoned victim of his seductions who killed him in a mixture of rage and hopeless passion to prevent him from marrying Eleanor.

At this point, having revealed this triad of triangles, the investigation comes to a halt. James, in a powerful counterplot, makes his suspicions of Redfield open and succeeds in winning the partnership in the firm and Mary Argyll's hand in marriage. Burton seems unable or unwilling to do anything to clear Redfield's name, and, at Mr. Argyll's request, lets the matter drop. No longer welcome in the Argyll home or firm, Redfield leaves Blankville and the law profession. The experience of suspicion has been a vertiginous one. Redfield, raised to be a gentleman, has not only had to become suspicious of everyone connected to Moreland, but has himself become the family's principal suspect. He has had the experience of "finding myself under the eye of suspicion, mingled in with the perplexing whirl of the whole, until I almost began to doubt my own identity and that of others" (*DL,* 54). Throughout the novel, Redfield doubts Burton's friendship and trust, and wonders if Burton is not actually scrutinizing him when he seems to be scrutinizing other people. Redfield's disorientation is twofold: he has lost his assurance of a place in the law profession, and he has lost his faith in his ability to read and assess members of his own class.

A dispirited Redfield goes to work as a postal clerk in the dead letter office in Washington, D.C. This turn of events, ostensibly a step down in the world, is of the utmost importance, for it is here that Redfield discovers the letter from Moreland's assassin to his mystery client. It is written in code, and doesn't make much sense to us at first: "It's too bad to disappoint you. Could not execute your order, as everybody concerned will discover. . . . That old friend I introduced you to won't tell tales, and you had not better bother yourself to visit him" (*DL,* 10). Redfield brings the letter to Burton, hoping he will be willing to reopen the case. Burton is willing, and it should hardly surprise us that it is a letter that sets the becalmed investigation in motion again. For, in a text that is shaped around the patterns of the gothic, secret letters are certain to shape plots, not simply to convey information. Letters of this sort are a part of the central passion of the gothic mode for telling secrets and bringing to light anything that has been concealed. And in the domestic novel, of which this text is also a variant, letters are the vehicle of erotic love; mothers, sisters, and lovers exchange letters that tell of the desire to close distances opened by geography. The opening scene of Redfield's narrative shows Eleanor waiting for Henry Moreland; the family puzzles and fusses over the mechanics by which Moreland might have sent an explanatory message with an overfine exactness that is the analog of Eleanor's erotic disappointment.

The dead letter is crucial to the investigation, though, not just because of the information it contains linguistically, but also because Burton is gifted in reading "chirographically," which is "reading men and women from a specimen of their handwriting" (*DL*, 206). After reading the letter, Burton knows about the hired killer's physical appearance, education, and spiritual state ("bad, from instinct, inheritance and bringing-up"). And, as we might expect in this novel so larded with explosive feelings, Burton concludes that the killer is a man of "powerful passion. If I could decide what that passion was, I might have a key to unlock the gate into some other matters" (*DL*, 206).

Looking to unveil that passion, Burton continues to investigate the murder along the lines of affection and jealousy in the community of suspects. No motives other than romantic ones are ever seriously entertained. The question of identifying the murderer has, in other words, been boiled down to this: Who most wanted to prevent Henry Moreland and Eleanor Argyll from marrying? As Burton returns to question Leesy a second time, he discovers a fourth romantic triangle that includes Moreland. Leesy says the father of the baby is a doctor — probably a fraud — who had tried to win Leesy's hand unsuccessfully. His name is George Thorley, and he married Leesy's cousin — possibly fraudulently — for spite, then abandoned her. And the reason he did not win Leesy's affections, of course, is that she was foolishly and unrequitedly in love with Henry Moreland. Thorley is a man with a jealous grudge against Moreland; furthermore, he is certain to be the author of the dead letter, since he is a self-taught pseudophysician with a "powerful passion" for Leesy and a history of fraud and skullduggery.

The letter that reopens the investigation also offers information on the economy of rivalry and jealousy that Burton and Redfield are reconstructing. For the letter makes it clear that Thorley was hired by someone else; its existence instructs Burton to find an overlap among the triangles in order to solve the mystery. To do that, Burton tracks Thorley to Mexico and extracts a confession from him. He discovers that the co-conspirator is James Argyll; Thorley had overheard him muttering his hatred for Henry Moreland and offered to kill him for a large sum of money. Burton brings the confession back to the Argyll family and unmasks James before them all — happily, before Mary Argyll marries him. For the sake of the "young ladies" and their "sacred feelings," James is simply ordered out of the country and allowed to escape. In the last pages of the book, Redfield reports that he later marries Mary, and that the two adopt Mr. Burton's clairvoyant daughter after Burton himself is murdered.

In this novel, a happy marriage is what stabilizes the plots and counterplots of the murder and its investigation. The murder is committed, of course, to prevent the marriage of Henry Moreland and Eleanor Argyll, creating a sort of narrative, as well as emotional, chaos in its wake. The structure of the story is such that the question "Who did it?" is entirely bound up in the question "Who will marry whom?"; this structure is exactly what requires us to define *The Dead Letter* as domestic detective fiction. The second half of the novel — the story of the investigation after the discovery of the dead letter — is a race between the detectives and a devious marriage plot. James has proposed to Mary not because he loves her, but because he needs to fund his high-stakes gambling. Burton and Redfield rush back from California with the confession that proves James a murderer, Burton anxious that "the marriage not be consummated which would seal my mouth; for if Mary had been married on my return, I should have considered it too late to reveal the truth" (*DL*, 300).

Burton's function in this novel is unclear in several respects: he is a detective so deeply undercover that only the chief of detectives knows that he works for the police; he refuses the money that is a normative part of police work; and he lets a proven murderer and thief go free so that two young women will not be upset by the trial and publicity. What is clear is Burton's work in realigning the erotic trajectories of the plot into proper patterns. He restores Redfield to his deserved standing in the family after exposing James's jealous counterplot, and he blocks the marriage of James to Mary by revealing James's role in the murder of Moreland. He is responsible for the happy ending of the novel, in which Mary and Redfield marry — Redfield having overcome his jealous passion for Eleanor — and become parents. The essentially conservative nature of Burton's role is evident in his squarely middle-class respect for the sanctity of marriage (even to a murderer) when he declares that a "consummated" marriage would "seal my mouth" and in his consideration of the sensitivities of young women when he lets James escape. Burton also exposes and expels Thorley, a man who poses as a physician and uses his small store of medical knowledge and his surgical instruments to murder Henry Moreland. The hybrid of domestic novel and detective plot is a form that allows Victor to make a connection between several interests of the professional middle class—the policing of crime in the narrative of surveillance, the purifying of the ranks of the professional class in the work of detection, and the education of the affections provided by the domestic novel.

Suspicion is more than a state of mind in detective fiction—it is the methodology of the detective, and by extension, of the narrative of investigation. In this novel, narrator, readers, and detective all immediately suspect James Argyll, yet the book spins on for another 279 pages after that first suspicion to its final confirmation. Burton tells us that the motto of all detective work is "learn to labor and to wait," and the latter imperative seems especially pertinent in the second half of the book, in which Burton and Redfield take a long, looping journey by steamer to California and Mexico. The narrative delay is of the sort that Peter Brooks illuminates so clearly by reading Freud. Brooks examines the two contradictory impulses of narrative desire—to drive forward to the ending and to pause in metaphor and subplot. The oscillation between the two produces the narrative "squiggle": that is "the arbitrary, transgressive, gratuitous line of narrative, its deviance from the straight line, the shortest distance between beginning and end—which would be the collapse of one into the other." If we had been able to confirm our suspicions right away, identifying James as the murderer, the story would end there, cheating us of the pleasure of our own suspicions, on the one hand, and the pleasure of yearning for the apprehension of the criminal (which is the ending in detective fiction). Brooks explains the erotic nature of narrative delay in this way: "We emerge from [Freud's] *Beyond the Pleasure Principle* with a dynamic model that structures ends (death, quiescence, nonnarratability) against beginnings (Eros, stimulation into tension, the desire of narrative) in a manner that necessitates the middle as detour, as struggle toward the end under the compulsion of imposed delay."[14] As in many novels, the possibility of narrative short-circuit is represented in *The Dead Letter* as what Brooks calls "the temptation to mistaken erotic choice"; Eleanor, the initial object of our narrator's passion, represents the "too perfect and hence annihilatory bride" for whom Redfield must find a less likely substitute. The novel is also troubled by the possibility of another kind of narrative short-circuit — the semi-incestuous marriage of cousins James and Mary Argyll — of the sort that threatens the "cessation of narrative movement," or, as Victor puts it, the sealing of Mr. Burton's lips.

However, there are many ways in which a narrative may discharge its ending prematurely, and many "temptation[s] of short-circuit from which the protagonist and the text must be led away, into detour, into the cure that prolongs narrative."[15] In detective fiction, short-circuit would block the detour into the investigation that reveals the full nature or the whole story of a crime. Our first object of suspicion, James, turns out to be guilty, but had he been arrested early, we might not have learned about the conspiracy with Thorley. Without the delay between suspicion and arrest, we would not, in other words, have much of a novel. James, of course, needs to thwart the narrative of investigation because he wants the story of the murder to remain incoherent; his temporarily successful attempt to smear Redfield is an effort to short-circuit the narrative into premature and mistaken resolution.

There is a third kind of delay (besides the suspension of certainty of James's guilt and the literal detour of Burton and Redfield around the tip of South America) in this novel. The dead letter from Moreland's assassin fell into a gap between a post office counter and wall and languished there for eighteen months before being forwarded to the dead letter office and into Redfield's hands. The figurative and literal gap in the postal service into which the dead letter fell is precisely the gap out of which *The Dead Letter* grows. There are several ways to understand this gap. It is an interruption of the communication between two conspirators — in other words, in the narrative of murder and cover-up, an interruption that allows the investigators access to a coherent plan. It is also a gap that permits the government access to the erotic lives of its citizens, for in becoming undeliverable, the dead letter becomes subject to governmental scrutiny.

The disturbing nature of that scrutiny is conveyed in the opening paragraphs of the novel:

Young ladies whose love letters have gone astray, evil men whose plans have been confided in writing to their confederates, may feel but little apprehension of the prying eyes of the Department; nothing attracts it but objects of material value — sentiment is below par; it gives attention only to such tangible interests as are represented by bank-bills, gold-pieces, checks, jewelry, miniatures, et cetera. . . . Sometimes, perhaps [a clerk] looks thoughtfully at a withered rosebud, or bunch of pressed violets, a homely little pincushion or a book-mark, wishing it had reached its proper destination. I can not answer for other employees, who may not have even this amount of heart and imagination to invest in the dull business of a Government office; but when I was in the Department I was guilty, at intervals, of such folly — yet I passed for the coldest, most cynical man of them all. (*DL,* 9)

Redfield distinguishes between two kinds of treasure to be found in these letters. One is the currency of the public sphere — monetary papers and gold — in which the postal service is officially interested. The second kind is the currency of the domestic sphere — preserved flowers, pincushions, bookmarks, and the erotic content or "sentiment" of the letters — in which the state is officially uninterested. But Redfield, we recall, is not an average government agent — he is a refugee from the professionalized vanguard of the middle class. His upbringing in the sentimental culture of mid-century has taught him to value the love letters of young ladies that he says are safe from the "eyes of the Department," just as his training in the law has taught him to be interested in the plans of "evil men . . . confided in writing." Redfield's rather disingenuous assurance that such letters are never read by the cynical clerks of the post office in fact points to a particular kind of surveillance that Victor imagines to be operating in postbellum culture. When the lawyer, cultural spokesman for the middle class on issues of crime, becomes employed by the government, the result is the sort of scrutiny of the erotic and the sentimental that Redfield — along with Burton, gentleman auxiliary to the city police — undertakes.

In this novel about the investigation of the middle class by the middle class, the lines of surveillance follow the dynamic of eros. As we have already noted, the investigation proceeds by tracing romantic and rivalrous triangles among Moreland's friends and enemies. Likewise, the investigation of Leesy Sullivan is an investigation of her erotic inner life that exposes her secret and unfulfilled desire for Moreland. When the detectives search for her in the city, Redfield actually enters her vacant room and waits for her in the dark, a scene that seems informed by the threat of rape. But perhaps the most powerful figure for the surveillance of the erotic is Burton's clairvoyant daughter, Lenore. She is eleven years old the first time we see her, and thirteen by the close of the novel, and though always referred to as a "little girl" and a "child," she is also a figuration or reflection of the sexuality of the adults around her. Redfield, on first meeting her, reports that "she was so every way charming that I held out my arms to kiss her, and she, with the instinct of children, who perceive who their real lovers are, gave me a willing yet shy embrace" (*DL*, 102). Lenore is afraid of James when she first meets him; James, realizing how dangerous her psychic perceptions might be to him, wins her over with all the trappings of courtship: "flowers and flatteries, and a dainty little ring for her forefinger"; and "on New Year's he overwhelmed her with presents; he took her out sleigh-riding with him, in a fancy cutter, which he declared was only just large enough for those two" (*DL*, 163).[16] Like Eleanor, whose name she shares, Lenore becomes the object of James's and Redfield's sexual rivalry; Redfield admits that "I was more hurt by her growing indifference to me and her increasing fascination for James than the subject warranted" (*DL*, 163).

When put into a trance by her father, Lenore is able to assist him in his detective work by psychically "seeing" the fugitives described to her and gathering information on their surroundings — the landscape, the information on street signs, their clothing — so that her father can track them down. These trances are traumatic experiences for Lenore; her father, a widower, admits that "her physician told me that I must desist, entirely, all experiments" with Lenore's "peculiar attributes" (*DL*, 100). Lenore does not enjoy these sessions with her father. When Burton suggests that "Father wants to put his little girl to sleep," Redfield tells us that "an expression of unwillingness just crossed her face, but she smiled . . . with the faith of affection" (*DL*, 102). On her way in and out these trances, Lenore's face and hands undergo "painful contortions" as her father's hands make "passes over her"; afterward, Lenore is "pale and languid . . . drooped against her father's breast" and is given wine to revive her. The scene of surveillance is also a scene of seduction (or in plainer language, molestation) by the father. If Lenore's perilous situation at the hands of both her father and James makes us ask "Where is her mother?" the only answer is that there are no mothers in the world of this book. The suggestion that Lenore, with her precocious sexuality and supernatural vision, is taking her mother's place shows how truly displaced the omniscient domestic novel mother is in this tale of crime and detection. The male detectives, in their attention to the erotic and moral life of the household, take on many of the mother's duties, but it is a sign of the waning of the sentimental domestic novel that all those powers are no longer held together in the awesome and entirely virtuous figure of Mother.

The yoking of the detective story to the domestic novel, then, allows Victor to write of the erotic life of the middle class as something undergoing—or requiring—new forms of surveillance in the postbellum period. Because her detective's motto is "learn to labor and to wait," and the domestic novel's mandate is the correction of erotic impulsiveness, the structure of *The Dead Letter* is marked by a series of delays and detours as the detective identifies, evaluates, and realigns the triangles of jealousy and desire. Implicit in the advent of detective fiction of this sort is a sense that misguided eros is pathological and dangerous. The structure of detective fiction proposes the sort of thing that Brooks calls a narrative "cure" to the explosive intersection of rage and desire that leads to murder within families. The detective novel, by fragmenting and obscuring the passionate story of murder, makes the main narrative of the novel—the story of investigation—fall into looping patterns of delay: reexamination of evidence, searches for witnesses, exploration of false leads. This structure provides for the kind of detour in which Redfield can correct his misguided infatuation with another man's woman and learn to transfer his love to a more appropriate object.

One structural feature in particular serves to redirect the energies of the protagonist of this kind of detective novel: the placement of the corpse. As David Lehman puts it in *The Perfect Murder*, the "corpse on page one, or near enough as to make little difference" appears "not only *at* but *as* the beginning" of the detective novel.[17] In *The Dead Letter*, page 1 gives us not a dead body but a dead letter; then, since the first half of the book is a retrospective narrative, we begin all over again, this time with Moreland's corpse. Both dead

body and dead letter are marks of broken or incomplete communication—the letter never reaches its destination, the corpse cannot
name its murderer—the sort of gap out of which narrative grows.
But the corpse as beginning shapes that growth in important ways.
In *The Dead Letter*—perhaps in all detective fiction—the corpse
represents a violent wish fulfillment of several, if not all the characters. Self-incrimination hovers close to Redfield's language as he
reports his feelings on seeing Moreland's corpse:

Who had dared to take upon himself the responsibility of unlawfully and
with violence, ejecting this human soul from its house?

I shuddered as I asked myself the question. Somewhere must be lurking a guilty creature, with a heart on fire from the flames of hell, with
which it had put itself in contact.

Then my heart stood still within me . . . her father was leading in
Eleanor. (*DL*, 28)

Redfield gives himself away with that admiring "who *dared?*" and
with the way he calls attention to his own heart in the same breath
with which he describes the heart of the murderer. Of course he
wanted, deep in that heart, to murder Moreland, and he is now faced
with the terrible evidence of his (imaginary) crime of passion. Moreland's murder, though, frees Redfield of his dangerous jealousy; the
corpse as beginning redirects Redfield's desire to apprehension of
the murderer rather than the elimination of his rival. The investigation of crime is a socially acceptable adjustment of eros, one that
controls and redirects misguided desire.

But we need to be careful when we talk about middle-class forms
of social control and the middle-class detective novel. Consider the
fact that Redfield's sublimation of rivalry into criminal investigation accomplishes what his murderous heart desired anyway; in the
end, he destroys James and marries the woman to whom this second
sexual rival was engaged. Detective fiction is, we must remember, a
blood relative of the gothic. That means that it works in the image of
the cipher, oscillating between the spoken and the unspoken, the revealed and the concealed. In its doubling of investigation and crime,
detective fiction is a genre that lets the author—and reader—have
her cake and eat it too. We get to see Moreland killed, and we get
to feel sorry for him also. We see violent jealousy sublimated into

investigation, but we see violent jealousy nonetheless. It is a commonplace to say that every character — including the narrator — in a detective novel is a suspect in the murders that occur in it. But as Umberto Eco has noted, "there is still to be written a book in which the murderer is the reader"; Lehman continues that thought with "the murderer as the reader? Never — which is to say, on some implicit, metaphorical level, always."[18]

To read detective fiction, now as in the nineteenth century, is to experience simultaneous repression and expression of murderous anger, unbounded treachery, and calculating greed. The appeal for the middle- and upper-class reader may be the fictive structure of surveillance and containment — but the appeal is also the violence and passion that are being investigated. Although the later use of the genre, with which we are more familiar, is the investigation of political and commercial corruption by the hard-boiled school, the first Americans to write detective novels picked the domestic sphere as the area most able to support the detective story and the area most in need of investigation. Those plots of intimate surveillance are not without political content and historical motivation, however, as the examinations of the themes of disguise and spying in the next chapter will reveal.

# 3

## The Loop of Surveillance in *The Figure Eight* and *Hagar's Daughter*

Metta Victor's *The Figure Eight* is a detective novel with a strikingly intricate weaving of tropes of disguise. It is narrated by Joe Meredith, a young man studying to be a doctor, who works to solve the mystery of the murder of his uncle and to regain the lost fortune of his angelic cousin, whom he loves. The absentminded Dr. Meredith has been poisoned in his home; at the moment of his death he was writing a treatise on nerve disorders, and with his last strength he left a cryptic message that includes the tracing of the figure eight that gives the novel its title. Joe Meredith feels certain that the scribbling is the dying man's attempt to communicate the whereabouts of the large cache of gold that is his entire fortune. Without the gold, his widow and daughter are destitute and will have to forfeit the family estate to their creditors and teach for their living. There are three suspicious characters in the household, all stock figures from the gothic. One is the young Cuban widow of the doctor; another is a sleepwalking governess who was clearly infatuated with her employer; and the third is the dashing and hard-hearted brother of the governess, with whom the widow has been flirting. The other inhabitant of the house is the beloved Lillian Meredith, the daughter of the doctor's first marriage, but she is a paragon of virtue and above suspicion. After the doctor's death, the house is rented out to a wealthy family, all of these characters are invited to live with them, so the household of Meredith Place is, like the Argyll household of *The Dead Letter*, seething with the erotics of love, jealousy, suspicion, and social ambition.

There are really two goals in this story: one is to bring the murderer to justice, and the other, which both the righteous and the criminal share, is to recover the missing sixty thousand dollars in gold. Although all of the suspicious characters seem guilty of one or both crimes for some period of the narrative, it turns out that Inez, the passionate and foolish Cuban child bride, is guilty of the murder, and Arthur Miller, the brother of the governess, is guilty of the theft, needing the gold to fund his ascent into high society. That gold, which had been mined in California by the doctor as a way to fund his research and secure his title to Meredith Place, is literally reminted as another kind of social currency.

Since the doctor's death, Miller has been steadily melting down the gold and casting it in dies stolen from the U.S. Treasury. The way he goes about his fraud is unusually fastidious and risky, for it was not necessary for him to steal dies from the Mint; the standard method for coin counterfeiting in this period was to take a plaster mold of a legitimate coin, and then cast cheap metals with the homemade mold.[1] Miller's work is an unusual kind of counterfeiting because he is not passing off valueless metal or paper; his coin is actual gold; its fakeness lies in the fact that it bears a fraudulent government imprimatur. This detail draws our attention to an important quality of Arthur's stolen money: it is both real and phony at the same time. His money supports another kind of counterfeiting; he leaves a trail of broken female hearts as he works his way up the social ladder through lying about his origins and making false promises about his intentions. He has convinced the daughter of the very rich family renting Meredith Place to marry him by displaying enough disposable income to come off as "a young man rising into wealth" and is exposed only on the eve of their wedding. As Inez pithily sums up his charade, "He *made money,* indeed!" (*FE,* 98).

The plot surrounding the gold is riddled with other kinds of counterfeit and deceit. Social aspirations drive many of the characters, and social performances are often key moments in the plot. Arthur is exposed by Inez in a combination of stakeout and *tableau vivant;* she knows where he has been doing his counterfeiting, and she gathers Arthur's sister, the sheriff, the father-in-law, and the bride-to-be before throwing open the door to reveal Arthur's handsome profile silhouetted against the flames of his furnace. But even as she unmasks Arthur, she masks herself, stating pointedly that this thief must be the murderer. Alongside these layers of falsehood and reinforcing their importance are many figures of reading and scenes of surveillance. The search for the gold is a matter of decoding the note the doctor wrote as he was dying, especially the figure eight it contains, and reading the clues written on the walls of the room in which the gold is hidden. All the main characters are simultaneously and surreptitiously searching the doctor's mansion for the gold, and they are all slyly watching each other do so in hopes of gaining clues and ideas.

The illegibility of the doctor's dying words shows a failed communication of the type that Sedgwick associates with the theme of the unspeakable in the gothic tradition. Indeed, the whole plot of searching is heavily gothicized and includes the governess sleepwalking around the grounds of the estate in a white nightgown (a clear reference to Wilkie Collins's 1860 *The Woman in White*), a tower room with secret cabinets containing the lost treasure, and a running concern that the house is haunted as its many inhabitants pop in and out of bedrooms and pass each other in the darkness. There are both vague and direct references to *Jane Eyre;* and the use of the governess figure is one of the most interesting aspects of the novel.[2] There is little love lost between Joe Meredith and the governess, for she has worked to keep him away from Lillian, and for most of the novel we find her a rather unsympathetic character. But there is one scene in which she spies on and interrogates Inez that shows her to have real potential as a detective. In the end, the governess breaks the murder case and forces Inez to confess, which would seem to make her some kind of prototype of a woman detective. She fits the later mold of a woman intimately involved with the case (she was in love with the victim and she is protective sister to the counterfeiter), both uncovering and disclosing information to protect people from the police and a family from disgrace. However, she still belongs to the older order of the gothic thriller, for she gathers much of her evidence and presents the case against Inez while in somnambulant trances.

Joe Meredith is, when all is said and done, the center of investigative consciousness in the novel. He is, like Redfield, driven to solve the murder and discover the hiding place of the gold by his love for a woman in the homicidal household and by his desire to clear his name when he is wrongly accused of the crime. Joe's social position is less certain than Redfield's; his father was "a spendthrift of no settled occupation" (*FE*, 14), and young Joe was boarded out in a string of wretched households. After his father's death, Joe was taken up—vices, ingratitude, and all—by his uncle, who tried to undo the boy's "pernicious training" with mixed success. Joe fell hard for his cousin Lillian, but also felt keenly the fact that such a match was entirely unwelcome to his uncle and aunt and chafed under the "Argus-eyed surveillance" of Lillian's governess. In his later teens, he began to study medicine, like his uncle and his grandfather, not because he enjoyed it, but because "I had no other way of proving my desire to please [my uncle], and my resolution to become industrious and reliable" (*FE*, 20).

Joe is a socially displaced figure: from a professional-class family, but raised in the rough world of urban poverty. Victor uses him to explore the social slippage that is both possible and necessary in a world so infused with suspicion and uncertainty. Joe investigates the murder in the same way he keeps from getting arrested: he uses disguise. He dresses as an itinerant laborer to escape from Meredith Place when, on the strength of his vicious background, he is accused of his uncle's murder. He stays close to the neighborhood so he can keep looking for clues, and hides out during the day in the attic of a feeble old woman. Later, he hangs up a physician's shingle in New York City and poses as Dr. John Milton, having just enough medical knowledge to fool his patients, meanwhile making himself familiar with the lives and habits of Miss Miller and her brother during a sojourn in the city.

His boldest stunt involves dressing up as "a mulatto waiter" so that he can attend a ball at Meredith Place and snoop around. This adventure in blackface starts as a lark, a break in the dull routine of hiding by day and skulking around the estate at night, and it is introduced in a lighthearted tone: he finds a black sheep, "and I think I may take to myself credit for the ingenuity with which I converted a portion of his fleece into a wig, and a mustache of which the most dandified Adonis of the colored race need not have been ashamed." He darkens his skin with walnut bark and finishes his costume with "a large red silk handkerchief, which I metamorphosed into a flaming cravat" (*FE*, 38). The figure he is cutting here is the minstrel-show character of the dandy, a poor man who has found sudden wealth or has class aspirations. Eric Lott argues that this character is deeply implicated in the antebellum minstrel show's "configuration of white class conflict through black characters," and that the black dandy is closely associated, through the songs he sings, with what Lott calls "the 'wrong' kind of miscegenation." [3]

One clue to how Victor might be trying to deploy this complex and disruptive type may lie in something Joe tells us after he finishes "blacking up." He reports, "I did not smile at my ridiculous figure; I never felt more solemn, more sad. . . . This was not a farce, but an awful reality in which I was engaged" (*FE*, 38). She has her class-displaced white man take on the persona not just of a black character, but a *blackface* character, and one associated with all kinds of threats to social categories to boot—and he finds that the charade expresses something solemn and real about his situation. This phenomenon is part of the complex of "love and theft" that Lott names in white Americans' embrace of blackface minstrelsy, but it is also an expression of the deep structures of insincerity and uncertainty in the world *The Figure Eight* represents. Michael Denning calls these kinds of disguises "ruses of the representation of social cleavages," a point that seems especially pertinent here, where Joe's blackface escapade is immediately followed by his assumption of the title of "Dr. Milton." [4] In the depiction of Meredith Place as a hotbed of phoniness and counterfeiting and of the successful detective as a master of disguise, there is a concentrated attention not only to the possibility of passing one thing off as another (or representing a social cleavage), but also the importance of doing it well.

If one part of coping with a world of "Argus-eyed surveillance" is to adopt disguises, the other is to become a spy. It is striking how often the word *spy* comes up in this novel, and how tender a subject spying is for anyone with aspirations to gentility, even a man of the world like Joe Meredith. Early on, he addresses us directly: "Let those who read these confessions not set me down as naturally deficient in honor or truth, that I assumed so often the character of spy and eaves-dropper. As it is necessary, in times of war, for some one to undertake these odious duties, it behooved me by any means at my command, to trace the guilty in order that I might relieve the innocent" (*FE*, 34). His reference to "times of war" would have made sense to his initial readers of 1869, not just because of the Civil

War itself, but also because of the popularity of spy memoirs in the postbellum period. Spies and military scouts took on a mythic aura in the war years and in postbellum culture; in addition to at least twenty spy memoirs published in book form in the first thirty years after the war, numerous accounts were printed in periodicals during and immediately after the war. As in detective narratives, these accounts highlight the moral ambiguity of the spy's work. Curtis Davis, examining the commonalities among spy memoirs, notes the energy with which spies offered justifications for their entry into a life of deception and lying—justifications that generally included service to a higher moral good.[5] But there is also in these narratives a real luxuriation in enumerating the various kinds and incidents of deception that the spy must practice. Spies from both sides detailed the differences in regional accents and customs that they learned to manipulate as they crossed into enemy territory. The adventures offered as most thrilling usually include elaborate disguises; spying is presented in these works as an improvised and dangerous theatrical production. Male and female spies crossed lines of color, gender, class, and region in their many disguises (one white woman posed as a male slave, another as a southern planter).[6] Spies, in other words, act out both the promise and the anxiety of a society in which individuals feel they are not bound to single identities of region, class, race, or gender and where anyone could be something other than what he or she appears to be.

Spy memoirs are very close to detective narratives in the taxonomy of popular genres in the postbellum literary field. *Spy* and *detective* were interchangeable terms in the literature of Civil War espionage, and that closeness was also apparent in the working-class dime novel. Michael Denning tells us that before the 1870s and 1880s, dime-novel detective series such as Old Sleuth centered on "anonymous sleuths who could assume any disguise" and that the celebration of this talent continued into the 1890s with the creation of Nick Carter, another master of disguise.[7] Both Denning and Marcus Klein see the legend of the infiltration of the Molly Maguires (an association of Irish coal miners suspected of assassinating mine bosses in the 1870s) by the Pinkerton operative James McParland as a defining source for the figure of the male detective.[8] Klein concludes that the most remarkable thing about McParland was that he "had been a 'detective,' nominally and according to general usage, employed by a 'Detective Agency,' but he neither analyzed nor ratiocinated nor in fact detected. He was a spy." Furthermore, McParland was in an entirely ambiguous position as the "agent of a plausibly immoral authority"; Klein argues that these paradoxes were exactly the traits necessary to the "new archetype" of the American detective, "appropriately and emblematically negotiating America after the Civil War and created in the particulars of a history," and "so fluently adaptable as to be beyond all moral considerations." [9]

The legend of James McParland expressed a new cultural preoccupation with both the necessity for and the morality of masking, passing, and spying as strategies for negotiating the upheavals of the extended postbellum era, especially the conflict between capital and labor.[10] Klein argues that McParland, as the hired detective-spy, initiated "a line which would extend forward to all of the stylized, morally neutral, entirely American tough-guy private eyes to come." [11] I agree that it is possible to trace a chain of influence from the early dime novel straight through to the hard-boiled school, but I would add that the work of Victor and Pauline Hopkins (and, as we shall see in the next chapter, Anna Katharine Green) shows that there were other contexts for, and other lines of development forward from, the spy-detective figure. Joe Meredith deploys his spying skills in a domestic setting and in the interests of the professional class. He, like the detectives that follow him in this tradition of detective fiction by women, is not morally neutral, but thoroughly enmeshed — emotionally, sexually, professionally, and financially — in the narrative of crime that he seeks to bring into coherency. Although he is more of a rogue than Redfield, both are shaped by the morality of the sentimental domestic novel, which is to say that both intervene on behalf of middle- and upper-class domestic ideology and know that to do so is both a duty and a pleasure.

In the domestic detective tradition, surveillance is an intimate act, and the story of uncovering a crime realigns and reaffirms the important bonds of love and duty. The next writer to take up the configuration that Victor worked out was Anna Katharine Green, who began publishing in the 1870s. But before turning to her work, I'd like to consider briefly Pauline Hopkins's use of detectives and detective fiction motifs in *Hagar's Daughter*, jumping out of chrono-logical order because her novel, though serialized in 1900, makes such interesting and socially critical use of the fusion of surveil-lance and intimacy that we have seen in Victor's fiction. In its serial structure and its use of multiple story-paper formulae it is also sty-listically closer to Victor's detective novels than to the more stable and generically integrated novels of Green and Rinehart.

The plot of *Hagar's Daughter* is notoriously convoluted, and, as Hazel Carby suggests, that very complexity of "intrigue" in the novel should be understood as part of a political and social critique.[12] Hop-kins combines a plot of passing for white with a layering of investiga-tive strategies, but, as Stephen Soitos argues, uses "the detective form to question the moral and cultural foundation that typical detective fiction supports through the reestablishment of the natural order."[13] Hopkins's strategy in deploying the tropes of gothic narrative is one that Goddu identifies as typical in African American literary tra-dition, where "the gothic has served as a useful mode in which to resurrect and resist America's racial history."[14] The ostensible crime in need of investigation is the murder of a young white woman by a powerful and charming villain named Benson with whom she had a child. An innocent young white man named Sumner has been ar-rested for the crime, and his fiancée, Jewel, asks Detective Henson of the Treasury Department to take an interest in the case. That first murder, though, was only part of a complex plan—straight from the female gothic—to take control of Jewel's fortune, and the same pair of conniving scoundrels poison Jewel's father and kidnap Jewel and an elderly black eyewitness known as Aunt Henny, which is one way the connectedness of the characters is inscribed.

As I have already noted, it takes a character intimately involved with the crime to solve it. Detective Henson is at a loss to find the two kidnapped women until a young black woman named Venus, grand-daughter to one woman and maid to the other, volunteers her ser-vices. Her psychic investment in their rescue is not only concern for their welfare, but also hatred for Benson. She declares: "I just made up my mind it was Venus for General Benson, and that I'd got to cook his goose or he'd cook mine."[15] Venus further suspects that her father is involved in the kidnapping, and she and Henson arrange for her to conduct her reconnaissance disguised as a young man named

Billy. Disguise, which we normally see working as a deliberate kind of self-estrangement or alienation, becomes in this novel a sign of connection, an acknowledgment of the fact that one could be recognized and would be known to the people under surveillance.

But what really is not known, and what really needs to be uncovered, is the fact that Jewel and her mother, Hagar, are Detective Henson's long-lost daughter and wife, and the villainous Benson is his estranged brother. All the events I have described are from the second half of the novel. The first half of the story includes the dramatic and unexpected disclosure that Hagar, ostensibly white, is of mixed ancestry and ends with Hagar and her daughter drowning as they attempt to flee from a slave trader, and with Ellis Enson, her husband, apparently murdered by his dissipated brother, St. Clair. But all these characters actually survive and come back under different names in the second half of the novel, unbeknownst to each other and to the reader until almost the end of the novel. The reliance on coincidence and the almost prurient desire for reunion that characterizes story-paper fiction have clearly shaped Hopkins's narrative structure here, as has her own abiding interest in conscious and unconscious passing. But by yoking those plot structures with the energies of the detective novel, Hopkins creates a painfully intricate narrative of not knowing.

The critique this novel makes is expressed through its string of surprises about connection and unanticipated intimacy. As Hazel Carby puts it in *Reconstructing Womanhood,* "the revelations and resolutions of popular fiction signaled the reestablishment of order in the social and moral fabric of the characters' lives."[16] But Hopkins deliberately thwarts the kind of emotional closure that is supposed to come at the end of both romances and detective novels by denying a reunion between Sumner and Jewel, having the latter die before Sumner can reaffirm the love shaken by the revelation that she is part black. The wedding that is the standard ending of family sagas and domestic detective fiction is replaced by the image of an irrevocably broken marriage. That discomfiting ending tells us that the revelation of truth is not always a comfortable thing, a lesson Hopkins also brings across in her innovative manipulations of the detective novel.

Stephen Soitos argues that "the interwoven irony of the passing theme demonstrates the duplicity of the prevailing social system.

Hopkins's plot structure of hidden identities, misinterpreted con-versations, compromising situations, and disguise—all stock ele-ments of detective fiction—begin to take on further meaning as they illustrate the immorality of a system based on racial prejudice and segregation."[17] I would add that this problem of interpretation is not something we simply observe, but is something we experience even more keenly than in most detective novels. Even very attentive readers have to ask themselves if Jewel is Hagar's daughter; for even if we suspect it to be true, we don't *know.* In reading this novel, we are less interested in finding out "who done it?" than in knowing "who are all these people?" Our experience of being fooled by dis-guises works at the level of the whole novel as well as with individual characters, for, as Carby argues, "the disguise of whiteness enabled Hopkins to write a 'black' story that unravels in the heart of elite Washington society."[18]

*Hagar's Daughter* shows how the tropes, conventions, and narra-tive structure of detective fiction can express questions about the social construction of reality. Hopkins shows a web of connections that establishes the intimacy and indistinguishability of white and black characters and names segregation and prejudice as impos-sible on epistemological grounds and futile on political ones. She ultimately familiarizes blackness, a result that is strikingly differ-ent from more famous uses of the gothic mode to depict stories of slavery and race mixing. The contrast with Mark Twain's *Pudd'nhead Wilson* is especially pointed, for while Twain combines the gothic trope of switched babies with a detective plot about fingerprints, cre-ating an airtight conundrum of race and criminality, he ultimately reveals, as Leslie Fiedler puts it, that "his specter is identical with Poe's and Don Benito's: 'the negro.' "[19] Likewise, Stowe's depiction of Cassy's gothic stratagem of escape was in part so effective with her initial readers because it resonated with white fears and stereotypes about African Americans as "unnatural" as well as supernatural. Alcott used gothic tropes in her abolitionist writing as well as in her thrillers, and an 1863 story called "M. L." is especially revealing of the resonance of estrangement even in a story that celebrates inter-racial love and marriage.[20]

*Hagar's Daughter* is ultimately only partly a detective story. But Hopkins's use of detective motifs, as well as the fact that she chose to experiment with them, suggest that we need to take the socially critical possibilities of domestic detective fiction seriously. Victor's novels do not present the sharp political point that *Hagar's Daughter* does, but they do represent a world of radical and disorienting falseness and treachery. In their emphasis on the need for surveillance and regulation of the erotic energies of sexual desire, rivalry, and love, domestic detective novels offer a view of the world as "a web of human iniquity" and continue some strains of the moralism of the sentimental domestic novel, combining them, as we shall see in Green's work, with the hygienic impulses of postbellum reform culture. Brodhead suggests that the middlebrow emerged first as a remnant of sentimental culture, and that is a helpful way of thinking about the emergence of domestic detective fiction. While this tradition drew on popular tropes and plots from story-papers and newspapers (especially gothic thrillers, detective memoirs, and spy narratives), the first full-fledged detective novels were published as hardbound volumes for a fairly well-to-do audience. These novels were about and for the consumption of the upper, middle, and professional classes; they offered a combination of traces of older themes like "disciplinary intimacy," a distinctive and complex narrative structure, and violent and transgressive subject matter like homicide, adultery, and counterfeiting. Much about detective fiction, with its plot conventions and its movement from chaos to solution, seems inherently conservative. However, the genre is also capable, because of its foregrounding of the epistemological constitution of narrative, of asking—and asking the reader to experience—questions about the construction of the social world and our reading of it.

# Part Two

ANNA

KATHARINE

GREEN

AND THE

GILDED

AGE

"I eschew prose. Poetry is my forte; story telling is not possible to me." Thus wrote Anna Katharine Green in 1869 to her friend and fellow writer Mary Hatch a few years after Green graduated from Ripley College.[1] The occasion was Green's first publication, of a poem called "Ode to Grant," and the most notable aspect of her declaration is that it seems to be utterly wrong. Green went on to become the most famous and prolific writer of detective fiction in America before Dashiell Hammett, and her first novel, *The Leavenworth Case*, was the best-selling novel of 1878.[2] Her statement — when read in light of the sheer volume of her detective prose, its success with readers, and the skill of its plotting and narration — seems so absurd that it begs investigation.

Hatch concludes, accurately, that "like George Eliot, she misconceived her own genius." Green's youthful embrace of poetry produced two volumes: a collection called *The Defence of the Bride* and a verse drama, *Risifi's Daughter.*[3] Both were published after Green was famous for *The Leavenworth Case,* and though *The Defence of the Bride* received some favorable reviews, both volumes soon were mentioned only as curiosities.[4] For as Green continued to write her mystery novels, she became a famous figure, and the tale of the young woman who "turned to prose only because the poetry, unfortunately, did not sell"[5] became a part of her legend. Such a figuration of Anna Katharine Green is interesting insofar as it reminds us of how, from its beginnings, the detective novel was understood to be a popular, and therefore artistically inferior, form. However, to sum up Green's career as that of a frustrated poet who sold out for cash is to miss the more complex algebra of gender and genre in the literary marketplace of Green's time. Green wrote a genre — detective fiction — that was from early on assumed to be masculine terrain, and in a mode — the gothic — with a scandalous history. She was a Victorian lawyer's daughter who ended up writing novels with a content and narrative structure that were, unlike an ode to the president, neither conventionally feminine nor genteel. Her work examines the question of what women are willing and able to say and what happens to those who tell what they know; the power to be gained and price to be paid for saying more than one should are frequent themes in her work. It is around those issues that Green's novels make their most socially critical points, using the themes and structures of detective fiction to identify the hypocrisies of domestic ideology. Her work often addresses the problem of the woman who wants to say more than she should, which seems to have been a problem faced by Green herself. Indeed, I would suggest that at the moment Green seems to be making a statement of individual artistic temperament, "I eschew prose . . . story telling is not possible to me," she is actually making a statement about the cultural restraints on the woman writer of the nineteenth century.

In standard histories of detective fiction, which see the detective story as a closed genre that "developed" by a series of internal reactions and innovations, Green has the honored but eminently forgettable place of a founder. She is, in fact, given the sobriquet of mother, grandmother, and godmother of the detective novel, which "sprang full-fledged from its author's head."[6] She is credited with many "firsts" (including, erroneously, being the first woman to write a full-length detective novel): the murder of a man while he makes out his will, the use of an icicle as a murder weapon, and so forth. She is also rightly credited with creating the first female detectives in American fiction. Although she appears in only three novels, Amelia Butterworth became the prototype of the amateur spinster detective and inspired Agatha Christie's creation of Jane Marple. In 1915, Green introduced another series character named Violet Strange, a New York debutante who works as a private investigator for wealthy families who find themselves troubled by crime and who have their own reasons—such as protection of their reputation or protection of a family member from prosecution—for hiring her in lieu of calling in the police.[7] *The Mayor's Wife* (1907) is narrated by a young woman who is hired to be a companion to the troubled wife of a mayor and ends up working as a kind of lay detective. There was, in fact, some precedent for the appearance of the woman detective; Green was probably acquainted with a British yellowback called *The Experiences of a Lady Detective* (c. 1861), and she would very likely have read Wilkie Collins's *The Law and the Lady* (1875).[8] She might also have been influenced later by the female detectives who appeared occasionally in American dime novels after 1880.[9] Detective fiction histories place her as an intermediary figure, a writer who brought together the transatlantic influences of Gaboriau, Poe, and Collins.[10] But Green has significance and interest outside the realm of detective fiction history; the phenomenon of her popularity adds to our understanding of the late nineteenth-century literary marketplace, and her novels document an intersecting set of cultural anxieties about class and gender at the turn of the century.

In her day, Green was depicted as a singular mix of contradictions; interviewers liked to play her subject matter, mayhem, off her demeanor, which was conventionally feminine. Several articles about her begin with passages of apprehension and relief: "I had not thought to meet a frail and diffident lady, who for the most part would talk to me about the felicities of her home, her husband, and her children, when in the city of Buffalo I sought out the author who had given to President Wilson what he called his 'most authentic thrills' "; or "She opens the door herself, a gentle woman. . . . It is a cozy, cordial room and all fear of the detective lady leaves you and you feel only an intense curiosity."[11] Assessments of the novels repeat two main points over and over: her novels are carefully plotted puzzles (the words *ingenious* and *clever* occur in almost every review), and they are punctuated by moments of suspense (*thrilling* is another Green key word). Some reviewers felt that the cerebral satisfactions and physical excitements of her novels reinforced each other: as one wrote, "she never fails to engage the interest of the reader at the outset of the tale, and to hold it unabated to the end."[12] But other reviewers despised her "melodramatic tone" (especially after Sherlock Holmes became popular in the 1890s), calling it a blot on the "ingenious planning and patient execution."[13] The two skills are gendered in these reviews: like science, the gift in the construction of a puzzle is masculine, and, like emotional display, the propensity toward terror is feminine. In 1903, the *Bookman* summed up this way of seeing things, opining that "had Anna Katharine Green been a man she would have written very fine detective stories indeed; . . . no woman can ever quite write a detective story as it should be written, for the good detective story is essentially logical."[14] The more gothic elements of her novels were frequently offered as evidence of a woman author in communication with her female reader-ship. The *Bookman* review goes on to complain about all the "horror and gloom" wasted on the description of the house (instead of the corpse) and the unhealthy abundance of "the gruesome and tragic."

Although "the gruesome" may have been classified as a female mode of discourse, however, it was hardly ladylike reading or writ-ing, and it is on this point that the hybrid qualities of Green's fiction become important to placing her work culturally and to understand-ing precisely how it defied the social and generic conventions of its time. When Green wrote of crime in the gothic mode, she engaged the complex issues of gender and class that ran through the literary marketplace of the late nineteenth century. Green clearly saw her-self as an heir to Poe and the detective story, paying direct tribute to him in at least three novels. She also owes a good deal to the Vic-torian sensation novel, particularly to its treatment of the problem of female entrapment. In those ways Green is just like Metta Victor; both drew on those traditions in writing full-length detective novels. Both also drew on the structure and themes of the domestic novel, though Green did so in a more sustained and systematic way. But there is also evidence of a substantial gap in the relative status of *The Dead Letter* and *The Leavenworth Case*—a gap that, ironically, is visible only when we look at the similarities of the two writers.

The texts of both writers share a number of thematic concerns and narrative patterns: false identity and hypocrisy, concealed stories of secret marriages or improper infatuations, secret messages and secret writing, the desire to unearth what is concealed, the compul-sion to confess, the drive to reconstruct the story that has been cut off or made incoherent. As in Victor's novels, the public and private spheres stand in uneasy relation to one another in Green's work, and many of the crimes and mysteries center on events or documents of events that are somehow both public and private: marriages and marriage certificates, wills, letters sent through the United States mail. In most of Green's thirty-four detective novels, the investiga-tion is conducted in whole or in part by a member of the professional or moneyed classes, usually acting as a buffer between the police and the members of the household, who may or may not be con-cealing cold-blooded murder behind the ethos of privacy in middle-class domestic culture. The work of the middle-class investigator, in

Green's novels as in Victor's, is a project in the surveillance and re-alignment of the erotic connections within the bourgeois household, a project that causes the detectives some inner torment about the scruples of listening at doors and reading other people's mail. Almost invariably, one of the secrets they discover is a secret marriage.

In addition, there are a number of striking similarities of plot in *The Leavenworth Case* and *The Dead Letter*. Both are narrated by young lawyers who become amateur sidekicks to police detectives and who are infatuated with one of the women of the household under investigation; both households include sisters or cousins named Mary and Eleanore, and both include a young Irish seamstress who flees the scene of the murder and is sought by the police. Green's novel also shares with Victor's *The Figure Eight* a wealthy patriarch murdered as he sits writing at his library table and a lost key, the possession of which makes someone look guilty. Surprisingly, I have not found any reviews noting the congruences between Green's work and Victor's, similarities so particular that they smack of plagiarism on Green's part.[15] The silence about the parallels between the two novelists suggests that they had very different readerships, with Victor's books hovering closer to the world of the dime novel, and Green's anchored more firmly in the literary world of the middle class.[16] Green's work was published in hardcover by such firms as Putnam's, Bobbs-Merrill, and Dodd, Mead; only two of the novels were issued in serial form in magazines before publication as single volumes.[17] These books had much the same status in the literary marketplace that the detective novel has today—light reading for the educated—and were part of the spectrum of "railroad fiction," books republished in paper covers and sold at train stations.[18]

Articles about detective fiction written at the turn of the century indicate that dime novels were considered to be the purview of pubescent males of all classes, while novels and short stories (particularly Green's) were understood as entertainment for middle- and upper-class adults. An article entitled "The Detective in Fiction" from 1902 offers a complicated portrait of the readership of detective fiction a few decades after Green and Victor wrote. In it, Arthur Maurice argues, in a lighthearted way, that "most men who have reached mature years can look back and recall the memory of an urchin who has been detected in the surreptitious reading of some paper-covered novel of sensational adventure," a discovery usually made by schoolmasters who did not appreciate the charms of dime novels like *Red Light Will, the River Detective.* A "boy's literary likes and the dime novel are only partially relevant to" the question of full-length detective novels, Maurice adds, but "the emotions which inspired fifteen or twenty years ago affection for the heroes of Cap Collier or of Old Sleuth are the same which underlie at a later day a liking for Gaboriau's Lecoq or Dr. Doyle's Sherlock Holmes." Maurice goes on to make an analogy between social class and groups of detectives: dime-novel detectives "Old Rafferty, Chink, Sleuth, Butts and all of that ilk may be designated as the *canaille,* the proletarians; Poe's Dupin, Gaboriau's Lecoq and Pere Tirauclair, and Dr. Doyle's Sherlock Holmes are the patricians; they represent the *grand monde:* between these two extremes are the detectives who belong to the *bourgeoisie* of detection and they of course are of the greatest number. An excellent type of this middle class is the Mr. Gryce of the stories of Anna Katharine Green."[19] While it is hard to know whether or not he means us to extend these class categories to the readership of the books, the piece as a whole suggests that he does. In an article written in 1899, Kathleen Woodward argues against critics who dismiss detective fiction as "irrelevant to literature" and appealing only to a "lower type of audience"; she also uses Green as an example of a writer engaging major questions of nineteenth-century culture in works of "detective *literature*" that fall on the cusp between serious and light reading.[20] We might take these remarks as a description of a growing middlebrow sensibility in the late nineteenth century, the development of a taste in entertaining reading that preceded the burgeoning of a middlebrow culture of self-improvement in the early twentieth century that Joan Shelley Rubin has documented.[21]

The distance within the marketplace between dime novels and hardbound detective novels probably accounts for Green's success in borrowing so extensively from Victor's two stories without detection. There is another, perhaps even more interesting, question raised by the congruences of their texts: If *The Leavenworth Case* and *The Dead Letter* are so similar, why did Green's become a best-seller and a landmark in detective fiction history while Victor's is known mainly to book collectors? Green's detective novels found a middle-class audience when Victor's very similar stories apparently did not. While, as argued in the previous chapter, Victor's detective fiction explores and applauds the emergence of the professional class in the postbellum period, it was Green's story of a young lawyer rooting out the pernicious side effects of merchant capitalism that won a niche in the middle- and upper-class popular market.

The crucial difference between the detective fictions of these two writers has to do with the incorporation of the domestic novel into their formulae. In *The Dead Letter,* the domestic plot is present only in a skeletal way, contributing the structure of courtship and the wedding-as-ending; the tone of the book is consistently more sensational than the work even of E. D. E. N. Southworth, herself at the gothic-domestic crossroads. Green takes the concerns and tropes of the American domestic novel far more seriously; her work is best understood as a hybrid of the detective story and the domestic novel. For reasons sketched out earlier, that genealogy is complicated, for the detective novel is a specialized form of gothic fiction, and the domestic novel of mid-century was often written against the prevailing Richardsonian-gothic plot of seduction. At the same time, writers such as Stowe, Alcott, Southworth, and Hopkins valued the gothic for what it could express about social conditions in the nineteenth century. Stowe and Alcott both used the gothic in the service of their abolitionist writing, allowing it to amplify the moral discourse at the heart of the domestic novel. What the detective novel and the domestic novel share is a desire to address problems of immorality and social anomie; the domestic detective novel names many of the same problems as the domestic novel and frames them even more urgently, as matters of violent crime clearly in need of police intervention.

Mary Kelley's articulation of the moral impulses of domestic fiction is very helpful in mapping the congruences of the domestic novel and the emergent detective novel. In her discussion of the intention of the domestic writers ("moralists *non pareil*") to offer blissful and inspiring pictures of family life as "a critical institution for the maintenance and reform of the social fabric," Kelley emphasizes the elements of the "dark vision of nineteenth-century America" that also inhere in the novels. Villainy within the domestic novel is scripted as selfishness, and the self-centered man is a constant prob-

lem: "impious, abusive of his privileged position as head of household, a trifler and despoiler of woman's sexual virtue," and driven by
an "obsessive quest for wealth and social position." The domestic detective novel presents the consequences of the same kind of villainy,
arguing over and over that greed for money and power—usually,
but not exclusively, masculine greed—leads to murder. And like the
domestic novel, while the domestic detective novel's moralism is
evident, its politics are a more complicated matter. The crucial question about the domestic novel, and the one most actively explored
in the feminist scholarship of the past twenty years, is that of its relative subversiveness or conservatism. Kelley traces those positions to
the work of, on the one hand, Alexander Cowie and his description
of the domestic novel as "a sort of benign moral police" regulating
female behavior and attitudes to a highly conservative standard, and,
on the other, to Helen Papashvily and her analysis of a rebellious assertion in these texts that "female superiority had to be established
and maintained." [22] She resolves those two antithetical positions by
arguing that there is a certain level of disjunction between the intentions of the novelists and the novels themselves; the texts assert both
a conservative argument for female deference and a subversive—
and thus self-subverting—critique of masculine culture. Likewise,
the domestic detective novel asserts contradictory moral positions:
that merchant capitalism corrodes the structures of society *and* that
the feminine values of the upper middle class are the best hope for
reform; that the home is a sanctuary from the ravages of competition *and* that the home must be opened to investigation by the state.

Green herself seems to have read the domestic novel as a genre of
conservatism, and she often depicts sentimental culture as a culture
of limitations for women. Nevertheless, her vision of domestic life
as plagued by secrecy, betrayal, and greed has to be understood as
coming out of the social critique offered by the domestic novel of
mid-century. Gillian Brown's work requires us to rethink our understanding of the nineteenth-century ideology of separate spheres,
suggesting that even in that ideology's period of ascendancy, separa-
bility was more a proposition than a *fait accompli*.[23] Green's novels,
which focus on crime within families and within homes, depict an
inseparability of private matters and public interests, of sexual desire
and career ambition, of paternal authority and the rule of law. They

thus resonated with the anxieties and experience of the middle and upper classes.

Green's novels also contain a level of moral discourse that made them familiar to mid-century middle-class readers. And they adhere to the conventions of domestic realism, especially in their consistency of narratorial perspective and the linear progress of the main narrative. Despite gothic obtrusions and pervasive gothic energies, the surface of the narrative remains quite stable. Although most of her novels are not built around the bildungsroman plot so central to the domestic novel, they do often present motherless women under great stress as they attempt to define an independent self. Even in the novels narrated by male characters or investigated by male detectives, Green is always most interested in the stories of women's lives, and women's writing and authorship are frequently at issue in those stories. The women in her novels have secrets they are afraid to talk about; Green explores what is at stake in reading, writing, and speech for women who know things they should not or cannot tell. She uses the narrative structure of detective fiction to express these particular problems of knowing and telling. Detective fiction, as crystallized from the gothic mode by Poe, has two strands of narrative: the story of an investigation of a crime and the story of how and why a murder was committed. The two strands are in a tense and shifting relationship, for the goal—and the method—of the investigation is the reconstruction of a narrative of the murder, but the story of the murder does its best to remain inaccessible, incoherent, unknowable.[24] The detective story shows its gothic nature in the fact that it is constantly working in two directions at once: toward revelation, but also toward concealment. It also shows its gothic energies in its abiding interest in clues that are texts, and thus it can be encoded, misread, or erased. And as we saw in the case of *The Dead Letter,* the doubled structure allows for a kind of double-talk; many of Green's novels simultaneously challenge and uphold the ideals of true womanhood, just as they simultaneously subvert and assert the epistemological certainties of a realist narrative in the course of an investigation.

Although Green was not associated with the reform politics of Alcott or Stowe (indeed, she took a public stand against woman suffrage in 1917), she did use her novels, with their mix of domestic and gothic tropes, as a kind of social criticism. The two chapters that follow offer readings of two of her novels and attempt to outline both the literary and historical components of the popularity of Green's work. The reading of *The Leavenworth Case* focuses on the narrative structures of detective fiction and their uses in Green's critique of the limitations placed on women — and women writers — under Victorian domestic ideology. The reading of *That Affair Next Door* explores Green's creation of an upper-class female detective within the context of turn-of-the-century social reform movements.

# 4

## *"A Woman with a Secret"*

### KNOWING AND TELLING IN

### *THE LEAVENWORTH CASE*

The actual writing of *The Leavenworth Case* was itself a matter of domestic secrecy. Anna Katharine Green, born in 1846, was the youngest daughter of James Wilson Green, a criminal lawyer who practiced at various times in Manhattan, Brooklyn, and Buffalo. She graduated from Ripley College, of Vermont, in 1866 and returned to her father's household, which included Green's stepmother, Green's unmarried elder sister, and her brothers and their wives. During this period Green set seriously to writing and to attempts at publication. Mary Hatch states that Green had been writing stories and poems since she was eleven years old, and wrote daily, even during vacations and house parties and after evening social calls, often late into the night. The sense that Green was a passionate, even compulsive writer is heightened by a letter Green wrote to Hatch describing — in terms reminiscent of Alcott's "blood & thunder" — the idea for *The Leavenworth Case,* which came to her in a dream: "It is so passionate, so strong, so subtle, so dread, dark, and heart-rending it ought to be written with fire and blood. It will require all my enthusiasm, study, and power, and then I may fall short, but I believe I shall someday try."[1] According to Patricia Maida, whose research on Green's life includes interviews with Green's daughter-in-law, James Green encouraged his daughter to write poetry but strongly disapproved of the idea of novel writing.[2] Therefore Green wrote *The Leavenworth Case* in secret, confiding only in her stepmother, and showing the manuscript to her father only after it was completed.[3] Since Hatch tells us that Green's work habits were rigorous, including long hours at her desk and extensive rewriting, we have a sense that this was no small secret to keep, especially for the two and one-half years it took Green to write the novel.[4] Secrecy was her subject as well as her method, for *The Leavenworth Case* is the story of secrets so danger-ous that people would murder to keep them from being told.

The situation of the writing of *The Leavenworth Case* suggests another reading of Green's statement that "story telling is not pos-sible to me," one that hears in her words the censorious voice of genteel literary culture, a culture that marked the gothic mode, in particular, as inappropriate for women writers and antithetical to the ideals of domesticity. Green wanted to tell stories that seemed impossible to tell; she seemed compelled to say things that she be-lieved were perhaps best left unsaid. Her stories became narratives of secrecy and disclosure, structured in complex, doubled ways that repeat that very deep sense that the heart of the story is "not pos-sible" to tell.

*The Leavenworth Case* opens with the announcement that a mur-der has occurred.[5] Horatio Leavenworth is found dead, shot once through the back of the head and slumped over his writing table in the library of his New York City mansion. The coroner is about to begin his inquest into the death, and the police and a detective are on the scene. Leavenworth's secretary, Trueman Harwell, has gone to summon someone from the family law firm because Leavenworth's two wards are felt to need someone "capable of advising them" in the aftermath of the murder. Harwell goes in search of Mr. Veeley, the senior partner of the firm and a family friend, but (because Veeley is out of town) has to settle for Raymond Everett, a youthful junior partner and our narrator. The novel is subtitled "A Lawyer's Story," and like Victor's *The Dead Letter,* it focuses on a young professional struggling to understand his proper role within the larger structure of the middle and upper classes.

The tone of the summons is ominous, but Raymond eagerly fol-lows Harwell to the Leavenworth house, where he meets Ebenezer Gryce, the police detective in charge of the investigation, a "portly, comfortable personage" with a facility for judging character and for assessing the complexities of human situations. Gryce senses Ray-mond's place in the investigation immediately, as their first conver-sation indicates:

"The jury have just gone up-stairs to view the body; would you like to follow them?" [asks Gryce]

"No, it is not necessary. I have merely come in the hope of being of some assistance to the young ladies. Mr. Veeley [head of the law firm] is away." [replies Raymond]

"And you thought the opportunity too good to be lost," he went on; "just so. Still, now that you are here, and as the case promises to be a marked one, I should think that, as a rising young lawyer, you would wish to make yourself acquainted with it in all its details. But follow your own judgment."

I made an effort and overcame my repugnance. "I will go," I said. (*LC*, 4–5)

Gryce points out to Raymond a young lawyer's own selfish inter-est in the case and suggests a course of action — gaining as much inside knowledge as possible — that will further his reputation and career; Raymond's reaction to Gryce's assessment, like his reaction to Leavenworth's corpse, is "repugnance." Raymond has entered this case with a very conventional imagination, that of a professional and a gentleman. Dispatched to lend support both masculine and profes-sional to the two nieces Leavenworth has raised since they were or-phaned as young girls, he comes to the scene of the murder expecting to find "nothing more terrible . . . than a tender picture of the lovely cousins bowed in anguish over the remains of one who had been as dear as a father to them" (*LC*, 40). He is as certain of his own recti-tude as he is of the young ladies' virtue, but, as Gryce tells him, "you don't begin to know what kind of a world you are living in" (*LC*, 43).

Raymond finds a scene in the Leavenworth mansion that shocks his gentlemanly sensibilities. He sees jurymen and police officers traipsing all over the house and the coroner setting up a public in-quest in the dead man's front parlor. The evidence points to some-one living inside the house. The exterior doors and the windows of the house remained locked from the inside all night; in his shaving stand, Leavenworth kept a pistol, which, on examination, proves to have been recently fired and hastily cleaned; Leavenworth must have known and trusted the person whose footsteps he heard coming up behind him through his own bedroom and into the adjoining library, since he did not turn his head as he was shot. The nieces are under a cloud of suspicion though no one has quite dared to mention their names, shaking Raymond's expectations of tender scenes of filial devotion and his certainty that the home is a place for seclusion and intimacy. The sense of disorientation is rendered as an almost psychotic episode:

As the strongly contrasting features of the scene before me began to impress themselves upon my consciousness, I found myself experiencing something of the same sensation of double personality which years before had followed an enforced use of ether. As at that time, I appeared to be living two lives at once: in two distinct places, with two separate sets of incidents going on; so now I seemed to be divided between two irreconcilable trains of thought; the gorgeous house, its elaborate furnishing, the little glimpses of yesterday's life, as seen in the open piano, with its sheet of music held in place by a lady's fan, occupying my attention fully as much as the aspect of the throng of incongruous and impatient people huddled about me. (*LC*, 9)

Raymond's sense of reality splits along the divisions that his genteel worldview makes between the public and private spheres, the world of crime and the world of comfort, the world of official inquiry and the sacrosanct privilege of the elite.

Raymond is further distressed by what he discovers when he is sent upstairs to fetch one of the cousins to testify at the inquest. As Gryce and Raymond reach the landing outside the bedroom door, they overhear a voice, a woman's voice, accusing someone of something: "I do not accuse your hand, though I know of none other which would or could have done this deed; but your heart, your head, your will, these I do and must accuse, in my secret mind at least; and it is well that you should know it!" (*LC*, 42). Raymond, who has walked up the stairs expecting "to meet the stricken nieces of a brutally murdered man" (*LC*, 42), is so shocked by what he hears that he literally covers his ears, as if to protect himself from knowing more. But his sentimental assumptions are not going to serve him well, even if his concept of honor will. For inside the room is not the tender denouement of orphaning that opens so many domestic novels, but a pair of women accusing each other of murder. To find out which one is guilty will require a delicate style of surveillance and investigation.

Apparently because Raymond is behaving like such a gentleman, Gryce recruits Raymond to help him investigate the relationship between these two women in a kind of undercover operation. Gryce outlines the "disadvantages under which a detective labors. . . . I cannot pass myself off for a gentleman. , , , I have even employed a French valet who understood dancing and whiskers; but it was all of no avail" (*LC*, 106). "I can enter a house, bow to the mistress of it, let her be as elegant as she will, so long as I have a writ of arrest in my hand, or some such professional matter upon my mind; but when it comes to visiting in kid gloves, raising a glass of champagne in response to a toast — and such like, I am absolutely good for nothing. . . . But it is much the same with the whole of us. When we are in want of a gentleman to work for us, we have to go outside of our profession" (*LC*, 107). Just as a detective cannot act like a gentleman, a gentleman is also, as in Victor's novels, reluctant to act like a detective. Raymond thinks to himself, "[A] spy in a fair woman's house! How could I reconcile that with my natural instincts as a gentleman?" He says he will help, but "any hearkening at doors, surprises, unworthy feints or ungentlemanly subterfuges, I herewith disclaim as outside of my province; my task being to find out what I can in an open way, and yours to search into the nooks and corners of this wretched business" (*LC*, 121). Despite his scruples, Raymond, like Meredith and Redfield before him, performs all the disclaimed activities in the course of the novel; in the world Green writes of, there is a pressing need for gentlemen to rethink their blind valuation of privacy. There is also, in this case, a personal motivation for Raymond's eventual acceptance of Gryce's assignment: in the course of the next few pages he falls helplessly in love with Eleanore, and investigating the crime will allow him to clear her name and to spend time with her. As he walks up the stairs to meet the Leavenworth nieces for the first time, Raymond recalls his mother's admonition to "remember that a woman with a secret may be a fascinating study, but she can never be a safe, nor even satisfactory, companion" (*LC*, 42). Raymond, in his charmingly obtuse way, advises us that this "wise saw" is "totally inapplicable to the present situation." Of course, as Raymond is to find out, the problem of a woman with a secret is at the heart of the matter, and the first of these women is Eleanore Leavenworth.

Eleanore is brought to testify after Harwell, the secretary, claims she came to him for instruction in loading, firing, and cleaning the gun that her uncle kept in his shaving stand. There are several other things the coroner wishes her to explain as well: why she ordered the servants to move the body before the authorities arrived on the scene; whether she removed a piece of paper from her uncle's writing table while the body was being moved; why her monogrammed handkerchief, stained with pistol grease, was found under one of the cushions of the library sofa; and exactly how she feels about the fact that her uncle chose Mary as his sole heir when she and her cousin were children. Eleanore's manner on the witness stand is so haughty and defiant that suspicion begins to settle on her. Things look even worse when an officer dispatched to keep an eye on her activities follows her into an upstairs bedroom and catches her in the act of hiding the missing key to the library door in the ashes of the fireplace.

The newspapers begin to print news of the suspicions surrounding Eleanore, and Raymond decides that he must act quickly to clear her name, to restore the proper distance between the private world of an upper-class woman and the public arena of inquests and newspapers. Fortunately, Henry Clavering, a man whom Gryce wants Raymond to befriend and observe, makes an unexpected visit to Raymond's office and provides the first break in the case. Raymond failed in his earlier attempts to win over the taciturn Clavering, but he learned an important secret: that Clavering called on Eleanore on the night of the murder, and that the butler is not certain that Clavering left the Leavenworth house afterward. Thus, it is in a context of suspicion that Raymond greets his visitor.

Clavering has come for a professional consultation on a point of law. Reading from a memorandum book, Clavering tells the story of a friend, a fellow Englishman, who married an American woman in secret. The marriage was performed by a minister—since deceased—and was properly witnessed by a friend of the bride and by the minister's hired man, since disappeared. The bride insisted that her groom leave the country immediately after the ceremony and that he keep the marriage a secret until she decided to announce it publicly. Clavering wants to know if such a marriage is legal and binding. Raymond explains that it is, but that the friend may have trouble proving the matter in court if the wife denies that the ceremony ever took place. Even Raymond realizes that "the friend" is only a fictitious front, and that Clavering is referring to a secret marriage involving himself. At Clavering's request, Raymond writes and signs a legal opinion, which Clavering carefully copies into his book. Then, to Raymond's surprise, Clavering hands the sheet of paper back to him, saying, "[R]eceive back this opinion into your own possession, and in the day you think to lead a beautiful woman to the altar, pause and ask yourself: 'Am I sure that the hand I clasp with such impassioned fervor is free?' " (*LC,* 142). Clavering takes his leave, and Raymond wonders if the purpose of the visit was to warn him that Eleanore is already secretly married to Clavering.

The scene constitutes a moment of revelation for Raymond, for Clavering's visit reveals that at least one of the murder suspects is married. His story is more than "a clue"—a piece of physical evidence or a snippet of overheard conversation—for it points directly to a secret that, if understood, might explain the murder. Clavering's story is the first solid lead in the case, and Raymond's pursuit of it will eventually disclose the secret of the Leavenworth nieces. Clavering challenges Raymond in his role as a lawyer by requiring him to issue a legal opinion, and in his role as a suitor by suggesting that he beware of bigamous marriage. Clavering also challenges Raymond as a narrator, for he reads his story of marriage out of his own book. Clavering's visit is the first point at which the concealed story of the murder breaks through into the narrative of the investigation. In his insistence on the written opinion and his careful copying of it, Clavering points to the importance of the written word in the moment when the two narratives merge. Raymond, at this point, does not appreciate that importance, but he soon will, for he is about to discover that a letter can provide a motive for homicide or can even become the agent of murder.

After their interview, Clavering departs for England and Raymond meets with Gryce. Gryce discloses that when Eleanore hid the library key in the ashes of the fireplace, she also attempted to burn a document of some kind, possibly the piece of paper she is said to have removed from the scene of the crime. The scorched paper proves to be a letter, stained with blood and torn into strips. The title of this chapter is "Patch-Work," and in a process similar to piecing fabric, Raymond arranges the strips into a sequence that allows the sense of the letter to be retrieved. Even though all of the strips are damaged, and several are missing altogether, Raymond is able to discern that this is a letter written to Horatio Leavenworth by Henry Clavering. It contains a complaint against one of the nieces and was written on the first of March, three days before Leavenworth was killed.

Even more interesting than the content of the letter—which reveals only that Clavering had become tired of waiting for his marriage to be acknowledged and had decided to force his wife's hand—is the textual treatment of the letter. In the original editions of the text, facsimiles of the paper strips were bound in between the pages of the book; most later editions include an illustration of the torn letter. The facsimile clue allows the reader to play along with Raymond as he pieces the fragments of the letter together, but the reproduction is not strictly necessary because the body of the text includes versions of the letter as Raymond reconstructs it. The first such version quotes Raymond as he reads the words and word fragments on the strips aloud; there are dashes to indicate where pieces are missing, and the presentation retains some of the format of the letter, such as the indentation of the signature. A second version of the letter, also a quotation of Raymond reading, includes phrases and words "interposed" to render the original sense of the letter. This version is more clearly set off from the body of the narrative and is a representation of the letter as well as an iteration of its contents, because it mimics the letter's placement of date, salutation, and signature. Certainly, this manner of presentation, even of letters being read aloud, is a literary convention. Here, though, the persistent representation—as distinct from simple iteration—of the letter stresses its status as a written text. Each of the three representations draws our attention to the fact that the letter is a mutilated text: not only are certain words obscured by bloodstains and scorching, but whole sections of text are lost, and have been made so deliberately. The content of the letter reveals a connection between Clavering and one of the nieces, and its mutilated condition demonstrates that someone is working to efface that secret. The scene of the letter's reconstruction seems to be another of those moments when the two parallel plots of the mystery novel—the story of the murder and the story of the investigation—come together. Like Clavering's visit to Raymond's law office, this occasion seems to offer a glimpse into the narrative structure of the mystery novel. What Raymond reconstructs is not simply a letter from Clavering to Leavenworth; it is also a message from one plot to the other. The letter exposes the concealed story to the narrative of investigation. And the mutilation of the letter indicates that the story of murder contains a force working desperately to disassemble its own narrative.

Clues, like this letter, allow the reconstruction of the murder plot but are also traces of the same destructive and disorganizing force that surrounds the act of murder and the game of evasion. In this novel, the clues—these points where the concealed plot pierces the investigative one—are often concealed or misleading texts. Such texts do more than simply move the plot forward with the information they contain, for in this novel letters and documents are also important as objects, perhaps because they provide tangible evidence of the existence of the concealed narrative of murder. Intense interest in the text as object (as distinct from the verbal information it offers) is at the heart of the novel's preoccupation with mutilated, inverted, illicit, erroneous, or forged texts. Most of the important clues in the case have some connection with books, letters, or the written word. We have seen Eleanore's monogrammed and soiled handkerchief, Raymond's desire to keep Eleanore's name out of the newspapers, Clavering's memorandum book and calling cards, and the torn letter about love and the Leavenworth nieces. We will also see a secret marriage certificate, illicit and misleading love letters, a forged suicide note, pages torn from a diary, a secret name scratched backward on a windowpane—by the end, even the name tags on underwear are unreliable. The most thorough investigation of the meaning of textual mutilation comes in the aftermath of the second murder in the novel, to which we now turn.

Through the careful work of Gryce's operatives, Raymond is able to confirm the details of Clavering's story of a secret marriage, but he discovers that Clavering's bride is not Eleanore but Mary. Suddenly, Gryce's and Raymond's suspicions shift to Mary Leavenworth, who may or may not have acted in cahoots with Clavering to murder her rich uncle. Gryce has continued his search for Hannah Chester, a maid in the Leavenworth household who disappeared on the night of the murder. A tip from a neighbor indicates that Hannah is hiding—or being held captive—at the country home of Mrs. Amy Belden, and the focus of the investigation shifts to that house.

Mrs. Belden's home is the site of sentimental domesticity in this novel: Mrs. Belden, while a humble seamstress, is notable for a "refinement in her speech and manner . . . combined with her motherly presence and gentle air" (*LC,* 206), and her household is infused with Christian virtue, combining "simplicity" and "cosiness" with habits of womanly industry and charity in feeding tramps and other needy strangers. This generous, nurturing woman and her home could have come out of a domestic novel, except for the fact that she is under suspicion of aiding and abetting a murderer. Raymond poses as a boarder and feels a "startled embarrassment . . . not remote from shame" (*LC,* 208) on realizing the depth of the cynicism that his prying indicates, but the Belden house also becomes the site of the most energetic and productive spying that Raymond and Gryce's operatives will do. It is the most suspicious place in the whole novel, and we might think of it (and other houses like it) as a measure of the extent to which Green rewrites domestic spaces as sites of deception.

Raymond starts to search for clues of Hannah's presence and Mrs. Belden's role in what begins to look like a conspiracy. He discovers several—including the name "Mary Clavering" etched backward ("Yram Gnirevalc") on a windowpane and the letter *H* embroidered on a stocking in Mrs. Belden's workbasket. Raymond is doing a fine job of snooping around and chatting up Mrs. Belden when she shyly asks him for legal advice. She was entrusted, she explains, with a set of documents belonging to two young ladies. She agreed not to destroy or release the documents without the consent of both women. But just that day, one of the women has written demanding the destruction of all the papers. Raymond advises Mrs. Belden that she is under a contractual and a moral obligation to continue holding the papers, even though her correspondent reports that her circumstances are dire. Raymond, of course, is wondering how to get a look at these documents, since he correctly surmises that they are papers belonging to Mary and Eleanore Leavenworth and contain incriminating evidence that Mary wishes to have destroyed. (In fact, the papers include the certificate of marriage between Clavering and Mary, several smuggled letters from Clavering, and pages torn from Eleanore's diary containing her entries for the weeks of Mary's courtship and marriage.) Late on the first night of Raymond's stay, Mrs. Belden slips out of the house with a small tin chest, and Raymond follows her through the village and into the forest beyond. He does not know what she is up to, and suspects that she is leading him away from the house deliberately. When they reach an abandoned barn, though, he realizes that she has come to hide the box of papers. In the stormy darkness, Raymond uses the light of matches to search the barn, and accidentally sets the old structure on fire. The chapter containing this incident is entitled "A Weird Experience," and it is indeed gothic in tone and structure and marks a looping departure from Green's tight plotting and domestic realism. Raymond's account of this little adventure has an improbable, dreamlike quality: lightning suddenly illuminates the scene at a crucial moment, and Raymond twice passes Mrs. Belden on the road without being recognized. The second time, on the way back to her house, she stands watching the fire, believing that she is responsible for it, and says, "like a person speaking in a dream, 'Well, I did n't mean to do it'" (*LC,* 218). Raymond does not say "like a person talking in her sleep," suggesting that it is not Mrs. Belden who is dreaming, but himself.

The incident operates as a nightmarish replay of Raymond's pursuit of "a woman with a secret." It also dramatizes his anxiety about his role as "a spy in a fair woman's house," for in searching the barn, he sets it on fire and destroys it. Mrs. Belden thinks the packet she hid has burned up in the fire, and she says, "with a certain satisfaction in her voice . . . 'the thing is lost now for good.'" Her affect suggests, if we read this episode as being dreamed by Raymond, that if his wishes were truly fulfilled, he would rather *not* uncover the concealed secrets of the Leavenworth case. The episode is interesting but completely unnecessary to the plot, for Raymond already knew that Mrs. Belden had the papers in her house and could have found them there. What it does, in its sequence of documents hidden, discovered, and almost destroyed, is draw our attention to the gothic power of secret writings and written secrets and to their vulnerability to mutilation and destruction.

The next set of events marks the beginning of the acute phase of the novel's preoccupation with mutilated texts. With the aid of the undercover operative — his name is Q, short for Query, and his business card consists only of a printed question mark — Raymond learns exactly where Hannah is hiding. Q lures Mrs. Belden away from the house so Raymond can interview Hannah alone. But when Raymond finally reaches Hannah, after breaking down her bedroom door, he discovers that she is dead. The scene that follows resonates with an earlier scene in which Eleanore proves her innocence to Raymond's satisfaction by kissing her uncle's corpse. Eleanore challenges the unspoken accusations of the police by invoking the belief of "olden times," when "they used to say that a dead body would bleed if its murderer came in contact with it" (*LC,* 93). Raymond vows his confidence in her innocence by taking her hand in his and pressing it on the chest of the corpse. The scene they enact is one of the corpse mystified and animated, capable of exposing its killer: "If I . . . should be the thing they accuse me of," Eleanore asks, "would not the body of the outraged dead burst its very shroud and repel me?" (*LC,* 93).

By contrast, Hannah's corpse is a figure of stillness and silence, but one that is absolutely fascinating to Raymond. His description of her body is long and repetitive—it goes on for three full pages, carrying across a chapter break, as if Raymond cannot stop looking at, cannot stop talking about, this dead body. Part of the fascination seems to be sexual, an example of what David Brion Davis calls "the strange nineteenth-century obsession with corpses," an obsession that draws disturbing parallels between the erotic beauty of classical marble figures and a cold, defenseless female corpse.[6] Raymond's description of the scene of Hannah's death is colored by sexual, if not necrophilic, longing. Raymond tells us that "contact seemed to be necessary." His eye dwells on her "pallor," her "fixity," the "marble-like repose" of her body "amidst the tumbled clothes of the bed" (*LC,* 223). This last suggestion, that Hannah's bed was—or could be—the site of sexual activity as well as death is reinforced by Raymond's careful note of her hastily discarded garments, "left just as she had stepped from them in a circle on the floor" (*LC,* 223). Having made sure that we understand that Hannah is scantily clad, if at all, Raymond tells us that "tearing down the [bed]clothes, I laid my hand upon her heart." Even after he thus discovers that her heart has stopped, he says, "[A]s I gazed, the look of expectation which I perceived hovering about the wistful mouth and half-open lids attracted me, and I bent above her with a more personal interest" (*LC,* 225).[7]

The sexual subtext of his examination seems to be part of a more general sense that investigations of women's houses are sexually charged projects. We recall that when Raymond first becomes enthralled with Eleanore, he has overheard one cousin accuse the other of murder while he stands outside their bedroom door; when he enters, his description freezes them into a *tableau vivant* as he attempts to read the meaning of their body postures. Just before he discovers Hannah's corpse at Mrs. Belden's house, Raymond again finds himself outside a woman's bedroom, only this time, he does the accusing: "Hannah Chester," he shouts, "you are discovered." Raymond breaks down her locked door and encounters a silent corpse where he had expected a source of important testimony. Even though he "listen[s] at the lips" of the dead woman, she has no words for him, and Raymond must admit to the "downfall" of "all the plans based upon this woman's expected testimony" (*LC,* 225). Hannah's murder is far more central and far more deeply felt than Leavenworth's; while Leavenworth's death sets the police investigation in motion, it is Hannah's death that forces Raymond to confront the darkness of the heart of a murderer.

Hannah's death seems, for the moment, to threaten the future of Raymond's investigation. When Raymond speaks to Q, however, Q reports that he observed, through the window, Hannah taking a dose of medicinal — or poisonous? — powder before she went to bed. Raymond speculates at first that Hannah committed suicide, triggered by something written on the piece of paper he finds burned to ashes in the washbasin, and later that she was poisoned by Mrs. Belden. Based on the odd and secretive way Mrs. Belden had treated the mail the day before, Raymond and Gryce suspect that Mary mailed two letters to Mrs. Belden's house — one that instructed Mrs. Belden to destroy the papers and one that contained the fatal poison that killed Hannah. What remains mysterious is what the letter said that convinced Hannah to swallow the poison.

Hannah, searched out for her account of the fatal night, is now a silenced witness to two murders — Leavenworth's and her own. When Raymond laments that "Hannah, the girl, was lost in Hannah the witness" (*LC,* 225), he is describing the motive for her killing as well as the frustration of his investigation. Hannah is perhaps the most important example of "a woman with a secret," and her silence is complete. Mrs. Belden swears that she is "in utter ignorance of what [Hannah] saw or heard. . . . She never told, and I never asked. She merely said that Miss Leavenworth wished me to secrete her for a short time" (*LC*, 237). Hannah, in other words, has been sent to Mrs. Belden's for safekeeping, along with the secret documents of Mary's courtship and marriage. Hannah's body seems to have undergone the specific kind of commodification that Teresa Goddu sees as the hallmark of the blending of gothic and domestic modes in critiques of the marketplace.[8] In this detective novel, that commodification takes on a particular intensification. As Raymond puts it, "Hannah, the girl" is subsumed to "Hannah the witness," in a process that makes Hannah all witness, a young woman so strongly linked to the idea of testimony that she becomes a kind of text herself. Hannah's death illustrates the same principle that Susan Gubar sees in Lily Bart's suicide: "the terrors not of the word made flesh but of the flesh made word."[9]

Written texts and the female body are conflated at another crucial point in the novel. Clavering's letter to Leavenworth was intended to force a confession of marriage from Mary. However, by the time it surfaces in the novel, as a sheet torn and stained with blood, it becomes an emblem — more specifically — of the consummation Clavering desires. The marriage, according to both Clavering and Mrs. Belden, was never consummated because Mary sent Clavering away immediately after the legal ceremony. Their marriage, then, has only been constituted on a sheet of paper (the marriage certificate in Mrs. Belden's care) and has not yet been consummated on the sheets of a bed. Even though Raymond asserts that this marriage is legal and binding, an unconsummated marriage seems to be a rather tenuous claim and one that would be easy to annul. Perhaps Mary intended to keep her options open, for she did not seem entirely joyful when she went to see Mrs. Belden after her marriage: the new Mrs. Henry Clavering was "frightened . . . now it was over, as if with her name she had parted with something of inestimable value" (*LC*, 256).

The reason for Mary's fear and the real value of her Leavenworth name become clearer later, but for now we can see that the mutilated letter depicts marriage as a phenomenon wherein a legal document is made incarnate and a woman's body becomes a kind of legal text. The changing of her legal name is one sign of the process, the marking of the nuptial bed sheets with the blood that testifies to her virginity (and thus to the paternity of any heirs) is another.[10] Mary attempts to stall the consummation of the marriage because there is another legal document—her uncle's will—vying for her loyalty, and her reluctance is evident in the signature she leaves on Mrs. Belden's window: her new name, but in cipher. Meanwhile, Clavering becomes impatient and writes the letter intended to force a confrontation between Horatio Leavenworth and Mary. For Clavering, the bone of contention is not simply Mary's name, but Mary's body itself. The language of the letter is colored by Clavering's sexual frustration as he writes possessively about Mary's face, her voice, her figure. He demands that Leavenworth interrogate her "to her cruel, bewitching face," and he centers the letter on the image of the thorn of a rose, conjuring up its ability to prick and draw blood. Clavering intends to start a conversation between Mr. Leavenworth and his niece in which Mary will reveal that they are married, but by the time we see the letter, torn and bloodied, it is more like an enactment of the postponed consummation than an invitation to it. The letter, which takes on the character of both the bloodstained bedsheet and the bride's torn hymen, testifies—contrary to the teachings of domestic ideology—that marriage is violent and an act of possession.

Whoever tore the letter has symbolically wed Mary Leavenworth. But did Clavering tear the letter? And if he didn't, to whom is Mary wed in this way? Many things about this letter are mysterious, not the least of which is the way the attempted destruction—the tearing—enacts precisely the information that should be effaced. The connection of the female body and the written text brings us toward the most gothic principles of this novel: as Mary says of her marriage (still enacted only on paper, but soon to demand institution in the flesh), "How can I keep it secret . . . some deeds are like ghosts. They will not be laid; they reappear; they gibber; they make themselves known whether we will or not" (*LC,* 257). Mary herself imagines her secret to be embodied—or, rather, horrifyingly disembodied; unlike Clavering, who imagines a proper marriage to be a union of the flesh as well as a written contract, she is terrified by the joining of words and flesh.

Throughout this novel, women keep secrets and often must fight to do so. Suppression of secrets is a positive necessity—we see it in

Eleanore's willingness to stand accused of murder in order not to reveal her suspicions of Mary, in Mrs. Belden's silence about Hannah and about Mary's wedding, and, of course, in Mary's desperate attempt to keep her marriage a secret. Suppression of secrets invariably means suppression of written documents. Eleanore first comes under suspicion when she refuses to speak for the official court transcript at the coroner's inquest; later she is extremely distressed to see her name published in the newspaper as "strongly suspected" and "under a cloud" (*LC*, 90). She and Mary, in turn, are accused of having stolen a document from the library table; in any case, Mary gathers up incriminating papers and secret letters for Mrs. Belden to conceal. The most dramatic keeper of secrets, though, is Hannah Chester, who, more than anyone else, is the "flesh made word." Even her name, Chester, associates her with the tin "coffer," or chest, in which Mrs. Belden keeps the secret documents.

Hannah's corpse becomes the sign of all that remains unrevealed about the death of Horatio Leavenworth. Raymond reports: "I looked across the room to the closet where lay the body of the girl who, according to all probability, had known the truth of the matter, and a great longing seized me. Oh, why could not the dead be made to speak? Why should she lie there so silent, so pulseless, so inert, when a word from her were enough to decide the awful question? Was there no power to compel those pallid lips to move?" (267). As he moves closer to the corpse, he begins to feel something "like anger" at the "mockery" with which the "closed lips and lids confronted my demanding gaze" (*LC*, 267). According to Raymond, Hannah is not simply unable to speak; her corpse, somehow, is unwilling to tell what it knows.

Hannah's silence signals more than the frustration of Raymond's investigative plans; it stands for a problem in the process of narrative in which people know things and cannot or will not tell them. Hannah dies in her bed, between white sheets and under a "patchwork quilt" (*LC*, 223), a detail significant in light of the fact that "Patch-Work" is the name given to the project of piecing together the torn letter from Clavering to Leavenworth. Hannah's silence is thus placed somewhere below the patchwork surface of the reconstructive investigation; she is a silenced clue, a mute and mutilated signpost that points toward the solution of the murder plot. Like the ashes in the washbasin in her bedroom, Hannah's presence points toward an absence—specifically, the absence of sensible narrative. That silence, in both death and life, concerning the story she knows seems connected to Green's remarks about her own writing shortly before she began this novel: "story telling is not possible to me." Hannah, as the woman who cannot tell, is a figure for the woman writer, a connection that becomes even more apparent from the results of Raymond's final interrogation of her corpse.

As Raymond stands over Hannah's body, wishing he could "compel those pallid lips to move," he spies an envelope protruding from underneath the corpse. Inside is a letter scrawled in pencil, apparently the work of the servant, as it is "rudely printed" and filled with errors of spelling and syntax. The suicide note reads:

I am a wicked girl. I have knone things all the time which I ought to have told but I did n't dare to he said he would kill me if I did I mene the tall splendud looking gentulman with the black mustash who I met coming out of Mister Levenworth's room with a key in his hand the night Mr. Levenworth was murdered. He was so scared he gave me money and made me go away and come here and keep every thing secret but I can't do so no longer. I seem to see Miss Elenor all the time crying and asking me if I want her sent to prisun. God knows I'd rathur die. And this is the truth and my last words and I pray every body's forgivness and hope nobody will blame me and that they won't bother Miss Elenor any more but go and look after the handsome gentulman with the black mushtash. (*LC*, 267)

There are several peculiarities to this letter. If Hannah was employed as a carrier of the secret love letters between Mary and Clavering specifically because she could not read, it seems strange that she should be able to write her own confession. The errors in spelling seem bizarre and inconsistent: Hannah includes the silent *k* of "known," but cannot spell the name of the people she works for; she can spell "ought" correctly, but not "prison." Also, Hannah does not identify the man with the black "mushtash"—Henry Clavering—even though she knew him by name.

When Gryce examines the letter, he notices that although the paper is the size of "commercial note," it has been cut from a larger sheet in order to remove the manufacturer's stamp. The letter is, in fact, a fraud, and positively not the work of Hannah's hand. Gryce and Raymond realize this when Mrs. Belden reports that during Hannah's stay, the girl was working to improve her handwriting and had advanced, proudly, from the crude printing she had used in the past to cursive writing. Furthermore, an inventory of the house reveals that the paper on which the "confession" was written did not come from Mrs. Belden's supplies. The suicide note, as Gryce puts it, "is the work, not of a poor, ignorant girl, but of some person who, in attempting to play the *rôle* of one, has signally failed" (*LC*, 273). The entire investigation now hangs on the question of a single sheet of paper; according to Gryce, "the clue to this murder is supplied by the paper on which the confession is written. Find from whose desk or portfolio this especial sheet was taken, and you find the double murderer" (*LC*, 284).

The note makes Hannah a writer — or makes her out to be a writer — but an ignorant and clumsy one. The question of women's literacy is an important one in the novel; it comes up almost every time women write. When Mary is leaving her uncle's house soon after the inquest, she decides to write a letter in the carriage, a letter Raymond calls an "illegible scrawl" and she calls "a crazy-looking epistle" (*LC*, 79). Later, Raymond describes a barely intelligible note he receives from Eleanore in the following way: it reads " 'Come, Oh, come! I —' there breaking off in a tremble, as if the pen had fallen from a nerveless hand" (*LC*, 88). After she is married, Mary scratches her new name on a windowpane, but backward, in an inscription that simultaneously announces her new identity and disguises it. Women's command and mastery of written documents are also questioned in Clavering's interview on the importance of the written certificate to the legitimacy of his marriage, in the illogical preservation of the damaging pages of Eleanore's diary, and in Mrs. Belden's anxiety about her duty as the keeper of Mary's secret papers.

By contrast, the men in the novel are comfortable and competent writers. Much of the investigative work is conducted by letter, and men seem to read and write in an untroubled way. Clavering's visit to Raymond, while it includes a challenge to Raymond's role as the narrator of the story, is also conducted in an atmosphere in which the writing of a legal opinion is seen as a professional and transparent act of communication. Trueman Harwell, Horatio

Leavenworth's "amanuensis," is professionally literate, for he answers Leavenworth's business correspondence and takes dictation for his employer's book on "the question of international communication" between China and America. When Leavenworth dies before the manuscript is completed, Mary asks Everett Raymond to finish the work from Leavenworth's notes. The book, which is based on Leavenworth's experience in the tea trade, is a public and collaborative effort of three men—Leavenworth, Harwell, and Raymond—as opposed to the secret, personal notes and diaries that the women write.

The principle that women are incompetent writers is at play in the attempt to frame Hannah as a suicide and Clavering as a murderer. Women are also constructed as dangerous and destructive writers when the search for the unique paper on which the fraudulent confession was written leads directly to Mary Leavenworth's desk. Both of those depictions seem to be expressions of the anxiety about what women writers can and should say that Green expresses when she writes that "story telling is not possible to me." The class dimensions of Green's figurations are also worth noting. Hannah, whose name so closely echoes Anna Green's own, is a domestic servant who knows things and is eager to learn to write. Although sewing is often presented as a figure for women's writing in middle-class novels, the figure of the seamstress in the nineteenth century is associated both with scandalous gossip and with prostitution. Mary Leavenworth is a moneyed young woman who seems bent on silencing the voice of her seamstress. Taken together, Hannah and Mary enact a drama of self-censorship and reception anxiety in the work of a middle-class woman writer.

Because she is a figure of knowing as well as of writing, the silencing of Hannah's voice is a sign that something is seriously wrong in the world of this novel. Within a literary text, the destruction of an enabling figure of writing is a particularly alarming kind of murder. The killer in this novel has now murdered two writers: Horatio Leavenworth, who writes for and about the marketplace, and Hannah Chester, the seamstress who knows the deepest secrets of the Leavenworth household. The apprehension of the murderer is in a double sense a matter "of an especial sheet of paper," for the fate of the killer depends on the correct tracing of that sheet; and, because he or she kills writers and mutilates texts, the continued safety of other sheets including those of Raymond's narrative—might come to depend on the capture of the murderer.

The discovery of the source of the "especial" sheet of paper seems to wrap up the case against Mary Leavenworth. Raymond has learned the details of Clavering and Mary's courtship and marriage in his interrogation of Mrs. Belden. "Mrs. Belden's Narrative," as the chapter in which she tells her story in the first person is entitled, reveals that Mary Leavenworth and Henry Clavering have been writing to each other, using her as a private postmistress. In her narrative, Mrs. Belden confirms what Raymond already suspected, that Clavering wrote to Horatio Leavenworth when he grew impatient with Mary's refusal to announce their marriage. Mary, according to Mrs. Belden, is enamored of fairy tales but has some strictly unsentimental ideas about her own life. When Mrs. Belden asks her why she simply does not risk being disowned by her uncle, Mary replies: "You don't understand. . . . Mr. Clavering is not poor; but uncle is rich. I shall be a queen. . . . Oh, it sounds mercenary, I know, but it is the fault of my bringing up. I have been taught to worship money. I would be utterly lost without it. And yet . . . I cannot say to Henry Clavering, 'Go! my prospects are dearer to me than you!' " (*LC*, 243–44). With this outburst, Mary expresses her personal dilemma and the central dilemma for the novel in its final pages—if a woman chooses money for its liberatory power, will she later regret giving up love, which requires a sacrifice of self and of ambition to be at its sweetest?

The sources of the money in question and of Mr. Leavenworth's idiosyncratic hatred of the English lie in Leavenworth's own marriage. According to the history that Mr. Veeley calls "The Story of a Charming Woman," the "very ambitious" young Leavenworth gave up his chance to marry a wealthy society lady because he fell in love with a young woman in England. This young woman's past included a marriage to a drunken and abusive Englishman, and the poor health brought on by this abuse and the death of their child killed her within two years of her wedding to Leavenworth. Her death broke Leavenworth's heart; he became fixed in his hatred of Englishmen, and "money became his idol, and the ambition to make and leave a great fortune behind him modified all his views of life" (*LC,* 172). It was some time after this change of heart that Mary and Eleanore be came his wards, so that they were raised in a luxurious but gloomy style by their uncle.

The money Mary stands to inherit, then, is both the product and the emblem of Leavenworth's heartbreak. In this sense greed is a masculine response to grief and loss, and the acquisition of money is both a compensation for and a denial of disappointment. In a configuration central to the domestic and the sentimental novel, Mary must choose between love and money — she may become the wife of the man she loves, or she may control a large fortune. The choice is between dependence as a wife and independence as a spinster, and the terms of the choice are so absolute that Mary would have to resort to murder to create other possibilities for her life.

Mary feels that she is entitled to her uncle's money; she tells Mrs. Belden, "I have always been brought up to regard myself as his heiress . . . I have been taught to worship money. I would be utterly lost without it" (*LC,* 243–44). Mary's sense of identity is built on the fortune she will inherit, an attitude that is more masculine than feminine in this context. Mary's dilemma, in other words, is a problem of gender peculiar to the moneyed classes; she must choose between a feminine self — dependent wife — and a masculine one — heir. Unwilling to choose between love and money, dependence and independence, femininity and masculinity, Mary murders the strongest figure of masculine authority, her uncle. In murdering him, or conspiring to murder him, Mary has committed a shocking and unexpected crime: shocking because it is a patricide, unexpected because murderous calculation is so far outside the range of emotions and actions allowed to heroines of domestic fiction. The murder of Hannah only deepens Mary's villainy, for the servant was someone Mary was bound to protect. By implicating Mary in the murders, Green suggests that, contrary to the vision of domestic ideology, even the most "respectable" women of the bourgeoisie can and do commit murder in cold blood.

Yet, the characters in the novel are reluctant to believe that Mary Leavenworth plotted or committed the murder of her uncle. Before he issues a warrant for Mary's arrest, Gryce stages a scene of accusation designed to smoke out any co-conspirators or the real killer if

Mary is innocent. Gryce finds a garret—the most "lugubrious spot" in the Leavenworth mansion—that has several rooms opening off of it: it is "surrounded by several closed doors with blurred and ghostly ventilators over their tops which, being round, looked like the blank eyes of a row of staring mummies" (*LC*, 295). Gryce is working by the process of gothic logic—he wants to expose the deepest secrets of the household, and so he comes to a place that is full of doors and transoms, to a place that seems to be occupied by mummified or unburied corpses. Indeed, it is a place that seems ripe for the kind of gothic disclosure Gryce seeks: "something unearthly and threatening lay crouched in the very atmosphere" (*LC*, 295). Gryce puts each of the suspects in one of the adjoining rooms, then proceeds to twist the gothic convention of "the unspeakable" by telling, loudly, of the case against Mary Leavenworth and accusing her, in a final cry, of both murders. Gryce has triggered a gothic principle—compulsive confession—deep in the heart of the story: Raymond reports that "something like a suppressed cry was in the air about me. All the room appeared to breathe horror and dismay" (*LC*, 299). That cry breaks free when Trueman Harwell—the secretary—runs from his room shouting, "I am the murderer of Mr. Leavenworth. I! I! I!" (*LC*, 301).

In a confession later composed in prison, Harwell claims he committed murder because he was secretly in love with Mary and wanted to protect her from being disinherited. His idea began when he read the crucial letter from Clavering by accident and was solidified when he overheard Leavenworth threatening to disinherit his favorite niece. Later, he observed Leavenworth writing a letter to his lawyers that would exclude Mary from his will; to stop him from mailing it, Harwell took the pistol from his employer's bedroom and shot him through the back of the head. He cleaned the gun with the handkerchief he found on the floor, which bore Eleanore's monogram, though it was Mary who had been carrying it during the tearful argument with her uncle. Worried about throwing suspicion onto either niece, Harwell hid the dirty handkerchief under a sofa cushion. He left the library with the key, the dangerous letter to the lawyers, and the damning letter from Clavering. He frantically chewed up the first of these letters, but the second, he explains, "had blood on it, and nothing, not even the hope of safety, could induce me to put it to my lips" (*LC,* 321). Taking his cue, apparently, from Poe's "Purloined Letter," Harwell disposed of the second letter and the key by putting them "in plain sight, trusting to that very fact for their being overlooked" (*LC,* 321). He tore the letter into "lighters" and left them in a vase of similar strips of paper, then attempted to leave the library key in the lock of the door. Later, he changed his strategy and, in attempting to destroy the two objects in Mary's fireplace, bungled the job. The result was that Eleanore appeared to have been in possession of the key and letter. Harwell says he was able to maintain a calm and detached facade by deliberately "blott[ing] from my consciousness" the occurrences of the fatal half hour of the shooting and by answering all the other questions truthfully.

Harwell is haunted, however, by one event of that night. As he left the library he encountered Hannah, who noted his strange look and the key in his hand. As he told her that their employer had been shot, he realized that she was certain to figure out that he was the killer. Harwell also realized that Hannah was in love with him—a state he calls an "unreasonable susceptibility to my influence" (*LC,* 319). Although she swore, "I won't tell . . . I will keep it to myself, I will say I didn't see anybody" (*LC,* 319), Harwell feared she could be made to talk by the police. He convinced her to go away by promising to marry her if she did as he told her and kept silent about what she had seen. Harwell's story explains the stubbornness of Hannah's silence, and he goes on to tell how he murdered her. "Hannah's existence," he explains, "precluded all sense of personal security. . . . I had but sent a trailing flag of danger out into the world with this wretched girl" (*LC,* 324, 320). He forged the confession, then enclosed it and the packet of poison in a letter that "played upon her ignorance, foolish fondness, and Irish superstition, by telling her I dreamed of her every night and wondered if she did of me" (*LC,* 326). Harwell's letter promised that the enclosed powder would give her "the most beautiful visions" if she would burn his letter, take the powder, and go straight to bed.

This last revelation explains the deepest mystery of Hannah's death—how she was persuaded to take poison—and connects her death to the central dilemma about women, marriage, and self-sacrifice. Hannah willingly consumed poison because she longed for romantic visions—not just the ones Harwell promised her, but also the vision of herself as a wife bound to her husband by a secret. It is a role she seems to have relished, especially in the scene of their parting. "Remember, you are to say nothing of what has occurred, no matter what happens," whispered Harwell. " 'Remember, you are to come and marry me some day,' she murmured in reply, throwing her arms about my neck" (*LC*, 319-20). Hannah struck a bargain, at least in her own mind, that she would marry the man she admired if she did not tell her story. Hannah was murdered by sentimental illusions about herself and Harwell. Perhaps she thought her love could overwhelm and redeem his crime; perhaps she believed that the secret would bind them closely together; perhaps she believed a wife is at her best when she is standing by her husband in adversity. In any case, Hannah's desire to become Harwell's wife was a folly that ultimately killed her.

The delusional power of sentimentality also plays a role in Harwell's murder of Mr. Leavenworth. In a confrontation with Mary after his confession, Harwell declares that "love, love, love was the force which . . . lent me will to pull the trigger" (*LC*, 308). He has cast himself as the hero in the drama of Mary's disinheritance, responding to Mary's rhetorical call for help during the confrontation with her uncle by murdering the powerful old man. He had entertained hopes of marrying the woman he thus rescued from shame and poverty—only too late does he learn that she is already married to Clavering. Even if he cannot marry her, Harwell hopes to haunt her like an important suitor from her past. In precisely the kind of gothicization of money that Goddu identifies just under the surface of domestic fiction, Harwell says, "[Y]ou can never forget the love of Trueman Harwell . . . every dollar that chinks from your purse shall talk of me" (*LC*, 308). But Mary rejects his claims on her heart by rejecting the love offering of her inheritance. "From this day," she swears, "Mary Clavering owns nothing but what comes to her from the husband she has so long and so basely wronged," and she initiates her marital devotions by removing her diamond earrings. Harwell now realizes that a role as Mary's lover, even a spurned lover, has been a romantic illusion and concludes, "I have given my soul to hell for a shadow!" (*LC*, 308).

Harwell's delusions run even deeper than an unrequited hope for romance, and we are warned that Harwell's face bears "a look whose evil triumph I cannot describe" and "the lurid light of madness"

(*LC*, 308). Harwell is not simply a double murderer, he is the figure for a satanic relationship with writing—a sort of antiauthor. Hired as a secretary, he becomes discontented with the "monotonous" copying of manuscript pages as he is emotionally drawn to his employer's niece; after he reads Clavering's letter, he recalls, "I wrote and wrote and wrote, till it seemed as if my life blood went from me with every drop of ink I used" (*LC*, 315). He wants, it seems, to write some other narrative than the one he has been hired to copy. He begins this narrative by killing a literal author, Horatio Leavenworth, and he does so to prevent Leavenworth from finishing the letter that will change his will. He consumes, like a predator, one letter and mutilates another. After the murders, he not only continues to work at the scene of the crime, he even takes his late employer's seat at the table. He then murders a second, figural, writer by means of a deceitful claim of love and forges a text intended to usurp Hannah's own narrative of what she saw and heard in the Leavenworth house. He is the force that actively disassembles the narrative of the murder to keep it from being reconstructed by the investigators. A figure of chaos and diseased narrative, his insanity takes the form of delusional plotting and psychopathological sentimentality.

His one realized aspiration to authorship, the written confession that forms the next to last chapter of the book, shows the degree to which he believes he can plot his and other people's lives. He reports that when he read Clavering's letter, "I was virtually the arbitrator of her [Mary's] destiny. Some men would have sought her there and then and, by threatening to place it in her uncle's hand, won from her a look of entreaty, if no more; but I—well, my plans went deeper than that. I knew she would have to be in extremity before I could hope to win her. She must feel herself slipping over the edge of the precipice before she would clutch at the first thing offering succor" (*LC*, 314). This passage pinpoints the origins of the murder plot that Raymond and Gryce have sought to recover. That plot, Harwell discloses, originated in the moment when he planned to cast Mary in the role of a helpless, endangered woman—the role, in other words, of a typical heroine of a gothic novel.

By her depiction of Harwell's manic plotting, Hannah's fatal trust in romance, and the unfair dilemma of love and money thrust on Mary, Green seems to critique the sentimental domestic novel as a delusional discourse with tragic consequences. It is perhaps surprising, then, that *The Leavenworth Case* takes such a conventional turn after Harwell's confession. In the last chapter, Mary is cured of her haughtiness, for the shame of the accusations about her have taught her true humility. Mary and Eleanore seek, and receive, each other's forgiveness, and Clavering apologizes for the anxiety he caused Raymond by his visit. In the book's last sentence, Raymond indicates that he marries Eleanore soon after the end of the novel. Nowhere is the sentimentality of the ending more apparent than in the story of the inheritance money. Mary offers to give her inheritance to her cousin, since it would have been willed to Eleanore if Harwell had not murdered their uncle. Eleanore, though, refuses "to accept property so stained by guilt," and the cousins decide to use the money to create a charity that will benefit "the city and its unfortunate poor" (*LC,* 331). With the death of the avaricious merchant, Eleanore and Mary are freed to develop a relationship to money that is, by the terms of the sentimental novel, healthier and more feminine. Like Meg March Brook in *Little Women,* Mary and Eleanore realize that to escape the guilty stain of money, they must spend their wealth in a sustained act of self-denial, and that they must rely on their husbands to provide for their needs.

Furthermore, there is a closely connected reassertion of class solidarity at the end of the novel. The dissent and suspicions among the four principal characters — Mary, Eleanore, Clavering, and Raymond — are all caused by the mischief of a liminal class figure, the secretary who hovers between the ranks of servant and business professional. We can see how the more general concern with sincerity that underlies Alcott and Victor's work has by this point settled more exclusively on the problem of social climbing. The protective relationship of a lawyer and his upper-class clients is a central feature of the novel; their interests are mutual, even when the lawyer is required to review his clients' most personal affairs. Raymond's work restores the Leavenworth daughters to both respectability and morality, rescuing them from the unhealthy world of the excessively rich. The ending reestablishes the novel as one of solidly middle-class values and literary genre: while the middle of the story is full of gothic obtrusions and energies, in the end domestic realism is triumphant.

But it is also possible to imagine a very different ending for this novel; without Trueman's confession, the story would have ended with Mary's arrest for murder. The story that Green does not stick by — but manages to sketch out — is the story in which Mary is discovered to have killed her uncle after all. In a detective novel such as *The Leavenworth Case,* the reader follows the plot of investigation as it examines suspects and generates possible motives and scenarios for the murder. Most of these scenarios are mistaken and are, sooner or later, abandoned by the detectives. The longer a particular scenario is in play, however, the more the reader will begin to trust that it is the solution to the crime. The structure of detective fiction furnishes something like the narrative equivalent of serial monogamy: first there is one suspect, then there is another. And, as Eleanore puts it, "the finger of suspicion never forgets the way it has once pointed" (*LC,* 96). In her detective novel, Green can make Mary both guilty and innocent, for although Harwell confesses to the crime in the last pages of the book, the bulk of the narrative has been a case against Mary.

Detective fiction with its stable endings and unstable middles, its gothic fascinations with secrets, its ability to point to many and contradictory villains, is ideally suited for a veiled and ambivalent kind of social critique. When merged with the moral discourse of the domestic novel, that critique takes as its subject the roles of and rules for middle- and upper-class women. While Green's novels are ultimately conservative in their espousal of class solidarity and middle-class notions of self-sacrifice and female virtue, they also take seriously the troubles and injustices done to women. They may declare the middle-class home as a place best left to the middle class, but they also argue for a need for intervention in its erotic and pecuniary affairs, especially as they affect women. The privilege of the middle and upper classes is the ability to hire or attract agents of their own class, like lawyers, to moderate the investigations of the police. In the first of Green's novels, that detective figure is a man, but later she began to use women amateur and private detectives to tell the stories of the suspicious bourgeois home.

# 5

## *"A Woman's Hand"*

### GOOD WORKS AND THE WOMAN DETECTIVE

Many of Green's female characters are like Mary Leavenworth, defiantly wanting things they are not supposed to want. In an article about the appeal of crime to the popular imagination, Green writes that "greed for one's own self" is the root cause of all crime, but she does not seem entirely to condemn her female characters' attention to their own interests.[1] As Barbara Welter has observed, Green was very interested in the "plight of these strong and passionate women" in a world remarkable for its "paucity of alternatives" for them.[2] More difficult to discern is the precise nature of the social critique that Green offers in her detective fiction. The plots of Green's novels include many subjects that were rallying points for women's activism: poverty among female textile workers, prostitution, male drunkenness, wife beating, desertion and neglect in marriage, and the inequality of property rights for women.[3] Green herself took a public stand against woman suffrage in 1917, but, like other "antis," did so out of the firm conviction that the vote would not ultimately serve the best interests of women.[4]

Her novels, then, reflect the complexities of the reform impulse in the late nineteenth and early twentieth centuries, for they show the thinking of a woman who was both against suffrage and against the unequal treatment of women in work and marriage. Like many of the reform projects associated with the mid-century woman's movement, Green's insertion of the detective figure into the domestic sphere is an emphatic assertion of—rather than a break with—the conventional role of woman as defender of morality and overseer of class identity. As Green depicts them, surveillance and investigation overlap with upper-class attentiveness to the fine points of social distinction in language and dress and the more narrowly female skill of reading and monitoring the emotional lives of those around them. Green's detective stories argue that there is an urgent need for such regulation of family life; the domestic world her novels depict is one in which jealousy, selfishness, and greed are submerged but have every expectation of erupting into deadly rages and murderous plots.

Similar ideas about regulation were on the minds of those who worked in social reform movements in the postbellum period. In *Domestic Tyranny,* Elizabeth Pleck argues that the 1870s saw a shift toward greater acceptance of government intervention in family matters, in large part because of the postbellum intensification of violent crime inside and outside the home. The middle class saw the family "facing a major crisis," whose particulars included the struggle over woman suffrage, the acceleration of immigration, and the apparent rebelliousness of the youngest generations.[5] The most important development in the history of upper- and middle-class reform during this period was the rise of what Timothy Gilfoyle calls "preventive societies," including antiprostitution associations and organizations for the prevention of cruelty to children.[6] These societies were set up as private philanthropic corporations and vested by state legislatures with policelike powers, which, for child cruelty societies, included the authority to investigate reports of neglect and abuse, to arrest violators, and to remove children from their parents' custody. These agencies were supposed to work alongside local police, and many of their field officers, according to Pleck, were former policemen and firemen. But Gilfoyle stresses that in practice the philanthropic groups did not work harmoniously with the police and often seemed to verge toward vigilantism in their pursuit of offenders.

In an effort to expose disorder and violence within the family, the child cruelty movement thus joined the new ethos of investigation in urban police work to the established ideology of domestic morality from the older temperance movement, with its emphasis on the effects of men's drinking on their wives and children. That blending is interesting for the ways it gives a context for the domestic detective novel, which yokes another expression of bourgeois morality, the domestic novel, with the investigative narrative of detective fiction. In fact, the popularity of this fiction helps us to see that the reform impulse of the late nineteenth and early twentieth centuries was paralleled by a strong investigative impulse.

While in reality the targets of the child cruelty societies were the urban and immigrant poor, there were other reform movements that took up the middle-class family as a more central cause. William Leach has identified a strain of 1870s social ideology that he calls "the cult of no secrets," which believed the root cause of misery in marriage to be ignorance about the scientific facts of sexuality and reproduction. The underlying critique was of rampant hypocrisy in the middle and upper classes, and the movements that came out of that critique included dress reform and advocacy of birth control and sex education.[7] This period also saw property law reform that strengthened women's economic independence within marriage and attempted to loosen the judicial and social prohibitions against divorce.

All these different efforts to reform married and family life were, to a greater or lesser extent, arguments for greater scrutiny of domestic arrangements by some authoritative social body, usually the courts. Gilfoyle's and Pleck's studies of social policy against vice and against family violence also reveal a willingness within the upper classes to embrace government intervention and regulation after the Civil War. Nancy Cott's recent work on marriage law in the last third of the nineteenth century exposes the deeply embedded connection between concern about marriage and concern about business practices in that period. She argues that the question of whether marriage was a public or a private matter was a vexed one in the late nineteenth century, and that "the public/private divide was a central ideological instability that dogged legal approaches to both property questions and marital ones."[8] Cott shows that this larger debate was expressed in an intensified legal scrutiny of common-law marriage, bigamy, and Mormon polygamy. With its focus on domestic arrangements and its assignment of police agents as investigators of family secrets, the domestic detective novel should be seen as part of the late nineteenth-century struggle to redefine *public* and *private*, particularly as those terms applied to marriage.[9] Green's novels capture that historical moment when surveillance of private life seemed both desirable and possible, though the details of who should be doing the investigating (the police, professional social workers, or old-style reformers) remained unresolved.

Green's detective stories are not reform novels in the tradition of the temperance novel, or even of the city-mysteries novel. As a group, however, Green's novels depict the late Victorian middle and upper classes as both deeply flawed and unable to confront or acknowledge their violent proclivities. Although we see the same kind of valorization of the professional class in *The Leavenworth Case* that we saw in Victor's detective stories, men of the merchant and professional classes are often the villains in Green's novels. The wealthy in Green's novels are easily corrupted by their desire to avoid scandal and their love of money. Liminal figures—social climbers and those in such ambiguous roles as gentleman's secretary or lady's companion—are especially complicated and make good detectives and passionate murderers. These novels are full of seductive elopements and bigamous marriages; again and again, the reappearance of a deserted spouse (usually a wife) motivates the bigamist to kill. Women of all classes are vulnerable to these men, and they are usually injured, robbed, or murdered by those who should, according to domestic ideology, be protecting them: husbands, brothers, legal guardians. The professional or amateur detective's job is to repair the damage caused by these corrupted relationships as well as to expose them, and that fictional task shares something with the rise, out of reform culture, of surveillance of and intervention in the private sphere.

The resonance with the reform impulse is perhaps deepest in the novels narrated by one of Green's series characters, a middle-aged spinster named Amelia Butterworth who appears in three novels: *That Affair Next Door* (1897), *Lost Man's Lane* (1898), and *The Circular Study* (1900). The character narrates the first two tales of her involvement in the investigation of homicide, and reveals a good deal about herself in the process. She wants us to know that she is "of Colonial ancestry and no inconsiderable importance in the social world" (*TA*, 19). The portrait is full of sly humor: Miss Butterworth prides herself on being orderly, straightforward, energetic, dignified, and unsentimental, but she reports to us that she overhears others call her "a meddlesome old maid" (*TA*, 5) and even "the ogress" (*TA*, 42). She is sensitive to how she is seen by other people, and she uses the social typing of the unmarried woman to her advantage; in order to intimidate or disarm people she wants to interrogate, she plays the part of the doughty Victorian and the absentminded spinster by turns. She is generally impatient with the younger generation of her class, calling two of them who come under her care "giddy things" and complaining, "I have no patience with the modern girl, she is made up of recklessness and extravagance" (*TA*, 64). She herself is made of very stern stuff; she tells us that "the path of duty has its thorny passages, but it is for strong minds like mine to ignore them" (*TA*, 78). Her style is proudly old-fashioned, and she evaluates everything from hats to indictments in moral terms. She represents the nineteenth-century ideal of high principle; on at least three occasions she declares that her only motive in investigating a murder in her neighbor's house is a sense of obligation to the "cause of justice" (*TA*, 27). In her fierce sense of duty and her precise sense of etiquette, she is an embodiment of Victorianism, always on the lookout for faults to correct.

Miss Butterworth would seem an unlikely advocate for women's rights, remarking as she does that "we [women] have lost our manners in gaining our independence, something which is to be regretted perhaps" (*TA*, 312). Yet, although her sense of class is the central feature of her identity, she has a strong conviction that women's lives are meant to amount to something. Her long-dead father is an important figure for her not only because he supplied her with such a good bloodline, but also because he predicted that she "would live to make her mark." Early on in the first novel in which she appears, *That Affair Next Door*, she tells us that up until she became involved in the case, she had not felt that she had any "special gifts" (*TA*, 23). Once she discovers her talents in logic and interrogation, she is unwilling to suppress them, despite resistance from the police detective, Ebenezer Gryce (from *The Leavenworth Case*). Gryce comes to admire her techniques and what he calls her "woman's knowledge" of "women's matters" (*TA*, 62, 59), but through most of the novel he is patronizing and sarcastic. Butterworth reports that when she suggests that they discuss the case on something like an equal footing, "the natural proposition of an energetic woman with a special genius for his particular calling, evidently struck him as audacity of the grossest kind" (*TA*, 58). She claims that "any interest I may take in this matter is due to my sense of justice" (*TA*, 62), but she is clearly goaded by the sense of male prerogative Gryce exudes. He engages in a good deal of banter at every meeting, but under the humor is the clear implication that she is, because female, incompetent in matters of crime; he quips that "a woman's kind heart stands in the way of her proper judgment of criminals" (*TA*, 174). That particular wise-crack causes Butterworth to declare herself not his "coadjutor" but his "rival," who hopes to see him "hopelessly defeated" (*TA*, 175). She makes good on her threat by conducting her own investigation and keeping her discoveries to herself; at one of the low points of their relationship he is reduced to an inelegant "imperative *tell me*" in an effort to get her to share her discoveries. Green's female detective is, ironically, so much of a Victorian lady that she feels she must challenge the idea that police work is men's work.

Butterworth's love of order, her habit of faultfinding, and her precision in etiquette are manifestations of that upper-class female identity, and they work in concert to help her to read the signs of guilt and mendacity in the people connected with a crime. *That Affair Next Door* is built around the problem of mistaken identity, and that plot implies that the first job of the female detective is to sort out who's who as well as who did it. The murder in question occurs in the Gramercy Park townhouse of the Van Burnam family, wealthy leather merchants who live next door to our Miss Butterworth; by her strict standards the family is slightly *arriviste*. The house stands empty while the patriarch and his daughters are in Europe, but one night Butterworth, who protests that she is "not an inquisitive woman" (*TA*, 1), sees a man and woman enter the house, using a key. The next morning a woman is found dead, crushed under a fallen cabinet of expensive bric-a-brac. Later, the police discover that she was killed by a hatpin stuck through the base of her skull; the cabinet seems to have been used to crush her face beyond recognition. Other clues make it seem likely that she is the wife of the wild son of the family, Howard Van Burnam, but he insists the woman is not his wife. Detective Gryce's suspicion wavers between Howard and his virtuous brother, Franklin, who turns out to have exchanged love letters with his brother's wife before their marriage. Gryce first involves Butterworth because he hopes she can identify which of the two brothers entered the house; that question is the first instance of the problem of mistaken identity.

Butterworth, however, quickly compounds the investigation when she suspects that the corpse itself has been mistakenly identified as Louise Van Burnam. She declares that she senses "a woman's hand" in the affair, and comes to believe there were actually two women in the Van Burnam mansion that night. Howard, she thinks, had a mistress, whom Louise murdered. She believes Louise switched their clothing, crushed the woman's face, then escaped, assuming the identity of her victim. Butterworth works out the set of inversions and reversals that allowed Louise to make the switch, most of which concern the clothing the two women wore. She traces the escapee, only to discover that she has constructed the switch backward, and that Louise Van Burnam is indeed the victim, and the second woman, Olive Randolph, is the escapee. That isn't the last layer of the plot of mistaken identity in this novel, however. It turns out that the murderer is none of the earlier suspects (the Van Burnam brothers or Olive Randolph), but instead a friend of the family named John Randolph Stone, who had intended to kill Olive Randolph but mistakenly stabbed Louise Van Burnam in the dark. Olive makes the switch of identity only to conceal the fact that she is still alive.

John Randolph Stone's motivation for killing Olive brings us to the second main plot of the novel—social climbing. Years before, Stone had, under the name John Randolph, married Olive in a small town in Michigan, but abandoned her to move to New York, where he was promptly taken up into society. His humble origins were known, but his "great distinction of manner" and "his deliberate intent to please" (*TA*, 156) have made him "universally admired" (*TA*, 250). He is, in particular, admired by the wealthy and pure-hearted Miss Althorpe, and he wins her hand. Only weeks before he is to marry this gem of New York society, Olive arrives unexpectedly in the city. Thinking fast, Stone seems to welcome her, outfits her in anonymous new clothes from a department store, and takes her by a series of conveyances to the dark and empty Van Burnam mansion, claiming it is a house he has bought for her. What in fact he has done is to create a body and a murder scene with little connection to himself, and he then drives the hatpin into the neck of the woman he thinks is Olive Randolph.

Unbeknownst to him, however, he is not the only social climber in the mansion that night. Louise Van Burnam, who once worked as a governess to families like the Van Burnams, had "set her heart on ruling in the great leather-merchant's house and she did not know how to bear her disappointment" (*TA*, 253) when her marriage to

Howard Van Burnam caused them to be "cut dead" by the family. She determines to win the acceptance of the patriarch by staging a scene on his arrival from Europe in which she will seem piteous and appealing. That is why she is in the house that night when John Randolph Stone attempts to eliminate the obstacle to his carefully cultivated social and economic ascent.

Olive Randolph is also, in a less callous way, a social climber. She grew up poor, and cast "longing looks at the great school building where girls like myself learned to speak like ladies and play the piano" (*TA*, 369). When John Randolph Stone, passing through town, seduces her, Olive is "intoxicated" with him and sees him as her ticket out of the "unsatisfied life" her mother and grandmother had led before her (*TA*, 369). She is therefore quite happy when her father forces Randolph to marry her, although she is quickly disillusioned. "Had I been older or more experienced in the ways of the world, I would have known . . . that there is no witchery in a smile lasting enough to make men like him forget the lack of those social graces to which they are accustomed" (*TA*, 371). Her remarks indicate that John Randolph Stone will be marrying up by wedding Ella Althorpe, and married down when he became attached to Olive Randolph. Once Olive realizes the class difference will destroy their marriage, she launches a campaign of self-improvement that continues even after he deserts her. By the time she gets to New York, she is cultured enough to secure a position as lady's companion to Miss Althorpe.[10]

All this social movement makes the work of investigating the crime more difficult. Miss Butterworth switches, in the course of constructing her theory and following her leads, the identity of the victim and the escapee. Both women are a similar type in Miss Butterworth's universe—the adventuress—and so she confirms her suspicion that she has Louise Van Burnam before her (when she has instead Olive Randolph) when she notices that the victim's hands, while "white and smooth . . . lacked the distinctive shape and nicety" of "a lady's hands" (*TA*, 247). She is, by her lights, understandably confused by the presence of not one but three social climbers in the case.

In this novel, as in Dreiser's *American Tragedy*, the drive to succeed encompasses treachery and murder, especially when there is an embarrassing woman in the way. John Randolph Stone is not the only one with a troublesome woman on his hands: the Van Burnams have Louise. When her body is discovered, the Van Burnam men refuse to acknowledge its identity. When the detectives tell Franklin Van Burnam that they have found a "young lady" dead in the parlor, he resists their request that he look at the body, declaring that she must be a scrubwoman or a thief—certainly not a lady, and certainly not anyone he would recognize. Her own husband claims not to know her, despite the matching of hair color and birthmarks. Although it is clear to our detectives that both brothers recognize her, they "absolutely refuse to acknowledge her" (*TA*, 52) in death as in life; with "brutality," Howard allows her body to be taken to the city morgue and exposed to the "ignominy of the public gaze" (*TA*, 54). Later, Howard Van Burnam admits that the dead woman is his wife; he then lies at the inquest and says that he accompanied his wife to the house that night, placing himself falsely under suspicion in order to prevent speculation about what she was doing in a dark house at night with another man. No lady, in other words, could die as Louise Van Burnam died, and those scandalous circumstances are the final confirmation of the family's assessment of her character.

This defense of family honor makes Butterworth's and Gryce's jobs extremely difficult. At the inquest, Howard spins an elaborate, and entirely false, tale to account for certain facts about Louise's movements in the company of a man. All the various reports of a man and woman are actually of Olive Randolph in a veil and John Randolph Stone wearing Franklin Van Burnam's duster. But both Gryce and Butterworth base their theories on pieces of Howard's testimony; only Olive Randolph's final narrative clears away Howard Van Burnam's fictions. The Van Burnams' stonewalling operates in concert with the lies of John Randolph Stone; at the narratological level, the Van Burnams are as guilty as the murderer of obstructing the detectives' work in reassembling the story of the crime. In Green's hands, a story of social climbing becomes not a narrative of female impurity, but a discourse on the hypocrisy and hardheartedness of men.

As we might expect in a novel with such elaborate proliferations of mistaken identities and concern about social climbing, clothing— or, in the more evocative term of the period, costume—has a central place in the crime and its investigation. Any solution of the murder involves sorting out who was outfitted at Altman's, who was wearing Franklin's duster, who switched the clothing on the corpse, and how and why all the various swappings and disposals of clothing took place. Butterworth's skills in reading evidence first make themselves known when she examines the clothing of the murder victim. "Store-made, but very good" (*TA*, 12), she declares after fingering the skirt, a conclusion that was significant in the days when wealthy women still had their dresses made by hand. She can likewise read a particular set of underwear for clues about its expense; not only can she tell it is handmade, she can also discern that it has "tucks such as you see come from the hands of French needlewomen only" (*TA*, 246). She knows that the petticoat of an extravagant woman like Louise Van Burnam would be "as well made as many women's dresses" (*TA*, 204) and so might be worn (by the escaping Olive Randolph) outside the skirt to disguise the dress. There are also humorous comments about the costume of minor characters; one woman who keeps a boarding house puts on airs about her respectability but reveals her vulgarity in the "wretched taste as regards colors" (*TA*, 220) in her interior decoration and dress. Coincidental with that lack of taste is her "utter ignorance of social distinctions"; the woman looks "with an equally inquiring air" (*TA*, 221) at Butterworth and at her accompanying maid and is easily fooled into thinking the two are related.

Her own taste in clothing makes the point that wealth and respectability are not interchangeable in Butterworth's mind. She is appalled by the consumerism and fashion snobbery of the Van Burnam daughters, and she does not seem to think that the expensive handmade underwear is in "the nicest taste." She herself dresses in clothing that is "rich rather than fashionable."[11] Subdued and well-made clothing earns her admiration, and the novel outlines a particular zone of respectability that a woman of any class can enter by wearing neat, simple clothing. Like Lily Bart pursuing Percy Gryce in *The House of Mirth*, Butterworth's conspiratorial maid, Lena, looks "the picture of all the virtues" (*TA*, 220) when she puts on a plain gray gown. This is also the costume that Olive Randolph acquires as soon as possible after her escape from the murder scene (and is an early clue that she is a redeemable woman). Because they both wear gray dresses, Gryce mistakes Olive for Lena at one critical juncture, another instance in which confusion about class and identity hinders the investigation. As with the murder itself, Gryce discerns only one woman ("the girl in gray") where in fact there are two. He does not, like Butterworth, have the training to see the distinctions of dress and manner between a lady's companion and a lady's maid.

As in *The Leavenworth Case,* the making of clothing becomes a recurrent metaphor for female storytelling. In one scene, while sitting at the bedside of a feverish Olive Randolph, Butterworth picks up Olive's knitting and begins to work at it while she simultaneously works at her theory of the murder. Olive, who has a great deal to hide at this point in the novel, becomes highly agitated at this activity and begs Butterworth to stop—later, Butterworth is dismayed to see the knitting unraveled. The exchange is a familiar instance, by now, of the attempts of a criminal to prevent the detective from weaving together the loose ends of evidence and clues. Eventually, however, Olive turns Butterworth from accuser to ally, and by the end of the novel she emerges as an innocent woman with a good story to tell. The vehicle of her expression is the making of an elaborate, even eloquent costume—a formal white gown.

Acquiring such a dress becomes important after Olive resolves to reveal the identity of the murderer. Once confronted by the police with her presence at the scene of the murder, she refuses to tell what she saw and begs to be allowed to reveal the identity of the murderer in her own way. That way involves making a spectacle of herself at John Randolph Stone's wedding to Miss Althorpe by appearing in that white gown and stepping up to the altar before the intended bride can make it down the aisle. This event is the dramatic climax of the novel and the culmination of Olive's outrage at desertion, bigamy, and murder; it is a carefully planned moment of revenge. Without hinting at what she plans to do, Olive brings Butterworth with her to pick out the "richest" white satin and trimmings to bring to a dressmaker: "You know what a young girl requires to make her look like a lady. I want to look so well that the most critical eye will detect no fault in my appearance" (*TA,* 354). Throughout this episode Olive has a look of "brooding horror in her eyes" (*TA,* 356), for by assuming the costume of a bride in this context, Olive Randolph enters into the realm of the gothic. John Randolph Stone believes that he murdered his first wife, so her appearance at his wedding seems like a visitation from the dead. Olive embodies the gothic principle of the return of the repressed and the figure of the speaking corpse. She later says that she was "maddened by hatred" (*TA*, 394) when she decided to stage this scene, and indeed the drama is one of triumphant anger. Not only has she outlived Stone's attempt to murder her, she has also humiliated him before the society he has worked so hard to enter. But perhaps only her husband would understand the subtler revenge of her costume: with Miss Butterworth's help she has been transformed into exactly the class of woman Stone has always wanted to marry.

We see the gothic employed here, as elsewhere, as the language of a woman's anger. Olive's hatred for John Randolph Stone is "boundless," and she confesses that she wanted to "revenge myself upon him in some never-to-be-forgotten manner" (*TA*, 394). That last description suggests that the gothic mode is important to Olive as another kind of revenge, this one against the assembled mass of high society. Olive has been snubbed, deserted, left for dead, and misidentified by the people of, and climbers into, the social aristocracy of New York. In various literal and metaphorical ways, no one of that class recognized her, but in the midst of her gothic spectacle they cannot take their eyes off her. Her revenge is that of the forgotten, and it works on behalf of Louise Van Burnam—the other dead bride—as well. Olive, in staging her terrifying scene, also stages a morality play that exposes Stone as a cad and his admirers as fools.

Olive Randolph, like Cassy in *Uncle Tom's Cabin,* is a successful orchestrator of a gothic scourge, but not all of Green's heroines are able to use ghost stories to such good advantage. In *The Mayor's Wife* (1907), a woman becomes extremely anxious when she realizes that her brutish first husband is not dead as she thought, but alive and working for her second husband, the mayor. Terrified that she will be exposed as a bigamist, destroying her husband's career and her child's chances in life, she becomes depressed and withdrawn. She makes up tales of ghosts in the house to account for her nervousness as the first husband mentally tortures her, but the fictional hauntings work only as restatements of her problem (a prior attachment one cannot escape). She cannot, like Cassy or Olive, use the gothic against the man who is wronging her because she has cast herself as the heroine and the man as the vengeful apparition; one's role within a gothic script can ensure defeat or victory. Olive herself, for a time, is in something like the position of a haunted gothic heroine. She tells us that after witnessing the murder of Louise Van Burnam, she was "horrified past all power of speech and action" (*TA*, 386) and "tongue-tied" (*TA*, 387) at the realization that her husband intended to kill her. She at first attempted to begin a new life under a new name and to forget the whole horrible crime; amazingly, "enough sense of duty remained in my bruised and broken heart to keep me from denouncing him to the police" (*TA*, 394). But the discovery that John Randolph Stone is to wed Ella Althorpe rouses her from her willful silence and forgetting; she realizes that her more noble duty is to "save Miss Althorpe from an alliance with this villain" (*TA*, 394). Right after the murders, Olive is terrified that her husband, like all murderers, "cannot help haunting the scene of his crime" (*TA*, 391) and imagines him looking through the windows and lurking around doorways. The fact that she shakes off her fright and instead becomes an avenging ghost is a mark of her courage and moral development.

The wedding scene is an abrupt gothic obtrusion into a narrative that in other ways follows the conventions of domestic realism (the Van Burnam house, for example, is not presented as a haunted house, although it is the scene of a murder). Olive's use of the highly symbolic language of the gothic to articulate the horror of seduction, desertion, and murder thus stands out in sharp contrast to Miss Butterworth's no-nonsense style. One would expect Miss Butterworth to disapprove of the use of such a display, since the gothic tradition was associated in the nineteenth century with everything antithetical to conventional upper-class life: the mass culture of the sensational press and cheap magazine fiction, certain strains of radical urban politics, the superstitions of immigrant culture, and the folk culture of the uneducated. And one might predict that, after her outburst, Olive Randolph would be sent off to an asylum to live out the rest of her days in madness, since there could be no lasting place for such an irrational and vulgar mind in Butterworth's world. Surprisingly, we learn in the epilogue that Butterworth develops a strong attachment to the young woman and brings her to live with her in Gramercy Park.

It is not entirely clear what inspires Butterworth's new regard for this young woman whom she previously distrusted so thoroughly, but the key seems to be Olive's besting of Gryce. Butterworth delights in the way that Olive refuses simply to name Stone as the murderer during her interrogation, and reminds us of it as a benchmark of female triumph over Gryce in her next narrative, *Lost Man's Lane*. Like other of Green's women who know things but will not tell them, Olive is in a position of power after she stops being afraid to say anything and begins planning how to say what she must. She is her own woman — or more precisely, her own narrator. She holds out against Gryce's pleas and his demands, stages a dramatic ending to the investigation, and tells the story of her life in a first-person account entitled "Secret History." She is a woman with a secret, but she makes sure it emerges as someone else's shame, not her own. In deploying the gothic, she casts herself as the avenger, not the haunted lady. Butterworth's admiration for Olive Randolph might be that of one strong-minded narrator for another. In a genre in which women are primarily victims and villainesses, both Butterworth and Olive find powerful and moral places for themselves; each, as Butterworth's father predicted, "makes her mark." The police cannot solve the crime without them, and the novel as a whole argues for the necessity of "women's eyes for women's matters" (*TA*, 59).

There is another important implication in the alliance of Butterworth and Olive, one apparent in the language Butterworth uses to describe their friendship: "Olive Randolph has, at my request, taken up her abode in my house. The charm which she seems to have exerted over others she has exerted over me, and I doubt if I shall ever wish to part with her again. In return she gives me an affection which I am now getting old enough to appreciate. Her feeling for me and her gratitude to Miss Althorpe are the only treasures left her out of the wreck of her life, and it shall be my business to make them lasting ones" (*TA*, 399). The reciprocal affection of a young woman and an older one, the prediction of permanent attachment, the shared abode, and the desire of the older woman to work for the happiness of the younger all point us in the general direction of an erotic bond, and more precisely toward a mother-daughter relationship. There is a trace of a maternal pattern in Butterworth's earlier dealings with Olive Randolph: she tends the young woman during an illness — undressing, bathing, and feeding her — and she takes Olive shopping for the bridal costume, just as a mother might outfit her daughter for a wedding. Butterworth is a spinster and a childless woman; Olive is a motherless daughter, literally and figuratively. Her mother died when Olive was a girl, but perhaps more important in this novel, she offered her daughter only a negative example with her "useful but unsatisfied life," like her own mother's before her (*TA*, 369). Butterworth, especially at this point of discovering detective work, offers an example of a life that is useful, contented, even exciting. Butterworth's adoption of the social climber is the sort of happy ending that naturalizes the desire to be taken up into the ranks of the wealthy that we see over and over again in the popular novel of the nineteenth century. In this case, though, it is important to note that the ending also fulfills the plot of the female gothic, in which mothers and daughters search for each other.

*That Affair Next Door* includes most of the important elements of the female gothic, although they are rearranged and attenuated. Our protagonist, Amelia Butterworth, is not the young innocent of a Radcliffe or Brontë novel whose experience in investigation is an experience in terror. However, it is clear that she is completing a passage of development (the chapter in which she first displays her powers of logic is called "Amelia Discovers Herself") when she rebels against the belittling paternalism of Ebenezer Gryce. Although the endpoint of her quest is not the discovery of her own mother, the events of the story require this spinster to rework her relation to the social and psychic category of motherhood. She is, even before the ending, a powerful mother figure in the eyes of the many "motherless girls" in the novel: a monster to the Van Burnam daughters, who call her "the ogress," and, in the beginning, a dangerous inquisitor of Olive Randolph.

Green develops the female gothic plot more thoroughly and systematically in other of her novels — most notably in Amelia Butterworth's second adventure, *Lost Man's Lane*. In that novel, Butterworth is recruited to investigate the goings-on in a reportedly haunted house — the house, tellingly, where the daughters of one of her deceased schoolmates now live. The plot includes a midnight burial, imprisonments, secret staircases and rooms, a ghostly carriage, a muttering crone, and a strange young man whose hobby is vivisection. Butterworth's work results in the freeing of the daughters from the thrall of a wicked mother who made her children bury her in the cellar. The twist in the female gothic plot, here and in *That Affair Next Door,* is that the protagonist is not a young girl discovering sexuality, but an older woman investigating its excesses and abuses. Still, Amelia Butterworth is always bumping into younger women who want mothering, or into mothers who are not doing their job.

That pattern is not confined to the Butterworth novels; as a whole, Green's stories are marked by the number of mothers who are quietly or more problematically missing. Younger women like Mary Leavenworth are often, as Barbara Welter observes, "trapped and haunted" because they are too proud, ambitious, and passionate for the narrow opportunities allowed them.[12] They are motherless and in danger, and they encounter in their travails mother figures who are troubling as often as they are comforting. In an interview late in her career, Green made an offhand remark that suggests that the female gothic plot was for her more than a matter of formula. When asked if she had ever been frightened by her own books, she replied, "I had such an experience when I was writing *The Forsaken Inn.* A woman dies in a locked room, which is never opened. Fifteen years later another woman crawls through the passageway to the room. I knew what she was going to find there, and when she was half-way through I was so frightened I could not take her any further. I had to lay the manuscript away for a while."[13] Green was herself a motherless daughter from the age of three, and we can imagine the psychological resonances of such scenes for her. It is telling that a writer frequently criticized for the gruesomeness of her descriptions of death and violence would find this particular scene—a classic moment of female gothic terror—too frightening to finish. The preoccupation with dead mothers and haunted daughters raises a larger, less personal question: Why was the eighteenth-century female gothic interesting and profitable to write in the late nineteenth century?

Green's highly popular revival of the female gothic plot, which was, as I will argue in part 3, continued into the 1940s by Mary Roberts Rinehart, seems to speak to a problem among women in the decades surrounding the turn of the century: the struggle between the older generation of Victorian matrons and the first generation of

New Women. Carroll Smith-Rosenberg describes those relations as marked by "resentful words, lingering guilt, and consequent alienation." She writes that the New Woman "repudiated" her mother's world because "the normative world offered her [the unmarried woman] no haven other than the role of the spinster aunt or the poorly paid . . . schoolteacher." At the same time, Smith-Rosenberg argues, New Women "replicat[ed] the emotional world and single-sex institutional construction of their mothers."[14] Like Butterworth, those unreconstructed Victorians may have worried that the "modern girl" was "made up of recklessness and extravagance" (*TA*, 64). The conflict was even sharper between those older women who resisted universal suffrage and the younger generation who continued the struggle for it; the campaigns for and against suffrage, over time, took on a generational dimension. Carrie Chapman Catt, one of those younger generations of suffragists, described the antis in terms that stress their inertia as well as their wealth: they were "mainly well-to-do, carefully protected, and entertained the feeling of distrust of the people usual in their economic class."[15]

Green herself became engaged in a generationally tinged skirmish in the fall of 1917 on the editorial pages of the *New York Times* as she and another writer, Gertrude Atherton, exchanged rather heated letters on the eve of the referendum on full woman suffrage in New York State.[16] Green began by writing an "appeal to the men of this state to vote against the Woman Suffrage Amendment" that included all the main arguments of the female antis. She felt that the push for the amendment during wartime was selfish, "bringing confusion and the utmost distraction into politics at the very time when all such confusion and distraction should be avoided." Sounding like Amelia Butterworth at her most sanctimonious, she wrote, "a true woman waives her rights in times of stress, whether that stress be domestic or public. If there is one virtue hitherto considered as characteristic of the sex it is that of self-forgetfulness." She saw the tactics of the suffragists, especially their picketing of Wilson's White House (they "humiliate the nation and insult our President"), as evidence that "the graces which once adorned [the young girl] are fading from our sight. Her modesty is already gone." Gertrude Atherton, who came from the West, where suffrage had recently been won in several states, was best known for writing novels that brought the

New Woman to the frontier.[17] She replied with a prosuffrage statement and included an attack on Green that was both personal and
literary. Atherton pointed out Green's age (seventy-one) and added
that it had been thirty-nine years since she had published her most
famous novel, *The Leavenworth Case*. She assessed Green's fiction
according to the values of Jamesian literary realism, offering the
opinion that while Green was "inventive," with "plots bubbling out
of her like steam out of a geyser," she had "never been compelled,
like other women writers to study life and study it at first hand"
and had chosen to live in the "backwater" of Buffalo. Some readers
found Atherton's comments unseemly, judging from other letters
the paper published. Green's own reply was sarcastic ("how can I in
the short time left to me master the contents of such a lengthy letter?") and high-handed (she thanked Atherton for proving her contention that "when a woman talks politics she loses that nice hold on
her emotions that is the first requisite of statesmanship"). Atherton's
impertinence and Green's scolding response make this exchange a
small portrait of the conflict between iconoclastic New Women and
traditional Victorians—except for the fact that Gertrude Atherton
was herself sixty when she attacked Green for being too old and too
out of touch to understand the needs of younger women. The jabs at
Green make no sense from a woman only ten years her junior, except
to the extent that Atherton was not only taking the part of younger
women but, in her letters, playing the part of a rebellious grand-
daughter as well. For Atherton, a woman raised in the West and a
writer who embraced the literary possibilities of the New Woman,
Green might indeed have seemed at least a generation older than
herself.

The exchange between Green and Atherton suggests that Green
had become in her later years an advocate for and a symbol of social
and political conservatism. That does not mean she was not a critic
of Gilded Age culture; the complexity of that position is suggested
in *That Affair Next Door*. Butterworth, as I have noted, is a brisk, unsentimental Victorian of the blue-blood (rather than bluestocking)
variety, who helps out at the Orphan Asylum but seems not to be
interested in politics or business. And while Olive Randolph is not
precisely a New Woman, her attempts to make a better life for herself
include getting what education she can, leaving her father's home,

and learning the typing skills that allow her to become economically independent. Butterworth begins the novel in a state of firm suspicion about young women in general and Olive Randolph in particular; the happy ending of the novel is a fulfillment of the hope that a young woman might turn out to be like oneself after all. What she seeks to reestablish is nothing less than the female world of love and trust that, Smith-Rosenberg argues, was valued by the younger as well as the older generations of women at the turn of the century. The desire for reconciliation may be a conservative, nostalgic impulse, but it needs to be understood in the context of a critique of masculine attitudes, assumptions, and privilege. The villains of the novel are men, young men who are successful capitalists with hard hearts and no sense of shame; even the male detective is arrogant and unwilling to listen to a woman's advice.

Many of Green's novels express a sense of anxiety and longing in the relations between older and younger women; uncertainty about the fate of those younger women is often the central mystery and the main source of the thrills she was famous for. The female gothic thread, a tale of terror spun out of a frightening ambivalence, may have been successful for Green because it could express—without precisely articulating—the simultaneous wishes for continuity and for rupture in the relations of New Women, Progressives, and their Victorian antecedents. The gothic novel has always been, to some extent, about the relation of the present to the past. In its early period, it was sometimes gleeful, sometimes nostalgic about the passing of the aristocracy; later, the gothic novel itself would become a dreaded sign of pre-Enlightenment, pre-Industrial ways of thinking, as Jane Austen records in *Northanger Abbey*. The persistent return of the repressed and animation of the dead are central to the gothic; the past refuses to slip away quietly and continues to affect the present. David Reynolds and Karen Halttunen have shown that the gothic had its uses in articulating American political and social anxieties throughout the nineteenth century;[18] at the moment of Green's gothic revival, its usefulness included the struggle between old and young, between atavistic and progressive forces. That Green chose to figure the upheavals of the Gilded Age as a problem of mothers and daughters shows how thoroughly domestic her imagination and vision were.

We can also see in the pairing of a gothic storyteller with a brisk realist a sort of allegory of the domestic detective novel's development under Anna Katharine Green. Taking the solidly middle-class themes of the domestic novel and combining them with the criminal interests of the detective story, she offered a popular genre that seems to have appealed to the appetites of the middle and upper classes in ways that the dime novel did not. The mixture of gothic and realist modes seems to have spoken to the many anxieties clustered around the state of class and gender relations at the turn of the century. Without being entirely soothing, for they dramatized the corruptibility of the upper classes, the greed of the middle-class capitalist, the hypocrisy of the seemingly respectable, and the dire situations of women, these detective novels seem to have expressed those ruptures and fears in a way that was both thrilling and deeply satisfying to their readers.

# Part Three

MARY

ROBERTS

RINEHART

AND THE

MODERN

ERA

*W*hen Mary Roberts Rinehart decided, in 1907, to try to publish in book form the manuscript of her second detective
serial, *The Circular Staircase,* she "picked a publisher by the simple
method of taking a story by Anna Katherine [*sic*] Green from the
book case, noted the name of Bobbs-Merrill of Indianapolis, and
sent [the manuscript] off."[1] With this gesture, Rinehart placed Green
as her direct antecedent and acknowledged her as the creator of an
identifiable tradition in detective fiction. Rinehart's mysteries — sixteen novels and dozens of short stories — are built around the same
cluster of concerns and conventions as those of Green and Victor.
She writes of murders and investigations within upper-middle-class
households; of jealousy, rivalry, and deceit among near relations;
and of women who seem fully capable of killing members of their
own families. One of the most distinctive features of Rinehart's mysteries is her use of spinsters as narrators.

Although clearly inspired by Green's spinster narrator Amelia
Butterworth, Rinehart goes further in creating female detectives
who are interested parties to the murder because it took place in
their house or because someone they know has been accused of the
crime.[2] Her novels foreground the tension between the concerns
of the family and the mission of the police: the narrator generally
works against the police, challenging their assumptions and refuting
their conclusions about the family they are investigating, initiating
her own inquiries, sometimes even obstructing an investigation she
feels has gone awry. Even more than Green, Rinehart is interested
in the state of suspicion as an epistemological and psychological
experience. The wealthy narrators of these novels must learn to suspect the nieces and nephews they have raised or the neighbors they
have known all their lives; they must learn to watch and to read the
comings and goings of their households in an impolite way; they
must learn to ask indiscreet questions and invade the privacy of their
families' rooms and belongings. Suspicion, as Rinehart explores it,
is the precise opposite of gentility; many of her spinsters find the
experience not only disorienting — as did Raymond Everett of *The*

*Leavenworth Case* and Richard Redfield of *The Dead Letter*—but also ultimately liberating. Rinehart's narrator-heroines are altered by their experiences in criminal investigation; Rinehart examines those changes by constructing retrospective narratives.

Rinehart's backward-glancing heroines are what gives her work the label, among detective fiction connoisseurs, of the "Had-I-But-Known" style. The epithet, which comes from a satiric poem by Ogden Nash, is not a flattering one. Rinehart began writing in 1905; by 1940, when Nash published the poem, her style apparently seemed hopelessly old-fashioned to aficionados of the hard-boiled style of Hammett and Chandler. More important, though, there was a hardening of the gender line in detective fiction in the early twentieth century in America. The hard-boiled school was considered an essentially American subgenre and an entirely masculine one. The "classical" or "golden age" style was understood as British, realistic in a mannered sort of way, clever rather than violent, and far more feminine than the American hard-boiled school. Rinehart and her imitators wrote novels that were American, but gothic instead of hard-boiled. They were not like Agatha Christie either, for their work is characterized by suspense, violence, and stormy emotions. Despite the fact that Rinehart's work did not fit the increasingly rigid boundaries of genre and subgenre, she continued to be extremely popular, writing more best-selling novels than any other American author between 1895 and 1944.[3] As early as 1946, however, Howard Haycraft, an early and abiding voice of authority in detective fiction history, called Rinehart's style "a school of mystery writing the less said about the more chivalrous."[4] Later, Julian Symons quipped that these are "the first crime stories that have the air of being written specifically for maiden aunts."[5]

The "Had-I-But-Known" epithet signaled the waning, in the mid-1940s, of the female gothic revival begun by Victor and Green.[6] Like Green, Rinehart uses female gothic conventions to comment on the structures of women's lives in general and on the relations between generations of women in particular. During the decades in which she wrote, the status of women in American society and even the meaning of the female in American culture were in turmoil; radicals, liberals, and conservatives all understood the woman question, in all its versions, to be at or near the center of political, familial, and artistic ideas of progress, modernity, and traditionalism. Like Green, Rinehart portrays the clash of ideas of what a woman could and should be in part as an argument between men, but largely as a generational struggle between mothers and daughters.

While Green's female gothic plots are often attenuated, Rinehart's are fully developed and shape both the narration and the plots of her novels. Her most characteristic moment is of a woman searching through a vast and frightening house, a moment of physical terror and mental excitement. The woman may be middle-aged or in her twenties, but she is always witty, ethical, and difficult to deceive. In Rinehart's hands, the gothic plot is one of rebellion and disillusionment; the heroine comes to learn that all is not well, that figures of authority are neither able to see nor willing to confront evil, and that she is the only one who can identify the source of the terror and violence and stop it from spreading. Architecture is Rinehart's main and multivalent metaphor. The haunted house is a figure for the female self, for the hypocrisy of the bourgeois family, and for the restrictions of "woman's place." It becomes also a metaphor for a generic tension in her work between the brisk and humorous realism of the narratorial perspective and the supernatural terrors of the events of the story. Although many of the narrators begin to investigate strange goings-on in their houses in order to debunk rumors of ghosts, they find that the secrets they uncover are not easily laid to rest. The gothic plot of a Rinehart novel at first appears to be nonsense but soon demands to be taken very seriously.

Taken as a group, Rinehart's novels present a portrait of the manners and values of the upper class of the early twentieth century that rivals, in its vividness and specificity, the one created by Edith Wharton. Although there is a kind of voyeurism possible in any kind of reading, these stories welcome a certain kind of reader: someone who is a member of the white, native-born bourgeoisie, or someone who wishes to pass in fantasy or reality for one. To read a Rinehart mystery is to be constructed as a confidante. The humor of the novels is often racist and class-specific; while Rachel Innes, the narrator of *The Circular Staircase,* makes fun of many of the conventions of her class, she does so — as her name implies — very much as an insider. We are expected to find Innes's exasperation with her weak-willed, temperamental Irish servants familiar and funny. About the way a cook quits her employ, Innes reports dryly: "[T]hat night the cook's sister had a baby—the cook seeing indecision in my face made it twins on second thought" (*CS*, 8). Innes seems to expect a nod of acknowledgment from readers of her own race and class when she quips about black servants, "[I]t was always my belief that a negro is one part thief, one part pigment, and the rest superstition" (*CS*, 29). These novels are told by and for people knowledgeable about certain structures of class identity and obligation, about particular notions of propriety, and about characteristic patterns of hostilities in the households of the very rich.

Rinehart writes about the inner life of the professional class, and particularly about their own sense of themselves as both privileged and normative. She is especially interesting on the question of wealth, which is frequently a precarious matter in these novels: uninsured banks collapse, stock markets crash, trusted partners embezzle, and entire fortunes are run off with. But if money is not to be relied on, class identity is. The older female investigators in Rinehart's novels are, like Amelia Butterworth, both trained to read for the minutiae of accent, dress, and deportment in other people and determined to teach their dependents the importance of class conformity. The parallels between detecting crime and keeping house are clear in Rinehart's novels, and the function of the female detective is to remove all noxious influences from the home. Her most interesting novels, two of which I discuss at length in this part, are ones in which the narrator not only questions the hypocrisies of her class but also mounts a personal rebellion against them. Rinehart's novels are conservative in many ways, but they are not uncritically nostalgic; as Jan Cohn puts it, if many of her social ideas are not radical, they are at least "up-to-date."[7]

Mary Roberts Rinehart grew up somewhat anachronistically in a family still under the influence of the sentimental culture of Victorianism with which Green, Alcott, and Victor grappled. Mary Roberts was born in 1876 into a rigidly religious household struggling to maintain the facade of gentility even as the family sank into poverty. Her early experiences gave her insight into the small and large hypocrisies of this type of middle-class household; the recurrent subject of her later books is the lies and secrets generated in the disparity between the ideology of domesticity and the practical realities of people's lives. Her paternal grandmother, a strict Presbyterian, seems to have brought her antebellum sensibilities with undiminished force into that postbellum family. Although they lived in a fairly fashionable section of Allegheny, Pennsylvania, Rinehart's grandmother was a dressmaker who worked out of their home and her father was a salesman of wallpaper and sewing machines. The house had an immaculately kept front parlor for the customers and dark and cluttered back rooms where the sewing was done (*MS*, 5), an arrangement emblematic of the family's attempts to cling to bygone — or perhaps mythical — affluence and gentility. Her mother grew up on a small farm but became so fastidious that she insisted on warming the silver knives and forks before meals in cold weather. She was a tireless housekeeper, and made an exhausting series of slipcovers and draperies to keep their front parlor looking smart (*MS*, 16, 38–39). In the midst of this attention to appearances, Rinehart's father secretly drank, eventually committing suicide.

Rinehart wanted to go to medical school to become a doctor like the woman doctor who opened a practice in her neighborhood and served as a role model (*MS*, 22–23). Too young to attend immediately after completing high school, she decided to prepare for medical school by studying nursing. Her mother was resistant: "[T]hat I should be coming face to face with life, life and death . . . was a horror to her" (*MS*, 44). On her first day at the hospital, she was sent to clean up an operating room, and encountered an amputated foot tossed into a bucket. In her autobiography, Rinehart makes an aside to the reader as she offers this gruesome anecdote. "Not pleasant reading, that," she acknowledges; then she adds this very revealing question: "but why always the evasion, the fear of acknowledging what we know exists, goes on? A big emergency hospital deals with life itself. It cannot evade" (*MS*, 53). She asserts that "those years in the hospital entirely changed my sense of values. There is no credit to me in this. It is simply that I know what others must only surmise" (*MS*, 46). What she came to know were not only the workings of the human body, but also human "brutality, cruelty, and starvation" (*MS*, 46). When Rinehart was a girl, her mother would take her across the street rather than share the sidewalk with a local woman who had had a child out of wedlock (*MS*, 36). During her training,

Rinehart was sent to the home of a terminal cancer patient and re-membered with anger that "no one save the doctor entered it, for her daughter was illegitimate. . . . She had had a child and had had the courage to acknowledge it, so she was dying alone" (*MS, 76*).

She married a doctor from the hospital and "retired" from nurs-ing to run his practice and raise their children. She claims that she began to write only after she and her husband went twelve thousand dollars into debt in the stock market crash of 1904. Cohn calls this claim—that she wrote only to earn money—"the Rinehart myth" and sees it as a part of a sustained performance of conventional femi-ninity.[8] Even late in her life Rinehart wrote, "I did not want a career. The word has never been used in the family and never will be. . . . My early determination never to let my work interfere with the family life continues. . . . The family came first; it always has, it always will" (*MS* 86, 89). Cohn sees a strategy here: "The Rinehart myth, built up over a quarter century of interviews and essays and expressed most fully in *My Story* is of crucial importance in understanding Mary Roberts Rinehart. Only within the protective structures of that myth, only as a wife and mother whose writing was undertaken for the good of the family could Mary defy the Victorian culture into which she had been born."[9] Cohn's argument resonates with what we know, especially from the work of Mary Kelley, about the careers of domestic novelists such as Susan Warner and E. D. E. N. South-worth.[10] In their cases, writing became acceptable only when seen as an extension of domestic duty; in what amounts to a loophole in the ideology of the separate spheres, the very fact that these women wrote for money left their femininity unthreatened by their author-ship. Rinehart resembles Victor in her facility and commercial suc-cess in a number of genres: mysteries, romances, domestic novels, plays, travel pieces, comic fiction, and wartime journalism. Hers was the kind of fame that was produced by mainstream magazine culture in the decades before television. She exuded a low-gloss matronly glamour and was asked, as a voice of good sense and good taste, to comment on many social and political issues, including woman suf-frage (which she actively supported), prohibition, and the New Deal (which she did not), and her own experience of undergoing a radi-cal mastectomy for breast cancer, which she wrote about in the hope that it would save other women's lives.[11]

Rinehart's work is solidly middlebrow; her detective plots are complex enough to satisfy educated, habitual readers but are not as thematically or philosophically demanding as the high modernist or realist novel. Rinehart began publishing in *Munsey's* and *All-Story*, and later became a regular contributor of fiction to the *Saturday Evening Post, Good Housekeeping*, the *Ladies' Home Journal*, and *Cosmopolitan*.[12] In her insightful study of middlebrow culture, Joan Shelley Rubin identifies an agenda for improvement in many sectors of middlebrow literature and entertainment. Rinehart's fiction presented itself as escapist pleasure for this same type of reader, and seems, judging by the placement of serials and the reviews of novels, to have been largely consumed as such. If, as Rubin argues, "the terrain of middlebrow culture [in the 1920s, 1930s, and 1940s] proved solid ground on which the genteel outlook could be reconstituted," we have to see Rinehart's stories of upper-class crime as challenging some aspects of that outlook, particularly the pieties of Victorian gender ideology and the smugness of the unthinking bourgeoisie.[13] The fact that her fiction is contained within the structures of the detective novel and the thickly layered sensationalism of the gothic mode seems to have made her work both stimulating to middlebrow readers (and many slumming highbrows) and acceptably sanguine about upper-class culture's chances for perfecting itself.

At the same time, Rinehart and her work have an interesting and complex relationship to highbrow literature of the early twentieth century. In her attention to material detail and the nuance of manners of the moneyed classes, her interest in their secret transgressions, and her fierce sense of irony and social comedy, she resembles Edith Wharton. Lacking is Wharton's superior sense of human psychology, patience in unfolding a plot, and ability to create a richly nuanced emotional setting for the drama of her novels. Rinehart's plots are crowded, her dialogue is often snappy but rarely memorable, and she is too willing to fall back on cultural stereotypes and literary clichés. Although a perfect example of a middlebrow writer with an upper-class readership who could count Theodore Roosevelt and Woodrow Wilson among her friends and admirers, she also included Dorothy Parker and Gertrude Stein in her audience. Parker might have been attracted by Rinehart's humor, which could be very pointed on the subject of men, and Stein was a longtime reader of her detective novels.[14] In her own experimental murder mystery, *Blood on the Dining Room Floor*, Stein restates Rinehart's themes and preoccupation with retrospection in passages like this: "There have to be changes in the country, there had to be breaking up of families and killing of dogs and spoiling of sons and losing of daughters and killing of mothers and banishing of fathers. Of course there must in the country. And so this makes in the country everything happening in the country. Nothing happens in the city. Everything happens in the country. The city just tells what has happened in the country, it has already happened in the country."[15]

While Rinehart was a literary celebrity, she was not part of the literati, and her career suggests a quite different profession of authorship, to borrow Amy Kaplan's phrase, than Wharton's.[16] In her autobiography Rinehart takes care to place herself outside the educated elite and the highly professionalized: "We knew no writing people"; and "there was no one to tell me how to write, or what. . . . I worked alone and marketed my manuscripts where I could, if I could" (*MS*, 81). She mentions that she was unexpectedly invited to a grand dinner in honor of William Dean Howells's seventy-fifth birthday, only to find herself "pitchforked into literary America," and very much out of her element (*MS* 131, 451).[17] She comments repeatedly that she came out of a writerly ethos that was fading even from memory: "[M]y world, the world of writing and publishing, had been changing since the First World War. If romance still survived, it was almost completely overshadowed by the new school of realism that arose largely out of the disillusionment of the war" (*MS*, 464). When she talks about literary movements and trends she almost always focuses on questions of morals and public reaction, defending modernism by stating that "honest writers, writing for the adult mind, have been hauled into courts because their honesty might contribute to the forbidden knowledge of youth."[18] In both editions of her autobiography, she reveals a yearning to have been taken more seriously and even to have been a different kind of writer. After praising the "frankness" of "those men who headed the literary revolt" — Dos Passos, Fitzgerald, and Sinclair Lewis — and giving due to Cather and Wharton as the women who preceded them, Rinehart describes her own failure to "follow this new trend" successfully as a combination of acquiescence to her husband's "intense" and "almost violent" reaction to "the new realism," her own feeling that much of that kind of writing was "embittered" and "cynical," and pressure from her reading public to keep it supplied with murder mysteries: "my readers still wanted romance or crime from me, not stark reality" (*MS*, 464–66).[19]

Rinehart also tells us that the transgressive mode of writing for a woman is realism, not detective fiction. Although her mysteries often include quite grisly situations and descriptions, she never suggests that writing about murder was a moral issue for her or her readers. Rinehart presents realism as a dangerous kind of writing and insists that there were subjects she was afraid to touch. The grim social "drama" she saw in the hospital was, she contends, her first compelling subject. She saw things she wanted to write about — starved children, battered prostitutes, the failure of employers to visit employees who had been hurt on the job. "I could only have written of the hospital, but I could not write it. It was beyond me. It always has been beyond me. I would go to my little room on my off duty with a pencil and pad and bravely go to work: 'The ambulance is ringing furiously in the courtyard below.' Then I would stop. I was too tired, too ignorant. . . . I have never written it" (*MS*, 64). Rinehart did write about nurses and hospitals in her romance novels and her detective fiction, but apparently felt she hadn't conveyed what she had learned.[20] "I had at my fingertips a wealth of material I could not use. . . . Prostitutes and kept women . . . had poured their tragedies, hates, and passions in to my ears." (*MS*, 89). Predictably, she explains her reluctance in terms of domestic ideology: "I had my children to consider. They read what I wrote."

Behind that platitude (which is an especially illogical one, because her novels contain much more gruesome material than, say, *Main Street*) is a more serious problem in Rinehart's life as a writer. Cohn, as I noted earlier, sees Rinehart's assertions that "the family came first" as an enabling myth and a "protective structure" within which Rinehart could simultaneously launch her career and retain her position as a middle-class matron. Within that overarching mythology, Rinehart allows us to glimpse the frustration and interruption of her writing that motherhood and marriage continually posed. Rinehart could not write at home; she says, "I never worked when the boys were in the house, or their father. . . . The slam of the front door . . . the shout of 'Mother,' was the signal to stop" (*MS,* 88). Even after she had bought her family an enormous estate in Sewickley after her first big successes, Rinehart wrote in an office in Pittsburgh. She calls her office a "resort of desperation," her answer to "the frantic search of the creative worker for silence and freedom, not only from interruption but from the fear of interruption" (*MS,* 132). Money, initially the acceptable reason for Rinehart to begin writing, began to complicate her domestic affairs. Like Jo March, Rinehart became "a power in the house" with the success of her first novel. Cohn reports that at the height of her career, Rinehart made more from two short stories than her husband made in a year.[21] While insisting that their marriage was a strong one, Rinehart includes in her autobiography many vignettes that show the strain her career put on her marriage. The most pointed anecdote involves a diamond necklace that she coveted; after several arguments with her husband about it, "the necklace itself ceased to matter. . . . What I *did* want to assert was that the money that my husband had so carefully invested for me was mine, after all" (*MS,* 532–33). In the 1948 edition of *My Story,* written fifteen years after her husband's death, Rinehart reflects that "he wanted a wife, not a more or less public figure. In a way he was proud of my success, but he had resented its demands. And I have no doubt that I myself had given him only a divided allegiance" (*MS,* 476). Cohn observes that Rinehart's career "had to be fought for not only in public but at home" and argues that "the story of that struggle . . . is the real story of Mary Roberts Rinehart's life." [22]

Husband and children were not the only distractions from writing. Rinehart's mother suffered a massive stroke around the time *The Circular Staircase* was published; she lost her ability to read and speak and became "a child again." For the next sixteen years, she lived with her daughter. Rinehart describes trying to write once her mother moved in but being constantly interrupted with "small mute interrogations" and complaints that had to be put into words by Rinehart before they could be resolved. Rinehart laments, "I have worked most of a day and until she was in tears before the right question was found" (*MS,* 132), and explains that it was this mute, interrogatory mother who finally drove her from her study at Sewickley and into a city office. In *My Story,* her mother functions first as the restraining, even suffocating, force of convention, and later, in her aphasic period, as an emblem of Rinehart's feeling that it was impossible to integrate motherhood and writing.

Rinehart's experience of the conflicts in private and public aspects of American culture in the 1920s shaped her sense of what could and should be taken up in popular, middlebrow fiction. Cohn argues that "Rinehart was in her profoundest beliefs a part of that culture," that she "kept a sense of moral values very close to that of her readers," and that "she was not talking down to them, not even when she shaped her fiction to provide the escape she believed they needed." She had a clear grasp of the difficulties mothers could present to their daughters in the decades of the transition from Victorian to modern culture. She also knew the anxieties of class and gender that surrounded money, and she understood keenly money's many symbolic and emotional valences in a household. Born into a family with a strong sense of downward mobility, Rinehart became in middle age a member of the elite. She retained a critical perspective on that class even as she ascended into it.[23]

Ross MacDonald has written that the persona of a fictional detective provides authors with "a kind of welder's mask enabling us to handle dangerously hot material."[24] Rinehart's detective fiction is in fact able to convey some ideas that were, she says, "received by the magazines with disfavor": her critique of "the bourgeois point of view, the comfortable acceptance of things as they were, the emphasis on possessions, on comfort, on peace at any price" (*MS*, 123). In her detective novels, Rinehart depicts anyone striving for "comfort" and "peace at any price" as hypocritical, mendacious, blind, or an easy mark for others' dishonesty. Rinehart's critique is a liberal rather than radical one: her detective novels propose that an intelligent and slightly rebellious member of the middle class can identify the criminal activities being perpetrated behind a mask of respectability. As we have seen in the work of Victor and Green, the detective story, with its serial assertions of guilt and its doubled structure, allows the author to tell a story that is both conservative and subversive. Like theirs, Rinehart's novels have conventional happy endings marked by the resolution of a troubled courtship into marriage. But the more interesting and important features of such novels are the unstable middles and beginnings, in which little seems certain or knowable, and almost everyone seems to be lying.

# 6

# *"No Place for a Spinster"*

## THE ARCHITECTURE OF RETROSPECTION IN

## *THE CIRCULAR STAIRCASE*

*The Circular Staircase* was Rinehart's first best-seller, and it established her as a major figure in detective fiction.[1] It introduces the formula that she used with great success for forty years: a country house setting; a pair or set of crimes, conflicts, or mysteries that turn out to be intertwined; and an intelligent, resourceful female narrator. Rachel Innes is the first in a long string of these narrators. Although Rinehart never created a series detective, her female investigators are all cut from the same cloth. Innes, a spinster of a certain age, is the "foster-mother" of her orphaned niece and nephew, Gertrude and Halsey Innes. Her age is important to our understanding of her narrative. She seems to be about sixty in this story of 1908, which means that she was born in the late 1840s; she is, in other words, more than a generation older than Rinehart herself and a contemporary of Anna Katharine Green. She looks backward to what she remembers as a time when servants respected their employers and children obeyed their parents; she calls herself "an elderly woman with an increasing tendency to live in the past" (*CS*, 134). Although she is sharp-tongued and irreverent, her basic values are those of postbellum, sentimental upper-middle-class culture. Like the narratives of Victor's and Green's novels, hers is structured around the tensions produced when domestic ideology fails to mitigate violence and deceit within the home, and when its vocabulary cannot even describe the motivations and strategies of its members.

One summer when Gertrude and Halsey are young adults, Innes decides to rent a summer home in the country. The place she settles on is Sunnyside, an enormous mansion rented out by the owners after they have moved to the West Coast. That the owner, Paul Armstrong, is the president of the bank in which Gertrude and Halsey's inheritance is deposited seems to make the arrangement even more suitable. The architecture of the house is grand and elegant and accommodates all the needs of the leisured classes, with a special room for the trunks of houseguests, a lodge for a gatekeeper, and rooms for billiards and cards in its east wing. Halsey is delighted to discover what he calls "his entrance" to Sunnyside: a separate entrance to the card room from the grounds and a staircase to the second floor — the circular staircase of the title — that will allow him to slip into the house and up to his bedroom unnoticed after late nights of gambling and drinking. But despite the home's opulence, Innes never feels comfortable there: "[T]he architect had done away with partitions, using arches and columns instead. The effect was cool and spacious, but scarcely cozy. . . . There were long vistas of polished floor, and mirrors which reflected us from unexpected corners" (*CS*, 11). The house has flaws in its architecture that make it a perfect setting for a campaign of terror: too few partitions, making for a lack of differentiation or difference; too many mirrors, making for unexpected moments of doubling; and, as we shall see, too many ways to get into and out of it, and too many ways to move up and down through it.

From their first night at Sunnyside, Innes and her servants are terrorized by the sounds and sights of people who seem to be spying on them and trying to break into the house. Faces appear at windows, doors are rattled, metal golf clubs are thrown down the staircase; the servants are convinced that a ghost is at work, and most of them leave. Innes hopes things will get better after Halsey and Gertrude arrive — but things only get worse. In the wee hours of the night that the Innes children arrive with their friend, Traders' Bank teller Jack Bailey, a man is shot in the billiards room. The man turns out to be Arnold Armstrong, son of the owner of Sunnyside. One immediate question is, what was Arnold doing at Sunnyside? If he was the mysterious somebody at the windows, then why was he trying to break into his own house? The next questions are more painful, for Halsey and Jack Bailey have disappeared from the premises in what looks like guilty flight. Things look even worse for them when Gertrude admits to the police detective, Jamieson, that she is secretly engaged to Jack Bailey and that Arnold Armstrong had been paying her "unwelcome attentions" over the past several months. The dangerous erotics of this situation appear even more tightly drawn when we discover that Halsey is in love with Arnold Armstrong's sister, Louise, who is engaged to a business associate of her father's.

Rachel Innes is faced with two kinds of terror now. One is gothic in nature: the strange knockings, the faces at windows, the shadowy figures disappearing around corners in the hallways continue unabated. After the discovery of the body, Detective Jamieson assures Innes that "the ghost is laid." "Which," Innes goes on, "shows how much he knew about it. The ghost was not laid: with the murder of Arnold Armstrong he, or it, only seemed to take on fresh vigor" (*CS*, 51). The second species of terror is more personal: the creeping suspicion that Gertrude or Halsey is deeply involved in the murder of Arnold Armstrong. Innes cannot bring herself to believe that either of them is a murderer, but she is horrified to discover Halsey's revolver hidden in a flower bed on the morning after the shooting and deeply aggrieved when she senses that Gertrude is lying to her about many things. The two anxieties — the basically gothic fear of ghosts and the basically bourgeois fear of filial deceit — are really versions of the same thing in this novel, for both are centered on secrets within the home. Sunnyside *is* a haunted house, but the returning demon is not so much an unquiet soul as it is a repressed plot of greed, betrayal, and erotic impropriety.

Rachel Innes suggests a great deal about the relation of gothic conventions and upper-class principles in her depiction of superstition and suspicion. In her narrative and in her investigative practice, Innes draws a firm distinction between superstition and suspicion. Superstition is the discourse of the servants and their response to the chaotic situation at Sunnyside; to be superstitious is to be downwardly mobile. Thomas, the Armstrongs' black butler and the target of Innes's sarcastic remark about thievery, pigment, and superstition quoted above, is the very figure of superstition in Innes's narrative. When called on to explain why he will not sleep in the main house, Thomas says, "There's been goin's-on here this las' few months as ain't natchal. 'Tain't one thing an' 'tain't another — it's jest a door squealin' here, an' a winder closin' there, but when doors an' winders gets to cuttin' up capers and there's nobody nigh 'em, it's time Thomas Johnson sleeps somewhar's else" (*CS*, 9). Innes's sarcastic recording of Thomas's speech in dialect has a point beyond racial humor — she and Rinehart need to isolate Thomas as the character who most firmly believes that the story of Sunnyside is a ghost story. Thomas, along with the other servants, has a reading of the disturbed household that Innes wishes to abolish.

This is not to say that Innes's narrative is not gothic in nature; like Redfield's in *The Dead Letter,* Innes's story cannot even attempt to refute the gothic without engaging and even reproducing its fundamental principles. *The Circular Staircase* features not only a haunted house but also a veiled woman, a forced marriage, a secret room, and a corpse exhumed in the middle of the night. More important, there is a gothicism to the narrative structure itself; Innes's narrative voice is characterized by a habit of suspenseful pronouncement ("never after that night did I put my head on my pillow with any assurance how long it would be there; or on my shoulders, for that matter" [*CS,* 7–8]) that is a local version of the larger gothicism of simultaneously telling and not telling a story. Her suspiciousness is related to the gothic structures of secrecy and the narrative structure of suspense; when she notes, "I am particular about Mr. Bailey, because he was a prominent figure in what happened later" (*CS,* 29), she is both creating suspense and inviting suspicion. While Innes does not believe, as her servants do, that Sunnyside is haunted, she does know that it is the site of many secrets.

Suspicion — Innes's response to the disturbances at Sunnyside — is what leads her into the independent investigation that eventually solves the crimes. Innes is suspicious of everyone: the servants, the police, even her own niece and nephew. She does not consciously decide to launch her own investigation of her household; rather, she begins to gather information on fairly normal principles of middle-class femininity. On the one hand, she feels she must "discourage" the superstitions and panic of the servants; on the other, she is troubled by her sense that Halsey and Gertrude are involved in the crime. Although she does not believe that either of them killed Arnold Armstrong, she does not trust the police to look past the circumstantial evidence. Her first act of investigation is actually an act of domestic counterplotting against the police: she begins by concealing evidence that might incriminate her foster children. Like any mother in a domestic novel, she believes in the goodness of the young man she has raised, but when she finds Halsey's recently fired pistol, she sees "a network closing around my boy, innocent as I knew he was" (*CS*, 41). Innes decides to conceal the gun — along with a cuff link belonging to Gertrude's fiancé — from "the sharp-eyed detective . . . in a secure place until I could see some reason for displaying them" (*CS*, 41). Of course, Innes has a perfectly good reason to display those pieces of evidence at that moment: it is against the law to impede a police investigation. Her obstruction of the work of Detective Jamieson reveals a lack of faith in the police and the coroner that is uncharacteristic for a woman of Innes's race and class.

Something Innes discusses at the beginning of her narrative suggests that there is another failure of faith driving her investigation: doubts about the way she has raised her niece and nephew. At the beginning of her narrative, Innes tells us how she became the guardian of her brother's children; the background is necessary "to start my story" (*CS*, 3). She tells about the plight of a spinster suddenly endowed with children in an ironic tone; but there is perhaps a little resentment mixed with the self-deprecating humor: "All the responsibilities of maternity were thrust upon me suddenly; to perfect the profession of motherhood requires precisely as many years as the child has lived, like the man who started to carry the calf and ended by walking along with the bull on his shoulders. However, I did the best I could . . . I sent them away to good schools. After that, my responsibility was chiefly postal, with three months every summer in which to replenish their wardrobes, look over their lists of acquaintances, and generally take my foster-motherhood out of its nine months' retirement in camphor" (*CS*, 3). Innes has, in other words, mothered largely from a distance. But over the course of the winter preceding the rental of Sunnyside, that situation changes, for Halsey and Gertrude move into her townhouse after finishing their schooling. They have just come into the fortune their own mother left them, so Innes's responsibility has become "purely moral." Her most important responsibility is supervising Gertrude's debut and discouraging inappropriate suitors, duties she describes with a mixture of humor and exasperation. There is more than one hint that Gertrude and Halsey have the upper hand; Innes describes the ways the two "made me a properly equipped maiden aunt" and jokes that "by spring I was quite tractable" (*CS*, 4). It is the children's idea to rent a summer house in the country, for Innes has always enjoyed bucking "the perspiring hegira" of the upper class from the city at the beginning of the summer and "oottl[ing] down to a delicious quiet in town" (*CS*, 1).

So, as the violent and nerve-wracking summer at Sunnyside begins, the Innes family has already suffered a disturbance of power and privacy. Rachel Innes has had to give up the quiet of her independent life to supervise the morals and courtships of her brother's children, children who rebel against her traditionalism. The mysteries that surface at Sunnyside—the murder of Arnold Armstrong chief among them—are, Innes begins to discover, entirely bound up in questions about the household's erotic life. As it turns out, all the criminal activities connected with Sunnyside have something to do with Gertrude's courtship of Jack Bailey and Halsey's courtship of Louise Armstrong.

Immediately after Arnold Armstrong's murder, the newspapers report that the Traders' Bank, of which Paul Armstrong is president and Jack Bailey the head teller, has been stripped of its assets by massive embezzlement. Bailey's flight looks especially damning now; what makes it that much harder for Innes to bear is the fact that Gertrude and Halsey's inheritance has been entirely lost in the bank collapse. The desires to find out who is responsible for stealing their fortune and to either clear Jack Bailey's name or end his association with her niece are further spurs to Innes's investigation of the continued disturbances in the household. Several of those disruptions are troubling breaks in Innes's trust of her niece: she suspects that Gertrude lied to the police and stole Bailey's incriminating cuff link from Innes's collection of evidence, and that a limping Gertrude was the evasive quarry Jamieson chased down the laundry chute one day. Innes simply cannot figure out what her love-struck niece is up to.

Halsey, meanwhile, returns to Sunnyside but will not tell his aunt where Bailey has gone. His romantic plot—his courtship of Louise Armstrong—is connected with the "haunting" of Sunnyside in several ways. Louise turns up at Sunnyside in desperate straits: she has fled from her stepfather's house in California and is very ill. Innes nurses the young woman back to health, and in the course of this most sentimental of activities learns that Louise's stepfather is forcing her to marry a man named Dr. Walker whom Louise does not love. News arrives from California that Paul Armstrong has died suddenly, but Louise still insists that she must marry Dr. Walker, although it is plain that she loves Halsey. Innes begins to realize that Louise's actions are meant to protect some very important family secret and determines to find out what it is.

Meanwhile, the disturbances in the household have taken a more sinister and yet more gothic turn: Thomas, the butler, dies of fright — or superstition — when he sees the ghost of Paul Armstrong, and someone is knocking holes in the plaster walls of the third floor of the house. Detective Jamieson comes to stay at Sunnyside, although whether to protect or to scrutinize the Innes family is a matter of some uncertainty. Jamieson and Innes continue to watch each other and to trade information warily. Between the two of them, they uncover the secrets of the Armstrong family in the last quarter of the novel. The first is a criminal secret: Paul Armstrong, though already wealthy, "loved money for its own sake. . . . Not power, not ambition, was his fetish: it was money" (*CS*, 215). Paul Armstrong embezzled the assets of his own banks and framed Jack Bailey, his head teller, then placed the cash in a safe in a secret room at Sunnyside before leaving for California to await Bailey's arrest. He then faked his own death; Dr. Walker provided a medical school cadaver in return for cash and the right to marry Louise. Paul Armstrong's plan was to return to Sunnyside, retrieve his cash, and flee the country. However, he ran into an enormous problem; unbeknownst to him, his wife had rented out Sunnyside to give herself the spending money he was too miserly to provide. He was desperate to get into — and out of — the house undetected, and his attempts to do so account for some of the disturbances at Sunnyside, particularly Thomas's fatal fright on seeing the "ghost" of a man he thought dead.

The second secret of the Armstrong family is a moral one. Arnold Armstrong, out West on a dude ranch "where wealthy men send worthless and dissipated sons, for a season of temperance, fresh air and hunting" (*CS*, 328), wooed and married a local woman under a false name and false pretenses. After three months, "Aubrey Wallace" deserted his young wife. She died giving birth to their child, and her sister, Anne Watson, took over the care of the infant. Watson was determined to track down Aubrey Wallace to force him to support this son. Much to her surprise, she found him when she came to work as a housekeeper for the Armstrong family. She obtained some money for the boy's care by threatening exposure, but Arnold Armstrong soon turned the tables on her. He realized that the little boy was "the ruling passion" of Watson's life, and threatening to take custody of him, began to extort money from *her*. Arnold Armstrong was a bad sort all around; he was eventually thrown out of the house for forging his father's signature on checks.

On the night of Arnold's murder, the two family secrets—the father's theft and the son's depravity—collide. Arnold has figured out his father's money is hidden at Sunnyside, having found a note describing a secret room in the house. He is trying to break in through the card room entrance when he encounters Anne Watson. He strikes her with a golf club to obtain her keys; she runs away, enters the house through another door, finds Halsey's gun, and shoots Arnold Armstrong just after he enters the house. Because she knows Sunnyside so well, she is able to move quickly enough through the house that she appears to have been at its other end when the murder occurred.

What is important to us about the last sixty pages of the novel, in which these two secrets are brought to light, is the way Innes conducts her investigation. At the beginning of this last section of her narrative, Jamieson reminds her of a letter the police found in Arnold Armstrong's pocket after he was killed, a note folded and re-folded so tightly that the creases have worn away many words and parts of words. What Innes and Jamieson can tell is that the letter expresses the opinion that it would be possible to add an interior, secret room near one of the chimneys of Sunnyside. The note made no sense to Innes when she saw it earlier in the novel; then, she said, with a firm, middle-class sense of the right to property and privacy, "[T]here is nothing in that, is there? A man ought to be able to change the plan of his house without becoming an object of suspicion" (*CS*, 57). But when Jamieson shows it to her the second time, she has spent too many nights listening to thumping and rattling and discovered too many holes in the walls to see the Armstrongs' remodeling plans as insignificant. She makes, in other words, the connection between family secrets and domestic architecture that is the key to the mystery at Sunnyside.

Once she has made that connection, Innes begins to understand that she must move beyond simple suspicion into more active kinds of investigation. She does learn one of the two Armstrong family secrets by acting out the conventional obligation of the mistress of the household to visit an ailing servant in the hospital. Anne Watson, dying of blood poisoning from the wound inflicted by Arnold Armstrong, tells Innes the whole story of desertion and blackmail and confesses to the murder. But while this information comes to Innes when she acts within the role of a Victorian lady, the rest of her investigation is only rooted in the conventional duties of the lady of the house, not entirely delineated by them. Innes solves the greater mystery of the ongoing disturbances when she investigates the house itself, when she physically sounds the walls and puzzles out the architecture to locate the secret room. She is learning to look behind the conventional, ideal appearance of the bourgeois home. Just before she launches her most intense period of investigation, she says: "Certainly, in daylight, Sunnyside deserved its name: never was a house more cheery and open, less sinister in general appearance. There was not a corner apparently that was not open and aboveboard and yet, somewhere behind its handsomely papered walls I believed firmly that there lay a hidden room, with all the possibilities it would involve" (*CS*, 321–22). Her summer at Sunnyside has taught her how to read a house with new eyes and a new sense of the "possibilities" of its contents. At the beginning of her narrative, Innes remarks, in telling us about a room that "seemed undisturbed" but was not, "since then I have developed my powers of observation, but at that time I was a novice" (*CS*, 20).

This sensory education builds a skeptical sensibility; Innes reports that in measuring the rooms and the walls between them, she is looking for a "discrepancy between the inner and outer walls" (*CS*, 322). Over the course of her investigation, Innes discovers discrepancies not only in the architecture of the house and not only between the Armstrongs' projection of respectability and their actual wrongdoing, but also between what the ideology of Victorian femininity tells her she should feel and what she actually does feel. This experience is emancipating; she insists that "I never really lived until that summer" (*CS*, 361), and in a more extended passage, writes, "I remember wondering if this were really I, and if I had ever tasted life until that summer. I walked along with the water sloshing in my boots, and I was actually cheerful. I remember whispering to Mr. Jamieson that I had never seen the stars so lovely, and that it was a mistake, when the Lord had made the night so beautiful, to sleep through it!" (*CS*, 315). The transgressions of feminine propriety are numerous here: enjoyment of the water in her boots when she is supposed to be dainty, sensual enjoyment of the night when she should be afraid of it, communication on the subject of nocturnal activities with a man not related to her.

As she makes these remarks, she is undertaking an even greater transgression of propriety and femininity. She is, surprisingly, on her way to a graveyard to assist the detectives in a secret, unofficial exhumation of Paul Armstrong's coffin. Little could be more gothic and nothing less ladylike than digging up a grave in the middle of the night: "It's no place for a woman" (*CS*, 316), one of the men protests. As Innes explains, the exhumation of a body violates the sense of the "fitness of things" that the upper classes weave out of a sense of the sanctity of property and a watered-down Resurrection theology: "There is an air of finality about a grave: one watches the earth thrown in, with the feeling that this is the end. Whatever has gone before, whatever is to come in eternity, that particular temple of the soul has been given back to the elements from which it came. Thus, there is a sense of desecration, of a reversal of the everlasting fitness of things, in resurrecting a body from its mother clay. And yet that night . . . I sat quietly by . . . without a single qualm, except the fear of detection" (*CS*, 317). The exhumation reveals that the body in Paul Armstrong's coffin is not, as Innes testifies after examining its face, that of Paul Armstrong. The opening of the grave is a violation of a culturally constructed space, but it reveals that, in this case, the structure is concealing a fraud. It is thus a lesson that prepares Innes to read between and behind the walls of Sunnyside.

Innes is stepping out of the sphere of the moneyed woman, a transgression she draws attention to in her comic description of the effects of her midnight excursion on her shoes. Her boots are ruined, and she tries to hide them from her sharp-eyed maid by dropping them through one of the mysterious holes in the walls of the house. Her maid discovers them nonetheless, and their condition convinces the maid that someone else has been wearing them. In another incident, Innes figures her departure from norms of feminine decorum as a literal climb out of the house and onto the roof.

Having determined the location of the secret room on the third floor of the house, Innes speculates that the hidden entrance may be on the roof. She remarks that she has never been "fond of a height. The few occasions on which I have climbed a step-ladder have always left me dizzy and weak in the knees. . . . And yet—I climbed out on to the Sunnyside roof without a second's hesitation" (*CS,* 337). She goes on to compare herself to "my bear-skin progenitor, with his spear and his wild boar[;] to me now there was the lust of the chase, the frenzy of pursuit" (*CS,* 337–38). This passage echoes one from the opening pages of the novel, in which Innes writes, "[I]f the series of catastrophes there did nothing else, it taught me one thing— . . . were I a man I should be a trapper of criminals, trailing them as relentlessly as no doubt my sheepskin ancestor did his wild boar" (*CS,* 6). "The chase," as Innes sees it, is essentially a male activity. Indeed, when her dress catches and hinders her progress as she climbs up onto the roof, Innes frees herself of her uniform of gender and class, "ruthlessly" finishing its destruction by tearing off a broad strip of the skirt. Standing on the roof of Sunnyside, Innes experiences a sense of dominion in her ability to see and hear everything going on below her. She feels powerful enough to play with the "familiar fiction" of the madwoman in the attic and with the gothic conventions she has elsewhere tried to suppress.[2] After witnessing the paperboy throwing a rock at her cat, Innes walks to the very edge of the roof to scare off the boy, who thinks he is seeing a ghost in the twilight. Innes tells us with some pride that this gothic moment is the basis of the afterward famous stories of a "Gray Lady" haunting the mansion.

The point of the roof-climbing episode is precisely this experience in power, for the search for a roof entrance proves fruitless. Innes returns to the interior of the house and manages to find the way to release the catch of what looks to be a fireplace but is actually the door to the secret room. Once she enters, the door swings shut, and Innes is trapped in a pitch-black, airless "sepulchre," illuminated and ventilated only weakly by a pipe in the roof. She has stumbled into a most gothic situation, live burial, and there is little hope that she will be rescued, because she is the only one in the

house who knows where the secret chamber is. She is imprisoned by
the architecture she has investigated and the secret code of walls and
spaces she thought she had broken. Just as she begins to fear that
her air is running out, she hears the sounds of the household pursuing someone up the stairs; that someone—who turns out to be
Paul Armstrong—enters the secret room, locks the door, and tries
to silence Innes's screams by strangling her. She fights him off and
manages finally to shout to her family where she is and how to open
the secret door. The most terrifying moment for her is the moment
she is made "helpless" by a silencing hand over her mouth; in this
climactic scene, both terror and liberation are centered on the ability
to speak. Read together with the adventure on the roof that immediately precedes it, this scene is the depiction of the imprisonment of
the middle-class woman within the home. It is an entombment that
ends only when she is able to articulate the nature of the prison and
the location of the exits in language. *The Circular Staircase* places a
"sepulchre" in the innermost regions of the home and names a kind
of live burial at the heart of domesticity.

Something very interesting happens to Innes in the secret room; if
she does not die in that "sepulchre," she is symbolically transformed.
While she is sitting alone in the dark, she falls asleep, drowsy from
the stale air, then is awakened by the sound of the household in
pursuit of someone. Paul Armstrong comes into his secret room to
hide from his attackers; his relief at reaching this place of safety is
shattered when he accidentally brushes against Innes's hand, which
is "cold, clammy, death-like." He is, in fact, more frightened of her
than she is of him, and for a moment Innes imagines Armstrong's
feeling upon encountering "a hand in an empty room! He drew in
his breath, the sharp intaking of horror that fills lungs suddenly col-
lapsed. Beyond jerking his hand away instantly, he made no movement. I think absolute terror had him by the throat. Then he stepped
back, without turning, retreating foot by foot from The Dread in the
corner, and I do not think he breathed" (*CS*, 347).

In this scene, Innes becomes a "Dread"; by telling the story from
Armstrong's perspective, she makes herself out as a terrifying visitation from the grave. As when she acted the part of the madwoman on
the roof, Innes is a gothic figure here—terrifying instead of terrified.

Her ensuing struggle with Paul Armstrong is a drama of what Eve Sedgwick identifies as a central gothic theme: "the unspeakable."[3] Her articulation of the hidden space in which she is imprisoned is a gothicized speech, in part because she speaks it as a ghost, and in part because she is speaking of barriers and spaces, of secrets and exposure. Like Stowe's Cassy and Green's Olive Randolph, Innes has become an author as well as a reader of the gothic. At the beginning of her narrative, the gothic is a way of understanding and behaving that is to be resisted and abolished, but by the end Innes has embraced it as a powerful mode of expression.

The secret room at the center of the house is connected to a complex tradition of associations of inner spaces with the female body.[4] In the female gothic mode, as Claire Kahane points out, the analogy is not only of houses with women's bodies, but more specifically of rooms and wombs and tombs.[5] Kahane elucidates the female gothic convention of the discovery of a secret room in a way useful to our understanding of Innes's experience: "Following clues that pull her [the heroine] onward and inward—bloodstains, mysterious sounds —she penetrates the obscure recesses of a vast labyrinthine space and discovers a secret room sealed off by its associations with death. In this dark secret center of the Gothic structure, the boundaries of life and death themselves seem confused. Who died? Has there been a murder?"[6] Kahane argues that the discoveries the heroines make in these secret rooms form a pattern of concern about "dead or displaced mothers." Kahane's description would seem to apply to Rachel Innes's experience in limited ways: while in her secret room, "the boundaries of life and death themselves seem confused"—as, we might add, are the boundaries of identity and perspective, since Innes is not a young woman in search of her mother. The secret room-womb-tomb would not seem to mean the same thing to an elderly spinster that it means to a younger woman contemplating marriage and motherhood. The inner space might be more like a point where female abides than like a thruway for reproduction. But if the secret room at Sunnyside is not a place where the erotic struggle of "(m)otherhood" is worked out in the ways Kahane's analysis suggests, then why is Innes's experience so dramatically and thoroughly gothicized? To understand that, we need to understand more fully that something constructed as female storytelling and something constructed as female space are at stake in Innes's narrative.

Innes's investigation, as I have noted, proceeds through fulfillment of and challenge to her proper role as "maiden aunt," but her methods need also to be understood in relation to language and narrative. We recall that she begins to solve the mystery when she rereads the note found on Arnold Armstrong's corpse. As with the torn letter of *The Leavenworth Case,* this letter is mutilated, its meaning obscured by blanks and elisions. The note, which is about the secret room, neatly reflects its subject in the lacunae of its form. To understand this text, Innes must learn to read the blank spaces on the page as well as its linguistic content. When Jamieson says, with satisfaction, that "the lines are closing up"—meaning that a solution is at hand—he is missing the point that Rachel Innes sees. While Jamieson's metaphor suggests that the elimination of space (i.e., the closing of lines) will restore a coherent narrative, Innes's investigation turns to the discovery and articulation of a significant space—the secret room.

Her careful reckoning of the dimensions of the rooms and patient examination of the woodwork of the mantelpiece succeed where another investigator's methods fail. Unbeknownst to Innes or Jamieson, Jack Bailey has returned to the house disguised as a gardener; he also knows that there is a secret hiding place at Sunnyside, and he wants to recover Paul Armstrong's embezzled cash so that he can restore the deposits of the Traders' Bank and clear his own name. He is the person who has been knocking holes in the plaster in his attempts to find the secret room. Bailey's invasive probing is made into low phallic comedy in Innes's account of an assault on the female servants' bedroom. One servant reports being awoken by plaster "'hit[ting] me on the face. . . . The first thing I knew, an iron bar that long' (fully two yards by her measure) 'shot through that hole and tumbled on the bed'" (*CS,* 258).

While Innes does, before she has calculated the exact location of the secret room, once take a hatchet to a wall ("a supreme disappointment," she reports), this kind of physical penetration is otherwise entirely the proclivity of male investigators. Jamieson examines the interior length of the clothes chute by hanging from a rope; Jack

Bailey "thrusts" a ladder up this same tunnel. The house under investigation is figured at some level as a woman's body under heterosexual assault; that metaphor reinforces our sense that Innes's investigations are different in kind as well as in motivation from those of the official police. In this house, the female detective-storyteller is required not only to uncover its secrets, but also to claim and articulate its most interior space.

Ultimately, the experience in and escape from the secret room is the motivation for the narrative that Innes offers in *The Circular Staircase*. Innes writes her "inner history" because "the newspaper accounts have been so garbled and incomplete—one of them mentioned me but once, and then only as the tenant at the time the thing happened—that I feel it my due to tell what I know. Mr. Jamieson, the detective, said himself he could never have done without me, although he gave me little enough credit, in print" (*CS*, 2). She puts forward her narrative as a correction of the "garbled and incomplete" newspaper accounts of the murder investigation. She wants "credit"; she wants her "due" as an investigator of domestic crime, and she sets her written narrative against the versions of the story told by male reporters and male detectives that elide her experience deep within gendered architecture and the architecture of gender. Her narrative testifies that what is important to understand about the deaths at Sunnyside is her female experience of them, an experience that culminates in the discovery of the secret room.

Innes wants to tell "what I know"; *The Circular Staircase* is a personal and retrospective narrative, a sustained version of the act of articulation that freed her from her "sepulchre." In this novel, the retrospection extends out of the frame of the introduction and conclusion and shapes the telling of the story in ways that we are meant to notice, such as the suspenseful utterances noted earlier. Although they are devices that pull the reader forward, they actually are possible only when the narrator is looking backward. Innes's narrative is also marked at several points by passages that draw attention to themselves as performative acts of storytelling. When Innes remarks, "Liddy always screams and puts her fingers in her ears at this point" (*CS*, 346), she is preparing the reader to experience terror, but she is also reminding us that she has told the story several times before. Elsewhere, she tells us: "At this point in my story,

Halsey always says: 'Trust a woman to add two and two together, and make six.' To which I retort that if two and two plus X make six, then to discover the unknown quantity is the simplest thing in the world. That a houseful of detectives missed it entirely was because they were busy trying to prove that two and two make four" (*CS*, 336). The inclusion of this conversation between listener and storyteller is a sign not only that this is a retrospective narrative, but also that Innes's persistent retrospection is an integral part of her goal of correcting and revising the official—which is, in this novel, to say masculine—accounting of events. Innes is telling us the story of the "X" after solving for this unknown quantity, and she is telling us that she set up this algebra as a variant on male arithmetic. The process of discovery is mirrored in the process of storytelling; *The Circular Staircase,* in other words, is not just about solving a murder, it is about discovering the voice in which to articulate the story—or the X, or the secret chamber—that the men of the novel overlook.

That the process of finding the voice to tell these stories is at issue in Rinehart's novels is evident in the "had-I-but-known" moments for which she is most famous. Innes's narrative has several of them. An archetypal declaration occurs early on, when Innes says, in effect, "had I but known what terrible things lay in store for me, I would have avoided them entirely": "And so we sat there until morning . . . arranging what trains we could take back to town. If we had only stuck to that decision and gone back before it was too late!" (*CS*, 18). But, of course, if Innes had gone back, there would be no story to tell, so this is a somewhat disingenuous utterance, especially in light of her plans at the end of the novel to rent another summer house— "and I don't care if it has a Circular Staircase" (*CS*, 362). But what the "had-I-but-known" moment does call attention to is the "before and after" structure of the retrospective narrative. As she lives through the events at Sunnyside, Innes is afraid of them; afterward, she commands them in narrative form.

Her experience is not only one of terror and doubt, but also one of narrative education—of instruction in reading and writing.[7] What Rachel Innes has learned, in discovering the secret room first mentioned in Arnold Armstrong's letter, is how to read between the lines of the text that is her house. She solves the mystery by reading behind the "handsomely papered" constructions of the moneyed classes, and she gathers information by reading what at first appears to be a sign only of silence and incomprehensibility—a corpse. As in *The Dead Letter* and *The Leavenworth Case*, there is simultaneously a wish that the corpse could name its murderer and a horror that the corpse might speak. In *The Circular Staircase*, both the disinterred—and misinterred—body in Paul Armstrong's grave and the murdered corpse of Arnold Armstrong—by virtue of the letter it bears—have important things to tell investigators. Innes first begins to understand the principle of the tale-telling corpse when she realizes that "the murder of Arnold Armstrong was a beginning, not an end" (*CS*, 184). She has discovered something like a narrative principle for investigation; her declaration is another version of David Lehman's analysis of "the corpse on page one . . . not only *at* but *as* the beginning" of the detective novel.[8] The corpse as beginning is, of course, also a gothic principle of storytelling—the repressed returns, secrets come to light, and the dead speak from the grave.

But while we can see Innes gaining a gothic storytelling sensibility and a skeptical eye, we can also see that much of her work is in the service of domestic ideology. Like Detective Burton in *The Dead Letter*, she is responsible for bringing about a happy resolution of the tangles and disrupted courtships of the household. Even as she starts to understand a corpse as a beginning, she is busily writing a conventional ending to the novel. Her investigations result in the clearing of Jack Bailey's name, and at the end of the novel, Gertrude is making plans to marry him with a glad heart and her aunt's blessing. Innes's investigation also exposes and thwarts Paul Armstrong's plan to trade his stepdaughter for Dr. Walker's assistance and silence; the end of the novel finds Louise and Halsey making plans for their wedding also.

Innes's investigation has, even more than Burton's, been motivated by her desire to screen her foster children's suitors and to ensure their happiness with mates of whom she approves. Her function, both as maiden aunt and as detective, is to realign the erotic connections between the characters into proper patterns. She has an authority, as head of her household, to regulate other people's behavior that amounts to a sort of authorship. In particular, she must investigate the misdeeds of the male members of the Armstrong and Innes households. What needs to be abolished and controlled are certain kinds of male behavior—greed and dissipation—that work against the ideology of domesticity. The story of Arnold Armstrong is one of seduction, abandonment, and blackmail; he is a young man who takes marriage lightly and uses a foster mother's love of his own son to extort money. Innes learns this story only after Arnold is dead, and so can do nothing (except to promise to care for the child after Anne Watson dies). There is, however, a threat that Halsey, with his love of fast cars and games of chance, might turn out the same.

One reason that Sunnyside is so unsettled may be because of the way its architecture accommodates masculine shenanigans. As Halsey says while admiring "his" entrance—the door between the grounds and the card room—and the circular staircase from there to the second floor: "[T]he architect that put up this joint was wise to a few things. Arnold Armstrong and his friends could sit here and play cards all night and stumble up to bed in the early morning, without having the family send in a police call" (*CS*, 12). This accommodation is a fundamental flaw in Sunnyside's architecture: such behavior should be discouraged rather than condoned. The circular staircase is a sign of masculine vice, and it is fitting that both Arnold and Paul Armstrong are killed on it.

The second story of masculine vice—and this one she thwarts—is one of greed; Paul Armstrong is guilty of the same kind of "fetishistic" love of money that Horatio Leavenworth exhibited. Love of money for its own sake is a vice that is specifically masculine in these novels, and hoarding of it is the terrible secret that causes such disruption of the domestic sphere of *The Circular Staircase*. The disruptions include not only the dissolution of order among the servants and the suspension of such customary events as regular meals and quiet nights, but also the distortion of relations between family members. Paul Armstrong is ready to sell his daughter into marriage with a man she does not love in order to escape with his loot, a despicable misuse of his right to determine whom his stepdaughter may marry. He is a force of erotic evil—arranging a bad marriage between Louise and Dr. Walker and blocking a good one between Louise and Halsey—just as Innes is a force of erotic propriety, investigating the character of Gertrude's fiancé, bringing together Halsey and the long-suffering Louise.

The investigation of the disruption of the middle-class household ends up by indicting not outsiders, not even insiders, but the very head of the family. Innes, acting out her responsibilities as head of her own household, is the proper person to investigate the depraved head and heir of the household of the Armstrong family; like *The Dead Letter* and *The Leavenworth Case*, this is a novel about the investigation of the upper class by the upper class. Innes's authority to identify and correct the erotic misbehavior of the people around her seems to be of a piece with her authorship, since her narrative ends with such a contented reestablishment of bourgeois normalcy. As I have noted before, however, we need to tread very carefully when we start to read the domestic detective novel — with its doubled structure and gothic bloodlines — as prescriptive of order rather than descriptive of chaos. As we shall see, this novel has a few more secrets to reveal.

After all has been exposed and her investigation is complete, Rachel Innes makes a very interesting remark about the happy ending she has brought about, one that begins to show us an answer to our earlier questions about the gothicization of the episode in the secret room. The evening after the investigation ends, Innes walks about Sunnyside looking for a good conversation, but she finds first one couple and then another embracing and making small talk. Innes remarks that the house is "no place for an elderly spinster" (*CS*, 353) and retreats to her bedroom. This remark is only the last in a series of similar objections in the novel. In the graveyard, as I noted earlier, one man objects that "it's no place for a woman" (*CS*, 316). And when Innes and Halsey go to investigate just what or whom the servants are hiding at the lodge, Halsey says, "[T]his is hardly a woman's affair. If there's a scrap of any kind, you hike for the timber" (*CS*, 122–23), a view that has its comic reversal when Thomas refuses to let Halsey upstairs to Louise's sickroom, saying, "It's a place for a woman" (*CS*, 124). Dr. Walker wants Innes out of the house so that he and his partner in crime can retrieve their swag; he pays Innes a social call and makes a thinly veiled threat: "[T]ake a warning. Leave before anything occurs that will cause you lifelong regret" (*CS*, 212).

All these questions about "a woman's place" are connected to the gothicism of the book, and posed, in this novel about a haunted house, as matters of architecture. Innes, in investigating the criminal activities of the house's owner, discovers that there is a secret place in the house, almost inaccessible, almost entirely unknown. Although this is Paul Armstrong's lair, it becomes Innes's "place": it is Armstrong who flees the room in fear of her, not the other way around. Innes's transformation into the ghost on the roof and "The Dread" in the secret room, and her insistence that her ghastly errand at the graveyard makes her "really live" begin to make sense when we consider them as answers to questions about a woman's place, and especially when we recall that the gothic is frequently a language in which women write about anger within the home.

Innes's experience of the gothic mode is in some ways similar to that of Cassy in *Uncle Tom's Cabin* and Olive Randolph in *That Affair Next Door*. Like those women, Innes is a character who, at different points, is by turns a ghost and a teller of gothic stories. Those are the positions of power within the gothic mode, and they can be used to avenge the wrongs inflicted by heartless and demanding men. When Innes portrays the secret room as a place that she wins through gothic terror, she is likewise using the gothic story to express an unacceptable kind of anger about the situation at Sunnyside. She has, of course, plenty of reason to be angry with Paul Armstrong, for he has essentially stolen her foster children's inheritance in his embezzlement scheme and he is at least one source of the disturbances in her household. More important, Innes's gothic rage in the secret room is linked to the larger dispute over her proper place. In fact, the men, with their strict sense of where women should and should not be, are the first to gothicize Innes; the paperboy sees her presence on the roof as a supernatural event, and, even earlier, a policeman leads Innes away from Arnold Armstrong's body, saying, "[C]ome, Miss Innes, you're a ghost of yourself" (*CS*, 37). For the men, a woman where she does not belong—on a roof, at a murder, in a man's secret room—is a gothic creature—a ghost, a ghost of herself, a Dread.

Innes, who is, after all, the one reporting these responses, may also agree that she is gothic when she steps out of her place; her explanation, however, might include the terrible anger at the barriers constructed between herself and what she wants to know. Her anger makes her gothic in a culture in which women are not supposed to be angry at proximate male authority figures such as Paul Armstrong, Detective Jamieson, and the other police and doctors in her home. Innes, we recall, was probably born in the 1850s, into a culture in which, as Jane Tompkins points out, women were encouraged to feel deeply but never to express anger.[9] Louisa May Alcott, whom we have noted as a writer of gothic fiction and as the earliest experimenter with detective fiction, was also one of the domestic novelists most interested in anger. In *Little Women*, Jo and Marmee must struggle to control their hot tempers, which in Marmee's case means learning to "fold [her] lips together" to hold in angry words. She is aided in her attempt to pick silence over wrathful speech by Father, who lays an admonitory finger across his own lips whenever he senses that his wife is about to fly off the handle. Jo, however, ends up writing her anger into her gothic tales. Alcott lays out the connections between the gothic mode, female rebellion, and anger, and between high literary traditions and male-style gentility, when she remarks, "I think my natural ambition is for the lurid style. How should I dare to interfere with the proper grayness of old Concord? . . . Mr. Emerson . . . never imagined a Concord person as walking off a plumb line stretched between two pearly clouds in the empyrean. To have had Mr. Emerson for an intellectual god all one's life is to be invested with a chain armor of propriety."[10] For the female writer of the female gothic as well as for its heroines, propriety is a heavy silence, and it is imposed or requested by the men in charge.

In the realm of gothic fiction, then, the silencing of women is a common motif of villainy, and the sort of anger that Innes expresses shapes the content of the story and often determines whether it will get told at all. Anger like hers is also the energy the gothic storyteller requires to overcome what Sedgwick calls the "massive inaccessibility" of information in the world of the gothic; it is a version of the "magic or violence" necessary to break down the barriers to narrative coherence that seem so crucial to the structure of the gothic.[11] In her reading of Harriet Jacobs's narrative of self-imprisonment, Teresa Goddu notes that most gothic texts "encode the difficulty inherent in speaking the unspeakable" and suggests that the act of writing horror inscribes both the pain of the experience and the power of reclaiming the experience for one's own purposes (especially the exposure of hypocrisy), a strategy Goddu calls "haunting back."[12] A fighting spirit is part of what makes Innes a successful detective; she says that she investigates the crime to protect her innocent niece and nephew, but most of her investigation is fueled by a determination not to be excluded or outdone by the police. Her gothic moment in the secret room is an explosion of her anger over her "place," the anger that has allowed her to overcome all the barriers—architectural, social, and psychological—to her investigations and that will compel her to write her corrective "inner history."

There is, however, an even more important pattern of exclusion and intrusion in Innes's narrative. Her narrative opens with a fairly detailed account of how she gave up her customary quiet and solitary summer in the city to rent a country house in order to please her niece and nephew. The language of the first sentence is strong: "This is the story of how a middle-aged spinster lost her mind, deserted her domestic gods in the city, took a furnished house for the summer out of town, and found herself involved in one of those mysterious crimes that keep our newspapers and detective agencies happy and prosperous" (*CS*, 1). Innes begins her story with an act of removal from her own home, a decision she calls "madness." What she has given up is her independence; that loss began several months earlier, when Gertrude and Halsey came to live with her. The issue is both literally and figuratively one of place: Innes has given up her "place" to rent another "place" for the summer, and she has, in the recent past, also taken on the place of mother to Gertrude and Halsey in a more active way. Her narrative begins and ends with remarks about her foster children squeezing her out of her independent place: at the beginning she tells us that Gertrude and Halsey insisted that she give up her "delicious quiet" in town, and at the end she tells us that the house has become "no place for an elderly spinster."

The anger she feels here is of a most unacceptable kind; she veils her resentment against Halsey and Gertrude in humor, and in the ultimately revealing denial: "I give myself credit for this . . . I never blamed Halsey and Gertrude for taking me there" (*CS*, 5–6). She is giving herself credit because she is resisting a dangerous temptation, one that would bring to the surface the long resentment of her sudden acquisition of "all the responsibilities of maternity"—something she likens to having a bull dropped on her shoulders (*CS*, 3). The deepest secret of this novel is secret female anger; Innes is able to express her resentment at being crowded from her architectural place and forced into a maternal place only in the veiling language of the gothic. The gothic mode allows her both to tell and not tell the story of secret anger; when she calls herself "The Dread" in the secret room, she joins gothic conventions to her ironic brand of humor with the effects of both terror and comedy, both admission and refutation of a frightening rage.

More than Green or Victor, Rinehart uses domestic architecture as an expressive language with which to tell her stories of crime within the Victorian household. Sunnyside's architecture has two meanings in this novel; it is as if there were two blueprints for this fictional house, and Rinehart has laid one over the other. According to one blueprint, the house represents the haute-bourgeois family in general and the Armstrong family, who commissioned it, in particular. The design of the house is a construction based on the needs and social aspirations of this wealthy family at the turn of the century. The disruption of the architectural integrity of the house—the attempts to break in, the damage to walls—both causes disturbances in the domestic routine of the inhabitants and indicates an even deeper rupture between the domestic ideal and the actual behavior of the men of the Armstrong family. The architecture of this house includes a secret room in which to conceal the greed and thievery of its owner. The second blueprint of Sunnyside shows it as a more metaphorical, less historically specific house: the house as female body, and the house of Innes's self. This is the house that the male investigators prod and probe their way through. It is in this house that the secret room is a place that belongs to Innes, a place that men cannot penetrate or abide in. It is the place for the spinster: a maiden room for a maiden aunt.

Likewise, Innes undertakes two investigations. One uncovers the Armstrong family secrets and disentangles the romances of her niece and nephew. It is an investigation that can be told in the language of the ideology of the separate spheres: a serious disruption of domestic harmony and erotic propriety has been caused by Paul Armstrong's greed. This is an investigation of the house of the first blueprint, the house constructed by the middle class, and it has a fundamentally conservative intent: the restoration of bourgeois domestic normalcy. The second investigation is a series of discoveries that Innes makes about herself, discoveries that deconstruct her place as a Victorian lady. This second investigation is subversive; its discovery of the secret room suggests that within the house of the second blueprint there is a secret, "spinsteral" place in which women do not have to be mothers. The second, metaphorical, blueprint and the second, subversive, investigation are loosely associated with gothic conventions and diction in the novel, while the first, more literal and conservative, blueprint and investigation are told largely in the language of domestic realism.

But, of course, there is really only one house in this novel. The two blueprints share the secret room, just as Paul Armstrong and Rachel Innes share it momentarily. Innes finds this metaphorical, womb-like space only after she finds the discrepancies in the stories that the Armstrong family tells about itself and the discrepancies in the architecture that houses the stories. The blueprints also share the circular staircase that gives Innes's narrative its title. While a sign of the dangerous accommodation of masculine dissipation that is at the root of the troubles at Sunnyside, the circular staircase is also a metaphor for the process of investigation in this novel. A spiral staircase is an indirect route and a structure of pleasurable delay: one first walks left, then right, in circles rather than in straight lines. The narrative of this story likewise moves along oblique, rather than direct, lines: the conduct and focus of Innes's investigations shift from literal to metaphorical, from gothic to domestic, from the secrets of the Armstrong family to the secrets of her family. The staircase is a sign of the extent to which her investigations will become circular and will double back on her. There is a circularity to the narrative as well: the story of the investigation is also the investigation of the story. The result of that investigation is not the punishment of the criminals, for the Armstrong men and Anne Watson are dead at the end of the novel and Dr. Walker has fled; the result of the investigation is the narrative of *The Circular Staircase*.

What makes Rinehart's architectural language complicated, and what allows her to use it to draw attention to the construction of the domestic sphere in historical and metaphoric ways, is her use of first-person retrospective narration. She is especially interested in the epistemological education of her detective-heroines and uses the narrative structure of retrospection to call attention to their growth as skeptical investigators of family life. The structures of retrospection and suspense also call attention to the process by which the heroine spins a narrative out of her investigation, including the ways she must surmount obstacles placed in her path by men and must supersede a false or incomplete version of the story told by men in the newspapers or in court transcripts. In the language of gothic conventions, these gendered obstructions are a version of the "massive inaccessibility" of information; by including them within a narrative structure of retrospection, Rinehart creates a type of detective fiction in which the story itself is the goal of the investigation. The story that is discovered and told is always explicitly a woman's story, an "inner history" of her victory over her own fear and the conventions of her class to discover the truth behind the "handsomely papered" constructions of a seemingly respectable household.

# 7

## *"I Suppose They Stood It as Long as They Could"*

MOTHERS, DAUGHTERS, AND AXE MURDER

IN *THE ALBUM*

Although Rinehart always classified her detective novels as "escape" both for her readers and for herself, they are in fact clearly engaged with some of the major social issues that concerned the middle and upper classes in the first decades of the twentieth century. Her leanings toward realism show themselves in her continuing interest in recording the transition from Victorian to modern culture in those decades, and that historical matrix of nostalgia, anticipation, and impatience may be the broadest context for her novels' preoccupation with retrospection. Questions of women's sexual freedom, economic independence, and class identity—all of which she understands as interconnected—are at the center of her mystery novels, especially those written after 1920.

Her favorite female figure for expressing and exploring the possibilities for women's lives in this period is the unmarried woman. Besides a dozen-odd spinster narrators, some of her detective novels feature spinster victims, spinster suspects, and spinster murderers. Among her most popular fiction was a long-running series of humorous stories in the *Saturday Evening Post* featuring a trio of middle-aged women. The ringleader of these bold, irreverent old maids is known as Tish; she is fearless, sharp-tongued, and despises hypocrisy. The spinsters of the "Tish" stories wear what they please (sometimes breeches), eat what they please (once, a mountain lion they caught), and go where they please (usually too fast in a motorcar).[1] In these tales, Rinehart creates spinsters who are independently

wealthy; their unshakable foundation of class- and race-bound respectability and their freedom from concern about money allow
them to flout convention whenever they choose. They do not regret
not having married and are perfectly content to be childless. Rinehart's middle-aged spinster detectives have similar backgrounds and
similar freedoms, though they exhibit more normative behavior for
women of their class. Later in her career, in such novels as *The Album*
(1933), *The Swimming Pool* (1952), and *The Yellow Room* (1945), Rinehart created a sort of borderline spinster, a young woman in her late
twenties who seems already to be "on the shelf" but who falls in love
with, and marries, the police detective investigating the crime in her
household. Rinehart's happy spinster is a figure of freedom and an
enabling persona of authorship, a woman in control of her sexuality,
her bank account, and her narrative. We can easily locate the origins
of the power of this figure in Rinehart's own difficulty in reconciling
her roles of wife, mother, and famous, well-paid author.

   The spinster was a culturally electric figure in the early twentieth
century, and of much interest to the middlebrow magazine culture of
which Rinehart was a part. Scores of articles by and about spinsters
appeared in mainstream magazines over the first three decades of
this century; the argument about whether spinsters were to be pitied
or envied was at heart a debate about women's control of money
and its effect on and place within heterosexual marriage. Indeed, the
spinster had been a figure of collective concern in American culture
since the 1860s, and, as historians Ruth Freeman and Patricia Klaus
suggest, has to be understood in the context of that discussion as
being always middle or upper class.[2] Freeman and Klaus argue that
near the turn of the century, the depiction of spinsters as redun-
dant shifted into a discussion, connected to eugenics and nativism,
about the unmarried gentlewoman as a cause or sign of the decline
of the white, educated middle and upper classes. The relation of the
debate to the reality of marriage rates is complicated: historians see
the highest proportion of never-married women — about 10 percent
of the population — in the cohort born between 1865 and 1895 (these
women would have reached adulthood between 1885 and 1915). That
proportion dropped to about 6 percent in the group born in the
years between 1895 and the beginning of World War I (reaching their
majority between 1915 and 1935). Marriage rates not only rose in the

1920s, but the median age at first marriage also fell.[3] However, as Nancy Cott explains, those facts about marriage have to be understood in relation to the rapid increase in the numbers of women entering the paid labor force and postsecondary educational institutions, and to changing ideas about female sexuality and psychology. Cott summarizes a series of acute arguments about the intersections of economic and sexual history in the 1920s and 1930s by arguing that "just when individual wage-earning made it more possible than ever before for women to escape the economic necessity to marry, the model of companionate marriage with its emphasis on female heterosexual desires made marriage a sexual necessity for 'normal' satisfaction."[4]

Cott's analysis of the issues surrounding the question of marriage in this period is borne out by the kind of discussion that took place in popular magazines of the period. Elizabeth Jordan, one of the wittiest and most energetic defenders of the unmarried state, saw a clear distinction between the spinsters of the nineteenth century and the spinsters of her own generation, and the difference was economic. She observed that her single status often evoked expressions of pity:

One explanation, of course, is that the economic independence of the average American woman is still little more than a quarter of a century old, and that most of us vividly remember the traditional spinster who lived with her married brothers or sisters, and did their housework and took care of their children because she could earn her living no other way. . . . [F]ood and shelter and clothing were given her with generous gestures and no admission or even realization that she was saving the family in actual dollars four or five times the amount the family spent on her. It was taken for granted that she was contented and grateful, though a few fitting words of appreciation from her were looked for at intervals.

. . . This type of spinster is almost extinct; but there are still a few of her left, and I warmly commend her as a fit object for the womanly sympathy so warmly and undeservedly poured out upon us all. She needs them. The average spinster does not, and it is of her that I am writing.

She is, as a rule, self-supporting, independent, very busy and surprisingly contented. . . . She makes a home for herself, which may be a hall bedroom, or a modest apartment, or an expensive and beautiful setting, according to her income. In the majority of instances she has the privilege of helping someone else — of supporting a mother or father, of educating a younger brother or sister, or of doing much more than this. She does it with her own money — the money she herself has earned."[5]

Jordan goes on in the article to ridicule concerns about the "starved nature" of women who do not marry or have children. She teasingly assures her readers that the attractive spinster is not bereft of romance ("even when she is swinging along in her late forties"), and that even the most "self-respecting and high-minded" spinster "learns a great deal more than she ever gets credit for knowing." In the era of popular Freudianism, the spinster was increasingly defined by experts and by the educated middle class as abnormal because sexually repressed.[6] The assumption that unmarried women were neurotic was a source of irritation and sardonic humor: as one spinster put it, to have dinner with married friends was "to be psychoanalyzed according to Freud, Adler, and a dozen others." She complained, "if I so much as give a youngster a friendly pat, I am trying to satisfy a 'thwarted maternal instinct' . . . I wonder where I kept it all these years? Perhaps it was just sitting around quietly, waiting for that thirtieth birthday; now it can show itself and chortle, 'I'm your thwarted maternal instinct. Don't pretend you don't know me. All your acquaintances say my place is with you. Better be satisfied with me and say nothing.' "[7]

One of the most striking patterns in the magazine articles of this period is the tracing of the history of spinsterhood as it is happening. Margaret Culkin Banning, writing in 1929, laments that "there was a period, which can be roughly calendared as a decade ago, when it was prophesied that the life of an unmarried woman in the world would give a richer yield than had been believed possible. It was as if a new vein in the mine of women's prospects had been discovered and there was the natural rush to share in its riches. . . . But now some of the old dubiousness about the spinster life seems to be surging back."[8] While she mainly discusses the inevitable dissatisfactions of any life choice, Banning makes her own contribution to what we might see as a topos of triumphant comparison: "The spinster of the last generation, that often pathetic figure, wearing clothes which must never be too conspicuous and were often a little shabby, the spinster for whom anything was good enough if it was warm and neat—because nobody was going to look at her twice anyhow—is gone forever. The single woman of to-day is . . . as well-dressed and well groomed as any woman in the world. . . . Just as the composite picture of the diffident or embittered old maid of the last century lingers in our minds, so the type of today begins to appear." Novelist Lilian Bell's article "Old Maids of the Last Generation and This" is one of the most expressive, if slightly hallucinogenic, chronicles of this sort. In it she traces the lives of women who were about forty years old when World War I began, and who were liberated by the war from a life of sewing, pickling, and babysitting for their relatives: "The businesslike, artloving, fashion-setting spinster of today burst from her thin-necked, anxious, service-without-pay chrysalis."[9]

In all these articles written by spinsters about spinsterhood, economic independence is always the crucial and determining difference between the Victorian old maid and the happily single modern woman. But the fact that the spinsters of the early twentieth century had to argue so repeatedly and so pointedly to differentiate themselves from the "diffident or embittered old maid" of one or two generations before suggests that the Victorian stereotype continued to have cultural currency well into the twentieth century. Elizabeth Jordan blames novelists for the persistent image of the "starved neurasthenic":

One is always picking up novels in which the hysteria of neurotic spinsters is described in detail, though one cannot imagine where the authors find their models. . . . It has been my privilege to meet an unusual number of human beings scattered over three continents. Among that vast number, I have known exactly one neurotic spinster. She was an extremely unpleasant person, who died years ago. I have always believed that this victim of repression was the sole model for the moaning sisterhood so frequently described by our authors. Many of them knew her, and evidently she left a lasting impression on their minds.[10]

Jordan's account begs the question of what cultural value such an out-of-date stereotype could have in the 1920s. All these writers indicate that the Victorian old maid would be instantly recognizable as a type in fiction or on the street: angular, emotionally and physically rigid, with thinning hair, bad teeth, a sour or mousy disposition, and a high collar (and their editors seemed to agree, including remarkably similar illustrations of the old maid with these articles). One could assume that this type was emotionally unbalanced, sometimes dangerously so. In highbrow literature, Wharton portrayed seething and ignoble emotion under the respectable facade of a nineteenth-century spinster ("precise, methodical, absorbed in trifles, and attaching an exaggerated importance to the smallest social and domestic observances") in her famous 1924 novella, "The Old Maid."[11] The idea that the seemingly moral spinster could have a bizarre, even violent, inner life had been so fully absorbed into the realm of common knowledge by the 1940s that murderous old maids could form the basis of one of the most popular and lighthearted stage comedies of the century, *Arsenic and Old Lace.*[12] The depiction of the nineteenth-century old maid as the dangerous or ridiculous product of female society and Victorian repression was, it seems, given new life by the arrival of psychoanalytic ideas on the broad horizons of middle- and upper-class popular culture in the 1910s and 1920s, and the value of the stereotype is in its iconographic representation of the new ideas about the benefits of heterosexual expression for women.

Nancy Cott argues convincingly that in the 1920s, "from popular, intellectual, and social scientific writers swelled a tide of scorn for 'Victorian' sexual morality, monochromatically conceived as repressive and hypocritical. . . . A new cultural apparatus formed around the revelation that sexual expression was a source of vitality and personality (not a drain on energy as nineteenth-century moralists had warned) and that female sexual desire was there to be exploited and satisfied."[13] The presumably celibate spinster became interesting in a new way as popular Freudianism hypothesized a causal connection between sexual repression, on the one hand, and neurosis and hysteria, on the other, a theory echoed by many in the male medical establishment. To talk about spinsters, then, was to talk about women's place in the economy and to talk about female sexuality. These potent cultural figures were in simple usage shorthand symbols of perfect morality, but they could, in the period when expression of heterosexuality "was almost a matter of conformity," easily be regothicized as figures of rebellion and emblems for the subversive and dangerous energies that always underlie repression. In particular, the spinster figure became conflated (sometimes partly, sometimes fully) with the newly evolving figure of the lesbian, and man hating was added as an explicitly stated ingredient in her embitterment.[14] Carroll Smith-Rosenberg contends that while the psychosocial category of "woman" signified "social danger and disorder" from the mid-nineteenth century forward, the "ultimate symbol of social disorder and of the 'unnatural' " was the stereotype of the "mannish lesbian" as it was constructed out of the anxieties occasioned by the second generation of New Women, who seemed to gain, in the 1910s and 1920s, an unacceptable degree of control over their sexuality, their finances, and, with the passage of woman suffrage, their civil rights.[15]

Rinehart's detective fiction engages this complex cultural pattern in ways both direct and indirect. It offers a portrait of what worried and amused the generation that spent its middle years in the midst of the transition from Victorian ideas of womanhood to modern ones. Rinehart includes several kinds of spinsters in her work: some, like Rachel Innes, are mild and contented rebels against certain traditions; others fit the dependent mold of the Victorian stereotype; others are unmarried women with independent means or their own income who live modern lives in the new style of spinsterhood of the 1920s and 1930s; others are eager to marry, and do so as soon as the right man comes along. Rinehart very rarely even suggests lesbian attachment or passion between characters, but her scariest Victorian spinster figure, Lydia Talbot of *The Album,* certainly gains in her power to frighten from all the resonances of a doctor's remark that she has led "an unnatural life." Rinehart's novels supply a fictionalized portrait of the encounter between the medical establishment and all these kinds of single women. Doctors are always male and almost always figures of control, scolding both younger and older women to make them conform to normative standards of deportment. In Rinehart's detective fiction, physicians attempt to soothe women's fear and anger with a combination of fatherly advice and injectable narcotics. Notably, almost all her doctors, including the most seasoned general practitioners, have some interest in psychoanalysis. They frequently act as foils to the amateur female detective, explaining in a ridiculously patronizing way why the narrator only thinks she is hearing and seeing sinister and bizarre phenomena in her home. In *The Confession,* for example, one nerve specialist doesn't believe our narrator's reports of an incessantly ringing phone: "He listened carefully. 'Ever get bad news over the telephone?' he asked."[16]

Rinehart's analyst figures are not entirely dismissable, however. Rinehart, even in her earliest works, alludes to such psychoanalytic concepts as the subliminal mind, the unconscious, hysterical amnesia, repression, the *idée fixe,* and compulsive neurotic expressions of inner conflicts. Of course, the mind itself has been since Poe a central and dominant subject for detective fiction, and both classical Freudian and Lacanian theory have found detective fiction rich material for analysis.[17] Rinehart is not systematic in the ways she deploys psychoanalytic material, but rather refers to an assortment of formulations from the nineteenth century alongside the newer ones introduced in the United States in the early twentieth century.[18] Although her novels usually seem to argue that psychoanalytic explanations for murder and theft are too mechanical to be truly insightful, she was, it seems, fascinated by the basic Freudian concept of a dynamic mind that could keep secrets from itself. She explores that model in *The Breaking Point* (1922), a novel about a man who suffers total amnesia after his involvement in a murder and is given a new identity by a sympathetic doctor.

Rinehart explores and draws attention to several of her main themes through the doctor and analyst figures. Most obvious is the way they function as a sign of her interest in the workings of the mind, which includes both an optimistic belief in the ability of a detective figure to learn and to know, and a pessimistic certainty of the ease of the formation and expression of criminal motives. She also uses doctors in a more historically specific way, showing them as male authority figures with a patronizing relationship to her narrators and to other women. Younger doctors tend to have their heads filled with modern analytic notions that half explain women's behavior without accounting for it in the ways that a female detective can. Older doctors are a good deal more insightful, but tend in their patronizing ways to try to discourage the female detective from asking too many questions or to disbelieve her when she discovers the truth. In both cases, doctors offer competing or muffling narratives that are never as good or interesting as the one the spinster detective can tell.

In this way, Rinehart's use of the doctor figure is quite different from Arthur Conan Doyle's: in the Sherlock Holmes stories, Doctor Watson may not be as acute as the detective he partners, but he is the chronicler of Holmes's exploits and the narrator of the stories. In Conan Doyle's work, Watson, the professional doctor, and Holmes, the amateur scientist, reflect the late Victorian faith in the ability of scientific methodologies to dispel mystery and in the applicability of medical or somatic theory to the study of criminal behavior.[19] Rinehart exhibits a certain early twentieth-century feminist skepticism in her formulation of an adversarial relationship between the spinster detective and the doctor. Indeed, when we compare her spinster detectives with their more famous British counterparts of the same period, Jane Marple and Harriet Vane, we have to see Rinehart's women as more willing to confront authority figures, more outspoken, and more physically courageous than Christie's or Sayers's.[20] The way Rinehart shows young and middle-aged women, figures who are continually marginalized in medical discourse in particular and in the construction of factual knowledge in general, besting doctors is probably her greatest break with her own class. If Victor (and, early on, Green), shaped detective fiction around the interest in and interests of the rising professional class, Rinehart decenters the doctor in her detective fiction.

Rinehart's spinsters make such good detectives of domestic crime because they are both participants in domestic ideology and figures with a vexed and irreverent relationship to it; they participate in family life, but see many of its affective structures—like marriage and parenthood—from a critical distance. The question about Rinehart's brisk, witty spinsters is whether they do not participate fully in the most sentimental strains of domestic ideology because they have not married, or whether they do not marry because they are unsentimental by nature. Within the domestic sphere, with its equation of woman's place with married motherhood, the happily unmarried woman constitutes an implicit critique of that construction of gender; as we saw in *The Circular Staircase*, that implicit critique can become an active investigation of the other constructions, falsehoods, and hypocrisies of the bourgeois household.

That critique, or subversiveness, has a narratological component as well in the novels in which the spinster detective is also the nar-

rator and apparent author of the text. As Tony Tanner and Joseph
Boone have argued, the construction of bourgeois marriage and the
structure of the novel have been closely linked projects of middle-
class culture.[21] Tanner calls marriage "*the* central subject for the
bourgeois novel" and defines marriage as "a means by which society
attempts to bring into harmonious alignment patterns of passion
and patterns of property." Because "for bourgeois society marriage
is the all-subsuming, all-containing contract," the novel always engages the subject of marriage, even if only to contest it, and is "coeval
and coterminous with the power concentrated in the central structure of marriage." Tanner is most interested in the play of contract
and transgression as figured by adultery, but he also observes that
"protagonists of the early English novels are socially displaced and
unplaced figures" who "threaten, directly or implicitly" the social
structure with, among other things, "the uncertainty of the direction in which they will focus their unbonded energy."[22] Boone takes
up the question of bonded or unbonded energies and narrative
more directly, connecting what Bakhtin calls the novel's presumption of a "homelessness of literary consciousness" with the structure
of courtship novels and the convention of wedding-as-ending.[23] By
looking at a number of texts from the American and British canon
of nineteenth-century literature, Boone establishes the kind of pattern we have seen in Alcott's thrillers, in Victor's *The Dead Letter*,
in Green's *The Leavenworth Case*, and in *The Circular Staircase*,
wherein the body of the novel, devoted to the courtship plot, has
a more or less realized potential to subvert many of the structures
of obligation, property, personal identity, privacy, and sexuality in
bourgeois culture; a conventional happy ending—in which heterosexual unions are legalized in a wedding—marks the limit of those
subversions or exposures. And Peter Brooks's work in Freudian narrative theory, as we saw in the discussion of *The Dead Letter*, helps
us to understand the erotic nature of the structures of delay under-
girding the courtship plot.[24]

The unmarried gentlewoman seems to be exactly the kind of "unplaced figure" of "unbonded energy" that Tanner identifies with
subversion. In the case of Rinehart's spinsters, the question of their
place—architectural and affective—is nearly as much of an issue in
their investigation of the upper-class household as their desire to un-

cover the secrets surrounding a murder. The spinster's unbonded-
ness within a sphere defined by pairing suggests her to be, structurally, an adulterator or infiltrator of the ideology of marriage; one
of her most important functions is to excise secrets about or within
marriages. At the same time, the middle-aged spinster in Rinehart's
novels has the responsibility to prevent a premature ending, which
might take the form of the conviction of an innocent person or the
quick arrest of a guilty one before the entire story comes to light,
or might take the form of mistaken marriages between characters.
Recovering the entire story of the crime and matching the correct
couples are usually overlapping processes of delay and realignment.

Rinehart's spinster narrator intervenes, in other words, at more
than one level of the narrative; she shapes the story and she tells the
story. She is also able to read between the lines of the stories that the
professional and banking classes tell about themselves. Her distinctive, retrospective style allows her to reproduce the process by which
she came to suspect that certain "handsomely papered" structures
concealed darker secrets, and how she came to know who was lying
to her. The story's gothicism allows her to draw attention to the barriers or constructions that conceal secrets, mask crime, and restrict
her access—because she is a lady, or should be—to information,
and to describe the cultural "magic or violence" necessary to break
them down.[25]

These patterns of spinsterhood, investigation, and narrative are
thrown into particularly vivid relief in Rinehart's 1933 novel, *The
Album*.[26] This novel is especially interesting on the subject of spinsters, because in it, one spinster investigates a murder committed by
another. In this work Rinehart focuses on the spinster as a symbol
of all that remained unresolved about women's roles and woman's
place in the transition from Victorian to modern culture, and she is
uncharacteristically focused on unhappy spinsters. Her central subject is the tenacity of the Victorian worldview among the women of
the upper classes, and she uses the pathologically repressed spinster
as a figure for all that can go wrong in the negotiation of women's
cultural and economic power. As in her 1917 novella, *The Confession,* in which a fastidious old maid murders her brother's mistress,
Rinehart shifts the terms that frame the pathological spinster as an

inside joke of the period, showing her less as an agent of Victorianism than as a product of its meanness and hypocrisy.[27] Her doctor feels that the root cause of the spinster's violent outburst was the shock of the "innocent" Miss Emily Benton learning about sex and reproduction. Our narrator, herself a middle-aged spinster, is more interested in the fact that the mistress was blackmailing the family to keep everything hushed up and thus draining away the inheritance that was Miss Emily's only means of support. Her Miss Emily is less overwhelmed than enraged when she kills the mistress; what our narrator finds fascinating and tragic is the fact that Miss Emily has a compulsive need to confess her crime even though she, like the narrator of Poe's "The Imp of the Perverse," has gotten away with the murder. Agnes Blakiston, the narrator, dedicates her narrative and investigative energies to replacing Miss Emily's written confession, so "merciless" to herself, with the detective-storyteller's version of absolution, situating the crime in a configuration of pressures and hypocrisies particular to Miss Emily's generation.

*The Album* is one of Rinehart's most sustained explorations of the conventionality of the life of the moneyed class; it is also, notably, one of her most violent stories. The juxtaposition of gentility and violence is the main point of the novel (and, arguably, of all Rinehart's detective novels); as the heroine realizes midway through the events of the novel, when little else seems clear: "[U]nder those carefully tended roofs, behind the polished windows with their clean draped curtains, through all the fastidious ordering of our days there had been unhappiness and revolt . . . hatred and murderous fury" (*A*, 261). Like *The Confession* and *The After House*, *The Album* is loosely based on a real murder case; in this instance, the notorious and unsolved Borden murders from the 1890s. The ways Rinehart alters and adapts the case for her detective novel are illuminating for what they tell us about both Rinehart's preoccupations as a writer and her interests as a social critic.

One morning in August 1892, a wealthy banker and mill director in Fall River, Massachusetts, named Andrew Borden was found murdered in the front parlor of his home; the body of his second wife, Abigail, was found in an upstairs bedroom. The victims had died from repeated blows to the head, face, and neck with a hatchet,

and the brutality of the murders, the boldness of the daylight attack, and the prestige of the victims added to the mystery and horror of the crime. Suspicion soon settled on Lizzie Borden, Andrew
Borden's thirty-four-year-old unmarried daughter, who admitted
being home at the time of the murders, but claimed she had neither
seen nor heard anything unusual before she discovered her father's
body near noon. She gave contradictory and evasive answers at the
coroner's inquest and was subsequently indicted by a grand jury. The
evidence against her was considerable: she was unable to give a con-
vincing account of her exact whereabouts in the Bordens' modest
two-story house at the time of her father's murder (she claimed to
have been "out in the barn," a shed not more than five yards from the
back of the main house, looking variously for lead to make sinkers
for fishing or for a piece of tin to fix a window screen). In addition,
she was cold to her stepmother even in death, and she was witnessed
three days after the murders burning a dress that she claimed was
ruined by stains from "brown paint." Although the prosecution presented a strong case based on the physical evidence and their belief
that she was motivated by a desire for her father's money, Lizzie was
acquitted of all charges.

The arrest and trial of Lizzie Borden fascinated the city of Fall
River and the surrounding region and was quickly picked up by the
New York City papers and the national press. The case resonated
with the questions of gender, class, race, and family structure that
were most at issue in American culture as the Victorian era gave
way to the modern period. In the arguments presented at the trial
and in the contemporaneous commentary on the case, the question of whether a genteel, native-born white woman could brutally
murder her parents for money was firmly connected to larger issues
about female capabilities of many kinds, especially those under consideration in the social debates over woman suffrage and female
education and employment.[28] The case presented a portrait of the
economic structure of family life that was at once peculiar to the
Bordens and expressive of broader concerns about women and economics in this period.

The prosecution argued that Lizzie and her elder sister, Emma,
had become concerned, even agitated, over the way their father was
handling his assets. The sisters discovered that Andrew had helped

his second wife's family by buying outright a house that belonged in part to Abigail's sister and deeding the property to Abigail. Emma and Lizzie demanded an equivalent gift, and their father gave them their grandfather's old house to rent out for income. If Lizzie and Emma come across as grasping, they may have developed that trait in response to their father's almost eccentric parsimony. Although he was a very wealthy man at the time of his death, with an estate of at least $300,000, he had begun his life as a poor relation to the rich and locally powerful Borden dynasty and had been an undertaker as a young man. His fortunes rose with the value of water rights and real estate as Fall River industrialized, and he became a successful businessman who sat on the boards of textile mills and banks, and a powerful landlord who built a large office building downtown and named it after himself. Despite his acquired fortune and old New England name, Andrew Borden never moved his family into the fashionable neighborhoods of the highly stratified city, keeping them in a modest house near the business district. The house had an awkward interior design and was missing some of the basic niceties of the urban upper-middle-class residence of the period, including gas, running water above the ground floor, and a proper bathroom.

Their father's unwillingness to participate in the norms of consumption and expenditure for his class must have put his daughters in an anomalous social position: they were of the ruling class but had little access to its resources. Their father seems to have provided enough of an allowance to see that Lizzie and Emma were respectably clothed, but Lizzie's main luxury in her young adult life seems to have been a tour of Europe she took in the company of several other young ladies from Fall River. There is some evidence that Lizzie felt this awkwardness; she belonged to a fashionable church and participated fully in its charitable and social functions. But she would not have been able to reciprocate in the sort of entertainments (supper parties, musical evenings) that her peers might have invited her to. Neither Lizzie nor Emma ever married, and we have to wonder how their father's disregard of the social culture of his class affected their prospects. While in some sectors of 1890s American society the unmarried gentlewoman was beginning to be understood as a symbol of independence and healthy rebellion against the Victorian past, Lizzie's life in conservative Fall River seems not to fit the early prototypes of the New Woman. She was not well educated, and she appears not to have sought a career of any kind, devoting her energies instead to her position on the board of the local hospital, the Women's Christian Temperance Union, teaching Sunday school, and other traditional occupations of the nineteenth-century spinster.

As unmarried women, Emma and Lizzie were financially dependent on their father not only for their present living but, through inheritance, for their entire futures. Had they been sons, their father surely would have taken them into one of his enterprises or given them some corner of his small empire to develop. But while Andrew might have been eccentric about money, he seems to have been entirely conventional in his thinking about its connection to gender roles. His single daughters could only hope to receive gifts of money and property during their father's life and, in the darker regions of their hearts, await his death. Their hostility toward their stepmother, which probably came from a number of sources, came to focus on her potential for redistributing property before Andrew's death and obtaining a substantial share of the estate after it. Before the dispute over Abigail's sister's house, Lizzie had called the woman who had raised her from four years old "Mother," but at some point afterward she began addressing her as "Mrs. Borden." [29]

Like the murders themselves, the story of the miserly patriarch hoarding his treasure against the demands of his daughters was an expression of the shadowy underside of the sunny middle-class ideologies of reciprocity, devotion, and generosity in family life. In its broad outlines and its small details, the Borden family history illustrated what those nineteenth-century ideologies stood guard against: the self-interest, material greed, and consequent antipathy that seemed to flourish under capitalism. This story was both disturbing and fascinating in its revelation of the primacy of financial considerations in the arrangement of the Borden family's emotional life. Although a shocking and aberrant event, the Borden murders resonated deeply with several of the central social questions of the day—especially the woman question—and it is little wonder that Lizzie Borden's trial and acquittal attracted national attention.

What is perhaps even more interesting is the way the case and the figure of Lizzie Borden lingered in the public imagination long after the trial. Gertrude Stein commented that on her return to America in 1934, "I was perfectly astonished to know that even the present generation knew the name of Lizzie Borden and that she had gone on living." [30] John Gill and Harriet Chessman have argued that Lizzie, who appears as the interlocutor of the narrative of *Blood on the Dining Room Floor,* was a figure of considerable fascination for Stein.[31] In 1936, Edith Wharton also wrote about Lizzie Borden in a story called "Confession," which explores the life an accused murderess might lead after her acquittal.[32] Rinehart's *The Album* (1933) came out in this same short period; the clustering of these works suggests that the case held an abiding interest for women of their generation.[33] They may have all been prompted to remember Lizzie Borden by the appearance of a series of biting essays by crime writer Edmund Pearson that were published over the period from 1924 to 1938, but, given the complexity of the phenomenon of cultural memory, it is difficult to state clearly whether those essays should be called a manifestation of interest in the murders in the late 1920s and early 1930s or a primary cause of that interest.[34] They do mark a clear point in the bibliographic history of the case: before the essays' appearance, there had been newspaper coverage of the murders, the arrest, and the trial, with an annual revisiting of the case by the *Fall River Globe* each August through Lizzie's death in 1927; there had been a book-length study of the case published in 1893 that quickly went out of print (because Lizzie bought up all the copies, legend has it); and there had been highly fictionalized retellings by Mary Wilkins Freeman and by Elizabeth Jordan in 1895 and by Pauline Hopkins in 1900.[35]

Pearson's writing on the case was both exhaustive and authoritative, and he has remained a major presence in the subsequent study of the case. He was convinced of Lizzie's guilt and gathered the complex details and contradictions of the case into a witty and engaging narrative of selfishness and deceit. Besides clarifying and recording the swirl of legend and rumor surrounding the case, his work is most significant for the way it demonstrates that the revival of interest in Lizzie Borden in the 1920s and 1930s was a product of the final stages of the transition from Victorian to modern American culture. He used his essays as a platform from which to poke fun at Victorian tastes and customs. In his descriptions of the scenes of the Borden murders, he gives scornful catalogues of the furnishings, noting that the sitting-room floor was "covered with the usual garish, flowered carpet, customary in houses at that time, and the wall paper was of a similarly disturbing pattern." He remarks that the guest-room furniture would be "familiar to most of us," with "all the heaviness of the Victorian style of decoration: the carpet with gigantic clusters of impossible roses, the ponderous bed with carved head- and front-boards in some dark wood." He continues in this vein, describing by evoking memories of the lingering Victorian past in his readers, commenting that on the bureau near Abigail's corpse were "a lace-covered pin-cushion and two white bottles or cruets, theoretically for scent or toilet water, precisely placed but purely ornamental, since nobody ever knew such receptacles to contain anything at all." [36]

The essays are especially fierce on the subject of Lizzie Borden herself, whom Pearson saw as a window onto the foolishness and fakery of Victorian womanhood, sarcastically describing the woman's rights advocates and "sob-sister" reporters who had defended Lizzie in the press as doing so "ecstatically" rather than logically. He felt that Lizzie had gotten away with her murders because the conventionality of the age had blinded both official authorities and the public at large, something he states most openly in one of his last pieces on the case, the introduction to his edited version of the trial transcript. There he writes, "It should be understood that all who came to the house after the discovery of the murders, whether they came as friends to fan the 'poor dear girl' and flutter about her, or whether they came as police officers to investigate and report, had but one idea. It was that some fiend, some unknown assassin had entered and done the ghastly deed." The combination of misogyny and disdain for the Victorians reaches its sarcastic climax as Pearson continues: "There were few careful or shrewd observers in the house that day. With friends and neighbors it was: 'Why Lizzie, you poor darling! It's God's own mercy that fearful creature didn't kill you too!' Less emotional persons were either handicapped by exaggerated ideas of gallantry; or were awe-stricken in the presence of an heiress; or else they were godly folk, blinded by sectarian prejudice. All that third and last class needed to know was that nothing but spotless virtue has ever surrounded a secretary and treasurer of the Young People's Society for Christian Endeavor." [37]

While there is a certain level of personal animosity in Pearson's discussions of Lizzie Borden, his ridicule of her and the genteel culture of the 1890s was very much an expression of certain intellectual developments of his day. As Wayne Hobson argues, we can see in Pearson's writing the typical patterns of the modernist critique of Victorianism: an "attack on what they now portrayed as the moral repressiveness, stultifying conformity, and empty materialism of American middle-class culture." Drawing on Anthony Hilfer's conclusions about the bohemian argument with America between the wars, Hobson argues that the Borden literature of the 1930s through the 1960s is characterized by this modernist "attack on conformity" and its accompanying theme of the "recovery of the buried life."[38] Pearson's work, the foundational material for all that followed, concentrates its energies on the attack on conformity. Rinehart, who surely read Pearson, produced a version of the Borden murders that much more carefully and imaginatively explores the connections between conformity and the burial of the inner life. *The Album* shows the possibilities of the Borden family story in the hands of a writer whose own central interests so closely parallel its themes: the place of the spinster, the relation of money and independence for women, the hypocrisy of domestic ideology.[39]

Rinehart's novel suggests a great deal about the reasons for the renewed notoriety of the Borden murders in the 1920s and 1930s, and, by extension, about questions of women and crime in those decades. Set in the early 1930s, *The Album* is in large part about the symbolic and emotional resonances of money, especially for women. It draws connections between monetary dependence and female conformity, on the one hand, and between knowledge, defiance, and the undoing of metaphorical live burials, on the other. It is one of Rinehart's most historical novels, for it not only engages actual historical events like the Crash, the early years of the Depression, gold hoarding, and Roosevelt's revaluation of paper money, but also examines the relation of the past and the present as an integral part of the mystery. Its depiction of spinsterhood, especially in the way it sets up a contrast between old- and new-style spinsters, echoes the patterns in other magazine fiction of the period. The main murder is a symbolic (if not actual) matricide, and, in its violence and intractability of solution, is a metaphor for the necessity of overthrowing the Victorian past. To Rinehart, Lizzie Borden, the daughter who killed her parents to gain their money and her independence, seems to express central facts about the status of women in this transitional period. In Rinehart's novel, there are Lizzie Borden figures who embody the repressive Victorian past and others who are expressions of a more modern, resistant present, a justifiably complex use of that daughter of the late nineteenth century.

Rinehart's reshaping of the Borden murders into a work of detective fiction shows her characteristic themes and concerns. *The Album* begins with the murder of an elderly woman in her bed; she has been hacked to death with an axe, and her two unmarried daughters come under suspicion once the initial hysteria about intruders quiets down. It is revealing that in her only explicit reference to the historical crime, Rinehart has her narrator muse, "[H]adn't Lizzie Borden been accused of having killed her stepmother with an axe?" (*A,* 276). The prosecutor's closing arguments explicitly stated that the murder of Andrew Borden was the more offensive and serious crime, and contemporary newspaper accounts and most subsequent retellings share that focus on patricide.[40] Rinehart's interest in the tensions of mother-daughter relations in a period of rapid social change reshapes the story into one about the murder of mothers, not fathers. As in the Borden case, the main family is a blended one, but in the novel the father is the stepparent, and a beloved one. The mother is the miser, hoarding the family fortune in a trunk under her bed, and that money is presumed to be the motive for her murder. The novel, like the actual case, includes two unmarried daughters living at home, but makes both of them suspects (in the real case, Emma Borden was away when the murders occurred) and has one of them, like Lizzie, give confusing inquest testimony while under the influence of prescribed morphine. Like the Bordens, Rinehart's Lancaster family is very particular about locking doors and windows, a habit that makes investigation of the crime both easier and more difficult. The murder occurs in broad daylight in August, as did the Borden murders, and the burning of bloodstained garments is an important part of the story. As in all Rinehart novels, the narrative of murder is only one layer in a total complex effect, and the Lizzie Borden parallels extend ultimately to the storyteller's own situation.

The setting of *The Album* is a small cluster of mansions in the close suburbs of an unnamed city. The Crescent, as this neighborhood is known, is inhabited by five families with very old money, some of whom are related. It is an enclave of Victorian bourgeois values and behaviors that are increasingly anachronistic as the Depression takes hold. The families of the Crescent retain the hairstyles and clothing of the 1890s, keep full staffs of servants, dress for dinner, and attend to the details of housekeeping with old-fashioned schedules, methods, and equipment. The householders of the Crescent adhere not just to the past, but to a kind of common culture that has evolved over time in the neighborhood. They all work very hard to maintain the outward elements of this culture (breakfast before eight, washday on Monday, the leaving of calling cards for visits after four o'clock), while at the same time keeping a sharp eye out for any deviance on the part of their neighbors. Surveillance is the connective energy in an otherwise formal set of relationships; it is facilitated by the maids' walks that run between the kitchens of these houses and allow for the transfer of gossip from kitchen to parlor, and their culture of discreet knowingness produces a number of widely known but seldom discussed secrets, many of which come to light in the course of the story.

The novel, narrated by the youngest resident of the community, a twenty-eight-year-old woman named Louisa Hall, depicts this deliberate anachronism as both stultifying and slightly creepy. Looking back on the place where she grew up, Louisa calls it "a strange and perhaps not very healthy human garden" (*A*, 14). All of the families display some peculiarity, especially when it comes to clinging to the past and holding grudges; one outsider declares that the place is marked by "old quarrels and freakish ideas" (*A*, 247). Mrs. Wellington leaves her husband periodically and takes up residence in a nearby hotel; the Daltons live together but do not speak for more than two decades after the wife discovers the husband's infidelity; the Talbots' matriarch has an obsession with keeping doors locked; the elderly mother in the Lancaster household requires a full schedule of fussing and coddling from her two unmarried daughters; and in the last household, a widow has worn mourning for more than twenty years and has prevented her daughter (Louisa Hall) from marrying so that she will not be lonely in her old age. We can see a pattern of women, especially the mothers, exerting power in de-

structive ways, but the Crescent itself sees most of this behavior as
outward expressions of inner rectitude.

The murder that sets the novel in motion would be shocking in
any setting, but it is especially so within the self-satisfied gentility
of this neighborhood. One summer afternoon, elderly Mrs. Lancaster, the querulous invalid with two daughters, is found murdered
in her bed, killed by repeated blows from an axe. Given the routines of the household, including the family's penchant for locking
doors and windows, the possibility of an unknown intruder seems
remote. Suspicion settles quickly, if horrifyingly, on the two daughters, Emily and Margaret, who claim to have been in their respective
bedrooms at the time of the slaying. The motive would seem to be a
desperate desire to put an end to the old lady's incessant demands;
her sister-in-law is the first to voice this view, remarking, "I suppose
they stood it as long as they could" (*A*, 29). When the police discover
that a large trunk in which the deceased was hoarding gold is empty,
the filial crime seems more pointed, and the portrait of a family
in violent turmoil broadens when Emily is herself found murdered,
shot with her father's gun. The entire Crescent is in distress: under
siege by the press, guarded and watched by the police, subject to fits
of suspicion about each other.

The narrator is herself involved in the events and anxieties of the
story. An old flame (Jim Wellington, also raised in this neighborhood) needs her help to keep certain falsely incriminating evidence
hidden from the police. In addition, her mother's house harbors
an important clue to the murders, the search for which puts her in
physical danger on several occasions. She also becomes romantically
involved with one of the police detectives on the case. But, as in
other Rinehart novels, the ways Louisa's investigation of the crime
resonate with a process of self-discovery are the most important
points of the novel. Here, that paradigm works especially neatly because Louisa Hall is coming to terms with the repressiveness of her
upbringing at the same time she is uncovering the suppressed facts
of the crime.

The concept of emotional and sexual repression is an explicit
one in Rinehart's and Louisa's sense of how the Crescent functions.
While Louisa introduces the idea lightly, making fun of newspaper
reports that refer to her as a "youngish spinster . . . who had been

abnormally repressed and was therefore by intimation more or less psychopathic as a result" (*A*, 15), there is ultimately a lot of credence given in the novel to the concept of repression leading to outburst. Helen Wellington, a daringly modern young woman married to the young heir of a Crescent family, is the character who is most an outsider to the neighborhood. Years before Louisa begins to see the place as an "unhealthy human garden," the more earthy and insightful Helen expresses a mixture of alarm and amusement about what might happen there, saying, "[Y]our Crescent scares me to death. Too much steam in the boiler and no whistle to use it up" (*A*, 113). Dr. Armstrong, a general practitioner with a grasp of basic psychoanalytic concepts, is certain that the axe murder could have been committed by someone from the neighborhood. He only half-jokingly describes the Crescent as a "fine neuro-psychiatric institute. . . . Look at that Talbot woman, with her mania, no less, for locking doors!" (*A*, 109). In a voice that echoes popularized Freudianism, he reasons that decades of the repression of rage and the rigid control of feelings create a pressurized psyche, one capable of being driven to "extreme violence."

In this novel, as in other artifacts of popular culture of the period, the concept of repression is most visible as a problem for and about women. Dr. Armstrong diagnoses the pathology of the Crescent as "too many virgins here now, and not only the unmarried ones" (*A*, 258), contending that the female sexual drive, if thwarted, will manifest itself in other, less healthy ways. Spinsters are the most obvious figures for repression in the novel, being both virginal and knowledgeable, and there are several who play important roles in the story. The main question of the first three-fourths of the novel is which daughter—Margaret or Emily—killed Mrs. Lancaster. While in both cases the motive for the killing would be the same (rage at the emotional and financial greediness of the mother), the meaning of the killing would differ somewhat depending on which spinster had turned murderess. Miss Emily Lancaster has always been eccentric—wearing only white dresses (like Emily Dickinson), never leaving the house except to walk to the library, doting on a canary. Although only middle-aged, she acts like an older woman, fussing over the small details of daily life. Like the Miss Emily of *The Confession*, she is generally understood to be mildly crazy, but had been assumed to be harmless up until the murders. She typifies the nineteenth-century style of spinsterhood—docile, helpful, and dependent—and she represents the current of madness that runs through twentieth-century figurations of that type. A plot that revealed her as a matricide would be one that focused on the unpredictability of the sweetly dithering old maid.

Margaret Lancaster represents a different type of unmarried woman, one emerging in the 1920s and 1930s. Like the self-described new-style spinsters quoted at the beginning of this chapter, Margaret is dissatisfied with the life of usefulness and dependency that spinsterhood still signals to her family. Margaret, "good-looking, intelligent, and restless," suffers the same limitations that her sister does, but "never had given up as had Emily" (*A*, 101). She longs for independence and does her best to carve out a more modern life for herself. She dresses fashionably, goes into the city regularly, and, as we discover, has been having an affair with one of her married neighbors. As it turns out, she had been engaged to this man many years ago, and her mother originally took to her bed to protest and prevent that marriage. If Margaret had done the killing, the murder would have expressed more clearly a generational conflict—not just between a daughter and mother, but the rebellion of the new-style spinster against older Victorian notions of womanhood.

In this novel, even maiden ladies have maiden aunts, and Emily and Margaret's is Lydia Talbot. She is older and sterner than her nieces, a "perfect specimen of the dependent female of the [eighteen-]nineties" (*A*, 16). She is dependent because her eldest brother, who had control of the family fortune, left her nothing in his will, and she has been reduced to circulating between her two sisters-in-law. (The one with whom she lives is Mrs. Jonathan Talbot, whose husband is in an insane asylum; the second, whom she helps care for daily, is the remarried widow of Lydia's eldest brother—and the murder victim—Mrs. Lancaster.) Lydia Talbot is "prim and late-Victorian" (*A*, 221), intimidating and morbid, the "high priestess of our funeral rites" (*A*, 317). She represents a dark side of women's power in Victorian culture, the sort of death-dealing propriety that Mark Twain parodies in his depiction of Emmeline Grangerford.

Lydia Talbot is, in fact, the murderer, and she kills three people in the course of the novel: Mrs. Lancaster, Emily Lancaster, and a maid named Lizzie Cromwell who goes in pursuit of her. Two of the murders are extremely grisly; not only does she use an axe to kill her first victim, she decapitates her last one and carries the head around in a satchel for a short time. We also learn that in the past she killed her brother's mistress, and that he took the fall for her, loyally accepting incarceration in an asylum. Her motivations are complex and unclear. She killed her brother's mistress, some feel, out of an incestuous jealousy. She kills Mrs. Lancaster partly out of hatred, partly to protect her brother, who has escaped from the insane asylum and whom the unpleasant Mrs. Lancaster is threatening to expose, and partly to get her hands on the money, which would make up for the inheritance she feels she and her brother have been robbed of through a forged will. The plot of this novel becomes convoluted around these points, but the confusion about Lydia Talbot's motivation only reinforces our sense that she is unpredictable and unknowable. Dr. Armstrong offers a psychoanalytic explanation, the "theory of murder being a reaction from extreme repression": " 'Like most of you, she lived an unnatural life,' he said. 'Maybe she started only by wanting to escape that, and the money would do that for her. But there was something else, too. She'd shot and killed that woman years ago, and her brother had suffered the punishment for it. That must have weighed on her for many years, and now came the old woman's threat to send him back to it, and she went plain crazy' " (*A,* 369). This medical explanation makes sense and offers partial truths, but it doesn't connect down to the deeper cultural and symbolic levels of the text. The only real resonance is with the phrase "unnatural life," which both expresses Rinehart's social critique of the life Victorianism prescribed for women and puts a name to the gothic horror of the story. Lydia is a transgressive, unplaced figure; besides shuttling between two households, she wears pads under her clothing to make her angular body appear more conventionally feminine (linking her to the "mannish lesbian" figure), and she "blacks" her face when she goes on her various nocturnal missions (suggesting a whole subterranean set of associations with the race prejudices of the period). She is also hard to place in terms of generational affiliation; she is actually one of the oldest of the three generations of women on the Crescent, but her position as a dependent places her functionally and emotionally in the position of a daughter.

In this novel, the blurred motivation suffices because Lydia is most important to us as an archetype: the madwoman in the attic. She is the superfluous female relative who, like Bertha Rochester, threatens to upset all the order of the domestic circle. We learn, near the end, that Mrs. Talbot's obsession with locked doors was a strategy to protect herself against Lydia, and that Lizzie Cromwell was Lydia's "keeper." Lydia is cruel and cunning, willing to kill Emily and Lizzie to hide the murder of her sister-in-law and gleefully framing others for her misdeeds. When she murders Lizzie Cromwell, she removes her victim's head so that she can swap clothes and identities for her getaway (becoming, in case we missed the point, another Lizzie); that act of appropriation, along with the fury of the axe murder, suggests that her propensities are not just violent but annihilatory. She is the embodiment of the Victorian past as well, and is a particular source of anxiety for our narrator, Louisa Hall.

Louisa is the fourth important spinster on the Crescent, and she is terrorized by the specter of the pathological spinster in ways both literal and figurative. Through a complicated series of events, Louisa's mother has been entrusted with the care of an old photo album, something Lydia Talbot wants desperately once she remembers that she left bloody fingerprints on it after the murder of Mrs. Lancaster. On three separate occasions, she breaks into the Hall house at night to search for the album and encounters Louisa, attacking her in the dark. She becomes the sort of unseen, demonic presence in the house that we have seen Rinehart employ elsewhere, made invisible by her spinster's black clothing, her trick of "blackening" her face, and the sneakiness learned from decades of minding her place. Along with Emily and Margaret, she is an image of Louisa's spinsterly fate if she remains in the neighborhood. Louisa's encounters with her, in the middle of the night on the top floor of the house where she has lived all her life, are encounters with the gothic female doppelganger, the repressed and returning madwoman. More specifically, Lydia, the woman who does not have a home or income of her own, is the most visible symbol of the displacements that characterize the life of the unmarried woman in this weirdly Victorian world. This question of what life on the Crescent means for women is the point at which Louisa's detective work and her personal narrative meet, and, as in *The Circular Staircase,* live burial operates as a central gothic trope and as a main point in the feminist critique. When she and Helen Wellington first met, eight years before the events of the story, Helen remarked that Louisa was "pretty well buried alive" and urged her to "beat it" (*A*, 18) while she still could. At the time, Louisa didn't see things her way, but the crime spree in her neighborhood opens her eyes to how the place has "contracted our lives." For its female residents, the anachronism of the Crescent is especially acute: "Out in the world women were taking their places and living their own lives, but our small rules of living and conduct ignored all that" (*A*, 275).

Once Louisa is able to see this "slavery of the unimportant" (*A*, 275), she begins to consider Emily and Margaret Lancaster as suspects. When confronted by evidence that Emily stole the money from her mother (which turns out to be true), Louisa at first resists, thinking "to accept that [Emily was a thief] was to revalue all the Crescent, to doubt every one of us, and to wonder whether under our cloaks of dignified and careful living we were not all frauds and hypocrites" (*A*, 264). If that statement is a familiar moment in Rinehart's mysteries, so is the next mental move that Louisa makes: "[I]f Emily had taken that money, it opened up something so dreadful that I was afraid to face it" (*A*, 275).

To understand why the idea of Emily Lancaster stealing from her mother so agitates Louisa, we need to consider Louisa's own life on the Crescent. Although twenty-eight years old, she has little independence, or even simple privacy, from her mother. She does not possess a house key, and she sleeps with her bedroom door open in case her mother needs her in the night. When Louisa needs, on behalf of Jim Wellington, to conceal a small object after the first murder, she realizes that there are no hiding places in a house that undergoes rigorous weekly cleaning. Indeed, about nine years before the events of the novel, her mother found a love letter in Louisa's bureau and thus discovered the attachment between her daughter and Jim. She forced them to break off the romance, and Jim married Helen instead of Louisa. The murders in the neighborhood force Louisa to review that old disappointment and her decision to fulfill her duty to her "still grieving mother" (*A*, 299). For Louisa, the mysterious events of the novel raise questions about the deals and decisions women of her class make, about the benignity of a mother's wishes, and about the motivations of matricide.

Louisa's greatest psychological crisis comes after the death of Emily Lancaster. She is brought to the point of nervous collapse by one moment in the scene of chaos and grief that follows the discovery of Emily's body on a path behind the houses: the picture of Helen Wellington, cigarette in hand, "strolling nonchalantly in her gaudy pajamas to where poor Emily lay dead" (*A*, 186). In ways she isn't able to articulate, Louisa is deeply disturbed by the "sheer contrast" between the two women, and we might attribute the source of the "strain" the image produces in her mind to her sense that she must choose between the two kinds of lives Emily and Helen lead. Emily represents spinsterhood, resignation to duty, the perpetuation of Victorian traditions of virtue, gender, and class; Helen, a lousy housekeeper, a rebellious wife, and a free spirit, lives a shallow but modern life of leisure. Louisa's comparison of herself with Helen is natural, given the fact that Jim married Helen instead of her. Louisa also sees herself in Emily. Despite his best efforts to calm her, Louisa becomes hysterical when Dr. Armstrong says, "[D]on't you let this get too far under your skin, Lou. You have your own life to lead, you know." Louisa replies "as I had never spoken before," exclaiming in front of her mother and the doctor, "I haven't lived any of my own life yet. I'm like Miss Emily in that. . . . I'm sick and tired of controlling myself. What does it lead to? A bullet in the dark, and nothing to carry away with one. No life, no anything. I wanted to marry and couldn't and now—" Here the speech ends as Louisa breaks down and her mother angrily leaves the room.

Helen Wellington, Emily Lancaster, and Lydia Talbot all represent possibilities of the kind of woman Louisa might become as she enters her thirties, and all three possibilities are deeply distressing. The woman she finds most interesting is Margaret Lancaster, with her independence and intelligence. The two women find an unexpected intimacy at the beginning of the novel, working together to remove evidence tending to incriminate Jim Wellington from the Lancaster house. One of the old secrets Louisa learns in the course of the novel is the story of Margaret's engagement to Bryan Dalton and her mother's adoption of invalidism to keep her at home, a story almost identical with Louisa's own thwarted romance. In a novel that makes so much of architecture as a symbolic structure, we cannot fail to note the significance of the fact that Louisa's bedroom "corresponds" to Margaret's in the floor plan of their twin houses. Over the course of the novel, Louisa comes to understand the correspondence between their situations as daughters of a particularly inflexible subculture of the upper class and, more specifically, as daughters of domineering and selfish mothers. It is therefore crucial to note that while Louisa admires Margaret most of all the women in the novel, she becomes convinced that it was Margaret who killed Mrs. Lancaster. Louisa's convictions about Margaret are fiercer and firmer than her suspicions about anyone else on the Crescent, an interesting twist in light of the fact that they are completely misplaced (Emily, whom Louisa is so reluctant to suspect of anything, turns out to be the one who stole the gold, and Lydia, as already noted, killed Mrs. Lancaster and Emily).

Her belief that the woman she admires is a killer has everything to do with Louisa's own circumstances. The murder and its investigation occasion a number of moments of memory and self-examination, and Louisa gradually becomes aware of how unhappy she is and why. Her involvement in the murder investigation allows her to see the literal and more figurative congruences between her place in her mother's house and the place of the putatively matricidal Margaret. At one level, she is learning about Margaret's secret past — her broken engagement, her continuing affair with the man after he marries someone else and remains in the neighborhood — and about the toll that years of caregiving have taken on her. She may fear that she, like Margaret, will end up killing her mother, or wish that she could. Over the course of the book, she begins to defy her mother in small ways; her refusal to attend a funeral leads to the following heated exchange:

> "Really, sometimes I wonder if all this trouble hasn't done something very strange to you."
>
> "I'm afraid it has, mother . . . I suppose it has taught me my right to live while I can. To live my own life, not yours, mother."
>
> She stared at me with incredulous eyes.
>
> "And that to me from my own child! All I have left, after years of sacrifice for her!" (*A*, 330)

Whenever they argue, which is often in this two-week period, Mrs. Hall makes a pronouncement of this sort, exclaiming, "I wonder how I ever bore a child so—so undutiful" (*A*, 114); and "[Y]ou seem to think you owe me no consideration whatever" (*A*, 94). Despite these manipulative scoldings, Louisa continues to distance herself from her mother, eventually marrying against her wishes and moving away from the neighborhood. To Louisa, the violence of the "troubles" reveals the danger of succumbing to the trap, baited with luxury, of trading independence for safety and comfort.

Her first moment of awareness that she has made a bad deal occurs as she prepares for bed on the evening after the murders: "I remember standing in the center of my room and looking about me. My sense of security was badly shaken that night, and suddenly I realized that I had given up everything else for it, had sacrificed to it my chance to live and even my chance to love. And for what? That my bed should be neatly turned down at night and the house run smoothly, with fresh flowers in the proper season and the table napkins ironed first on the wrong side and then polished on the right?" (*A*, 73). This understanding that obedience to her mother is commensurate with obedience to the norms and traditions of her class culminates in the argument with her mother about the funeral. When her mother huffs about the sacrifices she has made, Louisa replies: "Haven't I been the sacrifice, mother? Isn't this whole Crescent a monument to the sacrifice of some one or other? And to what? To security? Then where is it? To how things look? They don't look so well just now, do they?" (*A*, 330).

Rinehart's plot of matricide explores the sacrificial culture of the Crescent, which Louisa comes to understand as having "contracted our lives"—that is, the lives of all the women who live there. The men go off to their jobs, clubs, and golf games, but the women stay close to home, govern themselves sternly, and attend to the minutiae of remaining anachronistic. When all is said and done, this novel doesn't offer a precise picture of what a woman's life should be, but it does offer a clear sense of what it should not be. As Helen puts it, "[T]hat's living? To know how many napkins go into the wash each week?" (*A*, 122). Female sexuality is thoroughly embedded in these configurations of tradition and class, within this novel and in the culture at large. Strict regulation of female sexuality was a crucial and defining activity of the middle and upper classes of the Victorian era, a fact that added to the sense of conflict and turmoil that surrounded new definitions of women's sexuality in the post-Freudian period of the 1920s and 1930s.[41] The mother-daughter relationships in *The Album* are infused with this same understanding of conflict: arguments about behavior of all kinds and struggles over money are really about the mother's fear of deviance from class norms (or the breach of "appearances") and the daughter's desire for independence and a sense of progress. In *The Album*, sexuality is what mothers most need to control, and the withholding of money is the method of choice.

If adherence to tradition is the driving principle of all the older women's lives, then calculated subterfuge is the resort of the daughters. Liberation is a game of daughterly wits in this novel, and there are comic and far more serious versions of it throughout the book. Louisa reports that every trip home from boarding school was preceded by a bout of sewing to lower her hems and followed by another session to raise them back up. Mothers are not easily deceived, however, especially when it comes to any kind of alteration of the interior landscape of their households. In this world, every item is, as Helen notes, counted and recorded before and after each washday; all old clothing, household goods, and furniture are wrapped, precisely labeled, and stored in the attic. Early in the novel, Louisa describes the difficulty of discarding anything in her mother's house in a story about her pincushion, a once useful but now merely obligatory object (like the bureau ornaments Pearson describes so vividly). She relates that after her return home after graduation from boarding school, she attempted to throw it away, but discovered it the next day "firmly in its place again. . . . [I]t squatted there as if to remind me that life was short, but that it was still there; that it would always be there" (*A*, 73). The reappearance of the pincushion, never explained, drives her to hysterical laughter and tears and becomes "always symbolic" of the persistence of the status quo in her mother's household and the apparent impossibility of change or disencumbrance. Because of the sharp maternal eye, it is also extremely difficult to hide anything in the house, as Louisa's experience with her love letter has proved.

Since actually discarding anything old or adding anything new is well-nigh impossible, daughters and other troublemakers use sometimes elaborate schemes of substitution and replacement to outwit the mothers. Mrs. Lancaster puts on the most stubborn display of material and political conservatism in the novel with her hoarding of gold, which has many historical and cultural associations. She has lost her faith in banks, so she wants to keep her money at home, and she has lost faith in the monetary system, so she demands gold coin. Gold hoarding was a phenomenon of post-Crash nervousness, and demanding one's savings in specie was understood, at least in high-minded quarters, to be the height of selfishness and near-sightedness. In March 1933, President Franklin Roosevelt closed the nation's banks for four days to stop depositors from withdrawing their savings in gold.[42] *The Album* began running as a serial in April, just as the government imposed new restrictions on the withdrawal, foreign exchange, or private holding of gold, so a plot that included gold hoarding would have meant a great deal to its initial readers.[43] Mrs. Lancaster's greed is of the most ignoble sort; her determination to gather gold is at odds with the civic-minded, philanthropic values that are supposed to ameliorate the iniquities of wealth in this period.

In the world of American domestic fiction, an obsession with money for money's sake is a signally masculine vice, rendering Mrs. Lancaster an even more monstrous figure. Like a troll or hag from a Victorian fairy tale, she never leaves her treasure, which is connected by its location under her bed with sex and childbirth. By gothic convention, the chest in which the gold is stored is a metaphorical human chest, trunk, and—more to the point—womb. The layered associations of a trunk of gold make Emily Lancaster's thievery all the more interesting. In fact, it is hard for some in the novel to even view Miss Emily's removal of the money as a crime, wondering if it is "theft to take what will be yours someday and what you may feel you have earned a dozen times" (*A*, 291). Mrs. Lancaster is not just hoarding against the masses, she is holding out against her own daughters, denying them, in her conventionality and traditionalism, the means to live independently and more happily in the present. She wants them home with her so they can perform all manner of personal services for her, denying them marriage, career, or vocation. The money is valuable to both mother and daughters because it is both very concretely gold and very abstractly something else: to the mother, the virginity, loyalty, and labor of the daughters; to the daughters, the means of self-determination.

Emily outwits her mother by reversing the basic substitution her mother made (of real gold for the more theoretical asset of a bankbook), removing the gold in small amounts and substituting worthless lead to keep the moneybags misleadingly heavy. The weights she uses to fool her mother are dressmaker's weights, usually sewn into the hems of old-fashioned dresses to help keep ankles and calves covered, an especially cute trick for a daughter to play on a mother in this novel. Emily has devised a set of hollowed-out books to carry away the modest quantities of gold she purloins while sitting up with her sleeping mother, and she smuggles out her book-boxes under the guise of returning books to the library. In reality she is taking the gold to her own trunk, which is in a boarding-house room she has rented under a false name, claiming to be a nurse at a nearby hospital (thus professionalizing her status as a caregiver). In this make-believe world, where Emily has a job and a room of her own, she reads travel brochures and counts her own illicit hoard.

Her theft, or perhaps her mother's, initiates a long chain of devious and increasingly violent acts of substitution. After Emily's death, the trunk and its contents are stolen in a complex subplot, but end up in the hands of Lydia and John Talbot (the brother who escaped from the insane asylum). Lydia has one more killing to do; she must get rid of a nosy maid who knows everything, and she disposes of the corpse with the help of her brother. In a truly ghastly development that amplifies the hints of incest in their relationship, Lydia and her brother decapitate and undress the maid's body, swap its clothing with Lydia's, stuff it in the emptied trunk, and leave the trunk at a railroad station. In this way Lydia hopes to effect a clean getaway, since the police will believe that she is dead. These substitutions are linked by the gothic trope of feminized boxes, trunks, and chests as the hiding places of dangerous secrets and by the fact that they are in each case shameful (the unpatriotic hoarding) or criminal (the theft and the murder). These exchanges set up an economy of substitution, wherein the replacement item is close enough to the original to be plausibly counterfeit, and wherein the act of replacement is profitable or empowering.

Alongside that plot of linked substitutions is another game of wits, the one being played between Louisa and her mother. From the beginning, Louisa is certain that her mother knows more about the Crescent in general and the murders in particular than she is telling (which is true), and her mother senses that Louisa is not telling her about the extent and nature of her involvement with the private detective Jim Wellington has called in (also true). Just as Louisa develops theories in her mind and settles on various residents of the Crescent as suspects, so does her mother, who accuses Emily, Mrs. Talbot, and her chauffeur in turn, but won't explain her reasoning completely. During the daylight hours, Louisa continues to act the part of the dutiful daughter, "putting iced cloths on her [mother's] head . . . and raising and lowering the shades" (*A*, 109), but at night she waits for her mother to fall asleep and commences her own clandestine activities.

The first episodes concern the evidence that tends to incriminate Jim Wellington: a glove that Margaret finds near the crime scene (laundry marks inside indicate that it is Jim's). This glove is heavily symbolized in the text. On the one hand, so to speak, it is associated with the loss of virginity: it belongs to her first love and is given to her by Margaret, the adulterer, to hide ("slip it into your stocking," the older woman counsels); its fingers are phallically stiffened and covered with blood; and it is stained with an unguent with a "pungent, familiar" odor that Louisa can't place but her mother readily identifies (as shoe polish). On the other hand, the glove is presented like a letter, for Margaret gives it to Louisa sealed inside a white envelope, and Louisa immediately thinks of the love letter from Jim, the one her mother discovered ten years before, as she tries to think of a place to conceal it. On two successive nights, she creeps around her mother's house in the dark, moving the glove from one hiding place to another, like a teenager looking for a safe place for a tryst, and she is accosted by the private detective (the man she is about to fall in love with) just as she prepares to throw the glove into the furnace.

That she manages to outwit her mother and do what she wants with the glove is exciting for her, a triumphant rescripting of the incident of the love letter. Her encounter with Herbert Dean starts in motion a low-key courtship plot that ends in marriage, against her mother's emphatic wishes, and removal from the Crescent. If the heterosexual romance that the glove subplot and the novel's ending celebrate seems a little tame to us, we have to remember the historical context that codes Louisa's determination to make a love life for herself as liberatory. We should also be comforted by the facts that Herbert Dean is a good friend of the free-spirited Helen and that the prospect of marrying him induces Louisa to buy a chiffon nightgown, the sight of which causes her mother to make one of her meaningful exits from a room.

More immediately, her success with the glove gives Louisa the confidence to continue her "nocturnal investigations" of her mother's house. The competition for knowledge escalates between them and comes to center on the whereabouts of an old photograph album. About the same time Margaret gave Louisa Hall the glove, she gave Mrs. Hall this album for safekeeping. Because Lydia got bloody fingerprints on it during the murder but forgot to take it away from the scene, and because it contains the picture the police need to identify one of the suspects, it is a valuable and dangerous book. Margaret Lancaster, who believes the bloody fingerprints are her sister's and cut them out, wrapped the book in brown paper and gave it to Louisa's mother, and it ends up in the abandoned schoolroom of their house. At the request of the private detective, Louisa is searching the house for the album at night, and these campaigns are the occasions for her encounters with the wraithlike Lydia Talbot, who is likewise trying to find the book. The album, then, is both a graphic remnant of the Victorian past (and of Helen Wellington's observation that everyone on the Crescent looks as if they "had walked out of an album of the nineties") and an object of struggle between Louisa and her mother, on the one hand, and between Louisa and Lydia, on the other.

The struggle, of course, is not just over possession of the album, but also over control of *The Album*. From the beginning, Mrs. Hall has tried to stifle Louisa's interest in the case, making it clear that she knows certain secrets about the Crescent that she will not tell her daughter, and even warning her daughter that continued investigation will result in people getting hurt. Louisa sees her silence as a manifestation of the Crescent's "loathing of publicity, its distrust of the police, and its firm belief that every man's house is his castle" (*A,* 153). She also feels, looking back, that her mother "could have helped if she had wanted to" and that her refusal to tell what she knows about the Talbot family resulted in two of the murders. So, not only is Louisa's narrative a challenge to the supremacy of "appearances," it is also morally superior to her mother's silence as a product of the negotiation of gender, crime, and storytelling.

Louisa's narrative is the culminating substitution in the drama of replacement that the novel presents. The symbolic double of the defaced and hidden photograph album is Miss Emily's book-box, which is likewise cut into and likewise the repository of a carefully guarded secret. Both of these books are associated with and mutilated by female criminal acts, and both are what *The Album,* in the end, replaces. Read as Louisa's autobiography, *The Album* is the story of moving forward from the lingering Victorian past into the modern age and of eluding a monstrous mother without killing her, and it thus replaces both the script of maternal conservatism and the plot of matricide. The narrative Louisa offers is one in which analysis, investigation, and knowledge are ultimately liberating. She is a rebel, like Margaret, Emily, and Lydia, and what frees her from the unhappiness of women's lives on the Crescent is her ability to see the exchanges being demanded of her (of independence for security) and the ways she is being silenced. When she finds the photograph album in the room where she was schooled as a child, she reflects, "I was a child again, being told to be a little lady. I was an adolescent girl, curious about a thousand things which no one thought I ought to know" (*A,* 299).

However, Louisa lacks Margaret's, Emily's, and Lydia's destructive energies: she writes new texts instead of mutilating old ones. That kinship and difference are emblematized in Louisa's use of a scrapbook of press clippings collected by Lydia as she prepares her narrative of the murders and their investigation. Where Lydia could only cut up newspapers and assemble the fragments into a "neat and . . . lurid" book (or album), Louisa writes a rounded narrative, full of the self-reflexive retrospection and considerations of causes and effects that constitute epistemological education in Rinehart's novels. What keeps Louisa from becoming a murderess is her understanding that the controlling mothers of the novel are, in their own way, victims of the traditions and restrictions they impose on their daughters.

This understanding of and desire to address the situation of women is what differentiates Rinehart's critique of Victorianism from Edmund Pearson's misogynistic analysis of conformity. While she does frame her critique of "the slavery of the unimportant" as a problem of matriarchal conventionality and rigidity, she sees the resulting restrictiveness as a problem *for* women as well. Her evocation of Lizzie Borden in this story of daughters, mothers, and axes indicates the level of pathology and violence that she, like others in the period, associated with the Victorian past. Rinehart's fiction brings the female gothic plot of daughterly ambivalence and maternal power to the generational problem of women's history in the early twentieth century. In its layered stories of struggle over the daughter's sexual and economic status, Rinehart's popular fiction plays out, with narrative and symbolic density, the moment that Cott summarizes in this way: "Young women in the 1920s connected female heterosexual expression with bravado, pleasure, and knowledge, with a modern, and realistic approach to life. . . . The younger generation looked across the generational divide and saw Victorian sensibilities, as though the venturesome Feminists of the 1910s had never existed."[44] Rinehart's 1933 novel about the overthrow of the Victorian mothers is built on the same historical (mis)apprehension, one that was central to the changes in women's understanding of their place in the culture. The story's evocation of Lizzie Borden, the Victorian woman who killed her stepmother for money and independence, indicates how volatile and even violent a tale about this historical rupture could become, or had to be.

Yet, Lizzie is an alluring as well as a cautionary figure to Rinehart, who attaches one important Borden reference to her heroine rather than to the killer. Lizzie burned her dress, and Louisa tries to burn the glove; to be Lizzie, at that moment, is to be knowing, powerful, and mysterious. Stein stated most accurately—or as clearly as is possible—the ways Lizzie becomes a figure for mystery itself: "She held back nothing and she never lied but she never told anybody anything, that is integrity and is very American . . . it was all so American, the causes which were there which were almost a poem and at the same time were filled with evil meaning, and it was all so simple so evident so subtle and so open and nobody ever really came to know anything."[45] Stein invites us to see Lizzie as a cipher of telling and not telling and the case as an example of the pleasure of investigation and the triumph of mystery, and she is not alone in her sense of what Lizzie Borden means. Lizzie is a perfect, if troubling, muse for women's detective fiction in the late nineteenth and early twentieth centuries. She is a woman surrounded by both knowledge and silence, and she inhabits some realm where the unthinkable becomes possible, having got away with the kind of transgression and self-liberation that domestic detective novels (e.g., Green's *The Leavenworth Case* and *That Affair Next Door*) hint at but back away from.

In addition to inspiring such an experienced author of detective fiction as Rinehart, the Lizzie Borden case figured in (or perhaps prompted) experiments in detective fiction by Stein, Freeman, Wharton, and Hopkins. All connect Lizzie to issues of language and storytelling in quite direct and striking ways, reiterating the pattern we have already seen in women's detective fiction wherein issues of gender, crime, and narration are interdependent and conterminous. Hopkins's 1900 short story based on the Borden murders, "Talma Gordon," is especially interesting in this regard. A comparison of Hopkins's and Rinehart's treatments of the topic is instructive in regard both to the authors and to the traditions of women's detective fiction as a whole. As in *Hagar's Daughter*, Hopkins uses detective fiction's structuring themes of crime and ignorance as a way to portray and articulate certain aspects of race and gender relations at the turn of the century. Like Rinehart, she creates a plot that punishes the murderer, but one that also suggests that, under the conditions of injustice woven into the fabric of American culture, murderous ideas in a woman's head are understandable, if not justified. Like a Victor or Alcott story, "Talma Gordon" has the wildness of the sensational modes of the story-paper and dime novel from which it borrows, and incorporates plot elements from both gothic and adventure genres, including towers that get struck by lightning and catch fire, veiled ladies, and buried treasure. At the same time, this short story reveals through its compression and economy the same interests in intricate narration and in the hidden connections between seemingly disparate problems that characterize detective fiction in general and gothic-domestic detective fiction in particular.

"Talma Gordon" is a framed tale told by a prominent Boston physician to his dinner guests as his contribution on the subject of empire and racial "amalgamation."[46] The progression of the doctor narrating, one character reading another's letter, and so forth, leads

to a nesting of quotation marks four layers deep at some points in
the story, making us aware of the Chinese-box structure of the story
as a metaphor for the layers of secrecy surrounding the murders. The
story also borrows from the "locked room" type of detective story,
in which it seems that no one could have gotten into or out of the
room in which a body is found, and in which inaccessibility of information and inability of access reinforce each other. In the story the
doctor tells, we are introduced to the old, respectable, and unhappy
Gordon (read Borden) family of Massachusetts, which consists of
a mill-owning father, two grown daughters from a first marriage,
a second wife, and a new baby boy. One daughter, Talma, goes off
to Rome to study painting; the other, Jeannette, is left behind to
endure the slights of the stepmother. One night she overhears her
father describing changes he has made to his will since the birth of
his son; these mainly consist of transferring all the inheritance to the
boy and providing only a scant annuity for his daughters. Jeannette
confronts him, only to be told that she and her sister have inherited
from their mother a "trace of Negro blood," a "dire disgrace" (TG,
15) that their father has kept secret from everyone. Even their mother
did not know about her heritage, having been adopted by a white
family that decided to raise her as their own, and she goes into convulsions of shock and terror when her third child is born "dark as a
mulatto" (TG, 15) and she is accused of adultery. Both she and that
child died, and now that he has a male, white heir, Captain Gordon
can quietly finish his repudiation of his first family. While apparently unconcerned about the racial secret, Jeannette is infuriated by
the new will, not least because the money in question was brought
to the marriage by her mother, "money which mended the broken
fortunes of the Gordon house, and restored this old Puritan stock
to its rightful position" (TG, 6). She vows to kill her father, stepmother, and brother, but discovers when she gets to their bedroom
that someone has gotten there ahead of her and slit their throats.

Jeannette's sister, Talma, is tried for the crime; her indictment
rests on the quarrel she had with her father when he forbade her to
marry a young man she met in Rome, on the bad relations between
the daughters and the stepmother, and on the advantages to her of
becoming an heiress (the racial secret remains known only to Jeannette). Despite the popular sentiment against her, she is, like Lizzie

Borden, acquitted under a cloud of suspicion, and she and her sister both depart for Rome. Jeannette becomes ill and writes a deathbed letter to Talma about their mother, causing Talma to desert her lover and disappear from view. When she shows up at our doctor's sanitarium with tuberculosis some time later, the doctor secretly cables the heartbroken young man in an attempt to reunite the lovers. Talma, however, explains her refusal to marry by reading her sister's letter aloud and disclosing the secret of her racial heritage. Her instincts about her lover are right: he responds by crying, "I could stand the stigma of murder, but add to that the pollution of Negro blood!" (TG, 16). That scene produces two more surprises for the reader. First, someone else in the sanitarium confesses to the murders (a man avenging his father's death), and second, we learn in the last sentence of the story that our narrator, the doctor, is now married to Talma Gordon.

Many of the plot elements are familiar to us from the Lizzie Borden case, and the reshaping of those elements is very much in the tradition of Green and Victor. We are offered, in sequence, three plottings of the crime: first, Jeannette's desire to keep hold of her inheritance; second, Talma's wish to marry a man her father deems unsuitable (though we later extrapolate that the father feels his own daughter is unsuitable to marry a white man); and third, the resolution of this apparent parricide into a revenge killing by an unrelated party. The "correct" solution seems tacked on and infused more with the energies of a pirate tale than a domestic detective novel; it is at one level the now familiar backing away from the plot an upper-class woman's murder of her father or uncle. Read more obliquely, however, the solution is united to the main story by certain repetitions. Like Jeannette's letter, it is a deathbed confession, and it also concerns inheritance and race. The man who offers it goes by the Anglo-Saxon name of Simon Cameron, but he is an "enigma" of nationality and race. He is, he finally confesses, East Indian, and that detail, given the framing discussion of "expansion" and "amalgamation," stands out. Although the East Indian criminal was a favorite of Arthur Conan Doyle's, and although Hopkins relies on the cliché of the "old East Indian dagger" for Jeannette's intended murder weapon (itself a kind of foreshadowing), Cameron ultimately becomes, in Hopkins's fictive vocabulary, the person of color who can pass. He murders Gordon to avenge his own father's death. His father had been Gordon's mate and friend, and the two had buried their pirate treasure together. Gordon shot Cameron's father afterward so he could keep all the loot—a more outrageous version of a "custom" among pirate captains of killing the common sailors who buried their treasure to keep the location a secret. Cameron frames his motives as both personal and cosmic, saying, "[T]here is many a soul crying in heaven and hell for vengeance on Jonathan Gordon. Gold was his idol, and many a good man walked the plank, and many a gallant ship was stripped of her treasure, to satisfy his lust for gold" (TG, 17). Cameron is given the plans to the Gordon estate by his mother and discovers a secret passage that runs from the shoreline to Gordon's tower bedroom, and he swears by her deathbed to execute his father's killer. This plot echoes Jeannette's (both are motivated by their mother's deaths; both seek to punish Gordon's money lust) but adds one crucial material and metaphorical element in the secret passage made known by the mother. In fact, it might not be entirely fanciful to read Cameron and Jeannette as accomplices or even functional siblings, for Cameron does the killings, and Jeannette, on discovering the bodies, has the presence of mind to remove the new will from the room. Together, their actions punish past misdeeds and thwart Gordon's latest plan to disinherit racially mixed children (the first being, in effect, the killing of Cameron's father). Cameron's story also, as Hazel Carby puts it, "transform[s] Gordon from a heroic member of the 'founding families' into 'no better than a pirate.' "[47]

This story is reminiscent of *The Leavenworth Case* in its plot design of suspected sisters, discriminatory wills, documents snatched from the murder scene, thwarted engagements, and money-idolizing capitalists. And it is shaped by the rhetoric of the dime novel and of the middle-class African American domestic novel of the period. Yet, it also does something new with those plot devices, using them to comment on an actual murder case that would have been well known to its first readers. Especially effective, in that context, is Hopkins's use of the gothic conventions surrounding family secrets. Here, the dramatically nested, Chinese-box narrative is an indicator of the potency of the secret of the sisters' race; it is structurally and emotionally at the center of the story, and is so devastating that one sister can reveal it to another only on her deathbed, and even then only in a letter. Hopkins's story, published in her Boston-based *Colored American Magazine,* declares that, given a family murder that cannot be solved, the thing to look for is a racial secret, even in those old New England families who flaunt their *Mayflower* ancestry. The grim humor of this solution to the Borden family murders requires an understanding both of popular literary modes and of the contemporaneous history of black and white relations, and in that sense is very much in line with the goals of the magazine and with Hopkins's other venture into detective fiction, *Hagar's Daughter.* The framing device of the story, which sets up the doctor's narrative as his reply to a Boston men's club's discussion of imperialism and "its effect on the future development of the Anglo-Saxon throughout the world," (TG, 4) indicates that Hopkins saw the possibilities of using the mystery story as a form of social satire as well as social criticism.

While Hopkins was not as committed a writer of murder mysteries as Rinehart, she seems to have seen at least some of the same things in Lizzie Borden that Rinehart did. Talma Gordon, the Lizzie Borden who is suspected of the crime, is an artist, and Jeannette, the Lizzie Borden who wanted to murder, is the author of that all-important confessional text within the text, the deathbed letter. Lizzie Borden is a historical figure with primary associations with violence, insanity, and greed, yet she becomes for many women writers an at least momentary muse for work about the power of holding and revealing secrets and for daydreams about the overthrow of patriarchs and matriarchs. In Rinehart, to be a narrator and detective is to be a transgressing woman; in her long career as a woman author, she consistently drew a connection between writing and female rebellion. Her deeply ethical female detectives are always somehow criminal, too: they hide evidence, they lie to the police, they steal and pry, they break into other people's houses. Ultimately, these transgressions are vindicated and even celebrated, but unlike Sherlock Holmes, who does many of the same things with a sense of authority and confidence, Rinehart's detectives are often deeply fearful of being caught.

The analogy between the criminal and the author lies underneath all these equations of transgression and writing. When Stein writes of Lizzie Borden, "she held back nothing and she never lied but she never told anybody anything," she might be describing the female author of a detective novel, who, other than the criminal, is the only one who knows exactly how the crime was done and why. And when Stein points to "the causes which were there which were almost a poem and at the same time were filled with evil meaning, and it was all so simple so evident so subtle and so open and nobody ever really came to know anything," she could be describing the domestic detective novel, with its layers of gothicized symbols and its oscillations between concealment and revelation.

Despite the conservative tendencies of the detective fiction genre, and despite the limited insight of Rinehart's focus on the native-born, white professional and moneyed classes, we need to take the rebellious strain in Rinehart's characterizations of the detective-heroine seriously. In her framing of generational conflicts, she takes the side of the daughters, especially after 1920, when she became more interested in the situation of young women. In her depictions of women's lives, she gave the most interesting and fulfilling roles to spinsters more often than to matrons, and to bold young women rather than to settled matriarchs. Her female detectives literally and more figuratively seek to take apart the middle- and upper-class home. They pry up floorboards, break open chests and closets, and find the secret entrances to hidden rooms. They, more figuratively, dig up the past, pick the locks of family secrets, and unmask frauds and hypocrites. They look for discrepancies, they read between the lines, they search behind facades of familial harmony and moral rectitude to find hidden stories of sexual chicanery, tyrannical patriarchs and matriarchs, broken spirits, and suppressed female rage.

However, these deconstructive investigations produce as well as deduce. Like all investigators in the detective genre, Rinehart's detective-spinsters are reconstructing the narrative of a murder; their goal is to restore to coherency the fragmented narrative of the crime. Retrospection, which in these novels is not confined to a frame around the narrative but instead permeates the entire text, draws our attention to the ways the heroine's experiences are becoming coherent as well. At the heart of both *The Circular Staircase* and *The Album* is the triumph of our narrator's intelligence over the barriers placed between herself and the hidden story. These activities—investigating crime and narrating it—place Innes and Louisa at the edge of that configuration of class and gender identities named respectability. That positioning of her detective-heroine is perhaps the most serious of the thrills Rinehart was celebrated for producing.

Rinehart continued the nineteenth-century tradition of blending the gothic and domestic modes, but she also made that style resonate with the conflicts surrounding the woman question in the modern era. While she put herself at a distance from highbrow writers, she was a leading author throughout the decades we think of as modern, and her work may have appealed to her readers because of its use of the gothic detective novel formula to explore the relation between social conformity and the burial of the inner life that so thoroughly infused more elite and avant-garde cultural productions. It may have held special appeal for women because Rinehart is so exceptionally focused on what those questions meant for the women of her time and because she created a style of detective fiction that foregrounds the courage required in any woman's challenge to the status quo. We might think of her work as a kind of middlebrow modernism, one that could afford a reader a certain level of stimulating discomfort over the particular social ruptures and conflicts it presented, but which also offered the soothing assurances of solution in the end.

# *Afterword*

This book has focused on an almost forgotten tradition of women's popular writing, arguing that in the decades around the turn into the twentieth century, American women formulated a style of detective fiction that drew on the moral force of the domestic novel and the symbolic language of the gothic mode to critique the gender and class politics of maturing capitalism. These best-selling novels feature women learning about corruption and transgression, looking below the placid surface of things, and questioning appearances. They deploy the gothic mode as a language both of women's anger and of protofeminist epistemology, one that stresses the barriers to knowing and telling and the liberatory power of discovery through its dense concentration of conventions regarding secrets. Building on detective fiction's peculiar fascination with the reconstruction of fragmented plot, the later novels of this tradition show women becoming narrators and storytellers as well as detectives—all ways of taking control of narrative within the world of detective fiction. One of the arguments women detectives make once they have mastery over narrative and plot is that male power is problematic, and they make it through plots involving explicitly masculinized forms of chicanery, including sexual transgressions, the callous infliction of emotional pain, the selfish use or criminal acquisition of money, and attempts to silence women. The energies of these novels well up from two sources: a self-reflexive interest in narration and storytelling and an engagement with the upheavals and uncertainties of the long transition from Victorian to modern culture. The resulting fictions combine and recombine the historical and the literary in ways that offer a complex reading experience—both connected to the history of the moment and escapist, both anxiety producing and soothing, both narratologically dense and formulaic. That experience was structured, as in most popular literature, quite narrowly for the audience of its period, a quality that helps account for the popularity of these works in their own time and their current obscurity.

Up to this point I have been writing about the coherence of the domestic detective novel as a style and a tradition and its relevance to and resonance with the sexual and class politics of its day. But the work of genre study needs to include the study of declines as well as advents, and I will in these next pages attempt to sketch some account of the waning of this early wave of detective fiction writing, even as detective fiction as a whole became increasingly popular over the course of the twentieth century. Both the promise of women's detective fiction as a feminist discourse and the reduction of its cultural currency in the 1930s are indicated by an until recently obscure fact about Charlotte Perkins Gilman's literary career. In 1929, only a few years before her death, Gilman began shopping around the manuscript of a detective novel she had written entitled *Unpunished*. According to Catherine Golden and Denise Knight, editors of a 1997 edition of the novel, she wrote the book to bring her feminist social critique to a mass audience and in hope of making a big financial score in the popular fiction marketplace.[1] She failed to interest any publishers in the project, however, and the manuscript went unpublished for almost seventy years.

*Unpunished* is firmly in the tradition of domestic detective fiction. The murder that sets the novel in motion is the violent slaying of a lawyer named Wade Vaughn. He is also the villain of the novel, a man who delights in the evil that this novel, like other domestic detective novels, constructs as specifically masculine and patriarchal: the exploitation of people who are in one's care. The victims of his tyranny include clients whom he blackmails after learning their secrets and vulnerabilities and the daughters and grandchildren of a business crony. Gilman draws on gothic convention in portraying the multiple mechanisms of tyranny in a household ruled by an unscrupulous man, including coerced marriage to one of the sisters, confinement, rape, wife beating, and emotional abuse (all of which drive his wife, Iris, to suicide), the theft of the next generation's fortune, the silencing of women's speech and writing, and interference in the romantic prospects of the virtuous characters. Gilman also continues the line of cultural critique that focuses on hypocrisy, describing the repressive theatricality of the resulting life in this socially prominent family: to the outside world Wade Vaughn looks like a generous man supporting a mentally disturbed young wife, her crippled sister, and their two children from earlier marriages. The sister, Jacqueline, keeps her wits about her by writing a secret journal of Wade's iniquities and gathers the courage to fight back in a way that we have seen before, pivoting herself out of the role of the beset gothic heroine and into the role of the avenging ghost. Angered by Vaughn's plan to marry off his stepdaughter against her will, Jacqueline dresses up one night as her recently deceased sister, Iris, and scares Vaughn so badly that he dies of a heart attack.

Meanwhile, however, several of the clients he is blackmailing have also gathered the courage to act, and later that night Vaughn is poisoned, stabbed, strangled, and shot by a series of independently operating assassins. Gilman scholars who have commented on the work concur that the feminist message is contained in this satiric and grimly humorous plot of overkill. As Ann Lane and Golden and Knight argue, the real work of the detectives in this novel is the establishment of the innocence of all the murderers in the story: the last four because they can't be guilty of murder when their intended victim is already dead, and the first one (Jacqueline) because the homicide of such a monstrously perverse patriarch is justifiable.[2] The title cuts two ways: as a condemnation of Vaughn's long reign of terror and as a celebration of Jacqueline's going "unpunished" for the death of her family's tormentor. Apart from this subversion of the expectation that someone must always be punished for a murder in a detective story, Gilman's novel fits into the tradition of feminist critique established by the domestic detective tradition, deploying gothic conventions in ways that show the hypocrisy of the moneyed classes and the possibility of women gaining some measure of control over violent and oppressive circumstances.

The detectives in *Unpunished* are a husband and wife team, who, anticipating Nick and Nora Charles (of Dashiell Hammett's *Thin Man* series), find much to be amused about in the course of investigating the murder(s) of Wade Vaughn, as well as a good deal to be outraged over. Golden and Knight speculate that Gilman's manuscript was unsellable because editors would have found its "marriage of humor and pathos more than a little disconcerting."[3] Like the other scholars who have written on Gilman's work (including Lillian Robinson as well as Lane), Golden and Knight are clearly unaware of the tradition behind Gilman's style.[4] All seem to feel that the violence of the story, including the five murders of the villain and the plot of domestic abuse, are anomalous in Gilman's work and in women's writing of the period. Lane, for example, describes the lingering effect of *Unpunished* as "an uncharacteristic ghoulishness and bitterness."[5] However, a mix of humor, violence, and social criticism was the formula that made Green's Amelia Butterworth stories and all of Rinehart's detective stories popular. While we might argue about whether or not Gilman got the proportion of those elements right (especially damaging is the lack of attention to terror), we can't attribute the rejection of her manuscript to its violence or black humor, elements that should, in fact, have made her novel familiar to editors of popular fiction.[6]

The main problem for *Unpunished* was Gilman's timing. Nineteen twenty-nine, the year she began trying to place the novel, was also the year that saw the publication of Hammett's *Red Harvest* and, through it, the establishment of the hard-boiled detective story as a middle-class popular literary genre. Although the hard-boiled style did not instantaneously eclipse the domestic detective tradition, especially for established writers such as Rinehart, Gilman's experience suggests that the market for new writers of the domestic style was shrinking rather than expanding. While, as noted in the last chapter, imitators of Rinehart continued to publish recognizable extensions of the tradition into the 1960s, the market niche for those novels seems to have grown increasingly narrow and specialized after 1935. To understand the contraction of the domestic detective tradition in this period, we need to look to the rise of the hard-boiled novel; for, while it is too simple to say that one bankrupted the other, the fortunes of the two styles were closely linked by a number of historical problems and cultural developments.

The hard-boiled style developed along a quite different trajectory from the domestic detective novel. Although both traditions were at least initially worked out in the realm of the dime novel, the domestic detective style sprang up where the popular serial overlapped with the thematic concerns of the hardbound middle-class novel and almost immediately moved into that publishing market. The hard-boiled tradition came out of the dime-novel detective serials that were popular from the 1880s into the 1920s and was formulated, codified, and refined in the "pulp" magazines—cheap periodicals with a male audience—in the 1920s.[7] The most important incubator for the spare, violent, and pessimistic style was *Black Mask* magazine, where Hammett was considered the best of a seminal group of crime writers.[8] Only when Alfred A. Knopf published Hammett's serial, *Red Harvest,* as a clothbound volume did the hard-boiled style reach a broad middle-class audience of adult fiction readers.

Hammett's early novels, especially *Red Harvest* and its successor, *The Maltese Falcon* (1930), are regarded as radically innovative works, and have been since their initial appearance. Accounts of the development of the hard-boiled style almost invariably refer to Hammett's works as a "watershed" or, more tellingly, an "American revolution."[9] Raymond Chandler's famous essay "The Simple Art of Murder" is both an homage to Chandler and a manifesto of the hard-boiled school.[10] Chandler poses the problem that Hammett so thoroughly solved as a problem of realism. The British writers who dominated the form in the 1910s and 1920s, Chandler complains, wrote mannered novels with "a heavy crust of gentility" and with no basis in their own—or anyone's—lived experience. The genre had, in the hands of the British writers of what Stephen Knight calls the "clue-puzzle" (e.g., Agatha Christie, Dorothy Sayers, and their American imitators, S. S. Van Dine and Rex Stout), become entirely predictable.[11] No matter where one turned, there was "the same ingénue in fur-trimmed pajamas screaming in the night to make the company pop in and out of doors and ball up the timetable; the same moody silence next day as they sit around sipping Singapore slings and sneering at each other, while the flatfeet crawl to and fro under the Persian rugs, with their derby hats on" (SA, 12). Hammett, on the other hand, not only brought the authority of his work as a Pinkerton operative to the genre, he also "wrote scenes that seemed never to have been written before" (SA, 17).

Of course, Hammett's plots of revenge and betrayal, and his terse narration, barbed dialogue, and gemlike slang quickly became imitated and conventionalized themselves. His trench-coated ops and private eyes became and remain a globally recognized icon of American manhood in the twentieth century. That nationalistic armature within the figure of the hard-boiled P.I. is something Chandler recognized, praised, and helped to promote, making it implicit in his equation of British writing with artificiality and American with honesty, and stating it most directly as an issue of language. He points out that Hammett "had style, but his audience didn't know it," and asserts that "at its best it could say almost anything . . . . [T]his style does not belong to Hammett or to anybody, but is the American language" (SA, 16–17). Marcus Klein argues convincingly that Chandler's remarks and the impact of Hammett's fiction have to be understood in the context of the literary avant-garde of the period (including William Carlos Williams, Gertrude Stein, and the Young America group) and their valuation of American speech as "a banner and a cause, promising fresh knowledge."[12]

But if we are to understand the hard-boiled as a new, self-consciously American tradition, a pop-cultural manifestation of the growth of national culture and its export during the American century, we also need to understand how it was shaped by what came before it and what developed alongside it. William Marling writes that much about *Red Harvest* "reflects an awareness of narrative competition."[13] He analyzes that competitive streak as an issue of markets and audiences, as the hard-boiled style moved from the pulps to the mainstream novel and simultaneously had to compete with film. We might also take the idea of narrative competition in another way, thinking of the hard-boiled as a style written against British and Continental traditions of detective fiction, on the one front, and against the female tradition of the American domestic detective novel, on the other. The two enemies of the hard-boiled dick are conflated, to a certain extent, into a familiar demand that both the female and the effeminate are to be mistrusted and punished. Chandler faintly echoes Huck Finn explaining his reasons for "lighting out for the territory" when he writes that "Hammett took murder out of the Venetian vase and dropped it into the alley . . . it looked like a good idea to get as far as possible from Emily Post's idea of how a well-bred débutante gnaws a chicken wing" (SA, 16). Marcus Klein nicely expresses the conjunction of the projects of national celebration and gender correction undertaken in the hard-boiled style when he writes that it foregrounds "the Private Eye versus Dupin and Holmes and the other dandies of their stripe."[14] Chandler reveals the misogyny and homophobia that flavor the hard-boiled style of competitive play when he refers to Hammett's critics as "the flustered old ladies—of both sexes (or no sex) and almost all ages—who like their murders scented with magnolia blossoms" (SA, 18).

One point about the hard-boiled style that becomes clearer after studying the forgotten tradition of the domestic detective novel is the significance of John Cawelti's observation that "the creation of the hard-boiled pattern involved a shift in the underlying archetype of the detective story from the pattern of mystery to that of heroic adventure."[15] Cawelti, like Chandler, overlooks the body of work by American women, and draws the line of subgeneric difference between the British puzzle-centered novel and the *Black Mask* detective-centered story. Rinehart's fiction could be cast as an intermediate type, because it is interested in the patterns created by mystery (including the patterns of criminality that the study of mystery reveals) *and* in the psychological development of the heroine as she moves through a series of emotional, moral, and physical adventures. Cawelti's analysis is nevertheless accurate, however, for the whole point of the hard-boiled tradition seems to be to create a new kind of masculine hero, one able to resolve certain contemporary questions of gender, economics, and morality as well as to solve any mystery put before him. Chandler ends "The Simple Art of Murder" with an extended, lyric passage on the figure of the hard-boiled detective, the figure who contains that "quality of redemption" necessary to any art form. It is too long to quote in full here, but it begins in this way: "But down those mean streets a man must go who is not himself mean, who is neither tarnished nor afraid. The detective in this kind of story must be such a man. He is the hero; he is everything. He must be a complete man and a common man and yet an unusual man. He must be, to use a rather weathered phrase, a man of honor—by instinct, by inevitability, without thought of it, and certainly without saying it. He must be the best man in his world and a good enough man for any world. I do not care much about his private life; he is neither a eunuch nor a satyr; I think he might seduce a duchess and I am quite sure he would not spoil a virgin; if he is a man of honor in one thing he is that in all things" (SA, 20). As the last sentences of the passage indicate, Chandler is not talking about a generalized human being working as a detective, but is attempting to define a quite specific kind of male, heterosexual physical and moral entity. He calls for a "complete man" to inhabit a new kind of narrative; "the story [of] this man's adventure in search of a hidden truth . . . would be no adventure if it did not happen to a man fit for adventure."

If Chandler's sense of the fit of the man and his adventure seems somewhat circular, and if his description of the detective seems at moments strenuous in its distinctions, he needs to be understood as expressing a common, and complex, desire to redefine ideal manhood for the early twentieth century. Recent work in the cultural history of masculinity invites us to think about the hard-boiled detective as part of an intense interest in and concern over what it meant to "be a man" in the decades around the turn of the century. Gail Bederman describes the period from the 1880s through the 1910s as one of substantial change in concepts of ideal manhood for the native-born white middle class, in which the Victorian "discourse of manliness stressing self-mastery and restraint" gave way in the face of massive immigration and its challenge to old-line hegemony, the rise of consumer culture and its stimulation of many kinds of desire, and the concentration of capital and the resulting narrowing of opportunity to become "self-made." By 1910, Bederman argues, the level of anxiety over male identity and authority was such that middle-class men "adopted a variety of strategies to remake manhood," including attacks on feminism and feminists, the excoriation of all that seemed "effeminate," a selective extraction of "roughness" from working-class culture, and the careful construction of a kind of racialized "primitive" to revitalize white masculinity while reinforcing the supremacy of white "civilization."[16] Angus McLaren has made an intriguing study of the ways the new masculinity was delineated by negative example in the rhetoric of medical science, the criminal justice system, and the press that sensationalized certain trials and certain "discoveries" of deviance. McLaren's work makes clear that one of the central activities of this complex historical phenomenon was policing (rather than simply naming) the boundaries of optimal masculinity, an activity that is always a kind of intervention. "The notion that there was one essential form of masculinity was simply assumed by judges, journalists, and doctors. What they did not realize themselves is that the model of masculinity that they took as a given was one that they were actually helping to construct."[17]

The hard-boiled style, centered as it is on the plots, scenery, and language of deviance, corruption, and their punishment, might be profitably understood as both expressive of and participating in the policing of sexuality in the early twentieth century. It shares that status and task with the western, and, like it, eventually produced icons of aggressively American manliness (John Wayne on a horse, Humphrey Bogart in a trench coat) through film adaptations of the literary genre. The main difference between the two genres is in their sense of history: while the western is wildly nostalgic, the hard-boiled, at the time of its formation, celebrated all that was new and modern (though it has itself become an object of nostalgic fixation in the latter half of the twentieth century).[18] The hard-boiled detective and his language are streamlined, unsentimental, and smooth in every sense.[19] His modern masculinity includes the rejection of such old ideals of manliness as self-restraint; what checks his violent impulses or libidinal appetites is more his coolness than his conscience.[20] He is a loner, rejecting the nineteenth-century assumption that a man proves his virtue through his patriarchal governance of his family and his own ability to master complex and established systems such as a business or a political office. The hard-boiled detective works without the restraint or support of traditional anti-criminal institutions (e.g., the legal system), and his relations with the police are often fractious.[21] The manly hero of the early domestic detective novel, the gentleman lawyer, is no longer effective or admirable in the world of the hard-boiled, a shift signaled by the depiction of the effeminate, blackmailing attorney named Charles Proctor Dawn in *Red Harvest*.[22] The hard-boiled masculine style is new and unfamiliar in other ways. Despite Chandler's belief that the private dick is a "man of honor," it is always difficult to know exactly where he stands, since he is so often playing both ends against the middle, "just stirring things up," as the Op puts it in *Red Harvest*.[23] Even in the violent world in which this kind of figure operates, his most impressive feats are those of nerves and wits, not muscles. Indeed, the hard-boiled formula demands that he be beaten up or at least overcome by drugs in the course of his investigation.

How is it, then, that we perceive the hard-boiled detective as a man's man? The whole genre of hard-boiled writing—its structure, its paradigmatic plots, and its themes—all work to give the detective the upper hand over the types that most threaten modern masculinity: homosexuals, women, and nonwhites. The latter group, which includes Jews, African Americans, foreigners, and immigrants (especially Middle and Far Eastern men and women), are often given physical descriptions according to stereotype and referred to by racial and ethnic epithets, only rarely penetrate to the foreground of the story, and usually fill a role that is symbolic or metaphorical. For example, Chandler's *Farewell, My Lovely* (1940) opens with the murder of a black bar owner, which a police lieutenant dismisses as "another shine killing." The novel as a whole would seem to concur that this murder lacks real interest, for its only purpose is to get Marlowe enmeshed in the affairs of the white characters whose troubles are the important mysteries.

In the realm of the early hard-boiled novel, white superiority is so thoroughly assumed that, though objects of derision, non-WASP characters pose little serious threat to the detective.[24] Homosexual men, on the other hand, are villains who must be reckoned with. Or, given the limited taxonomy of gender types in the hard-boiled world, we could even put it another way and say that there is almost always something effeminate about the sinister characters in Chandler and Hammett. The bitter old men who hire the private detectives in *Red Harvest* and *The Big Sleep* are both invalids; one is confined to bed like a hysterical woman, the other resides in an overheated greenhouse full of orchids. Both have hired the detective to perform patriarchal duties they can no longer undertake (or never did properly in the first place), and the extent of their unmanning is measured by the Op's remark, on reading his client's "hot" love letters to a young woman, "I haven't laughed so much over anything since the hogs ate my kid brother" (*RH*, 203). *The Maltese Falcon* features several homosexual villains, the most memorable of whom is the "queer" Joel Cairo (*MF*, 42). Cairo comes equipped with perfumed handkerchiefs, trousers cut more snugly than fashion alone would dictate, and a "mincing, bobbing" (*MF*, 42) walk. He is irritating, condescending, and not nearly as smart as he supposes; he's the opposite of Spade, and we simply wait for him to get his comeuppance. But while the caricature of Cairo is pretty thin, more interesting for our discussion of the policing of modern masculinity are the details that he wears spats and a derby hat, both turn-of-the-century items of dress that indicate a concerted resistance to modern style, and that he carries in his pockets not just United States currency, but also that of Britain, France, and China. Just as his "much-visaed" (*MF*, 47) passport indicates, he is irrefutably cosmopolitan, which is to say antithetical to the ideal of patriotic American manhood.[25]

The archvillain Casper Gutman is represented as an aging version of Cairo: fat in a world where men of honor should be lean and muscular, with a "great soft egg of a belly" and a physique that seems to be built of "clustered soap bubbles." He styles his hair in "ringlets" and wears a dandified suit of clothes, including a pink pearl stickpin and patent-leather shoes (*MF*, 104). He has a live-in "punk," Wilmer, who does his gunslinging for him and tails his enemies, including Spade.[26] The relationship between Gutman and Wilmer ends up as an ironic parallel to the heterosexual alliance of Spade and Brigid O'Shaughnessy. Spade, in one of the most hard-boiled moments in the whole detective genre, refuses to cover up Brigid's murders and prepares to turn her in, saying, "I don't care who loves who. I'm not going to play the sap for you" (*MF*, 213), and arguing, "I couldn't be sure you wouldn't decide to shoot a hole in *me* some day" (*MF*, 214). Gutman, who struggled so irrationally against Spade's plan to let Wilmer take the fall for all of them (a plan made when they all seemed to be on the same side and the falcon seemed to be worth millions), pays for his old-fashioned sentiment dearly in the end, for Wilmer shoots him dead. ("He ought to have expected that" [*MF*, 216], observes Spade.)

An awareness of all forms of deviance, rebellion, and indulgence is an important part of the hard-boiled detective's store of knowledge, but insight into nonstandard sexual behavior especially bolsters his credentials as a cynic. In *The Big Sleep*, Marlowe confronts another live-in "punk," Carroll Lundgren, who is trying to hide the sexual nature of his relationship with his patron, a freshly deceased, blackmailing pornography dealer named Arthur Geiger. Marlowe knows, after surveying the house only briefly, that "you've got a nice clean manly little room in there. He shooed you out and locked it up when he had lady visitors. He was like Caesar, a husband to women and a wife to men. Think I can't figure people like him and you out?" (*BS*, 92).[27] In fact, Marlowe so prides himself on his ability to "figure" the homosexual that he passes for one when he first visits Geiger's place of business. (And reveals the narrowness of his conception when he jokes, "[I]f you can weigh a hundred and ninety pounds and look like a fairy, I was doing my best" [*BS*, 47].) At the same time, the hard-boiled detective's knowledge of homosexuality and bisexuality doesn't lead him to any level of acceptance of it, and homosexual characters are always punished in these novels.[28] The young "punk" seems to be the figure that most provokes the detective, perhaps because of the discomfort of being followed, or "shadowed," by a homosexual, an experience of doubling made even more complicated by the fact that the "punk" is doing the same thing to the dick that the dick does to his criminal quarry. Both Spade and Marlowe get special satisfaction from beating up these punks and taunting them about their various failings of masculinity.[29]

One of the characteristics that most clearly marks Gutman as an unmanly figure is his use of language, a verbal style shared by Joel Cairo and Poisonville's Charles Proctor Dawn. While he claims to value "plain speaking," Gutman is a master of circumlocution and euphemism. He rolls phrases in his mouth, constructing parallelisms like "And I'll tell you right out that I'm a man who likes talking to a man that likes to talk," a syntactical puffball that Spade deflates by answering, "Swell. Will we talk about the black bird?" (*MF*, 105). Although, as Chandler demonstrates in "The Simple Art of Murder" and in his own simile-studded fiction, language is the main beauty of the hard-boiled style, the linguistic aesthetic is minimalist — especially for the spoken word. In its most extreme form, hard-boiled dialogue looks like this phone conversation between two cops:

"Exit Arlie," he said.
"R.I.P.?"
"Yep."
"How?"
"Lead."
"Our lad's?"
"Yep."
"Keep till morning?"
"Yep."
"See you at the office," and I went back to sleep.[30]

This exchange exhibits the studied brevity and terseness that Peter Schwenger, in a discussion of masculinity, calls the "school of virility," an analysis Jane Tompkins picks up in her discussion of "the language of men" in the western.[31] Schwenger attributes the founding of this school to Hemingway and sees it as an effect of the fact that masculinity in modern literature and culture had to be "asserted," not just "assumed." This linguistic style can be summed up as "rough talk," shot through with slang and obscenities and distinguished by "a felt undercurrent of action."[32] In this context, speech that luxuriates in complexity is highly suspicious and distinctly feminine.

Feminine language in the hard-boiled novel is close to the kind of compulsive babble that gets people into trouble: "You talked too much, son," scolds the Op on nabbing a murderer in *Red Harvest*. "You were too damned anxious to make your life an open book for me" (*RH,* 59). Talking too much can be dangerous for other people, as when Dinah Brand sells the secrets of one of her lovers to another; or it can itself be a form of deception, as when Brigid O'Shaughnessy works a hyperfeminine throb into her voice to chant refrains like, "Help me. I've no right to ask you to help me blindly, but I do ask you. Be generous, Mr. Spade. You can help me. Help me" (*MF,* 35). In this style of detective fiction, a woman talking is always bad news. Hard-boiled heroes need to be especially careful about believing the stories women tell about themselves. Walter Huff, probably because he is not a P.I. but only an insurance salesman, ignores this principle in James M. Cain's *Double Indemnity,* listens to Phyllis Nirdlinger's tale of marital woe and newfound passion, and becomes exactly the kind of sap Sam Spade condemns, unable to extricate himself from the double-crossing narrative that a woman weaves around him.[33] Spade is smarter: he knows from the start that he should not trust Brigid O'Shaugnessy, because she tries to hire him with a trumped-up story in the women's literary line—a seduction plot involving Thursby and a make-believe underage sister. Women's stories are dishonest and ensnaring, and detectives prove that women lie and make them pay for lying.

The hard-boiled style's hostility to and mistrust of women can hardly be overstated; it is such an automatic impulse that the Op, though he personally seems to like Dinah Brand, appears to have driven an ice pick into her heart while he is fast asleep. The alloy of sex and danger these women present was, of course, not entirely new, but it seems to have been given fresh energy by the rearrangement of gender roles in the early decades of the twentieth century.

Estelle Freedman argues that the sexual psychopath was a new figure
in the public imagination after World War I, and concern over him
(it was mostly men who were the objects of anxiety) led to "sex
crime panics" in the late 1930s. Freedman attributes the rise of concern over violent and "insatiable" sex criminals to several sources,
including concerns about a collective loss of masculine status and
will stemming from the experience of unemployment in the Depression and the "disintegration" of the previously unassailable belief in
the existence and necessity of female purity in the wake of Freudian
formulations of human sexuality.[34] In the hard-boiled novel (at least
in the central cluster of works we have been concerned with here),
we do not see the figure of the male sexual psychopath, but we do
see female ones. If, as Freedman so carefully documents, the culture
at large feared that male appetites would rage out of control without
conventional domestic arrangements and women's moral authority
to hold them in check, the hard-boiled novel expresses an opposite
fear. The hard-boiled detective has to worry that women, freed from
those restraining Victorian ideals of purity, will themselves become
the sexual psychopaths: seductresses driven by greed and violent
rage and struggling to maintain the facade of sanity. In this class we
can include Phyllis Nirdlinger, a serial killer who begins by liqui-
dating children in efficient bunches and ends with a neatly linked
sequence of murder, marriage, and seduction; and Carmen Stern-
wood, a vicious, childlike drug addict who kills a man for refusing
her nymphomaniacal charms. We can think of the legions of crazy,
seductive, and two-faced women in the hard-boiled genre as echoes
of the central, baroque type.

The depiction and treatment of women in the hard-boiled formula may be the most significant departure from the earlier domestic detective style, and it represents, Richard Slotkin argues, an
inversion of the role of the "redemptive woman" in other popular
genres.[35] While it is true that "a woman with a secret" is made problematic in *The Leavenworth Case,* both Mary and Eleanor Leavenworth are exonerated in the end. Green's Amelia Butterworth novels
likewise work to show that women are misunderstood and that a
woman detective is required to bring out the truth of their situations. Rinehart explores this theme most fully with her self-narrating
detectives, structuring her novels so that the retrieval of a woman's

story is clearly equal in value to the solution of a crime. We might then understand the hard-boiled style's hostile depiction of women, women's language, and women's stories as a matter of "narrative competition," a renovation of the American detective novel to make it safe for modern men. With the full history of American detective fiction in view, we can read Spade's abandonment of Brigid O'Shaughnessy in the closing pages of *The Maltese Falcon* not only as a repudiation of her treachery, but also as Hammett's rejection of an ending that would be too much like that of a domestic detective novel.

William Marling suggests that the sources for the structural and thematic antagonism toward women lie in the broader patterns of gender and economics in the early twentieth century: "If women were to assume economic power and freedom, they would have to pay a price for it. They might, in the figuration Cain proposed, acquire economic power, but they must cede to men the right to serialize [i.e., commodify] desire, its discourse, and its relation to the new economy."[36] The new hard-boiled crime novel, Marling's arguments suggest, is the product of that "deal," an arena in which men cannot only work out models of masculine demeanor through the heroism of the private eye, but also dramatize a wish for the resubjugation of women in economic and sexual terms. Indeed, the woman who most needs punishing in the hard-boiled world is the woman who tries to make money, whether through criminal means (e.g., Phyllis Nirdlinger, Dinah Brand, or Brigid O'Shaughnessy) or through honest effort (e.g., Mildred Pierce). Punishment of women in these novels goes far beyond the arrest of the female thief or embezzler; the novel works to shame her (as in the ghastly closing image of Phyllis in her bizarre madwoman's getup) or to make her into a contemptible fool (like poor Mildred, too blind to foresee betrayal by her daughter, her husband, her business partner, and her lawyer).

We might, then, think of the hard-boiled style as beginning from some of the same questions about women, economics, and sexuality that Rinehart's later work does, but arriving at quite different conclusions. Changes in women's roles, the opening of new educational and vocational opportunities for women of the middle class, the reenvisioning of female sexuality—these features of early twentieth-century culture produced both *The Album,* in which female independence is offered as a simultaneously frightening and valuable proposition, and *The Big Sleep,* in which the modern girl is a sexual psychopath. It is clear that if the two subgenres were in competition for a long-term place in the popular imagination, the hard-boiled genre has won the match. Only the most serious mystery buffs have read Anna Katharine Green, and Mary Roberts Rinehart is, despite the fact that much of her work has remained in print throughout this century, only somewhat better known, usually through a half-remembered encounter with an old copy of *The Circular Staircase* found on the bookshelf of a summer cottage or urged on an adolescent girl by a sly grandmother. If *Little Women* is the domestic novel that managed to outlive its time, then *The Circular Staircase* is the domestic detective novel that has performed the same feat, though on a much more modest scale.

Any conclusions about why the hard-boiled style rose to such an important place in literary and film culture while the domestic detective tradition has slipped gently into obscurity are by necessity speculative. Complicating this attempt to trace generic history is the extent of change in the business of book and periodical publishing and in reading habits between the Civil War and World War II. The proliferation of new forms of popular entertainment for all classes makes it difficult to draw precise parallels between the cultural and market niche of the nineteenth-century dime serial and the twentieth-century hard-boiled novel. Without arguing that one tradition replaced another in any simple sense, I do think that the same cultural changes that made the domestic detective novel increasingly irrelevant also created a place for the hard-boiled tradition.

As we have seen, the domestic detective novel can be understood as part of the wide-ranging middle-class reform complex of the mid and late nineteenth century, a social and political phenomenon that was largely dismantled in the period between the world wars. We hear the passing of that way of thinking about crime, policing, and progress in the following famous exchange between the Op and the elderly, patrician Elihu Willsson in *Red Harvest:*

"I want a man to clean this pig-sty of a Poisonville for me, to smoke out the rats, little and big, It's a man's job. Are you a man?"

"What's the use of getting poetic about it?" I growled. "If you've got a fairly honest piece of work to be done in my line, and you want to pay a decent price, maybe I'll take it on. But a lot of foolishness about smoking rats and pig-pens doesn't mean anything to me." (*RH*, 42)

For the Op, the metaphor of cleansing and fumigating no longer describes his work or his role. He has no faith that his actions will eradicate corruption or restore a harmonious social system. Later, when he is almost finished in Poisonville, he tells Willsson, "[Y]ou'll have your city back, all nice and clean and ready to go to the dogs again" (*RH*, 203).

This pessimism is bone-deep in the structure of the hard-boiled crime novel, a quality that Fredric Jameson describes in a very early essay on Chandler as "a depressing fatality, like a circular movement narrowing down." This cynicism, Jameson argues, includes a "demystification of violent death" that not only strips away the symbolic struggle of good and evil traditionally associated with murder in literature, but also "involves the removal of purpose from the murder event." Instead of serving as the beginning of everything, or bearing "meaning and significance by the convergence of all lines upon it" (as Jameson sees in the classical style of British detective fiction, and we have seen in the domestic style), murder becomes intellectually uninteresting and "morally insignificant."[37] The domestic detective tradition remained loyal, at base, to the nineteenth-century, middle-class faith in rational thought, the effectiveness of human agency, and the redemptive power of good intentions—in all the conditions of progress. Those faiths make up its utopian strain (and here we turn to Jameson's later analysis of mass culture), the element that seems to turn the painful material of cultural anxiety into something compelling and soothing at the same time.[38] The hard-boiled style made its allegiances to a different historical sensibility and a different sense of history itself, one that suspected that the desire to make things better is always foolish, dangerous, or the front for some other plan.

It would be a mistake, however, to believe that the hard-boiled style is jaded, weary, and ultimately uninterested in the violence it portrays. Like the domestic style, the hard-boiled style is deeply engaged with the cultural anxieties of its period, especially in its attention to the turbulence surrounding gender roles and to the new prominence of concern over a link between sexual expressiveness and criminal violence. While its brutality is stylized, the sheer number of dead bodies generated by hard-boiled narrative, its insistent suspicion and cynicism about those deaths, and the intensity of its scenes of fistfights and shootouts all indicate that violence between men is also a serious concern. The hard-boiled style arrived as a new answer to the complex of sexual and economic issues that the domestic detective novel had worked to make sense of and control, just as other forms of crime writing, such as the execution sermon, had done earlier. By the mid-1930s, dramas of genteel systems of control reining in miscreants, of vexing questions about self-control, self-indulgence, and subtly distinguished styles of class identity in the context of the maturing capitalist economy had ceased to be the most interesting arenas imaginable for the detective. With consumerism ascendant, self-governance was no longer the optimal social or economic mode of the middle class, or the absorbing erotic problem it had been in the late nineteenth century. The structure and thematics of the female gothic mode were also increasingly outmoded in a period when the popularization of Freud made discussion of sex a much more public activity.[39] The American Freudianists' focus on the ills of sexual repression might have made the gothic mode's complex symbolic and narrative management of secrecy seem a little too obvious, and the emancipation of women might have made the metaphor of the haunted house less encompassing of women's experience and less trenchant.[40] Hammett's little-known second novel, *The Dain Curse,* features a number of gothic motifs within the basic structure of the urban, hard-boiled novel, including an old matricide, a family curse, and a secret community of religious fanatics.[41] However, the unevenness of this novel suggests the problem of recombining the hard-boiled style — which distances itself stylistically from the recursive, suspenseful, descriptive style of female gothic and domestic detective narrative — with gothic cliché.

Instead, the 1930s had a place for terse, tough stories about the social, political, and economic upheavals of the twentieth century and a need for a violent man to negotiate, if not control, the violence of men. The utopian element in the hard-boiled tradition is a belief not in progress but rather in its own detective. As Chandler puts it, "he is the hero; he is everything": a modern man who is already wise to the ways of modern women, unembarrassed by the sexual and material indulgence of the culture, and unafraid of violence.

Through the detective figure, we can make sense of the much-noted connection between popular hard-boiled fiction and elite modernism, for his voice is the voice of radical and fascinating subjectivity, of a self-sufficient man in a world of criminal collusion.[42] The fact that the hard-boiled tradition establishes the supremacy of the new masculinity at the expense of women and of men who "act like women" echoes larger ways in which the renegotiations of gender roles and sexual identities in the early twentieth century were mainly approached as zero-sum games. The fact that this "agent of regenerative violence" trailed, and still trails, such glamour is indicative of both the felt need for an honorably violent man and the essentially nostalgic need to, as Slotkin puts it, "imaginatively recover the ideological values, if not the material reality of the mythic Frontier."[43]

However, there is, even more than in the domestic detective novel, a strain of oppositional social criticism running through Hammett's and Chandler's work. The question of whether *Red Harvest* and *The Glass Key* reflect Hammett's leftist politics is a matter of some debate among scholars of the genre, but certainly the kind of corruption Hammett writes about, which comes from the top down and fuses politics and business to the criminal trades, is at least compatible with a Marxist critique.[44] The most open articulation of the critique of capitalism that lies just behind the hard-boiled tradition's dramas of gangsterism, bribery, and exploitation comes out of a police lieutenant's mouth in Chandler's *The Long Goodbye:* "There ain't no clean way to make a hundred million bucks. Maybe the head man thinks his hands are clean but somewhere along the line guys got pushed to the wall, nice little businesses got the ground cut out from under them and had to sell out for nickels, decent people lost their jobs, stocks got rigged on the market, proxies got bought up like a pennyweight of old gold, and the five percenters and the big law firms got paid hundred-grand fees for beating some law the people wanted but the rich guys didn't, on account of it cut into their profits. Big money is big power and big power gets used wrong."[45] This vision of the institutions of economic, legal, and political power polluting each other is the reason that metaphors of housekeeping, always near the surface of the domestic detective novel, no longer obtain in the world of the hard-boiled style. While the ideas of where corruption manifests itself and how radically it needs to be addressed are quite different in the domestic and hard-boiled styles, however, the belief that writing about crime requires a sharp, socially critical eye is something these two styles have in common. Both styles lead not just to the unmasking of respectable-seeming villains, but also to the unveiling of whole systems of hypocrisy in the normal functioning of American society. While Chandler does not use Metta Victor's metaphor of a "web of iniquity," he, like other hard-boiled writers, emphasizes the problem of rackets, sweetheart deals, and conspiracies—all problems of linkage and weblike connection between criminal and "legitimate" economic markets and power structures.

This socially critical edge marks the real difference between the clue-puzzle, on the one hand, and the domestic and hard-boiled styles, on the other. In the clue-puzzle, there may be adulterous bishops and other high-level hypocrites, but the motive for their pursuit and arrest is the preservation of a real or imagined felicitous status quo. The domestic and hard-boiled styles are much more seriously engaged with the histories of their moments and the shifting ideologies of their periods. The recent success of detective fiction by women, with writers such as Sara Paretsky and Sue Grafton becoming publishing superstars, is mostly understood to be a function of their rewriting of the male hard-boiled tradition, and rightly so. But we could also see a tie to the earlier tradition of writing by women through this quality of social criticism. The feminist critique of masculine assumptions of superiority that we saw in Rinehart and Green is argued forcefully at both implicit and explicit levels in the feminist hard-boiled style and its sister subgenre, the lesbian feminist detective story.[46] The kinds of crimes the female P.I. investigates lead directly to the questions about gender and economic ideologies, especially as they pertain to questions about what a woman can do with her life, that we have seen raised throughout the long history of American women's detective fiction.

Even if, as Bobbie Ann Mason has asserted, detective stories are like "sonnets, endless variations on an inflexible form," we might also understand that their conventions, tropes, and persistent preoccupations do not necessarily indicate a distance from history.[47] Like the gothic tradition from which it evolved, detective fiction is interested in evil, and capable of understanding evil to be historical and present—of naming its forms. It is also capable of exploiting our anxieties in their historical specificity. Structurally, the detective story is shaped by the relation of the subterranean and the apparent, the killer and the victim, the investigator and the liar, what is said and what can be proven. Over the last century and a half, it has become one of our favorite kinds of story to tell about ourselves, about what is wrong with us, how we come to know about it, and how we sometimes correct it.

# Notes

## Part One

1. E. D. E. N. Southworth, *The Hidden Hand*, 1859, ed. Joanne Dobson (reprint, New Brunswick: Rutgers University Press, 1988).

2. Southworth, *The Hidden Hand*, 312, 318.

3. There were several other women writing in this general style whom I do not include in this study. One was Mary Hatch, whose novels are more often about bank robberies than about the domestic murders central to the tradition I examine. Carolyn Wells (1870–1942), who was also an anthologist and children's author, wrote dozens of murder mysteries in a simpler, less gothic (and far less interesting) style than Green's or Rinehart's. Isabel Ostrander (b. 1883) wrote a number of novels that are more precisely thrillers than detective stories, though she was clearly influenced by Green. Leslie Ford (b. 1898), Mignon Eberhart (b. 1899), Dorothy Disney (b. 1903), and Mabel Seeley (b. 1903) are all associated with what detective fiction buffs call the "Had-I-But-Known" school, a style established by Rinehart. We could also include the Nancy Drew series as an offshoot of this style. I have not focused on their work because it lacks the literary and cultural edge that I see in that of the authors I do examine. I am also most interested in the roots of the domestic detective novel in postbellum culture; to discuss the work of these later writers is to take up a different set of questions having to do with the codification of detective fiction into genre and subgenre over the course of the twentieth century.

## 1. "To Trace a Lie, to Discover a Disguise"

1. See Roger Caillois, "The Detective Novel as Game," in *The Poetics of Murder*, ed. Glenn Most and William Stowe (New York: Harcourt, Brace, Jovanovich, 1983), 1–12. One strong example of criticism that works to immerse detective fiction in its economic historical context is William Marling's *The American Roman Noir: Hammett, Cain, and Chandler* (Athens: University of Georgia Press, 1995).

2. The fullest and most comprehensive work of this type is John Ca-

welti's *Adventure, Mystery, and Romance: Formula Stories as Art and Popular Culture* (Chicago: University of Chicago Press, 1976).

3. Although the consensus is that Poe is the originator of the structure of detective fiction, various critics have found sources for detective fiction as far back as Sophocles. See, for example, W. H. Auden, "The Guilty Vicarage," in *Detective Fiction: A Collection of Critical Essays,* ed. Robin Weeks (Englewood Cliffs, N.J.: Prentice Hall, 1980). Some find elements of detective fiction in the *Newgate Calendar,* in Godwin's *Caleb Williams,* and in Stendhal's *Le Rouge et le Noir.* Most agree, however, that Poe is the writer who pulled the story of murder and investigation into the structure that has defined the genre ever since. Richard Alewyn argues that all the structures important to "The Murders in the Rue Morgue" can be found in E. T. A. Hoffman's "*Das Fräulein von Scuderi*"; see his "The Origin of the Detective Novel," in *The Poetics of Murder,* ed. Most and Stowe, 62–78.

4. This historical outline has been laid down by Howard Haycraft, *Murder for Pleasure* (New York: Appleton-Century, 1941); and Julian Symons, *Bloody Murder* [formerly, *Mortal Consequences*] (New York: Penguin, 1972).

5. Raymond Chandler, *The Simple Art of Murder* (New York: Ballantine Books, 1972), 4, 16.

6. While it cannot be stated categorically that no men wrote full-blown, hardbound detective novels in the period between Poe and Hammett, it is true that women dominated the field in those years. At the turn of the century, Melville Davisson Post began publishing short stories featuring a lawyer with very few scruples about helping his guilty clients get off, even helping one to plan a murder that cannot be prosecuted. See *The Strange Schemes of Randolph Mason* (New York: G. P. Putnam's Sons, 1896). Jacques Futrelle published short stories at the turn of the century; their science-fiction bent is indicated by the nickname of his detective, "The Thinking Machine." Julian Hawthorne comes closest to detective fiction in the postbellum period. He published several fictionalized accounts of the exploits of Thomas Byrnes, the chief of detectives of New York City, between 1887 and 1888. These novels are stories of professional criminals and are not, in the judgment of historian Larry Hartsfield, suspenseful mysteries: "Hawthorne's major interest is in showing how and why the crime occurred, not in posing a mystery to be solved in the last chapter." Hartsfield also connects Hawthorne's work to the rise of urban realism; see his *The American Response to Professional Crime, 1870–1917* (Westport, Conn.: Greenwood Press, 1985), 51–52 and 112–18.

7. Quoted in David Lehman, *The Perfect Murder* (New York: Macmillan, 1989), 17.

8. Richard Wilbur, "The Poe Mystery Case," *New York Review of Books,* July 13, 1967, 27.

9. William Patrick Day, *In the Circles of Fear and Desire* (Chicago: University of Chicago Press, 1985), 50, 52.

10. Eve Kosofsky Sedgwick, *The Coherence of Gothic Conventions* (New York: Methuen, 1986), 4, 14.

11. Sedgwick, *The Coherence of Gothic Conventions,* 19–20.

12. Tzvetan Todorov, *The Poetics of Prose,* trans. Richard Howard (Ithaca: Cornell University Press, 1977). In his terminology, the two stories fall into the broader patterns of *fabula* (the story of the murder) and *sjuzet* (the story of finding out about the murder) that comprise many kinds of fiction.

13. Mary Roberts Rinehart, "The Detective Story" in *Mary Roberts Rinehart: A Sketch of the Woman and her Work* (New York: George Doran, 1923), 39–40.

14. Peter Brooks, *Reading for the Plot: Design and Intention in Narrative* (New York: Random House, 1984), 244–45.

15. Rinehart, "The Detective Story," 41–42.

16. Ann Radcliffe, 1826. The full sentence is: "Terror and horror are so far opposite, that the first expands the soul, and awakens the faculties to a higher degree of life, the other contracts, freezes, and nearly annihilates them." Quoted in Kate Ferguson Ellis, *The Contested Castle: Gothic Novels and the Subversion of Domestic Ideology* (Urbana: University of Illinois Press, 1989), xvii, n. 1.

17. Ellen Moers, *Literary Women: The Great Writers* (New York: Oxford University Press, 1985), 90.

18. Kathleen Gregory Klein, *The Woman Detective: Gender and Genre* (Urbana: University of Illinois Press, 1988), 57.

19. Kathleen Gregory Klein, "Habeas Corpus: Feminism and Detective Fiction," in *Feminism in Detective Fiction,* ed. Glenwood Irons (Toronto: University of Toronto Press, 1995), 173.

20. Kathleen Klein, *The Woman Detective,* 224.

21. The apogee of this style comes in George Lippard's *Quaker City, or The Monks of Monk's Hall: A Romance of Philadelphia's Life of Mystery and Crime* (Philadelphia: Leary Stuart and Company, 1845). See David S. Reynolds, *Beneath the American Renaissance: The Subversive Imagination in the Age of Emerson and Melville* (New York: Random House, 1988), 59–84. Lippard's work came straight out of the more pornographic, (e)visceral "horror-gothic" of the Matthew Lewis school, which is distinct from the "terror-gothic," which emphasizes the plot of pursuit and quest and is the type most closely related to the domestic detective novel. The terms were introduced by Ann Radcliffe herself (see n. 16, above) and are further problematized by Robert D. Hume in "Gothic versus Romantic: A Revaluation of the Gothic Novel," *PMLA* 84 (March 1969): 282–90. Some of the best criticism on the gothic, other than what I cite directly, includes

David Ringe, *American Gothic: Imagination and Reason in Nineteenth-Century Fiction* (Lexington: University Press of Kentucky, 1982); and Devendra P. Varma, *The Gothic Flame* (London: Arthur Baker, 1957).

22. Nina Baym, in her early work on the domestic novel, argues that the domestic novel was formulated in direct opposition to the Richardsonian novel of seduction, with its gothic plot devices and female victimization; see her *Woman's Fiction: A Guide to Novels by and about Women in America, 1820–1879* (Ithaca: Cornell University Press, 1978), 25–26.

23. Ellen Moers coined the term *female gothic,* using it as the title of her chapter in *Literary Women* on *Frankenstein* and *Wuthering Heights.*

24. On the question of the search for and confrontation with the mother, see Claire Kahane, "The Gothic Mirror," in *The (M)other Tongue: Essays in Feminist Psychoanalytic Interpretation,* ed. Shirley Garner, Claire Kahane, and Madelon Sprengnether (Ithaca: Cornell University Press, 1985), 335, 336.

25. For a more detailed discussion of the domestic novel as bildungsroman, see Nina Baym's introduction to *The Lamplighter,* by Maria Susanna Cummins (New Brunswick: Rutgers University Press, 1988), ix–xxxi.

26. Sedgwick, *The Coherence of Gothic Conventions,* 19.

27. We see the same synthesis of gothic and domestic in the more famous example of Charlotte Brontë's *Jane Eyre.* As Sandra Gilbert and Susan Gubar have argued, the central symbolic confrontation of that novel, Jane's discovery of the imprisoned madwoman, Bertha Rochester, is an encounter with Jane's "own imprisoned 'hunger, rebellion, and rage.'" See Sandra M. Gilbert and Susan Gubar, *The Madwoman in the Attic: The Woman Writer and the Nineteenth-Century Literary Imagination* (New Haven: Yale University Press, 1979), 339.

28. On the subject of social reform and the domestic novel, see Mary Kelley, "The Sentimentalists: Promise and Betrayal in the Home," *Signs* 4 (Spring 1979): 444.

29. Mary Kelley argues that the domestic novel is "finally, expressive of a dark vision of nineteenth-century America, and not, as they wished, of the redemptive, idyllic, holy land" ("The Sentimentalists," 445–46). Baym writes that in the work of domestic novelists, "home life is presented, overwhelmingly, as unhappy. . . . Domestic tasks are arduous and monotonous; family members oppress and abuse each other; social interchanges are alternately insipid or malicious" (*Woman's Fiction,* 27).

30. Ellis, writing about the eighteenth century, posits the general principle that "the conventions of the Gothic novel, then, speak of what in the polite world of middle-class culture cannot be spoken" (*The Contested Castle,* 7).

31. Teresa A. Goddu, *Gothic America: Narrative, History, and Nation* (New York: Columbia University Press, 1997), 119.

32. Louisa May Alcott, *Little Women*, 1869 (reprint, New York: Modern Library, 1983), 348.

33. Goddu, *Gothic America*, 120, 121, 96, 94.

34. My reading of this episode depends on Karen Halttunen's excellent essay on the gothic mode as political rhetoric, "Gothic Imagination and Social Reform: The Haunted Houses of Lyman Beecher, Henry Ward Beecher, and Harriet Beecher Stowe," in *New Essays on Uncle Tom's Cabin*, ed. Eric Sundquist (New York: Cambridge University Press, 1986), 118. For more on gothicism and the rhetoric of abolitionism, see Goddu's discussion of the relation between Stowe's text and Harriet Jacobs's narrative of hiding in the attic of her mother's house for seven years in *Gothic America*, 140–52.

35. Harriet Beecher Stowe, *Uncle Tom's Cabin*, 1852 (reprint, New York: Penguin, 1981), 516.

36. See Jane Tompkins, "Sentimental Power," in *Sensational Designs: The Cultural Work of American Fiction 1790–1860* (New York: Oxford University Press, 1985).

37. See Patrick Brantlinger, "What Is 'Sensational' about the 'Sensation Novel?'" *Nineteenth-Century Fiction* 37 (1982): 9–10, 6. See also Anthea Trodd's excellent *Domestic Crime in the Victorian Novel* (London: Macmillan, 1989); and Winifred Hughes, *The Maniac in the Cellar: Sensation Novels of the 1860s* (Princeton: Princeton University Press, 1980).

38. D. A. Miller writes extensively about the sensation novel's preoccupation with "the sympathetic nervous system," concluding that it is a component of the novel's interest in gender relations and an analogue of the novel's exploration of the plight of the woman shut up in a male "body," or institution. See Miller, "Cage aux Folles," in *The Novel and the Police* (Berkeley: University of California Press, 1988).

39. Literary scholars have not yet accounted fully for the decline of the sentimental domestic novel. Michael Denning, one of the few critics to address the question directly, attributes the decline of the domestic novel to "the breakup of the domestic ideology" caused by "the traumatic cultural effects of the Civil War," which altered the "well-regulated kinship networks, domestic routines, and Protestant certainties of the white middle-class household," along with the "'discovery' of the productive marginality of middle class women" and "the new visibility . . . of working women in the culture." He argues that the publication of Elizabeth Stuart Phelps's novel of labor, *The Silent Partner*, along with the appearance of popular serials about factory girls, mark 1871 as the "end of the sentimental hegemony." See Denning, *Mechanic Accents: Dime Novels*

*and Working Class Culture in America* (New York: Verso, 1987), 186–88. Laura Wexler provides a lucid account of post-1870 domestic ideology, arguing that the educational agenda of the middle-class women's novel became the institutional agenda of schools desirous of destroying cultural differences among Native Americans, African Americans, European immigrants, and the working class. Wexler, "Tender Violence: Literary Eavesdropping, Domestic Fiction, and Educational Reform," in *The Culture of Sentiment: Race Gender, and Sentimentality in Nineteenth-Century America,* ed. Shirley Samuels (New York: Oxford, 1992), 9–38.

40. Jacques Derrida couches this phenomenon as a question of law and violation in "The Law of Genre," trans. Avital Ronell, *Critical Inquiry* 7 (1980): 57: It is "impossible not to mix genres," he writes, since "lodged within the heart of the law [of genre] itself is a law of impurity or a principle of contamination."

41. Jane Tompkins, *West of Everything: The Inner Life of Westerns* (New York: Oxford University Press, 1992), 38.

42. Tompkins, *West of Everything,* 38.

43. According to Madeleine Stern, "V. V., or, Plots and Counterplots" first appeared in February 1865 in the story-paper *The Flag of Our Union* under the pseudonym A. M. Barnard and was then issued as a "dime novelette" by Thomes and Talbot of Boston. Citations of "V. V." are given parenthetically and refer to the reprint of the story in *The Hidden Alcott,* ed. Madeleine Stern (New York: Avenel, 1984).

44. The first work of excavation was done by Madeleine Stern, who tells the story of it in the introduction to the first collection she edited: *Behind a Mask: The Unknown Thrillers of Louisa May Alcott* (New York: William Morrow, 1975). Since then, Stern, in association with Daniel Shealy and Joel Myerson, has published four other collections, mostly of thrillers. The thrillers were recently compiled into a single two-volume set under the title *Louisa May Alcott Unmasked* (Boston: Northeastern University Press, 1995). Since Stern published her first collection of Alcott's thrillers, a great variety of Alcott's other works have been reprinted. Periodical fiction, excerpts from her adult novels, and essays make up Elaine Showalter, ed., *Alternative Alcott* (New Brunswick: Rutgers University Press, 1987). Alcott's novel *Moods* (1865; rev. 1882) has also been reprinted.

45. Richard Brodhead, *Cultures of Letters: Scenes of Reading and Writing in Nineteenth-Century America* (Chicago: University of Chicago Press, 1993), 80.

46. Brodhead, *Cultures of Letters,* 44, 79, 80.

47. Denning, *Mechanic Accents,* 188.

48. Edgar Allan Poe, "The Murders in the Rue Morgue," in *The Complete Tales and Poems* (New York: Random House, 1975), 141.

49. See Daniel Hoffman, *Poe Poe Poe Poe Poe Poe Poe* (New York: Random House, 1972), 121–22.

50. Goddu observes that this "spectacle of male voyeurism" concludes that Virginie is "property" and that the motive for her punishment is the fact that she acted as a "free agent in the marketplace," usurping men's right to control the women they commodify (*Gothic America*, 127–28).

51. More precisely, in the Alcott story, the detective arrives in the service of sincerity, rooting out and unmasking the "painted woman," who, as Karen Halttunen has shown, was a focal point of middle-class anxiety at mid-century. See Halttunen, *Confidence Men and Painted Women: A Study of Middle-Class Culture, 1830–1870* (New Haven: Yale University Press, 1982), xv. Many of Alcott's thrillers are worked around themes of theatricality, and Sarah Elbert (in *Hunger for Home: Louisa May Alcott's Place in American Culture* [New Brunswick: Rutgers University Press, 1987]) and Madeleine Stern have noted how she uses tropes of performance to critique norms of femininity.

52. Daniel A. Cohen, *Pillars of Salt, Monuments of Grace: New England Crime Literature and the Origins of American Popular Culture, 1674–1860* (New York: Oxford University Press, 1993), 191.

53. Cohen, *Pillars of Salt*, 192, 38.

54. Karen Halttunen, "Early American Murder Narratives: The Birth of Horror," in *The Power of Culture: Critical Essays in American History*, ed. Richard W. Fox and T. J. Jackson Lears (Chicago: University of Chicago Press, 1993), 67. The enumeration of the secular genres is from another related essay, "Humanitarianism and the Pornography of Pain in Anglo-American Culture," *American Historical Review* 100 (April 1995): 312.

## 2. "The Eye of Suspicion"

1. My source for Victor's biography is Albert Johannsen, *The House of Beadle and Adams and Its Nickel and Dime Novels*, vol. 2 (New York: Basic Books, 1980), 278–80. See also Lisa Maneiro, ed., *American Women Writers* (New York: Frederick Unger, 1981).

2. Frances F. Fuller and Metta V. Fuller, *Poems of Sentiment and Imagination* (New York: A. S. Barnes, 1851). The two were also included as "Sisters of the West" in Rufus Griswold's *Female Poets of America* (1851).

3. *The Senator's Son* is excerpted in *Hidden Hands: An Anthology of Women Writers, 1790–1870*, ed. Lucy M. Freibert and Barbara A. White (New Brunswick: Rutgers University Press, 1985). *Maum Guinea and Her Plantation Children* has been reprinted by Books for Libraries of Freeport, New York (1972). Her *Lives of Female Mormons: A Narrative of Facts*

*Stranger Than Fiction* (New York: D. W. Evans, 1860) is a hardbound novel that includes a polemical introductory essay against admission of the Utah territory to statehood unless the LDS church agreed to abolish plural marriage ("repulsive as slavery appears to us, we can but deem polygamy a thing more loathsome and poisonous to social and political purity" [vi]). The novel shows all the ways plural marriage wounds and corrupts, especially the way that Mormon women and men become accustomed to "let passion rule over conscience" (186–87) by repeatedly committing adultery. The fiction section is followed by an appendix of articles detailing yet more offenses (including incest). She does include, with feminist sarcasm, a list of "Maxims for Mormon Wives" from the *Deseret News,* as a demonstration of "the wretched and abject condition" of those women ("1st: Occupy yourself only with household affairs; wait until your husband confides to you those of higher importance, and do not give your advice till he asks for it"). She was not alone in her condemnation of Mormons and was voicing the consensus of a broad band of middle-class reform movements.

4. *Too True* (New York: G. P. Putnam's Sons, 1868) includes a robbery by an exiled German nobleman and his pursuit by the hardworking German immigrant security guard who is blamed for the crime. The novel includes an extended and extremely unflattering portrait of the *nouveau riche.* With its elements of gothic thriller (the story of the nobleman's past) and social comedy, it almost could have been written by Alcott in a very bad temper.

5. The publication history of *The Dead Letter* is somewhat cloudy. The National Union Catalogue lists three editions: Beadle and Adams in 1866 and 1867 and the Fireside Library (possibly as a Christmas edition) in 1878. Under his entry for *The Dead Letter,* Johannsen lists four series or journals in which the novel appeared: in serial form in *Beadle's Monthly* in 1866 [beginning at 1:1], as a "Fifty-Cent Novel," as a "Cheap Edition of Popular Authors," and in the "Fireside Library," no. 44 [1878]. However, Johannsen says in his profile of Victor, "In 1864 she published under the name 'Seeley Regester,' her novel 'The Dead Letter' which was reprinted in Beadle's Monthly in 1866" (*House of Beadle and Adams,* 2:279). I have decided to date the novel 1866, since the date 1864 is not corroborated even in Johannsen's own bibliography.

6. Metta Victoria Fuller Victor [pseud. Seeley Regester], *The Dead Letter* (New York: Beadle and Company, 1867), 69. Further references to this edition are in parentheses with the abbreviation *DL.* This book is much more difficult to find than most of the others I examine here; because it is a famous "first," it is prized by book collectors. A reprinting of the book with an introduction by Michele Slung (Boston: Gregg Press, 1979) has since gone out of print.

7. Larry K. Hartsfield, *The American Response to Professional Crime, 1870–1917* (Westport, Conn.: Greenwood Press, 1985), 42.

8. Thomas Byrnes, *Professional Criminals in America*, 1886 (reprint, New York: Chelsea House, 1969), v. See also Alan Trachtenberg, *Reading American Photographs: Images as History, Mathew Brady to Walker Evans* (New York: Farrar, Straus, Giroux, 1989), 28–29.

9. Examples of the detective memoir include George S. McWatters, *Knots Untied: Ways and By-Ways in the Hidden Life of American Detectives* (Hartford: J. B. Burr and Hyde, 1871); *Forgers and Confidence Men, or, The Secrets of the Detective Service Divulged* (Chicago: Laird and Lee, 1892); Phil Farley, *Criminals of America; or, Tales of the Lives of Thieves, Enabling Every One to Be His Own Detective* (privately published, New York, 1876); and Allan Arnold, *The Dwarf Detective* (New York: F. Tousey, 1883). See Hartsfield, *American Response*, 42–73. Also important are the detective exposés of urban vice exemplified by reporter Edward Crapsey's *The Nether Side of New York; or, The Vice, Crime and Poverty of the Great Metropolis* (New York: Sheldon and Company, 1872).

10. Marcus Klein, *Easterns, Westerns, and Private Eyes: American Matters, 1870–1900* (Madison: University of Wisconsin Press, 1994), 156.

11. Maxwell Bloomfield, "Law and Lawyers in American Popular Culture," in *Law and American Literature*, ed. Carl Smith, John P. McWilliams, and Maxwell Bloomfield (New York: Alfred A. Knopf, 1983), 125–73.

12. Southworth's *Ishmael* first appeared as a serial in a story-paper (the *New York Ledger*) and then, due to its popularity, was issued in two hardbound volumes by Grosset and Dunlap in 1864 as *Ishmael; or, In the Depths* and *Self-Raised; or, From the Depths*. See Maxwell Bloomfield's discussion of this novel in "Law and Lawyers in American Popular Culture" and in his *American Lawyers in a Changing Society, 1776–1876* (Cambridge: Harvard University Press, 1976), 186–89.

13. Brodhead, *Cultures of Letters*, 47. I am actually taking this phrase out of the context Brodhead constructs, for he uses it to describe not a person but the domestic novel itself, which becomes "a monitory intimate, another agent of discipline through love." But I find it exceedingly apt for the function of the lawyer here.

14. Peter Brooks, *Reading for the Plot: Design and Intention in Narrative* (New York: Random House, 1984), 104, 107–9.

15. Brooks, *Reading for the Plot*, 109.

16. Victor reveals a sneaky sense of humor — similar to that of Alcott — when she has James describe the "celestial" Lenore this way: "I like hearty little bread-and-butter girls, but not such die-away misses as that. She looks to me as if she read Coleridge already" (159).

17. Lehman, *The Perfect Murder*, 3.

18. Lehman, *The Perfect Murder,* 2. The Eco quotation is from his *Postscript to the Name of the Rose* (New York: Harcourt, Brace, Jovanovitch, 1984).

## 3. The Loop of Surveillance in *The Figure Eight*
### and *Hagar's Daughter*

1. See David R. Johnson, *Illegal Tender: Counterfeiting and the Secret Service in Nineteenth-Century America* (Washington, D.C.: Smithsonian Institution Press, 1995); Walter T. Nugent, *Money and American Society* (New York: Macmillan, 1968); Arthur Nussbaum, *A History of the Dollar* (New York: Columbia University Press, 1957).

2. Metta Victoria Fuller Victor [pseud. Seeley Regester], *The Figure Eight, or The Mystery of Meredith Place* (New York: Beadle and Company, 1869). Further references to this work are in parentheses with the abbreviation *FE.* When one young woman confides to her sister that she feels the house is haunted and, more accurately, that she can hear someone counting money in the night, her sister accuses her of reading ghost stories, but the suspicious one declares that she was reading "nothing worse than Jane Eyre" (*FE,* 78).

3. Eric Lott, *Love and Theft: Blackface Minstrelsy and the American Working Class* (New York: Oxford University Press, 1995), 134, 120.

4. Denning, *Mechanic Accents,* 146.

5. Curtis Carroll Davis, "Companions of Crisis: The Spy Memoir as a Social Document," *Civil War History* 10 (1964): 385–400. The article's footnotes comprise an excellent bibliography of spy memoirs.

6. Lyde Cullen Sizer argues of women's spy memoirs: "Just as much as spying itself, spy *stories,* fictional or factual, offered women an important avenue for revising or directly challenging gender convention." See Sizer, "Acting Her Part: Narratives of Union Women Spies," in *Divided Houses: Gender and the Civil War,* ed. Catherine Clinton and Nina Silber (New York: Oxford University Press, 1992), 114–33. See also Kathleen De Grave, *Swindler, Spy, Rebel: The Confidence Woman in Nineteenth-Century America* (Columbia: University of Missouri Press, 1995).

7. Denning, *Mechanic Accents,* 204. Denning outlines the dime-novel detective series or "libraries" of the 1870s and 1880s on page 139. He argues that in the case of Nick Carter and Frank Merriwell, "disguise is still central . . . [but] the disguises and accents of the earlier detectives had not been resolved in such an unequivocal and stable signifier" (204–5).

8. See Denning, "The Molly Maguires and the Detectives," in *Mechanic Accents,* 118–48.

9. Marcus Klein, *Easterns, Westerns, and Private Eyes,* 137, 134, 138.

10. Allan Pinkerton himself figured heavily in this cultural phenomenon, largely by his own design. While the meat and potatoes of most detectives was the recovery of stolen property and the investigation of adultery in divorce cases, Pinkerton searched out more glamorous fare. After ten years as a private detective in Chicago, with railroads and shipping companies as his clients, Pinkerton saw the future of detection in the outbreak of the Civil War. In 1861, he offered his services to protect President Abraham Lincoln and foiled an assassination plot in Baltimore that may or may not have had any basis outside Pinkerton's own ambition and imagination. During the war, Pinkerton headed the intelligence unit for General George McClellan, but lost that post when McClellan was dismissed. The legend of his contribution to Union intelligence, much of it created by Pinkerton himself in his memoirs, is both larger and more important than its reality. He claims to have run a "Secret Service" for the Union government and military during the war, though that service was not actually established until after the war. Through his shrewd self-creation as a hero-spy, Pinkerton positioned himself for investigations of the most serious national conflicts in the violent struggle between labor and big capital in the postbellum period. And through his careful creation of the detective as moral mediator between victim and criminal, Pinkerton was able to present the case of the Molly Maguires as a thrilling adventure and a patriotic service to ordinary men and women. He and his agency created themselves as the detectives of the public sphere on a national scale; the simultaneous message of comfort and threat the Pinkerton agencies traded on is contained in their symbol—a watchful eye over the motto We Never Sleep. See Allan Pinkerton, *Spy of the Rebellion: Being a True History of the Spy System of the United States Army during the Late Rebellion* (New York, 1883).

11. Marcus Klein, *Easterns, Westerns, and Private Eyes,* 138.

12. Hazel Carby, introduction to *The Magazine Novels of Pauline Hopkins* (New York: Oxford University Press, 1988), xxxvi–xxxvii.

13. Stephen Soitos, *The Blues Detective: A Study of African American Detective Fiction* (Amherst: University of Massachusetts Press, 1996), 60.

14. Goddu, *Gothic America,* 153. Goddu includes Frederick Douglass, Harriet Jacobs, Charles Chesnutt, Richard Wright, Ann Petry, and half a dozen others in her list of authors who use the gothic toward that end.

15. Pauline Hopkins, *Hagar's Daughter: A Story of Southern Caste Prejudice,* in *The Magazine Novels of Pauline Hopkins,* 226.

16. Hazel Carby, *Reconstructing Womanhood: The Emergence of the Afro-American Woman Novelist* (New York: Oxford University Press, 1987), 151.

17. Soitos, *The Blues Detective*, 70–71.

18. Carby, introduction to *The Magazine Novels of Pauline Hopkins*, xxxviii.

19. Leslie Fiedler, *Love and Death in the American Novel*, rev. ed. (New York: Stein and Day, 1986), 403.

20. Louisa May Alcott, "M. L.," in *Louisa May Alcott: Selected Fiction*, ed. Daniel Shealy, Madeleine Stern, and Joel Myerson (Boston: Little, Brown, 1990), 131–54; originally published in *Commonwealth* (Boston) 1 (January–February 1863). A wealthy white woman falls in love with the quietly dashing singer Paul Frere, who is passing as Spanish though he is actually the son of a slaveowner and his slave. He is found out only when, in gothic fashion, he leaves a page of a letter where a meddling gossip can find it; his bride-to-be sticks by him, and we hear that their subsequent casting out is the best thing that could have happened to either of them, but the sense of trauma and rupture that accompanies the gothic revelation remains.

## Part Two

1. Mary Hatch, "The Author of *The Leavenworth Case*," *Writer* 2 (July 1888): 160.

2. James Hart, *The Popular Book: A History of America's Literary Taste* (New York: Oxford University Press, 1950).

3. Anna Katharine Green, *The Defence of the Bride* (New York: G. P. Putnam's Sons, 1882); and *Risifi's Daughter* (New York: G. P. Putnam's Sons, 1887).

4. Interestingly, Green's poetry is highly narrative, and several of her long poems are historical. Before the two volumes were brought out, Green published poetry in *Lippincott's*, *Scribner's*, and the *Independent*. The most favorable review of *The Defence of the Bride* appeared in *Harper's* magazine, and later appeared facing the title page of *Risifi's Daughter*. *Harper's* wrote: "The ballads and narrative poems which form the greater part of this collection are vigorous productions . . . whose directness and straight-forwardness of narration are in strong contrast with the garrulity of most female writers. The author has the true story-teller's faculty for investing what she has to say with interest, and for keeping expectation on the stretch, and she delivers her messages with masculine force and brevity."

5. *Bookman* 37 (January 1910): 169.

6. Howard Haycraft, *Murder for Pleasure: The Life and Times of the Detective Story* (New York: Appleton-Century, 1941), 83–84.

7. Amelia Butterworth is the narrator of *That Affair Next Door* (New York: G. P. Putnam's Sons, 1897) and *Lost Man's Lane* (New York: G. P. Putnam's Sons, 1898) and appears in *The Circular Study* (New York: McClure's, 1900). Violet Strange appears in the short stories of *The Golden Slipper* (New York: G. P. Putnam's Sons, 1915). Her professional status— surprising for a woman, who should be dependent on her father or a husband for her income—is somewhat neutralized by the revelation that her earnings go to support a sister who has been disowned by the family.

8. The publication history of *The Experiences of a Lady Detective* is rather murky; see Michele B. Slung's introduction to *Crime on Her Mind: Fifteen Stories of Female Sleuths from the Victorian Era to the Forties* (New York: Random House, 1975). The stories in the book feature a police-woman named Mrs. Paschal who details her apprehension of bank robbers and jewel thieves. Collins's *The Law and the Lady* (London: Chatto and Windus, 1875) tells the story of a woman investigating a murder in order to exonerate her accused husband.

9. For a discussion of these female dime-novel detectives, see chapter 2 of Kathleen Klein, *The Woman Detective.*

10. See A. E. Murch, *The Development of the Detective Novel* (London: Peter Owen, 1958); and Barrie Hayne, "Anna Katharine Green," in *Ten Women of Mystery,* ed. Earl Bargainnier (Bowling Green, Ohio: Bowling Green State University Popular Press, 1981). Contemporary reviewers did some of the same kind of work: a review of her first novel rather half-heartedly endorses her work by saying, "It is not up to the standards of Poe's somewhat similar tales, but we commend it nevertheless to all who wish Poe's mantle had fallen on somebody, instead of being carried off into the skies"; review of *The Leavenworth Case, Literary World* 10 (January 18, 1879): 28.

11. Kathleen Woodward, "Anna Katharine Green," *Bookman* 70 (October 1929): 168. The second example is from the *Pittsburgh Dispatch* and was quoted in a brief article: "Anna Katherine [*sic*] Green Tells How She Manufactures Her Plots," *Literary Digest* 58 (July 13, 1918): 48.

12. Review of *Agatha Webb,* "A Good Detective Story," *New York Times,* July 29, 1899, 511.

13. Review of *The Leavenworth Case, Literary World* 10 (January 18, 1879): 28.

14. Review of *The Filigree Ball, Bookman* 17 (May 1903): 218. In 1893, the *Critic* reprinted a recent article from the *London Spectator* that declared "the marked inferiority" of women novelists of all kinds, especially in "imagination and construction." George Putnam, one of Green's publishers, protested against those statements, using Green's famous technical skill in plotting as his rebuttal. Putnam quoted from a letter Wilkie

Collins had written on reading *The Leavenworth Case* that praised the "fertility of invention, the delicate treatment of incidents—and the fine perception of the influence of events on the personages of the story"; "Wilkie Collins on *The Leavenworth Case*," *Critic* 22 (January 28, 1893): 52.

15. Green was actually accused of plagiarizing from a book called *All for Her* (New York: G. W. Carleton, 1877) by a correspondent for *Literary World* and in a letter from its author to the editor of that journal. The correspondent wrote in an 1886 issue of *Literary World:* "I have just learned that Mrs Anna Katherine Green Rohlfe [sic], obtained not only the legal points but all the best points of *The Leavenworth Case* from a novel called *All for Her,* which was published in 1876. It had previously, under the name of *St Jude's Assistant,* been submitted to the Messrs. Putnam [who published *The Leavenworth Case* in 1878] for publication, and declined." The book was also published—each time by different firms that the reporter does not name—under the titles *Little St. Jude's* and *A Cruel Secret; Literary World* 7 (March 6, 1886): 83–84. A few weeks later, a letter to the editor appeared over the anonymous signature of "The Author of *All for Her*" demanding that Green submit to public scrutiny her reckoning of the dates of the writing of her novel; *Literary World* 7 (April 17, 1886): 135. Green replied in an indignant letter—which was not published—that she felt moved to defend both herself and the Putnams from the attack on the following grounds: "First, that a writer who allows his (or is it her?) book to be issued at three different times, by three different firms, under three different names—as this writer is acknowledged to have done—has scarcely a record sufficiently clear to make it good taste, to say the least, for him or her to impeach the honor of one whose reputation, such as it is, has been honestly earned. Secondly, that the points upon which he or she professes to base the charge of plagiarism against me in my novel The Leavenworth Case, viz 'the development of a link in the story by the cross-examination of a witness at a coroner's inquest and the inverse order of the detective work' are such as are so common to detective stories wherever or by whomever written. . . . Thirdly, the book from which I am accused of borrowing ideas is and has been so totally unknown to me that I did not know that such a story existed till my attention was drawn to it some five days ago by the sight of the article in The Literary World" (open letter in her handwriting to the author of *All for Her* and *Literary World,* May 10, 1886, Beinecke Library, Yale University). There are, in fact, very few similarities between the two novels, except that there is a lawyer working as a detective, and an expertise in ballistics helps to solve the murder. *All for Her* is not even a detective novel in the usual sense, for we see the crime committed in the first chapters of the work, then watch as

the lawyer slowly tracks down the killer (his nephew). The novel seems to have been written by a man, or a woman masquerading as a man, but I have no hunch as to the actual identity of the author. The accusation was almost certainly a stunt to boost sales of *All for Her.*

16. The silence is even more striking in light of the fact that Beadle and Adams reissued *The Dead Letter* in 1878, the same year *The Leavenworth Case* was first published.

17. *The Millionaire Baby* was serialized beginning in April 1903 in the *Ladies' Home Journal,* and *The Mayor's Wife* was serialized in the same magazine beginning in January 1905.

18. Review of *One of My Sons, Bookman* 14 (January 1902): 448. Several of Green's novels were reissued in cheap editions and distributed by news-sellers to train stations: *A Matter of Millions,* 1890, Library of Popular Fiction (distributed by the American News Company); *Agatha Webb,* 1899, People's Library (distributed by the American News Company); *The Doctor, His Wife, and the Clock,* 1895, Leisure Hour Library. Green herself makes a reference to this kind of novel in *That Affair Next Door* when her narrator speaks dismissively of "one of those summer publications intended mainly for railroad distribution" (182).

19. Arthur Bartlett Maurice, "The Detective in Fiction," *Bookman* 15 (May 1902): 231, 232, 234.

20. Kathleen Woodward, "The Renaissance of Wonder," *Bookman* 10 (December 1899): 341.

21. See Joan Shelley Rubin, *The Making of Middlebrow Culture* (Chapel Hill: University of North Carolina Press, 1992). On the first page of the introduction, Rubin mentions detective fiction in a catalogue of the kinds of reading one could point to as middlebrow, but doesn't return to the topic.

22. Kelley, "The Sentimentalists," 436, 444, 446, 443, 440.

23. Gillian Brown, *Domestic Individualism: Imagining Self in Nineteenth-Century America* (Berkeley: University of California Press, 1990).

24. My sense of the double strand of detective fiction is based in part on Tzvetan Todorov's essay on detective fiction in *The Poetics of Prose,* trans. Richard Howard (Ithaca: Cornell University Press, 1977), 45. It has also been shaped by Mary Roberts Rinehart's argument that the detective story "consists of two stories running concurrently, the one which the reader follows, and the other a story submerged in the author's mind . . . every time this subcurrent story sticks its head above water, it makes a clew" (Rinehart, "The Detective Story," 39–40).

## 4. "A Woman with a Secret"

1. Hatch, "Author of *The Leavenworth Case*," 161. The letter is undated.

2. Patricia Maida, *Mother of Detective Fiction: The Life and Works of Anna Katharine Green* (Bowling Green, Ohio: Bowling Green State University Popular Press, 1989), 22.

3. Maida, *Mother of Detective Fiction*, 22. Later, according to Maida, he used his connections to help his daughter publish the novel by introducing her to the critic Rossiter Johnson, who brought the manuscript to the attention of George Putnam.

4. Maida uses a figure of six years for the writing of the manuscript (22). I take two and one-half years from a letter written by Green and included in Hatch, "Author of *The Leavenworth Case*," 161.

5. Anna Katharine Green, *The Leavenworth Case*, 1878 (reprint, New York: Dover, 1981). Further references to this edition are in parentheses with the abbreviation *LC*.

6. David Brion Davis, *Homicide in American Fiction, 1798–1860* (Ithaca: Cornell University Press, 1957), 164.

7. This last phrase was altered to "I bent above her as a friend might do" in an 1880 Putnam's reprint of the novel. Since this was a reprint by the original publisher of the novel, I would guess that the alteration is Green's or her editor's, not a simple typographical bowdlerization, but I do not know the circumstances of the editing. Its effect is certainly to dilute the sexual undertones of the scene. See *The Leavenworth Case*, Knickerbocker series (G. P. Putnam's Sons, 1880), 324.

8. Goddu, *Gothic America*, 94.

9. Susan Gubar, "'The Blank Page' and Female Creativity," in *The New Feminist Criticism*, ed. Elaine Showalter (New York: Random House, 1985), 299.

10. Gubar works many of her points from her reading of Isak Dinesen's story "The Blank Page" and its gallery of framed sheets from the marital beds of royal brides. Dinesen writes that the blood on the sheets "bore witness to the honor of a royal bride," and Gubar adds "one of the primary and resonant metaphors provided by the female body is blood . . . the bloodstains are the ink on these woven sheets of paper" ("'The Blank Page' and Female Creativity," 296).

## 5. "A Woman's Hand"

1. Anna Katharine Green, "Why Human Beings Are Interested in Crime," *American Magazine* 87 (1919): 39, 82–85.

2. Barbara Welter, *Dimity Convictions: The American Woman in the Nineteenth Century* (Athens: Ohio University Press, 1976), 135.

3. We see impoverished seamstresses in *The Leavenworth Case* and *A Strange Disappearance;* prostitution in *The Mill Mystery* (1886); wife beating in *Miss Hurd: An Enigma;* and desertion in the plots of *The Mayor's Wife, That Affair Next Door,* and *Miss Hurd: An Enigma.*

4. Green wrote a letter to the editor of the *New York Times* that was printed on October 30, 1917, and which I discuss at some length below. I have no evidence that Green was otherwise active in the antisuffrage movement in New York.

5. Elizabeth Pleck, *Domestic Tyranny: The Making of American Social Policy against Family Violence from Colonial Times to the Present* (New York: Oxford University Press, 1987), 78–79.

6. Timothy Gilfoyle, *City of Eros: New York City, Prostitution, and the Commercialization of Sex* (New York: Norton, 1992), 186.

7. William Leach, *True Love and Perfect Union: The Feminist Reform of Sex and Society* (Middletown, Conn.: Wesleyan University Press, 1989), 39.

8. Nancy F. Cott, "Giving Character to Our Whole Civil Polity: Marriage and the Public Order in the Late Nineteenth Century," in *U.S. History as Women's History: New Feminist Essays,* ed. Linda Kerber, Alice Kessler-Harris, and Kathryn Kish Sklar (Chapel Hill: University of North Carolina Press, 1995), 115.

9. The most pointed example is Metta Victor's 1860 antipolygamy novel, *Lives of Female Mormons.* Bigamy is a common plot device in domestic detective fiction, and the threat of discovery frequently precipitates murder.

10. She applies for, and wins, this position after the murders, when she is hiding under an assumed name. Because she falls ill immediately and is confined to her room, she has no idea that Miss Althorpe's fiancé is her husband, nor does John Randolph Stone know that his wife is living in Miss Althorpe's house.

11. Green, *Lost Man's Lane,* 51.

12. Welter, *Dimity Convictions,* 144.

13. *Literary Digest,* July 13, 1918, 48. *The Forsaken Inn* (New York: R. Bonner's Sons, 1890) is a short novel set in revolutionary America.

14. Carroll Smith-Rosenberg, "The New Woman as Androgyne," in *Disorderly Conduct: Visions of Gender in Victorian America* (New York: Oxford University Press, 1986), 257. Smith-Rosenberg's suggestive interpretation of the centrality of concern about daughters in the upper middle class is borne out in the careful social history of Mary Odem's *Delinquent Daughters: Policing Adolescent Female Sexuality in the United States, 1885–1920* (Chapel Hill: University of North Carolina Press, 1995); and of Kathy

Peiss's " 'Charity Girls' and City Pleasures: Historical Notes on Working-Class Sexuality, 1880–1920," in *Passion and Power: Sexuality in History,* ed. Kathy Peiss and Christina Simmons (Philadelphia: Temple University Press, 1989), 57–69, both of which document the ways female sexual expression was associated with urban working-class behavior and prompted various strategies of regulation by the middle and upper classes.

15. Carrie Chapman Catt and Nettie Rogers Shuler, *Woman Suffrage and Politics: The Inner Story of the Suffrage Movement* (New York: Charles Scribner's Sons, 1923), 271.

16. The exchange of letters seems to have been spontaneous rather than commissioned by the paper. The dates of letters in the *New York Times* are as follows: Green, "Women Must Wait," October 30, 1917, 14; Atherton, "Suffrage a Gain or Loss to Women?" November 2, 1917, 14; Green, "Anna Katharine Green Replies," November 4, 1917, sec. II, 2; Atherton, "The Woman Suffrage Issue," November 4, 1917, 14. The measure passed, and the New York State victory, coming as it did at the end of a year of successes at the state level, signaled the National Suffrage Association to pursue the federal amendment.

17. See her *Patience Sparhawk and Her Times* (New York: John Lane, 1897); and *American Wives and English Husbands* (New York: Dodd, Mead, 1898). Atherton wrote one novel, *The Avalanche* (New York: Frederick Stokes, 1919), that was published with the subtitle "A Mystery." It is not a detective novel formally and structurally; it is a portrait of a marriage under some stress. A wealthy San Francisco merchant thinks that his new young French bride is hiding a secret, probably adultery. He hires a private detective to investigate, but discovers that she has been gambling and is in debt to some rough characters. He and Atherton display a distinctly modern attitude toward marriage in the denouement, when he tells his wife: "You see, things always happen during the first years of married life. . . . I vote we treat it casually, as something that must have been expected sooner or later to disturb our — our — even tenor — and forget it." When his wife recriminates herself for having "stolen" jewelry from the safe to try to pay off her debts, her husband argues that "it was yours as much as mine" and blames himself for having behaved in a patriarchal style by giving her a limited allowance: "men have always driven women into a corner and they have had to get out by methods of their own" (227–28). While this novel just predates Dashiell Hammett's fictions of San Francisco, Atherton's private detective is anything but hard-boiled; he is a teetotaler and says things like, "Jimminy!" and "Lord, that's a poser!"; see 68–76.

18. Reynolds, *Beneath the American Renaissance,* especially on Lippard; Halttunen, "Gothic Imagination and Social Reform."

Part Three

1. Mary Roberts Rinehart, *My Story* (New York: Farrar and Rinehart, 1948), 94. Further references to this text are in parentheses with the abbreviation *MS.* Rinehart published one edition in 1931 and a second edition, with a long afterword concerning the intervening seventeen years, in 1948. The 1948 edition I cite retains the pagination from the 1931 edition. For a discussion of Rinehart's agenda in *My Story,* see Jan Cohn's excellent biography, *Improbable Fiction: The Life of Mary Roberts Rinehart* (Pittsburgh: University of Pittsburgh Press, 1980), xiii–xv. *The Circular Staircase* first appeared in serial form in *All-Story* from November 1907 through March 1908.

2. The Amelia Butterworth novels are *That Affair Next Door* (1897), *Lost Man's Lane* (1898), and *The Circular Study* (1900). The novel published by Bobbs-Merrill that seems closest to Rinehart's own themes and concerns is *The Mayor's Wife* (1907), which is narrated by the sort of sharp-eyed, unmarried woman Rinehart found interesting.

3. From a study by Irving Harlow Hart, cited in Cohn, *Improbable Fiction,* 203.

4. Howard Haycraft, *The Art of the Mystery Story* (New York: Simon and Schuster, 1941), 319.

5. Symons, *Bloody Murder,* 90.

6. Certainly the female gothic has continued throughout the twentieth century, in both high and low styles. What I am suggesting is that the particular blending of female gothic and detective fiction that is the subject of this book had lost much of its cultural currency by the end of the 1940s, a time, in the aftermath of World War II, when many of the gender conflicts of the first half of the century gave an appearance of being settled. While many of Rinehart's books are still in print, the audience seems to be small and to consist mainly of women who read Rinehart on the recommendation of older female relatives and friends or to revisit their own girlhood reading. (My evidence for this is entirely anecdotal, based on conversations with detective fiction buffs and writers over the last eight years.)

7. Cohn, *Improbable Fiction,* 232.

8. Cohn, *Improbable Fiction,* 30.

9. Cohn, *Improbable Fiction,* 30–31.

10. Mary Kelley, *Private Woman, Public Stage: Literary Domesticity in Nineteenth-Century America* (New York: Oxford University Press, 1984).

11. Rinehart commented on all of these issues in her autobiography, and on prohibition in "If I Had a Daughter" (*Forum,* March 1932) and "Can Women Stop Crime" (*Saturday Evening Post,* November 18, 1933); on woman suffrage in "Why Don't You Use Your Vote?" (*Ladies' Home*

*Journal,* August 1932). She was initially reluctant to discuss breast cancer publicly but claimed, with obvious pride, that the interview "I Had Cancer" (*Ladies' Home Journal,* July 1947) "amazed the editors. They report that no other article or piece of fiction ever had so enormous a public reaction" (*MS,* 522). In the way it urges women to undergo breast examinations and surgery the article brings together Rinehart's identity as a nurse and her later life as a celebrity.

12. In addition, from 1930 to 1932, she wrote a monthly column called "Thoughts" for the *Ladies' Home Journal,* a task she found aggravating: "Here many of the taboos still existed. There was to be no controversial matter in my page, and that in highly controversial times" (*MS,* 467).

13. Rubin, *The Making of Middlebrow Culture,* xviii.

14. Rinehart reports in the second edition of *My Story* that Dorothy Parker called Rinehart's statement about her grandmother ("Widowed early with five children, completely untrained, and with no openings outside of school teaching for women in those days, she fell back on her needle" [5]) "one of the most painful [things] she could imagine" (*MS,* 433). I cannot claim that Parker read Rinehart extensively, but the two share a similar sense of economy, pacing, and feminist acerbity. Rinehart's mysteries always contain comedy, but some of her funniest material is in her essays about camping with her sons and husband in the West, collected in *The Out Trail* (New York: George Doran, 1923). In one passage she cautions women not to succumb to the temptation to show off their camp cooking, writing that she once knew a woman "who made a delectable biscuit in a reflector oven, and for months on end in the summer her life was just one biscuit after another" (20).

Cohn discovered that when Rinehart sent Alice B. Toklas a copy of a new novel (*A Light in the Window,* 1948) shortly after Stein's death, Toklas replied: "It must have been before the 1914–1918 war that Gertrude discovered MRR. Anyway I can still see her coming into the room with a book at the rue de Fleurus and her saying she really writes very well — as if I knew what book she had under her arm. So thank you for the book and the happy memory it revives" (Alice B. Toklas to "Editor," Rinehart and Company, January 1948. Used by permission of the Alice B. Toklas estate.

15. Gertrude Stein, *Blood on the Dining Room Floor* (Berkeley: Creative Arts, 1982), 50–51. The novel was written in 1933 and first published in 1948.

16. Amy Kaplan argues in *The Social Construction of American Realism* (Chicago: University of Chicago Press, 1988) that Wharton sought to distance herself from the kind of popular, domestic, and gothic fiction that Rinehart produced. The terms of Wharton's strategy of rejection were the association of American women writers with cultural and literary senti-

mentality and sentimentality with commercialism and triviality (see 66–71). Rutger Jewett, in a letter discouraging Wharton from writing for the magazine market, wrote, "Work of high literary quality is not so good for these popular magazines as the typical lowbrow serial publication. Mary Roberts Rinehart and Kathleen Norris grind out ideal stuff—for serialization"; in R. W. B. Lewis, *Edith Wharton* (Harper and Row, 1975), 472. That said, it is also possible to argue that Rinehart saw the market-place for women writers in much the same terms—feminine literary discourse as popular and trivial, masculine discourse as artistic and enduring. While Rinehart might appear to have wholeheartedly embraced the female popular tradition in writing both detective novels and domestic fiction, she still looked with some ambivalence on the popularity of her detective novels. Like Wharton, Rinehart resented depictions of herself as a commercial writer; both writers—as Kaplan argues for Wharton—tried to make authorship a legitimate, serious form of work for women. Candace Waid, in *Edith Wharton's Letters from the Underworld: Fictions of Women and Writing* (Chapel Hill: University of North Carolina Press, 1991), argues that "for Wharton, 'the real' is a gender-related, sexually charged category," and that Wharton's 1922 introduction to *Ethan Frome* depicts women authors as writers of alluring but illusory and misleading stories (see 88–89). It is also interesting that when, in the introduction to *Ethan Frome*, Wharton speaks of the siren songs of the "insinuating wraiths of false 'good situations,'" she identifies dramatic plot as a female weakness. Rinehart, like Green, wrote fiction in which establishing the coherency and tautness of plot is the concern not only of the author but of the reader, the detectives, and even the murderer. But Rinehart shares Wharton's sense that reliance on "good situations" is the antithesis of art; she confesses, abashedly, that in her early efforts "to bolster up my faulty craftsmanship, I resorted to plot, that crutch of the beginner, that vice of the experienced writer. I devised weird and often horrible plots" (*MS*, 86). For more on the question of realism as a gendered discourse, see Alfred Habegger, *Gender, Fantasy, and Realism in American Literature* (New York: Columbia University Press, 1982).

17. Cohn reconstructs this event in some detail; see *Improbable Fiction*, 69–70.

18. Mary Roberts Rinehart, "The Chaotic Decade," *Ladies' Home Journal*, May 1930, 35.

19. Cohn argues that the collection of short stories titled *Married People* (New York: Farrar and Rinehart, 1937) and the novel *This Strange Adventure* (New York: Doubleday Doran, 1928) are the works that "give credence to Rinehart's statement 'in my heart I had always been a realist'" (*Improbable Fiction*, 210).

20. Mary Roberts Rinehart, *K.* (Boston: Houghton Mifflin, 1915).

21. Cohn, *Improbable Fiction*, 200.

22. Cohn, *Improbable Fiction*, 179.

23. I hasten to add that she also grew increasingly out of touch with the realities of middle- and lower-class life. During the Depression, when she was making approximately $100,000 a year, she wrote an article that was a misguided attempt to "rally" the American people from their economic discouragement by describing her own efforts to work hard and put her money back into circulation by buying houses and clothes. It drew what Rinehart claims was her first "unfavorable mail reaction" (*MS,* 469). The editorial was "A Woman Goes to Market," *Saturday Evening Post,* January 31, 1931: 6–7.

24. Ross MacDonald, *On Crime Writing* (Santa Barbara: Capra Press, 1973), 25.

## 6. "No Place for a Spinster"

1. Citations for quotations are in parentheses with the abbreviation *CS* and refer to the Carroll and Graf reprint (New York, 1985).

2. The phrase "familiar fiction" is from Gilbert and Gubar, *The Madwoman in the Attic,* 534.

3. Sedgwick, *The Coherence of Gothic Conventions,* 4.

4. See Gilbert and Gubar, *The Madwoman in the Attic,* 87–89.

5. Freud, in his essay "The Uncanny," explains male ambivalence toward the female genitalia by calling them the "entrance to the former *heim* [home] of all human beings, to the place where everyone dwelt once upon a time and in the beginning"; *On Creativity and the Unconscious,* ed. Benjamin Nelson (New York: Harper, 1958), 153.

6. Kahane, "The Gothic Mirror," 334.

7. Rinehart's interest in this kind of epistemological and narratorial education of her heroines is emphasized by the fact that though she wrote many novels that feature similar kinds of upper-middle-class spinsters, she never wrote a continuing series with a recurring amateur — or professional — sleuth as Green did.

8. Lehman, *The Perfect Murder,* 3.

9. Tompkins, *West of Everything,* 38.

10. From an interview in L. C. Pickett, *Across My Path: Memories of People I Have Known* (New York, 1916), 107–8. Quoted at greater length in Stern, introduction to *Behind a Mask,* xxviii.

11. Sedgwick, *The Coherence of Gothic Conventions,* 13, 20.

12. Goddu, *Gothic America,* 152.

7. "I Suppose They Stood It as Long as They Could"

1. The Tish stories appeared in the *Saturday Evening Post* between 1910 and 1937. They were collected in several volumes, including *The Amazing Adventures of Letitia Carberry* (Indianapolis: Bobbs-Merrill, 1910); *Tish* (Boston: Houghton Mifflin, 1916); and *More Tish* (New York: George Doran, 1921). See Cohn's bibliography of Rinehart's work in *Improbable Fiction* for a complete catalogue.

2. Ruth Freeman and Paula Klaus, "Blessed or Not? The New Spinster in England and the United States in the Late Nineteenth and Early Twentieth Centuries," *Journal of Family History* 9 (Winter 1984): 394–414. About the iconography of class they write, "Most commentators expressed little concern over working-class spinsters. These women had always worked and could, most believed, readily find employment in factories or domestic service" (394–95).

3. Nancy F. Cott, *The Grounding of Modern Feminism* (New Haven: Yale University Press, 1987), 14.

4. Cott, *The Grounding of Modern Feminism,* 158.

5. Elizabeth Jordan, "On Being a Spinster," *Saturday Evening Post,* April 10, 1926, 35, 214, 217. She explores the difference between being the dependent and having dependents more fully in "Family Parasites: The Economic Value of the Unmarried Sister," *Saturday Evening Post,* April 5, 1930, 35, 165–66. As the title suggests, she argues that economically independent women were still considered fair game for exploitation by their married siblings, though the gifts demanded now were cash loans, groceries, and clothing instead of housework. She also indicates that single women were still expected to care for and support their elderly parents, with disastrous consequences for their own old age.

6. See Christina Simmons, "Modern Sexuality and the Myth of Victorian Repression," in *Passion and Power: Sexuality and History,* ed. Kathy Peiss and Christina Simmons (Philadelphia: Temple University Press, 1989); Pamela S. Haag, "In Search of 'The Real Thing': Ideologies of Love, Modern Romance, and Women's Sexual Subjectivity in the United States, 1920–1940," in *American Sexual Politics: Sex, Gender, and Race since the Civil War,* ed. John Fout and Maura Tantillo (Chicago: University of Chicago Press, 1993).

7. Alice Ordway, "Thirty—and Single," *Atlantic Monthly,* February 1933, 252–53.

8. Margaret Culkin Banning, "The Plight of the Spinster," *Harper's Monthly,* June 1929, 88–97. Banning was an activist for women's education and the author of several dozen novels and hundreds of short stories.

9. Lilian Bell, "Old Maids of the Last Generation and This," *Saturday*

*Evening Post,* December 25, 1926, 18, 46. Bell was a Georgia writer and author of *The Love Affairs of an Old Maid* (New York: Harper Brothers, 1893) and several other novels.

10. Jordan, "On Being a Spinster," 217. Jordan's words have some weight, as she was editor of *Harper's Bazaar* from 1910 to 1913, then editor at Harper and Brothers from 1913 to 1918.

11. "The Old Maid" stands as Wharton's commentary on the 1850s in the retrospective quartet of linked novellas published as *Old New York* in 1924 (reprint, New York: Simon and Schuster, 1995). The description of "a typical old maid" is from page 128. "The Old Maid," with its interest in the spinster figure and in a long-kept sexual secret that constantly threatens to resurface ("the problem which, through all the years of silence and evasiveness, had lain as close to the surface as a corpse too hastily buried" [144]), could almost be, in its barest plot skeleton, a Rinehart story.

12. James Kesselring, *Arsenic and Old Lace* (New York: Random House, 1941). Rinehart rightly felt that the play had been stolen from her Tish stories; see Cohn, *Improbable Fiction,* 219.

13. Cott, *The Grounding of Modern Feminism,* 150.

14. For a study that looks at the porousness of those identities, see Tricia Franzen, *Spinsters and Lesbians: Independent Womanhood in the United States* (New York: New York University Press, 1996).

15. The question of whether female sexuality in the 1920s is best understood as a matter of conformity and the imposition of hegemony or as a matter of rebellion and threat to social order is one on which Cott and Smith-Rosenberg might seem to diverge. But I think the two arguments are reconciled when we keep in mind that types like the "Victorian old maid," the "mannish lesbian," the "New Woman," and the "flapper" were all ideologically loaded cultural constructions of the period and reactions to threatening changes in the economic and political power of women.

16. Mary Roberts Rinehart, *The Confession,* 1921 (reprint, New York: Kensington, 1989), 29.

17. Poe begins the first of his "tales of ratiocination," as he called his detective stories, with an extended passage about the detective's mind as the mind that "disentangles." One of the most important classical Freudian essays is Geraldine Pederson-Krag's "Detective Stories and the Primal Scene," which first appeared in *Psychoanalytic Quarterly* in 1949 and has since been reprinted in Most and Stowe, *The Poetics of Murder.* She argues that the allure and pleasure of reading detective fiction comes from the way it replays certain experiences of not knowing and then discovering "a secret wrongdoing." Lacan's *Seminar on "The Purloined Letter"* (also in Most and Stowe) has been central to a revival of interest in detective fiction as a complex linguistic form. Clearly, a well-trained Freudian or

Lacanian literary scholar could do fascinating readings of Rinehart's version of the family romance; of special interest might be the scopophilic curiosity of her virginal heroines.

18. Rinehart might have been introduced to Freudianist and other ideas from her husband's reading for his own work. Cohn tells us that Stanley Rinehart underwent some medical training in Vienna in 1910 and heard Freud lecture on infantile sexuality, ideas he found offensive (Cohn, *Improbable Fiction*, 58, 175). For histories of nineteenth-century psychology and early Freudianism in America, see Nathan G. Hale, *Freud and the Americans: The Beginnings of Psychoanalysis in the United States, 1876–1917* (New York: Oxford University Press, 1971), and *The Rise and Crisis of Psychoanalysis in the United States: Freud and the Americans, 1917–1985* (Oxford: Oxford University Press, 1995); Thomas Lutz, *American Nervousness, 1903: An Anecdotal History* (Ithaca: Cornell University Press, 1991).

19. In America, William Dean Howells made an amalgam of the physician, the psychologist, and the detective in his "Turkish Room Tales." These stories have received scant critical attention, but they show how blurred were the lines between the psychological and the supernatural in the decades surrounding the theorization of the human unconscious. The stories are collected in *Questionable Shapes* (New York: Harper, 1903) and *Between the Dark and the Daylight* (New York: Harper, 1907).

20. Miss Marple first appears in Agatha Christie's *Murder at the Vicarage* (1930). Harriet Vane is introduced in Dorothy Sayers's *Strong Poison* (1930); she had a predecessor named Miss Climpson in Sayers's *Unnatural Death* (1927). All three were undoubtedly inspired by Green's and Rinehart's characters. For a very interesting article on Sayers's development of a new "use" for the "superfluous" single women of post–World War I Britain, see Catherine Kenney, "Detecting a Novel Use for Spinsters in Sayers's Fiction," in *Old Maids to Radical Spinsters: Unmarried Women in the Twentieth-Century Novel*, ed. Laura Doan (Urbana: University of Illinois Press, 1991).

21. Tony Tanner, *Adultery in the Novel: Contract and Transgression* (Baltimore: Johns Hopkins University Press, 1979); Joseph Allen Boone, *Tradition Counter Tradition: Love and the Form of Fiction* (Chicago: University of Chicago Press, 1987).

22. Tanner, *Adultery in the Novel*, 15, 3.

23. Boone, *Tradition Counter Tradition*, 3.

24. Brooks, *Reading for the Plot*, 90–112.

25. The phrase "magic or violence" is from Sedgwick's *The Coherence of Gothic Conventions* and is discussed in chapter 1 above.

26. Mary Roberts Rinehart, *The Album*, 1933 (reprint, New York: Kens-

ington, 1988); originally serialized in the *Saturday Evening Post,* April–May 1933. References are to the Kensington reprint and are in parentheses with the abbreviation *A.*

27. *The Confession* was first published in *Good Housekeeping* in the summer of 1917. It was published in book form, paired with another story as *The Confession and Sight Unseen* (New York: George Doran) in 1921.

28. For a very insightful comparison of the treatment Lizzie Borden received and that meted out to Bridget Durgan, an Irish-born servant also accused of a brutal murder, see Ann Jones, *Women Who Kill* (Boston: Beacon, 1996), 195–237.

29. From Emma Borden's testimony at her sister's trial. Edmund Pearson, *The Trial of Lizzie Borden* (New York: Doubleday, 1937), 275.

30. Gertrude Stein, "American Crimes and How They Matter," in *How Writing Is Written* (Los Angeles: Black Sparrow, 1974), 103.

31. John Gill, afterword to *Blood on the Dining Room Floor.* Harriet Chessman explores the implications of Gill's insight in depth in chapter 5 of her *The Public Is Invited to Dance: Representation, the Body, and Dialogue in Gertrude Stein* (Stanford: Stanford University Press, 1989). Dennis Bass sees the presence of Lizzie Borden haunting Stein; his arguments are most persuasive in his discussion of her college essay called "In the Red Deeps," several sections of *Tender Buttons* (most directly in "A Petticoat"), and her 1921 poem "Curtains Dream." "The Gertrude Stein Connection," in *Proceedings: Lizzie Borden Conference* [Bristol Community College, 1992], ed. Jules Ryckebusch (Portland, Maine: King Philip, 1993), 117–36.

32. Edith Wharton, "Confession," in *The World Over* (New York: Appleton-Century, 1936). In their edition of her letters, R. W. B. Lewis and Nancy Lewis tell us that Wharton "wrote a little more than one act of a play" based on the Lizzie Borden case and on "Confession," but that "upon hearing from Sheldon that the subject had already been used, she gave it up." See *The Letters of Edith Wharton* (New York: Scribner's, 1988), 585, n. 2. The play Sheldon referred to may have been John Colton and Miles Carlton's *Nine Pine Street,* which starred Lillian Gish and premiered at New York's Longacre Theater in April 1933.

33. I am admittedly stretching the definition of a generation when I include Wharton (1862) with Stein (1873) and Rinehart (1876). But in the 1930s, these women were in their sixties and seventies and may have had a similar psychic distance from (and closeness to) the crime. Lizzie Borden herself was born in 1860.

34. Edmund Pearson, "The Borden Case," in *Studies in Murder* (Garden City, N.Y.: Garden City Publishers, 1924), 3–120, reprinted by the Modern Library in 1938; "The End of the Borden Case," *Forum* (March 1928): 370–

390, and in his *Five Murders* (Garden City, N.Y.: Doubleday Doran, 1928): 263–96; "The Legends of Lizzie," *New Yorker,* April 23, 1933: 20–22, and in his *More Studies in Murder* (New York: Harrison Smith and Robert Hass, 1936; *The Trial of Lizzie Borden* (Garden City, N.Y.: Doubleday Doran, 1937); "The Bordens: A Postscript," in *Murder at Smutty Nose and Other Murders* (Garden City, N.Y.: Doubleday Doran, 1938).

35. The book-length study was by a local reporter named Edmund Porter and was published under the title *The Fall River Tragedy* by a Fall River publisher, George Buffinton, in 1893. It was reissued by Borden scholar Robert A. Flynn's press, King Philip Publishing of Portland, Maine, in 1985. Freeman wrote her story, called "The Long Arm," specifically for a detective story contest along with J. E. Chamberlin. The story, in characteristic fashion, is set in a small New England village and is told from the point of view of a young woman falsely accused of killing her father. This Lizzie Borden figure works to solve the mystery of her father's death in order to clear her own name and discovers that the real murderer is the village seamstress, an elderly spinster, who killed the father because he had recently proposed to her lifelong female companion, and, as she puts it, "some bonds are as sacred as marriage." The story hasn't been collected in recent volumes of Freeman's work, but it was published in the long-out-of-print contest winners' collection, *The Long Arm and Other Detective Stories* (London: Chapman and Hall, 1895), and it appeared in *Pocket Magazine* 1 (December 1895): 1–76. In her letters, she expresses delight over receiving one particular letter after winning the prize: "I must tell you that Anna Katherine [*sic*] Green wrote me a letter of congratulation. Was it not nice of her?" Letter from Freeman to Charles W. Wilcox, in *The Infant Sphinx: Collected Letters of Mary E. Wilkins Freeman,* ed. Brent Kendrick (Metuchen, N.J.: Scarecrow Press, 1985), 175. Elizabeth Jordan's story, "Ruth Herrick's Assignment," appears in her *Tales of the City Room* (New York: Charles Scribner's, 1898) and is based on her experience as a reporter covering the trial. Pauline Hopkins's story, "Talma Gordon," first appeared in *Colored American Magazine* (October 1900) and was recently reprinted in Paula Woods's anthology *Spooks, Spies and Private Eyes: Black Mystery, Crime, and Suspense Fiction* (New York: Doubleday, 1995).

36. Pearson, "The Borden Case" (1924), 25. He makes the same point in slightly different language in his introduction to *The Trial of Lizzie Borden,* describing "the usual assortment of useless toilet articles: among other things, a lace-covered pin-cushion and two white glass bottles, supposed to contain 'toilet water' or something—always correctly at their posts and always empty. A guestchamber was hardly decent without them" (25).

37. Pearson, *The Trial of Lizzie Borden*, 28, 29.

38. Wayne K. Hobson, "Lizzie Borden and Victorian America: Shifting Perspectives, 1892–1992," in *Proceedings: Lizzie Borden Conference,* ed. Ryckebush, 176–77. Hobson bases this conclusion on the study of several nonfiction books on the Borden murders from this period and on the 1934 play *Nine Pine Street,* Agnes de Mille's 1948 ballet *Fall River Legend,* and Jack Beeson's 1967 opera, *Lizzie Borden: A Family Portrait in Three Acts.* Anthony Hilfer's arguments are in his *The Revolt from the Village, 1915–1930* (Chapel Hill: University of North Carolina Press, 1969).

39. I feel certain that Rinehart read Pearson's pieces on the Borden murders and other cases either in mainstream periodicals like the *New Yorker* and *Forum* (the second of which she published in herself) or in his several book-length collections. Interestingly, Pearson's *Studies in Murder,* which includes his first essay on the Borden murders, also includes an essay on the 1896 murders aboard the merchant schooner *Herbert Fuller,* another actual murder case that Rinehart used as the basis for a novel. *The After House* was serialized in *McClure's* in 1913 (and published in book form by Houghton Mifflin in 1914); in it, Rinehart proves that a supposed eyewitness to the murders lied in court. While the serial was still running, the man convicted on evidence given by this witness was paroled and later pardoned by Woodrow Wilson. As Jan Cohn puts it, "Rinehart's role in seeing justice done . . . was an even better story than the novel itself," and notes that Claudette Colbert played Rinehart in a 1957 ABC teleplay based on the tale (*Improbable Fiction,* 66–67).

Pearson's essay on these murders was written after Rinehart's novel. He does not mention her intervention in the frame-up, and he gives this slighting review of her book: "It is a rather confused and jerky novel about a triple murder on a private yacht. . . . What might have been a masterpiece of grim horror is dissipated into a second-rate tale about wealthy and fashionable folk" (*Studies in Murder,* 225). His comments indicate that the two were not friendly, and his abrasiveness reinforces my own sense that Rinehart wrote *The Album* as a response, in part, to Pearson's version of the Borden murders.

40. The prosecutor, Hosea Knowlton, referred to the murder of Lizzie's father as "the far sadder tragedy" and seemed to assume that the jury would find patricide utterly unthinkable. He argued that the murder of the father was a desperate act to cover up the murder of the stepmother: it "was done as a wicked and dreadful necessity, which if she could have foreseen she never would have followed that mother up the stairs . . . [and] slain her" (Pearson, *The Trial of Lizzie Borden,* 344, 345).

41. See John D'Emilio and Estelle Freedman, *Intimate Matters: A History of Sexuality in America* (New York: Harper and Row, 1988). The

middle and upper classes did not confine their regulation of female sexuality to their own women in the decades surrounding the turn of the century, but extended that work to poor and working-class women, as Mary Odem has detailed in *Delinquent Daughters.*

42. The view that hoarding was the primary cause of the Bank Holiday of 1933 is the traditional one, and was the argument Roosevelt used in justifying his drastic actions to the public. More recent historians have argued that beginning in February 1933, hoarding was caused by the fear that Roosevelt would devalue the dollar (which he eventually did), and that the more precipitate cause of the Bank Holiday was a large loss of gold by the New York Reserve Bank. See Barrie Wigmore, "Was the Bank Holiday of 1933 Caused by a Run on the Dollar?" *Journal of Economic History* 47 (1987): 739–55.

43. The context of patriotism would have been made inescapably clear to those initial readers. The second installment of *The Album* ran after an article entitled "The Economic Drive against America" that outlined foreign strategies to "create in this country hoards of gold, impounded to the credit of foreign countries, the first effect of which was the same as if Americans themselves were hoarding the gold, as they have been exhorted not to do" (*Saturday Evening Post,* April 15, 1933, 3).

44. Cott, *The Grounding of Modern Feminism,* 151.

45. Stein, "American Crimes and How They Matter," 103.

46. References to this text are in parentheses with the abbreviation TG and refer to the reprint in Woods, *Spooks, Spies and Private Eyes.*

47. Carby, *Reconstructing Womanhood,* 135. Carby reads this story even more emphatically than I do as having "situated the personalized family history within a wider imperialist history."

## Afterword

1. Charlotte Perkins Gilman, *Unpunished,* ed. Catherine J. Golden and Denise D. Knight (New York: Feminist Press, 1997), 216–17.

2. Ann Lane, *To "Herland" and Beyond: The Life and Works of Charlotte Perkins Gilman* (New York: Pantheon, 1990), xxxi; Golden and Knight, afterword to *Unpunished,* 216, 221.

3. Golden and Knight, afterword, 217.

4. Lillian Robinson, "Killing Patriarchy: Charlotte Perkins Gilman, the Murder Mystery, and Post-Feminist Propaganda," *Tulsa Studies in Women's Literature* 10 (Fall 1991): 273–85.

5. Ann Lane, ed., *The Charlotte Perkins Gilman Reader* (New York: Pantheon, 1980), 170 (from Lane's headnote to an excerpt from *Unpunished*).

6. Golden and Knight report that Gilman submitted the manuscript for review at Macmillan and G. P. Putnam's Sons, and that Gilman's daughter engaged a literary agent to try to place the manuscript after Gilman's death ("afterword," 235, n. 9, and 236, n. 10). She may have submitted it at more houses — likely prospects would have been Bobbs-Merrill, Grosset and Dunlap, and Doubleday Doran, all of which published detective fiction by women in that period.

7. For the dime-novel origins of the hard-boiled school, see Denning, *Mechanic Accents;* Ron Goulart, *The Dime Detectives* (New York: Mysterious Press, 1988); J. Randolph Cox, "The Dime Novel Detective and His Elusive Trail," *Dime Novel Roundup* (December 1985: 2–13). Richard Slotkin addresses the historical and thematic relation of the western and the hard-boiled detective novel in chapter 6 of *Gunfighter Nation: The Myth of the Frontier in Twentieth-Century America* (New York: Harper-Collins, 1992).

8. *Black Mask* was founded by H. L. Mencken and George Nathan in 1920, and passed through several hands until it was taken over by Joseph Thompson Shaw in 1926. Shaw worked deliberately and successfully to change the style and ethos of the detective story through his editing of Dashiell Hammett, Raymond Chandler, Lester Dent, Carroll John Daly, and others.

9. William Marling uses the term *watershed* in *The American Roman Noir,* 106; Julian Symons uses "The American Revolution" as the title of his chapter on Dashiell and Hammett in *Bloody Murder.*

10. Raymond Chandler, "The Simple Art of Murder," in *The Simple Art of Murder* (New York: Ballantine Books, 1972). Further references to the essay are in parentheses in the body of the text with the abbreviation SA.

11. The phrase "clue-puzzle" is from Stephen Knight, *Form and Ideology in Crime Fiction* (Bloomington: Indiana University Press, 1980), 107. For another critical angle on the British style of detective story, see Maria DiBattista, "The Lowly Art of Murder: Modernism and the Case of the Free Woman," in *High and Low Moderns: Literature and Culture, 1889–1939,* ed. Maria DiBattista and Lucy McDiarmid (New York: Oxford University Press, 1996), 176–93.

12. Marcus Klein, *Easterns, Westerns and Private Eyes,* 182–83.

13. Marling, *The American Roman Noir,* 113.

14. Marcus Klein, *Easterns, Westerns, and Private Eyes,* 183.

15. John Cawelti, *Adventure, Mystery, and Romance: Formula Stories as Art and Popular Culture* (Chicago: University of Chicago Press, 1976), 142.

16. Gail Bederman, *Manliness and Civilization: A Cultural History of Gender and Race in the United States, 1880–1917* (Chicago: University of Chicago Press, 1995), 12–19.

17. Angus McLaren, *The Trials of Masculinity: Policing Sexual Boundaries, 1870–1930* (Chicago: University of Chicago Press, 1997), 238.

18. Lee Clark Mitchell points out that Conan Doyle's first Sherlock Holmes story (*A Study in Scarlet*, 1887) contains a long framed tale about forced Mormon marriage in the American West, twenty-five years before Zane Grey's similarly plotted *Riders of the Purple Sage* (1912). See introduction to Zane Grey, *Riders of the Purple Sage* (Oxford: Oxford University Press, 1995), ix.

19. Marling makes an extensive analysis of the principle of "smoothness" in modernism generally and in the roman noir in particular, contrasting it with the "roughness" of older aesthetics. See his *American Roman Noir.*

20. I'm speaking here specifically of the early detectives of Hammett, Chandler, and the *Black Mask* school. Post–World War II practitioners of the hard-boiled school (e.g., Ross MacDonald and Walter Mosley) often include a much more conscience-driven, even old-fashioned detective.

21. Marlowe's relationship with the police is usually friendlier than the Continental Op's, and even in Hammett's fiction the P.I. turns over most miscreants to the proper authorities in the end. But in Hammett's novels, the police are often corrupt, with the Chief of Police of Poisonville trying to assassinate the Op.

22. The parallel between Charles P. Dawn and Gilman's blackmailing attorney, Wade Vaughn, is intriguing. The gentleman lawyer type is not very important to Rinehart either, suggesting that the valorization of lawyers by Victor and Green was specific to the emergence of the professional class as a new social category in the nineteenth century.

23. Although I noted in chapter 3 that the spy narrative was a source for the early domestic detective novel, many scholars trace the figure of the hard-boiled detective straight back to Allan Pinkerton, who established a reputation for expertise in infiltration that put his agents in great demand as strikebreakers and *agents provocateurs* in the decades around the turn of the century. Hammett worked for the Pinkerton agency for four years, and claimed to have been offered a bounty by an industrialist client for the death of an iww leader, which prompted him to get out of that line of work.

24. For the ways African American detective fiction writers such as Chester Himes and Ishmael Reed (in *Mumbo Jumbo* [New York: Macmillan, 1972]) parody the white detective, see Soitos, *The Blues Detective,* 41–42. Walter Mosley's Easy Rawlins series also renovates the racial framework of the mid-century hard-boiled novel with great success.

25. Hammett also refers to him as "the Levantine" (i.e., from the Mediterranean area including Greece, Turkey, Cyprus, and Egypt) rather than

by a specific nationality, though he carries a Greek passport. The film version of the novel makes Cairo's internationalism even more pointedly an issue of divided loyalties by having him carry passports from Greece, France, and Britain.

26. Both *punk* and *gunsel*, the terms by which Hammett and Chandler's characters refer to young men in the employ of villains, have definite connotations of homosexuality. Both were used in the nineteenth century to refer derisively to young tramps who formed sexual pairs with older men on the road; it was in the mid-twentieth century that *punk* came to mean a worthless, no-account young man. The connection to the world of the vagabonds is underlined when Spade taunts Wilmer by asking, "[H]ow long have you been off the goose-berry lay, son?" (120) — that is to say, in tramps' lingo, "How long has it been since you were stealing garments off clotheslines?" See *The Random House Dictionary of American Slang*, vol. 1 (1994). Tramps, vagabonds, and drifters became increasingly visible to mainstream culture in the Depression, and according to Estelle Freedman, they were associated with dangerous and deviant sexual values. See her "'Uncontrolled Desires': The Response to the Sexual Psychopath, 1920–1960," in *Passion and Power,* ed. Peiss and Simmons, 204.

27. Geiger's room, by contrast is "neat, fussy, womanish" with a "flounced cover" on the bed and perfume on the dresser.

28. Deviance from heterosexuality is not the only way a man can go wrong in the world of the hard-boiled. Sam Spade offers a cautionary tale about a man who succumbs utterly to a stifling conventionality. This man, named Flitcraft, is one day almost struck by a falling beam as he walks by a construction site, an intimation of mortality that makes him feel "like somebody had taken the lid off life and let him look at the works" (63). He decides to run away and remake his life, abruptly leaving his real-estate business, his wife and children, his comfortable home in a Tacoma suburb, and his Packard automobile — all "the appurtenances of successful American living" (62). But he is a man so "comfortable in step with his surroundings" that after a brief interval he finds himself settled in Spokane, remarried, and back in "the same groove he had jumped out of in Tacoma" (64). Steven Marcus offers an excellent discussion of this story from a philosophical point of view, but I would add that Flitcraft's apparent poverty of imagination is also a comment on the sense of forces of gender conformity in this period. Spade, and Hammett, indicate that the private eye is heroic because he is a nonconformist while still upholding certain principles of order and honor — all of which is in keeping with the modern masculine sensibility. See Steven Marcus, "Dashiell Hammett," in *The Poetics of Murder,* ed. Most and Stowe, 197–209.

29. But as we see elsewhere in the discourses of gender, the hard-boiled

style sounds a counter note in the midst of its establishment of the detective as the enemy of the homosexual. The descriptions of Spade's and Marlowe's fights with Cairo, Wilmer, and Lundgren contain a level of detail about the physical contact between the struggling men that is subtly but noticeably more eroticized than the mechanical descriptions of action scenes including these same detectives and straight men. When Spade disarms Wilmer at one point, we get two full paragraphs of commentary like this: "The boy, teeth set hard together, did not stop straining against the man's big hands, but he could not tear himself loose, could not keep the man's hands from crawling down over his hands. The boy's teeth ground together audibly, making a noise that mingled with the noise of Spade's breathing as Spade crushed the boy's hands" (*MF*, 120). Likewise, when Marlowe goes after Lundgren, he describes a moonlit making of something like the beast with two backs: "I took hold of my right wrist with my left hand and turned my right hipbone into him and for a minute it was a balance of weights. We seemed to hang there in the misty moonlight, two grotesque creatures whose feet scraped on the road and whose breath panted with effort" (*BS*, 93). In the midst of cleaning Cairo's clock, Spade pauses and smiles at his adversary with an expression that is "gentle, even dreamy" (*MF*, 46). I would suggest that the sexual undertone is part of the larger phenomenon of the eroticization of violence in the hard-boiled style (which we might contrast with the eroticization of fear in the female gothic). In addition, I think the "punk" figure might have to be understood more figuratively as one who shadows the detective — that is, doubles him — while the fat villain serves as the detective's diametric opposite.

30. This gem, from Hammett's "$106,000 Blood Money," is quoted by Marcus Klein in *Easterns, Westerns, and Private Eyes*, 181.

31. Peter Schwenger, *Phallic Critiques* (London: Routledge and Kegan Paul, 1984); Tompkins, *West of Everything*.

32. Schwenger, *Phallic Critiques*, 9, 22–31.

33. James M. Cain, *Double Indemnity*, 1936 (reprint, New York: Random House, 1989).

34. Freedman, "Uncontrolled Desires," 201–3.

35. Slotkin, *Gunfighter Nation*, 226–27.

36. Marling, *The American Roman Noir*, 150.

37. Fredric Jameson, "On Raymond Chandler," in *The Poetics of Murder*, ed. Most and Stowe, 146–47. This essay was originally published in 1970.

38. Fredric Jameson, *The Political Unconscious: Narrative as a Socially Symbolic Act* (Ithaca: Cornell University Press, 1981).

39. D'Emilio and Freedman, *Intimate Matters*, 234.

40. On American Freudianism, see D'Emilio and Freedman, *Intimate Matters*, ch. 10; and Hale, *Freud and the Americans* and *The Rise and Crisis of Psychoanalysis in the United States*. When I speculate about ways that the gothic mode and the domestic detective novel may have become obsolete, I am not arguing that the gothic mystery mode disappeared completely, but that it lost its centrality in the array of popular literary forms in the middle decades of the twentieth century. One visible development in popular literature is the way gothicism became attached to romance novels for women, creating a genre of historical "bodice busters" that was called, at least in the 1970s and 1980s "gothic romance." These novels feature heroines who have a lot of mysteries to figure out, but they really can't be called detectives in any meaningful use of the term. See Tania Modleski, *Loving with a Vengeance* (New York: Methuen, 1984). The current mode of truly popular gothic fiction is led by Clive Barker and Stephen King, who, interestingly, have recombined the horror gothic and the female gothic into a genre for young men. The presence of ghosts and vampires in postmodern fiction (including its most elite modes) has prompted some to identify a strain of "new" gothic. See *The New Gothic*, ed. Bradford Morrow and Patrick McGrat (New York: Random House, 1991).

41. Dashiell Hammett, *The Dain Curse* (New York: Alfred A. Knopf, 1929).

42. For example, Faulkner was influenced by Hammett, and worked on the screenplays of both *The Maltese Falcon* and *The Big Sleep*. One can see his interest in the detective story in *Intruder in the Dust*, and in the stories in *Knight's Gambit*, if not *Absalom, Absalom! Sanctuary* is the novel most clearly influenced by the *Black Mask* school. Albert Camus claimed Chandler as an important influence. See Stephen Knight, *Form and Ideology in Crime Fiction*, ch. 5.

43. Slotkin, *Gunslinger Nation*, 228. Slotkin reads detective fiction as one of the most successful of the genres of cheap literature that spread the literary-mythic tradition of the frontier throughout the mass culture of the twentieth century (194).

44. How far left Hammett really leaned is a matter of some debate as well. Hammett joined the Communist party in the late 1930s, and was famous for serving six months in jail for contempt of court after refusing to testify concerning the whereabouts of some alleged Communists who had jumped bail after being convicted under the Smith Act (Hammett was a trustee of the fund that had paid their bail).

45. Raymond Chandler, *The Long Goodbye* (New York: Ballantine Books, 1953), 227.

46. On Paretsky, Grafton, and the slightly earlier Marcia Muller, see

Kathleen Gregory Klein, *The Woman Detective,* ch. 10, and her study of Barbara Wilson, one of the most innovative of the urban lesbian detective writers, "*Habeas Corpus:* Feminism and Detective Fiction," in *Feminism in Women's Detective Fiction,* ed. Glenwood Irons (Toronto: University of Toronto Press, 1995), 171–89. See also Scott Christianson, "Talkin' Trash and Kickin' Butt: Sue Grafton's Hard-boiled Feminism," and Ann Wilson, "The Female Dick and the Crisis of Heterosexuality," in the Irons collection.

47. Bobbie Ann Mason, "Nancy Drew: Once and Future Prom Queen," in *Feminism in Women's Detective Fiction,* ed. Irons, 79.

# Select Bibliography

Alcott, Louisa May. *Little Women*. 1869. Reprint. New York: Modern Library, 1983.

———. "M. L." In *Louisa May Alcott: Selected Fiction*, ed. Daniel Shealy, Madeleine Stern, and Joel Myerson, 131–54. Boston: Little, Brown, 1990.

———. "*V. V.*, or Plots and Counterplots." In *The Hidden Louisa May Alcott*, ed. Madeleine Stern, 315–404. New York: Avenel, 1984.

Alewyn, Richard. "The Origin of the Detective Novel." In *The Poetics of Murder: Detective Fiction and Literary Theory*, ed. G. Most and W. Stowe, 62–78. New York: Harcourt Brace Jovanovich, 1983.

"Anna Katherine [*sic*] Green Tells How She Manufactures Her Plots." *Literary Digest* 58 (July 13, 1918): 48.

Anonymous. *All for Her*. New York: G. W. Carleton, 1877.

Atherton, Gertrude. *American Wives and English Husbands*. New York: Dodd, Mead, 1898.

———. *The Avalanche*. New York: Frederick Stokes, 1919.

———. *Patience Sparhawk and Her Times*. New York: John Lane, 1897.

———. "Suffrage a Gain or Loss to Women?" *New York Times*, November 2, 1917, 14.

———. "The Woman Suffrage Issue." *New York Times*, November 4, 1917, 14.

Auden, W. H. "The Guilty Vicarage." *Harper's* (May 1948). Reprinted in *Detective Fiction: A Collection of Critical Essays*, ed. Robin Winks. Englewood Cliffs, N.J.: Prentice-Hall, 1980.

Baker, Lafayette. *The History of the United States Secret Service*. Philadelphia: L. C. Baker, 1867.

Banning, Margaret Culkin. "The Plight of the Spinster." *Harper's Monthly*, June 1929, 88–97.

Bass, Dennis. "The Gertrude Stein Connection." In *Proceedings: Lizzie Borden Conference* [Bristol Community College, 1992], ed. Jules Ryckebusch, 117–36. Portland, Maine: King Philip, 1993.

Baym, Nina. Introduction to *The Lamplighter*, by Maria Cummins, ix–xxi. New Brunswick: Rutgers University Press, 1988.

———. "Melodramas of Beset Manhood: How Theories of American Fiction Exclude Women Authors." In *The New Feminist Criticism*, ed. Elaine Showalter, 63–80. New York: Pantheon, 1985.

―――. *Novels, Readers, and Reviewers: Responses to Fiction in Antebellum America.* Ithaca: Cornell University Press, 1984.

―――. *Women's Fiction: A Guide to Novels by and about Women in America, 1820–1879.* Ithaca: Cornell University Press, 1978.

Bederman, Gail. *Manliness and Civilization: A Cultural History of Gender and Race in the United States, 1880–1917.* Chicago: University of Chicago Press, 1995.

Bell, Lilian. "Old Maids of the Last Generation and This." *Saturday Evening Post,* December 25, 1926, 18, 46.

Bloomfield, Maxwell. *American Lawyers in a Changing Society, 1776–1876.* Cambridge: Harvard University Press, 1976.

―――. "Law and Lawyers in American Popular Culture." In *Law and American Literature,* ed. Carl Smith, John P. McWilliams, and Maxwell Bloomfield, 125–173. New York: Alfred A. Knopf, 1983.

Boone, Joseph Allen. *Tradition Counter Tradition: Love and the Form of Fiction.* Chicago: University of Chicago Press, 1987.

Brantlinger, Patrick. "What Is 'Sensational' about the 'Sensation Novel.' " *Nineteenth Century Fiction* 37 (1982): 1–28.

Brodhead, Richard H. *Cultures of Letters: Scenes of Reading and Writing in Nineteenth-Century America.* Chicago: University of Chicago Press, 1993.

Brooks, Peter. *Reading for the Plot: Design and Intention in Narrative.* New York: Random House, 1984.

Brown, Gillian. *Domestic Individualism: Imagining Self in Nineteenth-Century America.* Berkeley: University of California Press, 1990.

Byrnes, Thomas. *Professional Criminals in America.* 1886. Reprint. New York: Chelsea House, 1969.

Caillois, "The Detective Novel as Game." In *The Poetics of Murder: Detective Fiction and Literary Theory,* ed. G. Most and W. Stowe, 1–12. New York: Harcourt, Brace, Jovanovich, 1983.

Cain, James M. *Double Indemnity.* 1936. Reprint. New York: Random House, 1989.

―――. *Mildred Pierce.* 1941. Reprint. New York: Random House, 1989.

Carby, Hazel. Introduction to *The Magazine Novels of Pauline Hopkins,* xxix–l. New York: Oxford University Press, 1988.

―――. *Reconstructing Womanhood: The Emergence of the Afro-American Woman Novelist.* New York: Oxford University Press, 1987.

Catt, Carrie Chapman, and Nettie Rogers Shule. *Woman Suffrage and Politics: The Inner Story of the Suffrage Movement.* New York: Charles Scribner's Sons, 1923.

Cawelti, John G. *Adventure, Mystery, and Romance.* Chicago: University of Chicago Press, 1976.

Champigny, Robert. *What Will Have Happened.* Bloomington: Indiana University Press, 1977.

Chandler, Raymond. *The Big Sleep.* New York: Random House, 1992.

———. *The Long Goodbye.* New York: Ballantine Books, 1953.

———. "The Simple Art of Murder." 1944. In *The Simple Art of Murder.* New York: Ballantine Books, 1972.

Cheney, Ednah D., ed. *Louisa May Alcott: Her Life, Letters, and Journals.* Boston: Little Brown, 1928.

Chessman, Harriet. *The Public Is Invited to Dance: Representation, the Body, and Dialogue in Gertrude Stein.* Stanford: Stanford University Press, 1989.

Cohen, Daniel. *Pillars of Salt, Monuments of Grace: New England Crime Literature and the Origins of Popular Culture, 1674–1860.* New York: Oxford University Press, 1993.

Cohn, Jan. *Improbable Fiction: The Life of Mary Roberts Rinehart.* Pittsburgh: University of Pittsburgh Press, 1980.

Collins, Wilkie. *The Law and the Lady.* London: Chatto and Windus, 1875.

Cott, Nancy F. "Giving Character to Our Whole Civil Polity: Marriage and the Public Order in the Late Nineteenth Century." In *U.S. History as Women's History: New Feminist Essays,* ed. Linda Kerber, Alice Kessler-Harris, and Kathryn Kish Sklar, 107–21. Chapel Hill: University of North Carolina Press, 1995.

———. *The Grounding of Modern Feminism.* New Haven: Yale University Press, 1987.

Davis, Curtis Carroll. "Companions of Crisis: The Spy Memoir as a Social Document." *Civil War History* 10 (1964): 385–400.

Davis, David Brion. *Homicide in American Fiction, 1798–1860.* Ithaca: Cornell University Press, 1957.

Day, William Patrick. *In the Circles of Fear and Desire.* Chicago: University of Chicago Press, 1985.

De Grave, Kathleen. *Swindler, Spy, Rebel: The Confidence Woman in Nineteenth-Century America.* Columbia: University of Missouri Press, 1995.

D'Emilio, John, and Estelle Freedman. *Intimate Matters: A History of Sexuality in America.* New York: Harper and Row, 1988.

Denning, Michael. *Mechanic Accents: Dime Novels and Working Class Culture in America.* New York: Verso, 1987.

Derrida, Jacques. "The Law of Genre." Translated by Avital Ronell. *Critical Inquiry* 7 (1980).

DiBattista, Maria. "The Lowly Art of Murder: Modernism and the Case of the Free Woman." In *High and Low Moderns: Literature and Culture, 1889–1939,* ed. Maria DiBattista and Lucy McDiarmid, 176–93. New York: Oxford University Press, 1996.

Douglas, Ann. *The Feminization of American Culture.* New York: Doubleday, 1977.

"The Economic Drive against America." *Saturday Evening Post,* April 15, 1933, 3–4.

Elbert, Sarah. *Hunger for Home: Louisa May Alcott's Place in American Culture.* New Brunswick: Rutgers University Press, 1987.

Ellis, Kate Ferguson. *The Contested Castle: Gothic Novels and the Subversion of Domestic Ideology.* Urbana: University of Illinois Press, 1989.

Fetterley, Judith. "Impersonating 'Little Women': The Radicalism of Alcott's *Behind a Mask.*" *Women's Studies* 10 (1983): 1–14.

Fiedler, Leslie. *Love and Death in the American Novel.* Revised edition. New York: Stein and Day, 1986.

Fishel, Edwin C. "The Mythology of Civil War Intelligence." *Civil War History* 10 (1964): 344–67.

Fisher, Philip. *Hard Facts: Setting and Form in the American Novel.* New York: Oxford University Press, 1985.

Franzen, Tricia. *Spinsters and Lesbians: Independent Womanhood in the United States.* New York: New York University Press, 1996.

Freedman, Estelle. "'Uncontrolled Desires': The Response to the Sexual Psychopath, 1920–1960." In *Passion and Power: Sexuality in History,* ed. K. Peiss and C. Simmons, 199–225. Philadelphia: Temple University Press, 1989.

Freeman, Mary Wilkins. Letter to Charles W. Wilcox. *The Infant Sphinx: Collected Letters of Mary E. Wilkins Freeman.* Edited by Brent Kendrick, letter 173, p. 175. Metuchen, N.J.: Scarecrow Press, 1985.

———. "The Long Arm." In *The Long Arm and Other Detective Stories,* 1–66. London: Chapman and Hall, 1895.

Freeman, Ruth, and Patricia Klaus. "Blessed or Not? The New Spinster in England and the United States in the Late Nineteenth and Early Twentieth Centuries." *Journal of Family History* 9 (Winter 1984): 394–414.

Freibert, Lucy M., and Barbara A. White. *Hidden Hands: An Anthology of Women Writers, 1790–1870.* New Brunswick: Rutgers University Press, 1985.

Freud, Sigmund. "The Uncanny." In *On Creativity and the Unconscious.* Edited by Benjamin Nelson. New York: Harper, 1958.

Frohock, W. M. *The Novel of Violence in America.* Dallas: University Press of Dallas, 1946.

Garrison, Dee. "Immoral Fiction in the Late Victorian Library." *American Quarterly* 28 (Spring 1976): 71–80.

Gilbert, Sandra M., and Susan Gubar. *The Madwoman in the Attic: The Woman Writer and the Nineteenth-Century Literary Imagination.* New Haven: Yale University Press, 1979.

———. *No Man's Land: The Place of the Woman Writer in the Twentieth Century.* Vol. 1, *The War of the Words.* New Haven: Yale University Press, 1988.

Gilfoyle, Timothy. *City of Eros: New York City, Prostitution, and the Commercialization of Sex.* New York: Norton, 1992.

Gilman, Charlotte Perkins. *Unpunished: A Mystery.* Edited and with an afterword by Catherine J. Golden and Denise D. Knight. New York: Feminist Press, 1997.

Goddu, Teresa. *Gothic America: Narrative, History, and Nation.* New York: Columbia University Press, 1997.

Goulart, Ron. *The Dime Detectives.* New York: Mysterious Press, 1988.

Green, Anna Katharine. *Agatha Webb.* New York: G. P. Putnam's Sons, 1889.

———. "Anna Katharine Green Replies." *New York Times,* November 4, 1917: sec. II, 2.

———. *The Circular Study.* New York: McClure's, 1900.

———. *The Defence of the Bride.* New York: G. P. Putnam's Sons, 1882.

———. *The Filigree Ball.* Indianapolis: Bobbs-Merrill, 1903. Reprint. New York: Arno, 1976.

———. *The Forsaken Inn.* New York: R. Bonner's Sons, 1890.

———. *The Golden Slipper and Other Problems.* New York: G. P. Putnam's Sons, 1915.

———. *The Leavenworth Case.* 1878. Reprint. New York: Dover, 1981.

———. *Lost Man's Lane.* New York: G. P. Putnam's Sons, 1898.

———. *The Mayor's Wife.* Indianapolis: Bobbs-Merrill, 1907.

———. "Open Letter to the Author of All for Her." Green Papers. Beinecke Library, Yale University.

———. *Risifi's Daughter.* New York: G. P. Putnam's Sons, 1887.

———. *That Affair Next Door.* New York: G. P. Putnam's Sons, 1897.

———. "Why Human Beings Are Interested in Crime." *American Magazine* 87 (1919): 38–39, 82–86.

———. "Women Must Wait." *New York Times,* October 30, 1917, 14.

Grossvogel, David. *Mystery and Its Fictions: From Oedipus to Agatha Christie.* Baltimore: Johns Hopkins University Press, 1979.

Gubar, Susan. " 'The Blank Page' and Female Creativity." In *The New Feminist Criticism,* ed. Elaine Showalter. New York: Random House, 1985.

Haag, Pamela. "In Search of 'The Real Thing': Ideologies of Love, Modern Romance, and Women's Sexual Subjectivity in the United States, 1920–1940." In *American Sexual Politics: Sex, Gender, and Race since the Civil War,* ed. John Fout and Maura Tantillo, 161–91. Chicago: University of Chicago Press, 1993.

Habegger, Alfred E. *Gender, Fantasy, and Realism in American Literature.* New York: Columbia University Press, 1982.

Hale, Nathan G. *Freud and the Americans: The Beginnings of Psychoanalysis in the United States, 1876–1917.* New York: Oxford University Press, 1971.

———. *The Rise and Crisis of Psychoanalysis in the United States: Freud and the Americans, 1917–1985.* Oxford: Oxford University Press, 1995.

Halttunen, Karen. *Confidence Men and Painted Women: A Study of Middle-Class Culture, 1830–1870.* New Haven: Yale University Press, 1982.

———. "Early American Murder Narratives: The Birth of Horror." In *The Power of Culture: Critical Essays in American History,* ed. Richard W. Fox and T. J. Jackson Lears, 67–101. Chicago: University of Chicago Press, 1993.

———. "Gothic Imagination and Social Reform: The Haunted Houses of Lyman Beecher, Henry Ward Beecher, and Harriet Beecher Stowe." In *New Essays on Uncle Tom's Cabin,* ed. Eric Sundquist. New York: Cambridge University Press, 1986.

———. "Humanitarianism and the Pornography of Pain in Anglo-American Culture." *American Historical Review* 100 (April 1995): 303–34.

Hammett, Dashiell. *The Dain Curse.* New York: Alfred A. Knopf, 1929.

———. *The Maltese Falcon.* 1929. Reprint. New York: Random House, 1989.

———. *Red Harvest.* 1929. Reprint. New York: Random House, 1992.

Hart, James D. *The Popular Book: A History of America's Literary Taste.* New York: Oxford University Press, 1950.

Hartman, Geoffrey H. "Literature High and Low: The Case of the Mystery Story." In *The Poetics of Murder: Detective Fiction and Literary Theory,* ed. G. Most and W. Stowe, 210–29. New York: Harcourt, Brace, Jovanovich, 1983.

Hartsfield, Larry K. *The American Response to Professional Crime, 1870–1917.* Westport, Conn.: Greenwood Press, 1985.

Hatch, Mary. "The Author of *The Leavenworth Case.*" *Writer* 2 (July 1888): 159–62.

Haycraft, Howard. *The Art of the Mystery Story.* New York: Simon and Schuster, 1946.

———. *Murder for Pleasure: The Life and Times of the Detective Story.* New York: Appleton-Century, 1941.

Hayne, Barrie. "Anna Katharine Green." In *Ten Women of Mystery,* ed. Earl Bargainnier, 150–77. Bowling Green, Ohio: Bowling Green State University Popular Press, 1981.

Hobson, Wayne. "Lizzie Borden and Victorian America: Shifting Perspectives, 1892–1992." In *Proceedings: Lizzie Borden Conference* [Bristol Community College, 1992], ed. Jules Ryckebusch, 167–90. Portland, Maine: King Philip, 1993.

Hoffman, Arnold. "Social History and the Crime Fiction of Mary Roberts Rinehart." In *New Dimensions in Popular Culture,* ed. Russell B. Nye. Bowling Green, Ohio: Bowling Green State University Popular Press, 1972.

Hoffman, Daniel. *Poe Poe Poe Poe Poe Poe Poe.* New York: Random House, 1972.

Hopkins, Pauline. *Hagar's Daughter: A Story of Southern Caste Prejudice.* In *The Magazine Novels of Pauline Hopkins.* New York: Oxford University Press, 1988.

———. "Talma Gordon." In *Spooks, Spies, and Private Eyes: Black Mystery, Crime, and Suspense Fiction,* ed. Paula Woods, 3–18. New York: Doubleday, 1995.

Howells, William Dean. *Between the Dark and the Daylight.* New York: Harper, 1907.

———. *Questionable Shapes.* New York: Harper, 1903.

Hughes, Winifred. *The Maniac in the Cellar: Sensation Novels of the 1860s.* Princeton: Princeton University Press, 1980.

Hume, Robert D. "Gothic versus Romantic: A Revaluation of the Gothic Novel." *PMLA* 84 (March 1969): 282–90.

Hutter, Albert D. "Dreams, Transformations, and Literature: The Implications of Detective Fiction." In *The Poetics of Murder: Detective Fiction and Literary Theory,* ed. G. Most and W. Stowe, 230–51. New York: Harcourt Brace Jovanovich, 1983.

Jameson, Fredric. "On Raymond Chandler." In *The Poetics of Murder: Detective Fiction and Literary Theory,* ed. G. Most and W. Stowe, 122–48. New York: Harcourt Brace Jovanovich, 1983.

———. *The Political Unconscious: Narrative as a Socially Symbolic Act.* Ithaca: Cornell University Press, 1981.

Jeffreys, Sheila. *The Spinster and Her Enemies: Feminism and Sexuality 1880–1930.* London: Pandora, 1985.

Johannsen, Albert. *The House of Beadle and Adams and Its Nickle and Dime Novels.* 3 vols. New York: Basic Books, 1980.

Johnson, David R. *Illegal Tender: Counterfeiting and the Secret Service in Nineteenth-Century America.* Washington, D.C.: Smithsonian Institution Press, 1995.

Jones, Ann. *Women Who Kill.* Boston: Beacon, 1996.

Jordan, Elizabeth. "Family Parasites: The Economic Value of the Unmarried Sister." *Saturday Evening Post,* April 5, 1930, 35, 165–66.

————. "On Being a Spinster." *Saturday Evening Post,* April 10, 1926, 34–35, 214, 217.

————. "Ruth Herrick's Assignment." In *Tales of the City Room.* New York: Charles Scribner's Sons, 1898.

Kahane, Claire. "The Gothic Mirror." In *The (M)other Tongue: Essays in Feminist Psychoanalytic Interpretation,* ed. Shirley Nelson Garner, Claire Kahane, and Madelon Sprengthener. Ithaca: Cornell University Press, 1985.

Kahn, David. *The Codebreakers: The Story of Secret Writing.* New York: Macmillan, 1967.

Kaplan, Amy. *The Social Construction of American Realism.* Chicago: University of Chicago Press, 1988.

Kelley, Mary. *Private Woman, Public Stage: Literary Domesticity in Nineteenth-Century America.* New York: Oxford University Press, 1984.

————. "The Sentimentalists: Promise and Betrayal in the Home." *Signs* 4 (1979): 434–46.

Kenney, Catherine. "Detecting a Novel Use for Spinsters in Sayers's Fiction." In *Old Maids to Radical Spinsters: Unmarried Women in the Twentieth-Century Novel,* ed. Laura L. Doan, 123–38. Urbana: University of Illinois Press, 1991.

Kesselring, James. *Arsenic and Old Lace.* New York: Random House, 1941.

Klein, Kathleen Gregory. "Habeas Corpus: Feminism and Detective Fiction." In *Feminism in Detective Fiction,* ed. Glenwood Irons, 171–190. Toronto: University of Toronto Press, 1995.

————. *The Woman Detective: Gender and Genre.* Urbana: University of Illinois Press, 1988.

Klein, Marcus. *Easterns, Westerns, and Private Eyes: American Matters, 1870–1900.* Madison: University of Wisconsin Press, 1994.

Knight, Stephen. *Form and Ideology in Crime Fiction.* Bloomington: Indiana University Press, 1980.

Lacan, Jacques. "Seminar on 'The Purloined Letter.'" In *The Poetics of Murder: Detective Fiction and Literary Theory,* ed. G. Most and W. Stowe, 21–54. New York: Harcourt Brace Jovanovich, 1983.

Lane, Ann, ed. *The Charlotte Perkins Gilman Reader.* New York: Pantheon, 1980.

————. *To "Herland" and Beyond: The Life and Works of Charlotte Perkins Gilman.* New York: Pantheon, 1990.

Leach, William. *True Love and Perfect Union: The Feminist Reform of Sex and Society.* New York: Basic Books, 1980.

Lehman, David. *The Perfect Murder.* New York: Macmillan, 1989.

Lewis, R. W. B. *Edith Wharton.* New York: Harper and Row, 1975.

Lewis, R. W. B., and Nancy Lewis. *The Letters of Edith Wharton.* New York: Scribner's, 1988.

*Literary World* 7, nos. 5–8 (March 6–April 17, 1886). Articles on the Green plagiarism controversy.

Lott, Eric. *Love and Theft: Blackface Minstrelsy and the American Working Class.* New York: Oxford University Press, 1995.

Lutz, Thomas. *American Nervousness, 1903: An Anecdotal History.* Ithaca: Cornell University Press, 1991.

MacAndrew, Elizabeth. *The Gothic Tradition in Fiction.* New York: Columbia University Press, 1979.

MacDonald, Ross. *On Crime Writing.* Santa Barbara: Capra Press, 1973.

McLaren, Angus. *The Trials of Masculinity: Policing Sexual Boundaries, 1870–1930.* Chicago: University of Chicago Press, 1997.

Maida, Patricia D. *Mother of Detective Fiction: The Life and Works of Anna Katharine Green.* Bowling Green, Ohio: Bowling Green State University Popular Press, 1989.

Maio, Kathleen L. "'Had-I-But-Known': The Marriage of Gothic Terror and Detection." In *The Female Gothic,* ed. Juliann Fleenor, 82–90. Montreal: Eden Press, 1983.

Maneiro, Lisa, ed. *American Women Writers.* New York: Frederick Unger, 1981.

Marcus, Steven. "Dashiell Hammett." In *The Poetics of Murder: Detective Fiction and Literary Theory,* ed. G. Most and W. Stowe, 197–209. New York: Harcourt Brace Jovanovich, 1983.

Marling, William. *The American Roman Noir: Hammett, Cain, and Chandler.* Athens: University of Georgia Press, 1995.

Mason, Bobbie Ann. "Nancy Drew: Once and Future Prom Queen." In *Feminism in Women's Detective Fiction,* ed. Glenwood Irons, 74–93 Toronto: University of Toronto Press, 1995.

Maurice, Arthur Bartlett. "The Detective in Fiction." *Bookman* 15 (May 1902): 231–36.

Miller, D. A. *The Novel and the Police.* Berkeley: University of California Press, 1988.

Mitchell, Lee Clark. Introduction to *Riders of the Purple Sage,* by Zane Grey, ix–xxxvi. Oxford: Oxford University Press, 1995.

Modleski, Tania. *Loving with a Vengeance.* New York: Methuen, 1984.

Moers, Ellen. *Literary Women: The Great Writers.* New York: Oxford University Press, 1985.

Most, Glenn, and William Stowe, eds. *The Poetics of Murder: Detective Fiction and Literary Theory.* New York: Harcourt Brace Jovanovich, 1983.

Murch, A[lma]. E. *The Development of the Detective Novel.* London: Peter Owen, 1958.

Odem, Mary. *Delinquent Daughters: Policing Adolescent Female Sexuality in the United States, 1885–1920.* Chapel Hill: University of North Carolina Press, 1995.

Ordway, Alice. "Thirty—and Single." *Atlantic Monthly*, February 1933, 252–53.

Overton, Grant Martin. *The Women Who Make Our Novels*. New York: Moffat Yard, 1918.

Papashvily, Helen Waite. *All the Happy Endings: A Study of the Domestic Novel in America, the Women Who Wrote It, the Women Who Read It, in the Nineteenth Century*. New York: Harper and Row, 1958.

Pearson, Edmund. *The Trial of Lizzie Borden*. New York: Doubleday, 1937.

Pederson-Krag, Geraldine. "Detective Stories and the Primal Scene." In *The Poetics of Murder: Detective Fiction and Literary Theory*, ed. G. Most and W. Stowe, 13–20. New York: Harcourt Brace Jovanovich, 1983.

Peiss, Kathy. "'Charity Girls' and City Pleasures: Historical Notes on Working-Class Sexuality, 1880–1920." In *Passion and Power: Sexuality in History*, ed. K. Peiss and C. Simmons, 57–69. Philadelphia: Temple University Press, 1989.

Peiss, Kathy, and Christina Simmons, eds. *Passion and Power: Sexuality in History*. Philadelphia: Temple University Press, 1989.

Pinkerton, Allan. *Spy of the Rebellion: Being a True History of the Spy System of the United States Army during the Late Rebellion*. New York, 1883.

Pleck, Elizabeth. *Domestic Tyranny: The Making of American Social Policy against Family Violence from Colonial Times to the Present*. New York: Oxford University Press, 1987.

Poe, Edgar Allan. *The Complete Tales and Poems*. New York: Random House, 1975.

Porter, Dennis. *The Pursuit of Crime: Art and Ideology in Detective Fiction*. New Haven: Yale University Press, 1981.

Putnam, George. "Wilkie Collins on *The Leavenworth Case*." *Critic* 22 (January 28, 1893): 52.

Reppetto, Thomas A. *The Blue Parade*. New York: Macmillan, 1978.

Reynolds, David S. *Beneath the American Renaissance: The Subversive Imagination in the Age of Emerson and Melville*. New York: Random House, 1988.

Rinehart, Mary Roberts. *The After House*. New York: Houghton Mifflin, 1914.

———. *The Album*. 1933. Reprint. New York: Kensington, 1988.

———. *The Amazing Adventures of Letitia Carberry*. Indianapolis: Bobbs-Merrill, 1910.

———. *The Breaking Point*. New York: George Doran, 1922.

———. "Can Women Stop Crime?" *Saturday Evening Post* 206 (November, 18, 1933): 8, 98.

———. "The Chaotic Decade." *Ladies' Home Journal* 47 (May 1930): 35.

———. *The Circular Staircase*. 1908. Reprint. New York: Carroll and Graf, 1985.

———. *The Confession and Sight Unseen.* 1921. Reprint. New York: Kensington, 1985.

———. "I Had Cancer." *Ladies' Home Journal* 64 (July 1947): 8.

———. "If I Had a Daughter." *Forum* 87 (March 1932): 188–92.

———. *K.* Boston: Houghton Mifflin, 1915.

———. *Married People.* New York: Farrar and Rinehart, 1937.

———. *Mary Roberts Rinehart: A Sketch of the Woman and Her Work.* New York: George Doran, 1923.

———. *The Mary Roberts Rinehart Crime Book.* New York: Rinehart and Company, 1957.

———. *More Tish.* New York: George Doran, 1921.

———. *My Story.* New York: Farrar and Rinehart, 1931. Revised edition, 1948.

———. *The Out Trail.* New York: George Doran, 1923.

———. *This Strange Adventure.* New York: Doubleday Doran, 1928.

———. *Tish.* Boston: Houghton Mifflin, 1916.

———. "Why Don't You Use Your Vote?" *Ladies' Home Journal* 49 (August 1932): 5, 50.

Ringe, David. *American Gothic: Imagination and Reason in Nineteenth-Century Fiction.* Lexington: University Press of Kentucky, 1982.

Robinson, Lillian. "Killing Patriarchy: Charlotte Perkins Gilman, the Murder Mystery, and Post-Feminist Propaganda." *Tulsa Studies in Women's Literature* 10 (Fall 1991): 273–85.

Rosenheim, Shawn. "The King of 'Secret Readers' ": Edgar Poe, Cryptography, and the Origins of the Detective Story." *ELH* 56 (Summer 1989): 375–400.

Rubin, Joan Shelley. *The Making of Middlebrow Culture.* Chapel Hill: University of North Carolina Press, 1992.

Saxton, Martha. *Louisa May: A Modern Biography of Louisa May Alcott.* Boston: Houghton Mifflin, 1977.

Schopen, Bernard A. "From Puzzles to People: The Development of the American Detective Novel." *Studies in American Fiction* 7 (Fall 1979): 174–89.

Schwenger, Peter. *Phallic Critiques.* London: Routledge and Kegan Paul, 1984.

Sedgwick, Eve Kosofsky. *The Coherence of Gothic Conventions.* New York: Methuen, 1986.

Simmons, Christina. "Modern Sexuality and the Myth of Victorian Repression." In *Passion and Power: Sexuality in History,* ed. K. Peiss and C. Simmons, 157–77. Philadelphia: Temple University Press, 1989.

Sizer, Lyde Cullen. "Acting Her Part: Narratives of Union Women Spies." In *Divided Houses: Gender and the Civil War,* ed. Catherine Clinton and Nina Silber, 114–33. New York: Oxford University Press, 1992.

Sklar, Kathryn Kish. *Catherine Beecher: A Study in American Domesticity.* New Haven: Yale University Press, 1973.

Slotkin, Richard. *Gunfighter Nation: The Myth of the Frontier in Twentieth-Century America.* New York: HarperCollins, 1992.

Slung, Michelle, ed. *Crime on Her Mind: Fifteen Stories of Female Sleuths from the Victorian Era to the Forties.* New York: Random House, 1975.

Smith, Henry Nash. "The Scribbling Women and the Cosmic Success Story." *Critical Inquiry* 1 (September 1974): 47–70.

Smith-Rosenberg, Carroll. *Disorderly Conduct: Visions of Gender in Victorian America.* New York: Oxford University Press, 1985.

Soitos, Stephen. *The Blues Detective: A Study of African American Detective Fiction.* Amherst: University of Massachusetts Press, 1996.

Southworth, E[mma]. D. E. N. *The Hidden Hand.* 1859. Reprint, edited by Joanne Dobson. New Brunswick: Rutgers University Press, 1988.

———. *Ishmael; or, In the Depths.* Vol. 1 of *Ishmael.* New York: Grosset and Dunlap, 1864.

———. *Self-Raised; or, From the Depths.* Vol. 2 of *Ishmael.* New York: Grosset and Dunlap, 1864.

Spacks, Patricia Meyer. *Gossip.* Chicago: University of Chicago Press, 1985.

Stein, Gertrude. "American Crimes and How They Matter." In *How Writing Is Written,* ed. Robert Bartlett Haas, 100–105. Los Angeles: Black Sparrow, 1974.

———. *Blood on the Dining Room Floor.* 1948. Reprint, with afterword by John Gill. Berkeley: Creative Arts, 1982.

Stern, Philip Van Doren. *Secret Missions of the Civil War.* New York: Rand McNally, 1959.

Stowe, Harriet Beecher. *Uncle Tom's Cabin.* 1852. Reprint. New York: Penguin, 1981.

Symons, Julian. *Bloody Murder: From the Detective Story to the Crime Novel.* New York: Penguin, 1972. Former title, *Mortal Consequences.*

Tanner, Tony. *Adultery in the Novel: Contract and Transgression.* Baltimore: Johns Hopkins University Press, 1979.

Todorov, Tzvetan. *The Poetics of Prose.* Translated by Richard Howard. Ithaca: Cornell University Press, 1977.

Tompkins, Jane. *Sensational Designs: The Cultural Work of American Fiction 1790–1860.* New York: Oxford University Press, 1985.

———. *West of Everything: The Inner Life of Westerns.* New York: Oxford University Press, 1992.

Trachtenberg, Alan. *Reading American Photographs: Images as History, Mathew Brady to Walker Evans.* New York: Farrar, Straus, Giroux, 1989.

Trodd, Anthea. *Domestic Crime in the Victorian Novel.* London: Macmillan, 1989.

Twain, Mark. *The Adventures of Huckleberry Finn.* 1884. Reprint. New York: Penguin, 1985.

Varma, Devendra P. *The Gothic Flame.* London: Arthur Baker, 1957.

Victor, Metta Victoria Fuller [Seeley Regester, pseud.]. *The Dead Letter.* 1866. Reprint. New York: Beadle and Company, 1867.

——— [Seeley Regester, pseud.]. *The Figure Eight, or, The Mystery of Meredith Place.* New York: Beadle and Company, 1869.

———. *Lives of Female Mormons: A Narrative of Facts Stranger Than Fiction.* New York: D. W. Evans, 1860.

———. *Maum Guinea and Her Plantation Children.* New York: Beadle and Company, 1861.

———. *Passing the Portal.* New York: G. W. Carleton, 1876.

———. *The Senator's Son.* Cleveland: O. Tooker and Gatchel, 1853. Excerpted in Lucy Freibert and Barbara White. *Hidden Hands: An Anthology of Women Writers, 1790–1870.* New Brunswick: Rutgers University Press, 1985.

———. *Too True: A Story of Today.* New York: G. P. Putnam's Sons, 1868.

[Victor] Fuller, Metta V., and Frances F. Fuller. *Poems of Sentiment and Imagination.* New York: A. S. Barnes, 1851.

Waid, Candace. *Edith Wharton's Letters from the Underworld: Fictions of Women and Writing.* Chapel Hill: University of North Carolina Press, 1991.

Walsh, John. *Poe the Detective.* New Brunswick: Rutgers University Press, 1968.

Welsh, Alexander. *George Eliot and Blackmail.* Cambridge: Harvard University Press, 1985.

Welter, Barbara. "Murder Most Genteel: The Mystery Novels of Anna Katharine Green." In *Dimity Convictions: The American Woman in the Nineteenth Century,* 130–44. Athens: Ohio University Press, 1976.

Wexler, Laura. "Tender Violence: Literary Eavesdropping, Domestic Fiction, and Educational Reform." In *The Culture of Sentiment: Race, Gender, and Sentimentality in Nineteenth-Century America,* ed. Shirley Samuels, 9–38. New York: Oxford University Press, 1992.

Wharton, Edith. "Confession." In *The World Over,* 141–212. New York: Appleton-Century, 1936.

———. "The Old Maid." In *Old New York.* 1924. Reprint. New York: Simon and Schuster, 1995.

Wigmore, Barrie. "Was the Bank Holiday of 1933 Caused by a Run on the Dollar?" *Journal of Economic History* 47 (1987): 739–55.

Wilbur, Richard. "The Poe Mystery Case." *New York Review of Books,* July 13, 1967, 25–27.

Wilson, Christopher P. "The Rhetoric of Consumption: Mass Market Magazines and the Demise of the Gentle Reader, 1880–1920." In *The

*Culture of Consumption,* ed. Richard W. Fox and T. J. Jackson Lears. New York: Pantheon, 1983.

Winks, Robin. *Detective Fiction: A Collection of Critical Essays.* Englewood Cliffs, N.J.: Prentice-Hall, 1980.

Wood, Ann D. "The 'Scribbling Women' and Fanny Fern: Why Women Wrote." *American Quarterly* 23 (Spring 1971): 3–24.

Woodward, Kathleen. "Anna Katharine Green." *Bookman* 70 (October 1929): 168–70.

———. "The Renaissance of Wonder." *Bookman* 10 (December 1899): 340–43.

# Index

African Americans: in hard-boiled style, 206; and history of detective fiction, 249 n.24; stereotypes of, 50–51, 120–21, 131–32

Alcott, Louisa May, xiii, 2, 12, 13, 66, 68, 95, 121, 149, 163; abolitionist fiction of, 56, 230 n.20; *Little Women*, 16, 21, 24, 212; "M. L.," 56; thrillers of, 23, 224 n.44; "V. V.," 23–26

Anger: in detective fiction, 46; and female detectives, 148–50; gothic mode and, 18, 108, 197

Architecture. *See* Domestic space

*Arsenic and Old Lace,* 159

Atherton, Gertrude, 113–14; *The Avalanche,* 236 n.17

Austen, Jane, 115

Bahktin, Mikhail, 163

Banning, Margaret Culkin, 157, 241 n.8

Barker, Clive, 252 n.40

Barthes, Roland, 4

Baym, Nina, 222 n.22

Bederman, Gail, 204

Bell, Lilian, 158

Bloomfield, Maxwell, 33

Bodies: conflated with houses, 141, 151; conflated with texts, 45, 83, 85–86, 234 n.10. *See also* Corpses

Boone, Joseph Allan, 163

Borden, Lizzie: depictions of, 168–72, 178, 189–95, 244 nn. 31, 32; story of, 165–68, 246 n.40

Brodhead, Richard, 23–24, 26, 27, 227 n.13

Brontë, Charlotte, xiii, 13, 49, 222 n.27, 228 n.2

Brontë, Emily, 13

Brooks, Peter, 10, 40, 163

Brown, Gillian, 67

Cain, James M., 209–11

Camus, Albert, 252 n.42

Capitalism: critique of, 12, 18, 30, 66–67, 197, 214, 215. *See also* Greed; Money

Carby, Hazel, 55, 193, 247 n.47

Carter, Nick, 52

Catt, Carrie Chapman, 113

Cawelti, John, 203

Chandler, Raymond, 5–6, 201–4, 205–8, 212–13

Chesterton, G. K., 5

Christie, Agatha, 5, 61, 119, 162, 201

Class: ambiguity and detectives, 50–51, 74; climbing, 48, 95, 100, 103–6, 111; markers of, 106–7; policing of, 97–98, 214. *See also* Professionals

Clue-puzzle, 201

Clues, 79; texts as, 10

Cohen, Daniel, 27

Cohn, Jan, 121, 123, 127, 128, 238 n.14, 239 nn. 17, 19

Collins, Wilkie, 20, 49, 61, 62

Confusion: in detective fiction, 12; in detectives, 73, 144; in readers, 56

Corpses: necrophilia and, 81, 234

Catherine Ross Nickerson is
Associate Professor of American Studies
and English at Emory University.

Library of Congress Cataloging-in-
Publication Data

Nickerson, Catherine.
The web of iniquity : early detective fiction by
American women / Catherine Nickerson.
    p.    cm.
Includes bibliographical references and index.
ISBN 0-8223-2251-X (acid-free paper). —
ISBN 0-8223-2271-4 (pbk. : acid-free paper)
1. Detective and mystery stories, American —
History and criticism.    2. American fiction —
Women authors — History and criticism.
3. American fiction — 19th century — History
and criticism.    4. American fiction — 20th
century — History and criticism.    5. Women
and literature — United States — History.
    I. Title.
PS374.D4N532              1999
813'.087209 — dc21        98-8397
                          CIP